C. L. Skelton was born in Tynemouth in
1919. His varied career has included stage and
film acting, war service in the RAF, seven
years as a lay brother with a religious order,
hunting the Loch Ness monster and selling
insurance and brushes door-to-door in the
Scottish Highlands.

He has written screenplays and published
several previous books under a pseudonym.
This is his first major work of fiction under his
own name.

C. L. Skelton

Hardacre

A MAYFLOWER BOOK

GRANADA
London Toronto Sydney New York

Published by Granada Publishing Limited in 1978
Reprinted 1978, 1979 (three times), 1980, 1981 (twice)

ISBN 0 583 12786 X

First published in Great Britain by
Hart-Davis, MacGibbon Ltd 1977
Copyright © C. L. Skelton 1977

Granada Publishing Limited
Frogmore, St Albans, Herts AL2 2NF
and
3 Upper James Street, London W1R 4BP
866 United Nations Plaza, New York, NY 10017, USA
117 York Street, Sydney, NSW 2000, Australia
100 Skyway Avenue, Rexdale, Ontario, M9W 3A6, Canada
PO Box 84165, Greenside, 2034 Johannesburg, South Africa
61 Beach Road, Auckland, New Zealand

Made and printed in Great Britain by
The Anchor Press Ltd
Tiptree, Essex
Set in Linotype Plantin

Granada ®
Granada Publishing ®

To Debby who made me write

THE HARDACRE FAMILY

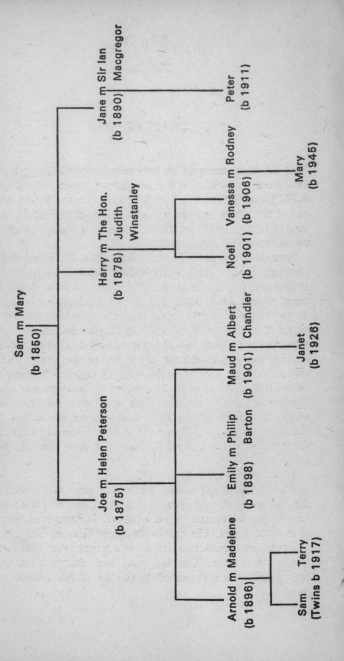

Sam m Mary
(b 1850)

Joe m Helen Peterson (b 1875)   Harry m The Hon. Judith Winstanley (b 1878)   Jane m Sir Ian Macgregor (b 1890)

Arnold m Madelene (b 1896)   Emily m Philip Barton (b 1898)   Maud m Albert Chandler (b 1901)

Noel (b 1901)   Vanessa m Rodney (b 1906)

Peter (b 1911)

Sam   Terry (Twins b 1917)

Janet (b 1926)

Mary (b 1945)

Book One

The Guttie

CHAPTER ONE

Sam Hardacre stamped his hob-nailed boots on the gut-soaked cobble-stones in an abortive attempt to restore the circulation to his freezing feet. His numb fingers, great red gobs sticking out of the filthy hessian strips that bound his hands, worked automatically, with an instinct born of many years spent standing behind a gutting bench.

Sam was a master of his trade. His left hand held the herring, his right the gutting knife, a razor-sharp piece of steel with a wooden handle bound with string. It was all one movement, as rhythmic as if it had been orchestrated: knife in, down the back of the fish leaving the bone on the left as it sliced the creature open, while his right thumb dug the gut from the body and into the gut bucket, and then, while the herring was still in the air on its way to the barrel, the knife was already ripping open the next. A layer of herring in the barrel and a pause while Sam spread a layer of salt and ice. A muttered oath as the salt bit deep into the open wound where the blade of the knife had slipped across his thumb half a barrel ago. A quick suck at the throbbing thumb, spit the muck into the gut bucket, and the next fish was already being ripped open.

'God it's bloody cold!'

And it would get colder. December was only weeks away; the day was dull and drab, posing the threat of a hard winter. The biting November wind whipped in from the dirty grey of the North Sea. The daily race of the Herring Drifters, each piling on its canvas in a desperate attempt to be first home to market, was over. The last boat had dropped her stained brown sails and was unloading the last of her baskets on the quay.

7

In November 1885 there was a depressing sameness about the fish quays of Britain. Grimsby, at the mouth of the Humber just south of the Yorkshire border, differed from the rest only in that it was larger, noisier, and more nauseating than most. Square wooden pillars supported long curved roofs; below them it was open on all four sides to the elements. The creaking and groaning of the derricks as they heaved their slithering contents from the fish-holds was followed by the screech of rope through pulley as the straining muscles of the seamen relaxed and the basket was run on to the quay. Then there was the constant mewing of the gulls, who carpeted the roofs of the sheds dirty white and grey with their excrement. The birds launched themselves into the air after every discarded piece of fish or offal, competing for the scraps with the flotsam of near-starving humanity who had found no work. The raucous shouting of the auctioneers, unintelligible to all save the buyers; the constant brawling of the casual labourers as they fought over what work there was to be had; and, on the landward side of the sheds, emaciated horses standing between the shafts of wagons and rattling away over the cobbles as soon as they had loaded. And everything overlaid with the stench of fish whose guts and slime covered building, boxes, carts, and men.

Sam Hardacre looked up for a moment, glancing at the fish porters who were busy filling barrels and heaving them to the gutting benches. A guttie's livelihood depended on these men. Sam was nearly out of fish. Another barrel would be his fourth, and at sixpence a time that would make a fair day's wages.

Damn the bloody thumb! It was slowing him down. Slice, gut; slice, gut; he glanced up again and caught the eye of a porter whom he knew.

'Fucking crook,' Sam spat contemptuously.

The porter caught his eye and nodded. Sam knew that it would cost him a halfpenny, but he would get his barrel; maybe even two.

Sam sucked his aching thumb and spat again as the porter dumped the barrel at his bench. He laid the ha'penny on the table and watched the porter's grimy hand close over it.

'Get us another one.'

'It'll cost yer.'

'Ha'penny.'

'Penny.'

Sam's knife came up, the point half an inch from the other man's nose. 'It won't only be fish gut on here if I don't see that other barrel.'

The porter ducked back and swallowed hard. 'There's no need for that, Sam, I was only joking. Thou'll get thee barrel.' There were not many men who would argue with Sam Hardacre.

'And thou'll get bugger all for thee asking,' growled Sam.

He grinned as the porter scuttled off, knowing that he would get his fifth barrel. Two shillings and sixpence, less a halfpenny, and add to that threepence from the guano or fish glue factory for the gut. He had had a good day. He would buy a mutton pie for their supper, fresh milk for the kids, and a glass of stout for Mary.

Even among that tough breed of men who, summer and winter, sweated and froze on the fish quays, Sam Hardacre was a commanding presence: six feet of weather-beaten brawn and muscle, close-cropped sandy brown hair, blue-eyed, firm-jawed, and carrying not one ounce of spare flesh. He had for thirteen years been tramping around Britain in the wake of the herring fleet. On that November Thursday in 1885, he had been working at Grimsby for a month. On the following Sunday he would leave, and with Mary and the children and his pony and cart, walk the fifty miles to Bridlington to be ready to meet the first boat in on Tuesday morning.

Sam was not looking forward to Brid'. Bridlington had no smokehouse, and he could earn nearly half as much again gutting for kippers as he could gutting, skinning, and filleting whitefish, but there were not many herring landed at Brid'. He consoled himself with the thought that it was not a long stay, two weeks only, and then on to Whitby; and there were still two more kippering days at Grimsby.

The porter brought Sam his fifth barrel.

'That's mine!'

Sam looked up at the owner of the voice, and his eyes narrowed. It was Bill Gormley. A huge man whose belly overflowed the string which supported his shabby, rough, grey serge trousers long since bereft of fly buttons, Gormley had lumbered over from his bench and was holding the little porter by the scruff of the neck.

'Tak it ta my bench, tha bloody little weasel,' he growled.

As the little man squealed, Sam put down his knife, picked up a handful of fish gut, and took a pace towards Gormley. The two big men stood facing each other over the head of the unfortunate porter.

'Keep out of this, 'Ardacre. It's ma barrel, and this bastard knows it,' snarled Gormley, releasing his hold on the porter.

'Tha'll leave that barrel where it is,' said Sam.

The porter stood rubbing his neck.

'Now get to hell out of here.'

The porter, with a frightened glance at both of them, scuttled away.

Sam turned back to Gormley. 'Now if tha wants this barrel, tha can bloody well come and get it.'

Gormley wanted that barrel, he wanted it very much. But he did not want it enough to welcome the idea of a fight with Sam Hardacre. The trouble was that it had now become a question of face, and face was very important if you wanted to survive on the fish quays.

With its usual carrion instinct, a small crowd had begun to gather, offering highly colourful advice to the two men. Gormley looked around him, he wanted a way out. He was beaten before he started, and he knew it, but he had to fight. Suddenly, fists clenched and arms flailing, he let out a roar and charged at Sam.

Sam moved; the gut in his left hand was rammed into Gormley's wide-open mouth, while his right sank up to his wrist in the other man's beer-sodden belly. Gormley doubled up in agony retching, spewing fish gut over the cobbles.

'Peelers!' cried a warning voice.

Two guardians of the law were strolling slowly down the quay. In a matter of seconds all the gutties were back at their benches bending to their tasks. One policeman paused as he was passing Sam's bench.

'Not on my patch,' he muttered.

Sam answered him with an expressionless stare, and the policeman moved on.

Sam had gutted his last herring. He stood waiting for the smokehouse clerk to check his work, pay him his wage, and collect his five barrels. It was ten hours since he had started; it would have taken less, maybe only nine, had it not been for his injured thumb. Still, threepence an hour was not bad pay. The clerk arrived and barely looked at the barrels, for he knew Sam and Sam's work; he counted five sixpenny pieces on to the gutting bench and moved on. Sam folded a piece of hessian and laid it on his forehead; he bent down and laid the broad leather strap attached to his gut bucket over this and stood up, heaving the stinking bin on to his back. As he passed Bill Gormley's bench, he spat contemptuously.

He carried his noisome load up the hill away from the quay, passing the row of ships' chandlers and sailmakers and pubs already doing a heavy trade as the men were paid off for the day. The women were there as well. Just now they would cost sixpence, by nine o'clock the price would have gone down to threepence, and by midnight a penny and whatever they could filch from your pocket. You did not need directions to find the guano factory. You just followed your nose in the direction of the most foul of all the foul smells with which the area abounded, and when it was strong enough to make you want to puke you were there.

When Sam arrived, the foreman, a new man, looked at his bucket.

'It's not full,' he said, 'but I'll gi' thee tuppence for it.'

'Tha'll gimme thruppence, or I'll tip bloody lot over tha sodding head,' growled Sam. 'Tha'll bloody soon find out if it's full or nay.'

'All right, all right, I was only joking.'

Like hell he was, thought Sam; if he had been new to the game, like as not he'd have got a penny, and the other twopence would have ended up in that greedy bastard's pocket.

Sam grabbed his threepence and made his mark. He was

finished for the day. Tomorrow morning at five o'clock the whole stinking business would start all over again.

Sam ripped the rags off his hands and flung them into the gutter. He stamped his way from the guano factory in the direction of his lodgings, about half a mile away. The lodgings occupied by the migrant workers rose in price commensurate with the distance between them and the stink of the factory, though when there was an easterly wind, everyone got a bellyful of the stench. First there were the rotting grey dwellings built right up to the cracked flagstone pavements; they were streaked with damp from broken gutters, had moulding planked doors, and their broken windows were stuffed with old rags or damp newspapers. The doors he passed opened directly on to a single room, which sometimes housed as many as ten. The only buildings of any substance were the smithy, with its smell of coke fires and the ring of hammer upon anvil, and the stables, open gaps between the buildings, reeking of horse manure.

At first there were as many as three pubs to the street, barely distinguishable from the houses which surrounded them except for the raucous noise from within as men and women sought oblivion in gin at a penny a glass.

As Sam neared his lodgings, the buildings began to give way to neater and more completely residential streets. Here the houses presented a solid face of red brick on either side of the street, with neatly painted doors and white pumice-stoned steps. They were two stories high and built in groups of eight. Between the groups were alleyways leading to a back lane. The lane was flanked by six-foot brick walls with gates leading into a paved yard behind each house, each of which contained a washing line, a coal shed, and a privy which housed an earth closet. Some of the houses in Reed Street were occupied by single families, but most of them were let off in single rooms, each house having two large ones in the front and two smaller ones in the rear. Sam's particular landlord lived in one of the houses on the block, half of which he owned. He let out most of his rooms to shopworkers and the more respectable of the not quite poor, but he had a few regulars among the migrants, all 'decent and respectable', one of whom was Sam Hardacre.

Most of the streets, and Reed Street was no exception, boasted their corner shop, where, with commendable loyalty, the inhabitants of the street did all of their food shopping. The corner shop sold practically everything edible – eggs, meat, cheese, pies, cakes; name it, and you would likely find it at the corner shop. Of course, each corner shop had its own particular speciality, and the shop at the corner of Reed Street made the best mutton pies in Grimsby. Sam went in.

'Give us a mutton pie,' he demanded, standing away from the counter so as not to leave any trace of his odour in the shop.

'Tuppence or fourpence?' asked the shopkeeper.

'Fourpence,' said Sam without hesitation.

'Had a good day, then, Sam?' The shopkeeper knew Sam well.

'Middling.'

'I've got a fourpenny one left over from yesterday, thou can have it for threepence if tha likes.'

Sam was tempted, but he turned the offer down, took the fresh one, and went out. He turned into the back lane and entered the yard of his lodgings by the plain wooden gate which had been newly painted since last year. He ducked carefully under the washing, which was hanging on the line to dry, so as not to stain it with his work clothes. He opened the brown back door and started to climb the bare wooden staircase past the plain, unadorned green and yellow walls.

Mary Hardacre had married Sam eleven years ago. During that period she had presented him with four children, three boys and one girl. Two of the boys, Joe and Harry, had beaten the odds stacked against them by society and their environment and had survived. The other boy had been stillborn, and the girl had lived for only six weeks. The death of his daughter was the only time in her life that Mary had seen Sam Hardacre cry. She had never lost the vision of him standing there, the tiny body clutched in his arms, the tears streaming down his cheeks, as he cursed the fates that had robbed him of the daughter he had wanted so dearly.

These same lodgings in Grimsby had been their first home. Sam had taken the day off to marry Mary, and in doing so had rescued her from the clutches of a drunkard of a father and a slut of a mother. The room was about eighteen feet square. It contained two beds with hard mattresses; they supplied their own blankets and pillows. The larger of the beds, of tubular iron with brass rails and knobs, was a good bed which had obviously started life in better-class surroundings than those in which it was now situated; this was where Sam and Mary slept, between coarse grey blankets, one of which Mary washed every week. The other bed was little more than a wooden pallet, about three feet wide, where the boys slept head to toe and took the inside berth against the wall in strict rotation.

There were four chairs and a scrubbed deal table. The chairs were a hodgepodge of fashions; one was a plain wooden kitchen chair, another an oak wheel-back which had seen better days, while the other two came from different upholstered dining suites long since disbanded. One of them still showed patches of the red and yellow regency striped damask which had once adorned it, but the other had been covered with a piece of discarded blanket which had been nailed to the frame with carpet tacks. The oblong sash window had a red plush curtain which was in surprisingly good condition, and it looked out of place against the rather seedy furniture. The most striking item in the room was the range – massive, shining, and black-leaded. On the right was the fireplace, which had two hobs that could be swung in over the fire, carrying either pan or kettle, and over the centre of the fire was a large soot-blackened hook from which the soup kettle could be hung. On the fire's left was the oven, with a heavy iron door and shining polished hinges. This was heated by the opening of a flue in the side of the fire; it was used for baking and on the rare occasions when they had a piece of meat to roast. Over the fireplace was a large mantelpiece surrounded by a green-plush, heavily tasselled pelmet, and to its right a large cupboard. A huge brass fender surrounded the whole of the range; it had a brass stool on each end, the lids of which opened to make a coal box. Their own possessions were stowed away in the cupboard and in the two wicker hampers, which had rugs thrown over them to provide additional seating. A couple of rugs on the floor and the aspidistra in an earthenware pot, which Mary took with them everywhere, completed the furnishings.

This was Mary's domain; anything and everything to do with the home was dealt with by her. She always spent the first day in any lodgings scrubbing floors, black-leading the range, pounding the mattresses, and searching for bedbugs. When everything was spotless, when every nook and cranny had been dusted or wiped down, then and not before she would prepare their first meal.

They ate reasonably well, and, by the standards of their times, they were not poor. Sam could count on average weekly earnings of around twelve shillings, and that did not include the odd pennies he received from the guano factories. The guano money was sacred. Every penny went into the Tin Box. This Tin Box was their treasure chest. It was old and battered and black with a gold line around its middle, but it occupied the place of honour, the centre of the mantelpiece. It contained their marriage lines, the children's birth certificates, and the guano money. That money was their emergency fund, to be used only as a last resort when all else had failed. Every now and then they had to dip into it, but this was done only after long and serious consultation. On 18 November 1885, the Tin Box contained four golden sovereigns, eighteen shillings in silver, two pennies, and one farthing.

Every evening around four o'clock Mary would start boiling big kettles of water, one on each hob over the coal fire. She would get the zinc bath from the corner where it stood on end and place it in the centre of the room in front of the fire. Then she would put the big zinc bucket near the door and fill them both. To do this she had to draw water from the tap in the yard next to the privy, and it took her eight trips carrying the heavy kettle up and down the stairs.

As soon as she heard Sam on the stairs, she spread yesterday's newspaper over an area of floor just inside the door. Sam came in.

'Hello, wife,' he said, stepping carefully into the centre of the newspaper.

He always greeted her as 'wife', proud of the fact that theirs was a more lasting and respectable relationship than those of most of his acquaintances, who seldom bothered to avail themselves of matrimony.

'Hello, husband,' she replied.

'Mutton pie,' he announced, handing her the paper bag.

She took it unsmiling. She expected no less from her man. Whatever the cost, he would make sure that there was at least one good, belly-filling meal each day.

'Where are the kids?' he asked.

'Playing in the back lane,' she replied.

Sam handed over the remains of his day's earnings. 'There's threepence for the Tin Box,' he said, 'and tha can send Joe out for a can of milk and a jug of stout.'

'Joe's got his paper round, Sam.'

'That's not till six, there's plenty of time.'

'Can we afford it?' Mary was always cautious.

'Do as I say, Mary.'

Sam stripped off his filthy hessian apron and dropped it into the steaming bucket while Mary ran downstairs to send the boy on his errand.

He was almost stripped off when she returned. She collected his outer garments from the newspaper where he had dropped them. His trousers she put over the brass fender to dry out, his socks and shirt she put aside to be washed. She took his long combination underwear over to the bed, where she examined it to see if any darning was needed, but they were all right so she laid them on the bed for him to wear again after he had got rid of his grime.

Sam grinned as he watched her putting the mutton pie into the oven and a pan of peeled potatoes on the hob. Mary was funny that way – she would never look at her husband naked if she could possibly avoid it.

So, there were only some parts of Sam that Mary knew with her eyes; the wind- and salt-tanned face weathered older than his thirty-five years; the strong browned throat above the dirty shirt collar; forearms bare in all weathers and marked with cuts and scars, old and new, of the fish knife.

16

His hands were a working-man's hands – broad enough to cover entirely her thin shoulders. Mary could not abide small hands on a man. Her father had them, and she considered them cruel and weak.

But now she turned her back on him, as he dropped his shirt to the floor and slipped the yellow-white combinations from his shoulders. The white skin of his back, untouched by the sun, was a stranger's skin, unseen and unknown save by her hands. Their marriage bed was in darkness and would always be so. Still, the skin was pale and youthful, and had he been a gentleman he would have seemed fair, even blond. As it was, he was nearer dark, with his brown face and hair too short to show any colour other than sand.

His blondness showed in his fair-haired older son and in his eyes, which salt and wind could not change, no matter how they might try. They were simple eyes, simple and plain in colour and in mood. Pure straight blue, light enough but warm, utterly honest, without depth or mystery. Mary saw them as small-boy eyes, more innocent than either of her children's, and wondered, when she was inclined to wonder, how they could have survived, or rather how Sam could have survived with them so blatantly reflecting honesty in a world where honesty was a dangerous virtue.

The answer was that Sam had been blessedly endowed with physical strength, enough to defend his small personal bastion of decency. He was a good six feet tall, with the useful muscularity of a survivor. Mary had been very fortunate. With Sam she and her children would be sheltered and safe. Without him, they most certainly would not.

Sam cautiously lowered himself into the zinc tub, and sitting there with his knees up to his chin he set to work with coarse household soap and scrubbing brush until all of his white body glowed as red as his face. He called Mary, and she came to do her part and scrub his back. She didn't mind doing this; with his private parts submerged, she had less aversion to approaching him than when he was standing with everything in full view. She held the rough towel in front of her face as he rose from his bath, then dropped it over his shoulders. Straightaway she busied herself setting the table, while Sam finished drying himself and put on his combinations and his spare corduroy trousers. He pulled a flannel shirt over his head and, tucking it into his trousers, went over to the front window. He pushed up the sash and stuck his head out to make sure there was no one in the street below. Then he took the zinc bath and pitched its contents out on to the road.

Their eldest son came into the room carrying the can of milk and the jug of stout. Joe was a miniature of Sam, though it was clear, even at ten, that he was not likely to be as big a man. He had many of Sam's features, each one just a little exaggerated. The sandy-brown hair was a little bit redder, the blue eyes a little bit paler, and the square jaw a little more aggressive. Joe at ten was well able to look after himself; when he spoke, he looked you straight in the eye, but it was a challenge, not a confidence. He did not walk, he strutted like a young bantam cock, and he had all of his father's aggression but lacked the gentler side of Sam's nature. Joe asked neither favours nor quarter and offered none. He and Sam quarrelled frequently but with that grudging admiration that is held for a respected adversary. Joe's respect for his father was never a matter of doubt, but his love was reserved for Mary. These things apart, Joseph Hardacre had neither fear nor affection for God or man.

Harry came in with Joe. Three years Joe's junior, warm and loving, he was a gentle child, completely out of place in the harsh environment into which he had been born. When they came into the room, Harry stood a little behind Joe; he always seemed to stand a little behind someone, wide innocent blue eyes peering enquiringly out of the soft oval of his face. His hair was much darker than that of his brother, almost as black as Mary's, and his lips still had the remains of their baby fullness, making him look all the more like his mother. He had Mary's hands, long and slender, though not yet marred by the callouses of years of housework. He was in all things the antithesis of Joe. Joe was the doer, Harry the thinker. Joe welcomed conflict as an expression of his manhood, Harry avoided it. Joe sold newspapers, Harry wanted desperately to read them. It was a near-incredible fact that, in that completely illiterate household, Harry had taught himself the alphabet and was already beginning to learn the written formation of simple words. Joe went out morning and night and sold newspapers, contributing a penny or two to the household budget and keeping alive his fierce independence. Harry would spend most of the day looking through the paper which Joe had brought home the night before, picking out the words he knew and maybe learning one or two new ones.

Mary loved Joe because he was to her another Sam, a man's man, ready and willing to accept whatever challenge a hostile world might offer him. Sam loved Harry because he was gentle like Mary, perhaps like his daughter would have been had she lived, and because Harry was the clever one who strived for learning. Sam would do anything to further Harry's desire to study and would, much to Joe's disgust, bring him little picture books to help him with his reading.

'When'll tea be ready?' asked Sam.

'Soon,' replied Mary.

'Come on then, lass, take tha porter,' said Sam.

He went to the cupboard and got out the 'Victoria and Albert' wedding mug and filled it with black beer.

'Where's thine, Sam?'

'A cup of tea with me mutton pie'll do for me,' he replied.

'Thou'll take thy half of the porter, or I'll toss it out of the window,' said Mary.

Sam did not argue. He knew that she would do it. He went to the cupboard, got another mug, and divided the porter between them.

'By gum, but that tastes good,' said Sam as he took a long satisfying pull at the black beer. 'Do thee lads want tha milk now?' he asked, turning to the children, who were sitting on the floor by the brass fender.

'Yes, Dad,' said Harry eagerly, jumping up and coming over to his father.

'No,' said Mary firmly. 'They can have it hot when Joe comes in from his paper round.'

Longingly, Harry eyed the enamel can containing the fresh milk, but he said nothing and went back to rejoin his brother at the fire.

Sam and Mary did not talk a lot, they had no need to. They never felt uncomfortable in each other's company. They sat silently drinking their porter, while the boys chatted around the fire. When the potatoes were cooked, Mary took the mutton pie from the oven and put it beside Sam's plate. He cut it carefully into four equal parts while Mary heaped potatoes on to the plates.

As soon as the meal was over, Mary cleared away the dishes, Harry went out into the yard for a bucket of water and washed up, while Joe, muffled up against the cold, left on his paper round.

Sam drew his chair up to the fire and took a small tin box and a clay pipe down from the mantelpiece. The tobacco in the tin was in three-inch oblong black slices. He took the top slice from the tin and rubbed it carefully between his hands, shredding the tobacco. Then he filled his pipe, making sure that every last scraping went into the bowl and, after testing it to see that it drew easily, picked up a spill of paper which Mary had previously put by the hob and lit up. If anyone had cared to ask Sam Hardacre what he lived for, he could quite likely have replied that the most satisfying thing in life was those first few puffs at the end of the day. For a blissful moment or two he smoked contentedly and in silence.

'Sam,' said Mary.

'Aye?'

'Thou's cut thy thumb.'

'It's nobbut a scratch.'

'It's more than any scratch,' she said.

Somewhat grudgingly he allowed her to inspect the wound.

'It's more than any scratch,' she repeated, 'and it's getting red.'

Sam grunted noncommittally.

'Harry,' said Mary, 'go to the corner shop and get a tin of Germolene. Take a penny with you.'

Germolene was a pink ointment, Mary's universal remedy. If any member of her family met with any cuts or rashes or bruises, they received a liberal application on the spot. As everything that had gone wrong to date had got better, Mary had developed a boundless faith in its power, refusing to listen to the suggestion that 'they'd have got better any road'. That was heresy.

Harry returned with the ointment and a farthing change. Mary put a large dollop of the stuff on Sam's thumb and then bound it with a strip of clean cotton rag. Her task completed, she pulled over another chair to the other side of the fire and sat watching her husband as he puffed away contentedly at his pipe.

It was nearly eight o'clock when Joe returned from his paper round. He proudly handed his mother two pennies and one halfpenny.

'Tha's done well today, Joe, lad,' Mary smiled at her son. 'Here, keep that for thee sen'; she pressed the halfpenny into the boy's hand.

'Well done, Joe,' grunted Sam. He then went and picked up the farthing from the table where it had lain since Harry's return with the Germolene. 'Here, Harry, tha can buy tha sen summat tomorrow.'

'Thanks, Dad,' said Harry beaming. He crawled under his bed and came out clutching his little red tin money box. 'I think I'll save it.'

Sam grinned; he had known that Harry would say that.

Mary cut four slices of bread and margarine and heated the milk for the boys. Fresh milk was reserved for the children; she and Sam had a cup of tea, strong and sweet, made with evaporated milk.

After the boys were in bed, Sam and Mary tidied up. Then Mary got into the red flannel nightdress which had been Sam's Christmas present to her last year. She took the pins out of her black hair and shook it out, letting it cascade down her back, where it nearly reached her waist. She sat on one of the chairs and submitted to the luxury of Sam giving her hair fifty brushstrokes, carefully counted. Sam then stripped to his combinations, and then, quietly, so as not to disturb the children, they climbed into their bed.

'Mary,' whispered Sam.

'Aye, Sam, what is it?'

'Thou's a good woman, Mary.'

'Thou's a good man, Sam Hardacre.'

They lay silent in the dark for a while, and then Mary reached out and found Sam's hand. Gently she ran her fingers over the horny skin, tenderly she caressed the scars and callouses.

'I hope thy thumb's not going to be bad.'

'It'll be reeght. Don't tha worry tha sen.'

Again there was a pause.

'Those lads, Mary, Harry and Joe.'

'They're fine boys, Sam.'

'Don't I know that? And that's why we've got to do summat for them.'

'How dost tha mean, Sam?'

'I don't want to see them working on bloody fish quay.' He said it almost every night.

'Joe could do it if he had to; I don't know about Harry.'

'It ud kill Harry.'

For a long time neither of them spoke.

'Sam,' whispered Mary. 'Sam, I've got summat to tell thee.'

Still there was no reply, so Mary went on. She had never said it before, and she did not know what made her say it then. They both knew that it was true, they had just never got round to expressing it.

'Sam ... I love you.'

But Sam was asleep.

CHAPTER TWO

The following morning at a quarter past four, Sam got out of bed, raked the ashes from the grate, and lit the fire. When the fire had caught, he put on a kettle of water and, while it boiled, got himself dressed. Then he made a pot of tea. He took Mary hers in the Victoria and Albert mug, quickly drank two cups himself, grabbed a hunk of bread, and, just before five, wearing his reefer jacket with the collar turned up against the cold, he left the lodgings.

Mary sat up in bed sipping her tea. She cupped the cheap gaudy mug in her hands, regarding it lovingly. It had been Sam's first present to her.

She had been sixteen when they met. It had happened here in Grimsby on the fish quay. Sam had just started with the gutting. Mary, with an old coal sack around her shoulders to protect her little body from the cold and wearing a pair of cast-off men's boots, holed and several sizes too big, had been, as usual, hungry.

Her black hair, greasy and unkempt, was tied in a clumsy knot at the back of her neck. Her forehead was tall and grey-white, overhanging a pair of great blue eyes lustreless with despair. Hollow-cheeked and empty-bellied, she peered around the men at their work, looking for some discarded scrap to damp down the gnawing hunger which was always with her. She was small, a little over five feet; her bones showed through her thin hands, the fingers of which terminated in dirty, cracked fingernails. In spite of this, there was a certain prettiness, almost beauty, to be seen beneath the grime. Her mouth was full-lipped. If she could have smiled, if her wide eyes could have sparkled, if her weary body could have found a morsel of comfort so that it might relax, and if she had had anything to live for other than mere existence, she would have been an attractive girl.

She had been thrown out of her room that morning by her father, with a cuff over the ear and strict instructions not to return without money and food. She had tried to find work, scrubbing or cleaning, fetching or carrying on the quay, but that day she could find none. There were only two other ways that a girl like Mary could get money or food. She could sell herself at the then-going rate of threepence, or she could steal. Both of these courses terrified her, but she feared even more the beating she would receive should she return home empty-handed.

She had ended up on the fish quay, wandering around aimlessly, watching the gutties bending over their tasks, the porters heaving the barrels and the boats unloading their catches and putting out to sea again. Three times she saw a fish fall from a basket as it swung ashore. Each time she was too late, twice beaten by vagabonds as hungry as herself and once by a ravenous sea gull.

The day wore on, and with it Mary was getting more and more hungry and more and more desperate. The boats had finished their unloading, and the scavengers had nearly all given up and crawled back to their hovels. She was practically alone with the men still working on the quay. Hunger is hell, and Mary's belly was begging to be filled.

She made her decision; there could be no other. She looked along the line of rough, tough men as they filled their last barrels; she made her choice.

Sam seemed younger than the others and somehow cleaner. She sidled up to his bench, trying to force a smile to her lips.

'You want a good time?' The words almost choked her.

'Try somebody else.'

'But I fancy you, mister.'

'Bugger off.'

She had worked her way around the bench until she stood next to the barrel of fish. Quickly she grabbed a handful of herring, but she was not quick enough. Sam's great hand had her by the arm.

'Please, mister,' she whined, 'they wouldn't notice a couple of herring.'

Sam felt the thin arm beneath his grip and looked down at

24

the great eyes, welling with tears over the grey, hollow cheeks. He dived into his apron pocket and pulled out a quarter of a pork pie wrapped in newspaper.

'Stop tha blubbing,' he said. 'Eat this and wait over there till I've finished.'

She stood with her back to one of the greasy wooden pillars and ate ravenously, picking out the crumbs from the newspaper to make sure that no scrap of nourishment escaped. She was for it now, she told herself. She had sold her body for a piece of pork pie. She stood there watching him with frightened eyes. Would it hurt, she wondered, and shivered at the thought. Some women seemed to enjoy it, did it just for pleasure, and other women had babies. God, she couldn't face that, what could she do with a baby? She'd kill herself. She tried to sneak away.

'Stay where thee are,' Sam growled, 'I'm nearly done.'

She stood terrified and motionless, trying not to think about it. Sam had finished his last barrel, and the clerk was paying him two whole shillings. Mary had never before seen so much money. Surely he would give her threepence.

'Reeght,' said Sam, heaving up his gut bucket.

Wordlessly they walked together to the guano factory, where Sam received another twopence, and then he led her on to Reed Street to the same first-floor lodgings. Meekly she followed him in, too frightened even to be impressed by the order and cleanliness of the room. She wished she knew what to do. Would it be now? Would she have to take her clothes off? All of them?

'Gimme thruppence first, mister.'

'Don't thee stand there talking bloody rubbish. I'm going to get out of this muck, so if thee don't want to watch, take this tanner, go to the corner shop, and get a mutton pie and a pennorth of tea. And if thee don't come back, I'll find thee wherever thee goes and ring tha bloody neck.'

When she got back to the room, Sam had washed and changed into a clean shirt and corduroy trousers. He had a fire burning with a blackened kettle sitting on it.

'Thou's taken thee time,' he snarled.

'Here's change,' she said, hoping that he might tell her to

25

keep it, as she reluctantly put the twopence on the table. 'Are thee going to give me some of the pie?'

Sam grunted, pocketed the change, and put the pie in the oven.

'There's water in the bucket,' he said. 'Tha'd better wash thee sen afore thou sits at my table.'

She did as he ordered. Then she stuffed herself with mutton pie, washing it down with three cups of tea. For the first time in weeks her belly was really full. Sam sat and watched her intently.

'How long is it since thou's eaten?' he asked her not unkindly.

'Had a bit of bread yesterday.'

'What age of a woman art thee?'

'Old enough,' she replied, and there was a touch of defiance in her tone.

'Ever done this before?'

'What if I have?'

'I want to know, have thee?'

'Hundreds of times.'

'Liar!' Then, after a long silence, he opened a tin trunk and pulled out a striped flannel shirt. 'Tha can sleep in that, get to bed now'; he threw the shirt over to her.

She stood petrified, clutching the shirt.

'Go on, get on wi' it,' he said, 'what art tha waiting for? Thou's done this hundreds of times, remember?'

She still had not moved. Sam walked over to the table and blew out the candle. After that, he went over to the fire and sat down with his back to her.

'Go on, get on wi' it, I won't look.'

In the darkness she quickly slipped out of her rags and put on the enormous flannel shirt, never for a moment taking her eyes off the still, silent figure silhouetted against the dying embers of the fire. She stumbled as she groped for the bed.

'Watch what tha's doing, thou'll knock summat over.'

She found the bed and crept between the blankets. She could hear him breathing and moving about in the dark as he took off his clothes. Then his figure blocked the glow from the fire, as he approached the bed. Now, this was it, it would have to be now! She held her breath as she felt his hand on top of the bed. Suddenly he ripped off the top blanket.

'I want this,' he growled.

'What for! What art tha doing?' Panic welled within her.

'Sleeping on the bloody mat! What the hell dost tha think I'm doing? Hundreds of times.'

Mary could still remember the wonder and the shock of waking up the following morning. For a while she thought she must be dreaming. Waking up in a real bed instead of the vermin-infested heap of rags in the corner of her father's room. Sam standing over her with a cup of tea in his hand. It had seemed like paradise. She remembered too how she had wondered at this man. He had fed her, given her his bed, slept on the floor, and never touched her. She knew that her body was not much to brag about, but every man wanted that ... perhaps when he was drunk?

'Here, drink this,' he said, handing her the cup. 'We've got a lot to do today. The closet's in the yard when tha wants it.'

He went out of the room, and she jumped out of bed. She pulled on the tattered rag of a skirt that she had been wearing, tucking the tails of Sam's shirt inside the waistband and rolling up the sleeves. Sam returned carrying a bucket of water.

'Thou looks a mess. Tha'll find a comb on the mantelpiece.' He looked her over. 'Thou'd better keep the shirt, I'm going to burn this lot.' He picked up the rest of her filthy clothes, boots and all, and flung them on to the fire.

She started to protest. They were not much, but they were all that she possessed.

'Shut up and comb tha hair.'

Meekly she obeyed.

While she was dragging the comb through her hair, he opened the tin trunk and pulled out something. It was the first time she ever saw the Tin Box. He opened it and took out a coin.

'Here,' he said, 'take this and go down to Willy Mackenzie. Thou can get thee sen a dress and socks and shoes and whatever tha can get for it.'

She looked at the coin. 'What is it?'

'It's a half sovereign, luv, ten shillings. Tha'll have to go barefoot, but it'll be the last time, and if Willy asks where tha gotten it, tha can tell him Sam Hardacre.'

She was about to leave when Sam stopped her. 'Hi, wait a minute. What's thy name?'

'Mary,' she replied, puzzled.

'Mary what?'

'I'm not sure. Me father's called Wilkins, but he says that he isn't really me father.'

'It'll do,' said Sam. 'Now get thee down to Willy's.'

Willy Mac's little pawnbroker's shop was still at the far end of Reed Street, though it was now being run by his sons. Willy himself was a little old Scot who had three sons. They were always clean and neat and always attended the local Presbyterian church on Sundays. Willy himself was the local bank, shop, and outfitter, and he was also a fence. He died a few years later in prison while serving four-years hard labour for being a receiver of stolen goods.

The local pawn served many purposes; it was one of the safest deposits in the country, and many a one who possessed a 'pearl of great price' would pawn it for a fraction of its value knowing that, as long as he kept up the interest payments of sixpence per pound per month, his jewel was as safe as if it were in the Bank of England. It provided the poorer people of the area a place where they could get cheap second-hand clothing and footwear and where they could raise a few pence on some little treasure to feed a hungry family. The customers represented a fair cross section of society. There was the middle-class youth who pawned his birthday present to buy himself a woman, looking this way and that as he went in for fear that he might be recognized. Then there were the regulars who would pawn a suit every Thursday and redeem it after they had been paid on the Saturday, in time to take their girls out. And there were also the thieves, most of them not villains but simply hungry human beings. It was through them that the pawnbroker was initially tempted and finally trapped into fencing stolen property. Finally there were the Marys.

Mary did not mind going to Willy Mac's. She had received many a kindness from him. Often he would let her pawn her old sack for a penny and never ask for interest. On more than one occasion he had given her food. Willy had a heart, and he never liked to turn away anyone who might be hungry.

Mary went into the shop with its high counter, the iron grille at one end where transactions concerning valuables took place, the two winged cubicles where the shy and the shady could conduct their business with a little privacy, and the shelves behind stacked with unredeemed pledges; there were clothes, walking sticks, musical instruments, almost any portable item that you could think of. In the midst of it all sat Willy Mac. Mary found him sitting on a high stool examining a watch through a magnifying glass.

Willy was angry. It was not often that he was fooled, but this was one of those rare occasions. 'Robbers,' he was saying, 'that's what they are, robbers. Four shillings, and it isn't worth fourpence. Never trust a sassenach, Mary. And what can I do for you, lassie? That's a nice shirt you're wearing; when you want to pop it, I'll give you threepence for it if you keep it clean.'

'I want some clothes, Mr Mackenzie.'

'Clothes, indeed? Now, Mary, clothes cost money. I might be able to find you an old shawl that I can't sell, but clothes cost money, and I fear that you'll need the bawbees.'

'I've got the money,' said Mary, showing him the half sovereign she was clutching.

'But that's an awful lot of money, Mary, where did you get it?'

'Sam Hardacre.'

Willie looked at her sadly. It was a pity about Mary. It had to happen to all of them, of course. There was little else that a girl could do if she wanted to go on living.

Mary could see what was in his mind. 'I didn't . . .'

'No, of course you did not,' he said. 'Still, Sam Hardacre's a nice laddie. You could do a lot worse. Well, Mary, what do you want?'

Willy was generous, and Mary found herself fitted out with an almost-new grey skirt, two blouses, a nice blue jumper, a grey cardigan, two changes of underwear, a pair of boy's socks, and some stout walking shoes.

She put on the skirt, a blouse, and the blue jumper and gave her old skirt to Willy to throw away; then, with the rest of her purchases parcelled up in newspaper, she left.

When she got back to the lodgings, she was surprised to find Sam still there and dressed in his blue serge Sunday suit.

'Well, tha looks a damned sight better now,' he greeted her.

'Are thee not working today?' she asked.

'No.'

'What are thee going to do?'

'Listen, lass, I mun ask thee summat. Does that want to stay here along of me?'

'Can I?'

'Aye, tha can if tha wants to.'

So that was it, she thought. She was to become his fancy woman. It would not last, of course, but it was a damned sight better than anything she had ever known.

'I'll stay,' her voice was toneless.

Sam breathed deeply. 'Reeght,' he said and grabbed her hand. 'Come on.'

'Where are us going?' she asked.

'Where the hell dost tha think us'ns going? We're going to Mission. I fixed it all up while thee was out. Tha can't stay here with me unwed, so we're going to get married.'

Even now, eleven years later, she could still see him standing there shouting it at her to cover his embarrassment.

It was eleven o'clock, the children were playing in the street below, and Mary was preparing Sam's jam butty and his can of tea. She did this every morning, and as soon as the tea was ready, she would run down to the quay and sit with Sam while he had his midday snack.

She was just about to leave the lodgings when Sam appeared.

'Sam!' she said, surprised. 'What's up? Were there no boats?'

'Oh, aye,' said Sam. 'There's plenty of boats. It's this.'

30

He held up his injured thumb for her to see. It had gone all blue, and a yellow pus was oozing from it.

He let her help him off with his working clothes. Then she bathed his wound in hot water, gave it a liberal application of Germolene, and tore strips off an old shirt to make a bandage.

When she had finished, she poured out two cups of tea, and they sat sipping them.

'What are we going to do, Sam?' She wasn't worried, it was just an enquiry.

'I thought that we might move on today, seeing that I'm not going to be able to do any more work. We could mebbe make Beverley tonight, and that would mean Brid' tomorrow, and we could catch the Monday boats.'

'Will there be any?' asked Mary.

'Oh, aye, the local ones'll be out, and there won't be many gutties there until Tuesday.'

'If thy thumb's right by then.'

'It'll have to be right by Monday,' said Sam. 'Where are the boys?'

'Out in the street. Shall I tell Joe to get Adam?'

'Aye, lass, we'd best be packing. We can be on the road in an hour.'

CHAPTER THREE

Adam, their brown Welsh mountain pony, was ready by six o'clock the next morning. Mary had managed to persuade Sam not to start that Friday and to try and rest for the balance of the day and make an early start on Saturday. Joe had bolted his bread and margarine, gulped down his tea while it was still too hot, and dashed off to the field, nearly a mile away on the outskirts of the town, where the pony was kept, heaving the heavy harness with him. Joe got a rope on Adam by bribing him with a crust of bread, then he led him to the corner of the field where their little cart was parked. He backed Adam between the shafts and tacked him up in his gleaming harness. Adam was strictly Joe's province. The boy spent a great deal of time polishing the harness, cleaning the cart, and plaiting string reins. Every day he would go out to the field and give Adam a good brushing, then reward himself by mounting the pony and having a brisk canter around the field. By half past five Joe had Adam ready; he straightened the pony's forelock over the red and yellow painted headband and started to walk him slowly back to the lodgings.

While Joe was away, the others were busy packing all their possessions into the two wicker baskets and Sam's old tin trunk. Everything was packed except Mary's aspidistra; she carefully took it down from its place of honour in the centre of the table, wiped its leaves, and wrapped its pot in a special piece of sacking against the November chill. The aspidistra was a subject of lighthearted banter on Sam's part. 'What dost tha want to bring that damned weed for?' he would say, as she carefully prepared it for its journeyings.

'But, Sam, it's the only bit of garden I've got,' would be her pathetic reply. But neither of them were very serious.

Saturday was a long haul, about thirty miles. Starting from Grimsby on the south bank of the Humber estuary, they headed northwest along the coast. They had about fifteen miles to go before they caught the horse-and-cart ferry which would take them across the Humber to Kingstone-upon-Hull and thus into Yorkshire. When they started, Joe walked at the pony's head with little Harry trotting along beside him; Sam and Mary walked behind the cart. The weather was, for once, kind to them, and they made good time, being well over halfway to the ferry when they made their noonday stop for a meal of bread and cheese washed down with milk drunk from a communal blue-enamel can. In fifteen minutes they were on their way again, only this time Harry was put on to the cart and allowed to rest his little legs. Just before dusk they arrived at the ferry, and as soon as they were on board and Sam had paid the fare, tenpence for the trip, Joe dug out Adam's nose bag and put it around the pony's head; then he climbed on to the cart and lay down beside his brother, who was by then fast asleep. The deck was dry, so Sam and Mary sat down on it, leaning against one of the cart wheels, for the twenty-minute crossing. Mary put her head on Sam's shoulder, and Sam lit his pipe, puffing away happily as the ferry pulled out, its paddle wheels churning the water into white foam.

When the ferry docked at Hull Corporation pier, the two boys were sound asleep. Sam and Mary grinned at each other, and Sam took the pony's head and led him off the ferry. Here he waited a few moments while Mary went into a nearby shop and bought two pounds of sausages, which she put on to the cart, taking care not to disturb either of the boys or the aspidistra.

They walked most of the way in silence. Neither Sam nor Mary was a great conversationalist, but they found a peace in one another's company which did not require words. There was little to see. Once they were away from Hull and the lights of the town, it was pretty black. Sam lit a candle lantern and hung it on the cart as they pressed on to the north. They arrived on the outskirts of Beverley at about eleven o'clock, but they did not continue into the sleepy little market town. They turned east, heading for the racecourse, the environs of which provided the best camping sites around. As soon as they stopped, Joe and Harry woke up.

As in all of the many migrant working families, each of

them had his own job in making camp. Joe of course attended to Adam and staked him out for the night. Sam lit a fire – they carried the fuel for this, replacing it each morning as they started. Once the fire was going, Mary and Harry set to preparing a meal while Sam created a not-too-attractive but quite serviceable shelter out of the tarpaulin and the cart.

They all ate ravenously, shifting the whole two pounds of sausages and a loaf and a half of bread between them, followed by tea. After the meal and after Sam had carefully doused the fire, they all huddled together under the cart and were soon fast asleep.

On Sunday they woke just as dawn was lighting the green and brown of the gentle rolling hills of the Yorkshire Wolds away to the west. They started packing for the remainder of the trip to Bridlington; this would take them on through the coastal plain, where the rich brown earth was freshly turned by the ploughs of the men who farmed the richest arable land in England.

They were surprised to find that they were in the middle of a group of small camps and stalls in various stages of erection. There were not many there, and the absence of litter indicated that the race meeting which had drawn them had not yet taken place. Most of the stalls followed a pattern of a wooden bench or counter under a striped or brightly coloured canvas awning with shelves at the back which would hold the wares offered for sale. The people who ran these stalls were another group of the many groups of migrant workers who swarmed all over Britain. They included the navigators – 'navvies', who built the railways and the bridges, performing incredible feats with tools no more advanced than a wheelbarrow and a pick; the hop pickers who became the fruit pickers and then the potato pickers; those, like Sam, who followed the fishing fleet; and these people, who went from race meeting to race meeting – bookmakers, touts, pimps, tipsters, and stall-holders. It was a fact that almost every weekend a whole section of the population packed its belongings and moved.

Sam was busy lighting a fire so that Mary could cook breakfast – it was to be porridge – when he was approached by a man.

'That's a likely looking couple of lads thou's got there,' he said, indicating Joe and Harry.

'They're all right,' replied Sam, geting on with his work.

'Dost tha think they'd mind giving me a hand? I'd see them right, of course.'

'What dost tha want them to do?' asked Sam.

'Well, I'm on me own, and I could do wi' a hand to get me stall up,' replied the man. 'I tell thee what I'll do; if they'll help me, I'll supply bacon and eggs all round for breakfast, if thy woman'll cook them.'

'That woman happens to be my wife, lawfully wed,' growled Sam.

'I'm sorry, I'm sure, Mr er ... ?'

'Hardacre.'

'Mr Hardacre, I meant Mrs Hardacre of course.'

'Thou'd better.' Sam turned to Mary, who had been standing listening to the conversation. 'Well, wife, what dost thou say? It'll mean a late start.'

'I'd love bacon and eggs,' said Mary, 'but ...'

'Two eggs and four rashers each,' said the man.

Mary nodded.

'It's a bargain, then,' said Sam. 'Tell thee what, we'll all help, and that way we'll get it done quicker.'

Rapidly they assembled the planks and trestles to make the counter and the work table at the back of the stall. Then they erected the wooden frame, tightening up the guys in their tent-pegs and pulling over the whole construction a covering, open to the front, of green-and-white striped canvas.

Forty-five minutes after they had started, they were all sitting around Sam's fire finishing up the promised bacon and eggs.

'Thanks, Mrs Hardacre,' said the man, taking a cup of tea from Mary.

'They were champion,' said Sam, wiping up minute bits of egg yolk with a piece of crust. 'That's a fine stall tha's got there, mister, what dost thee use it for?'

'I sell tea at a ha'penny a cup. I usually have me woman with me, but she's been taken poorly, so I'm on me own this trip. She's staying with her ma in Leeds.'

35

'Well, I certainly hope that she's soon well,' said Sam. 'Dost tha mind if I ask thee summat?'

'Go on.'

'When do races start?'

'Tuesday.'

'Then why dost tha put thy stall up on Sunday if races don't start till then?'

'Thou can allus do a bit on a Sunday, especially wi' young folk coming out for a walk in the afternoon, and there's allus plenty of folk around on a Monday, and they all want a cup o' tea some time in the day,' the man went on. 'Thou can get the best part of a week out of a three-day meeting.'

'Is it a good living?' asked Sam.

'We can't grumble. We never go hungry, and we get a holiday every year.'

'A real holiday?' Mary was impressed. 'Like wi' nowt to do?'

'Aye, we go to the seaside for a week, or if we're doing extra well, we might have two weeks. She looks forward to it all year.'

While they talked, the boys were busy. They took the breakfast things down to the brook, washed them, and stored them away on the cart. Joe went to get Adam and soon had him between the shafts and tacked up ready to go.

They said good-bye to their new-found friend and headed off north, away from the racecourse. The road from Beverley through Great Driffield and on to Bridlington skirts the eastern edge of the Yorkshire Wolds, vast rolling moors covered with lush pasture where the sheep grew the wool for what for hundreds of years had been the county's principal industry. For miles after they had left Beverley behind, they could still see the tall spire of the Minster of St John of Beverley. The road was flat and straight, and to their right was the large coastal plain containing some of the finest agricultural land in England, where two crops a year was the norm rather than the exception. Since the weather was holding and it was another pleasant day, once they were clear of the town, Sam led the horse with Mary by his side so that the two boys could play in the late autumn sunshine.

As they walked, Sam was silent for a long time. He gave the horse to Mary and lit his pipe, which was unusual for him, for he hardly ever smoked before evening. Once he had the pipe going to his satisfaction, he puffed away pensively.

'Tha's doing a lot of thinking, husband,' said Mary.

'Aye,' he replied.

She waited for him to elaborate, but there was no further response.

'How's thee thumb?' she asked at length. She had changed the dressing that morning, but the thumb had still looked red and inflamed.

'It'll be reeght by t'morn,' he replied. It was quite a while before he spoke again. 'It's a better life than gutting.'

'What is, Sam?'

'What that fella's doing at racecourse.'

'Gutting's all right. We manage.' She was beginning to see what was on his mind.

'Aye, we manage, but there's precious little to fall back on; I'd like to do a lot better for thee and for those lads. Just look at them over there, they were born to enjoy life, they don't want to spend their time on stinking fish quays. I wouldn't like to think that that was all they had for a future.'

They were out in the farm country now among the dark green hawthorn hedges and ditches. The two boys were tumbling about in the hedgerows, delighting in the clean country air and the freedom.

'Tha know, Sam,' said Mary, 'they're a damned sight better off in this life than they would be if you had to find work in the town. At least they get the fresh air, and every time they have to move on it's a sort of holiday for them. They're happy.'

'Now they are,' replied Sam, 'but I'm not thinking about now. I'm thinking about what's going to happen after.'

'After what, Sam?'

'After summat happens to me, or I get too old to work. What's left for thee and for them? The poorhouse?'

'That's gloomy talk, Sam Hardacre, there's lots of folk worse off than us; any road, they'll be able to support them sen soon enough, and when they do that, happen they'll look after their old mum and dad. I don't know what thou's worrying about, that sort of thing's a long way off.'

'But it gets closer every day, Mary. I can't even afford to be poorly. Even this bloody thumb's costing us money that we can't spare.'

Sam was depressed. It was unusual; Mary had seldom seen him that way. He had lost a day's work before on occasions, but it had seldom seemed to worry him. She realized that it was much more than the bad thumb that was responsible for his present mood and that the talk at the racecourse had unsettled him; but she held her tongue.

They walked on for several miles without a word passing between them. The boys, in boisterous high spirits, were enjoying the sunshine, while Sam, still alone with his thoughts, puffed away at his long-since-empty pipe. They kept going at a fairly brisk pace, for in spite of the sun it was quite chilly and would get colder after dark; and their late start had made it inevitable that they would not get to Bridlington and the comfort of their lodgings until quite late.

As they approached Driffield, they came to what was obviously the environs of an estate. A high red brick wall, behind which there were thick woods, effectively shut off another life style from the vulgar gaze of the likes of the Hardacres. Ahead of them a closed landau, drawn by a beautiful matched pair of shining black hackneys, turned out of a concealed drive and careened past them. The liveried coachman cracked his whip over the glossy rumps of his charges as they passed at a quick, high-stepping trot. A few yards farther on they came to a pair of wrought-iron gates set back from the brick wall. A pleasant-looking little gatehouse stood to one side, and from the gates a smooth, clean, gravelled drive swept away, flanked by tall elms, to whatever secret lay beyond. Sam stopped Adam outside the open gates and looked down the drive.

'That's where thou ought to live, Mary,' he said.

'Oh, Sam,' said Mary, returning his smile, 'I wouldn't know how to behave among all them posh folk.'

'Thou'd behave just the same as thou allus does,' he said. 'That's good enough for anybody.'

There was a hint of belligerence in his tone; Sam Hardacre

would defend his own.

The door to the little gatehouse opened, and a servant came out, looking enquiringly at the Hardacres.

'What are you lot doing, hanging around here?' he demanded as he started to close the gates.

'Watch it, lad, tha might be talking to tha next boss,' Sam spoke with mock ferocity. Then he laughed, 'Come, lass, we'll never get to Brid' at this rate. But we're not moving on account of thee,' he said to the servant.

It was all right again, Sam's depression had left him. It was quite dark by the time they got to Burton Agnes some five miles south of Bridlington, and the weather had taken a change for the worse. Dark clouds had blown in from the southwest, and the cold November rain combined with half a gale to make everything very uncomfortable. In spite of this Sam's spirits remained high. They loaded the boys on to the cart and covered them with the tarpaulin which writhed and heaved as some mysterious game was played out underneath. Mary grabbed her aspidistra and put it in a corner of the cart protected by the tin trunk. 'If they damage that, I'll break their necks,' she said.

Sam laughed. 'Well, lass, thank God wind's in our back,' he said as they marched one on either side of the now-reluctant Adam's head. But as the storm grew in intensity, even Sam's new-found good humour began to wilt, and their progress became a grim battle with the elements.

'There won't be many boats out tonight,' said Mary.

'There'll be some,' said Sam. 'Some of them'll 'ave got out before this came up. There'll be work tomorrow, thou'll see.'

'I'm glad thou's not a fisherman, Sam.'

'On a night like this I'm glad too, Mary.'

It was approaching ten o'clock when they finally arrived at their lodgings in Bridlington. They were cold, they were wet, and they were miserable, but their troubles were not yet over. It seemed like the last straw when their landlord told them that the present occupier of their lodgings would not be moving out of their room until the following day.

'But what the hell can I do?' said Sam. 'I've got Mary and the kids here. Is there anywhere else tha can bring to mind?'

'Town's pretty full, them as are still taking folk,' said the landlord, 'and tha don't want to be wandering about chancing it on a night like this. I tell thee what, I've got an empty stable. There's a stove in there, you'll be dry and warm, and I'll only charge thee for the coal. You can have your room tomorrow for sure. What dost tha say, Sam?'

'Is there owt to sleep on?' asked Sam.

'There's plenty of clean straw,' said the landlord. 'I'm sorry I haven't got any beds. It's not my fault, you know, I didn't expect you till Monday. You can stick your pony in one of the stalls if you want.'

'What dost tha think, Mary?'

'Well,' said Mary, 'as I see it we haven't got any choice, and don't worry, Sam, we aren't the first family to have slept in a stable.'

'Mary,' said Sam reprovingly; he was easy to shock in these matters.

And so, much to the delight of the boys, who loved the idea, it was settled. Sam lit the stove, and Mary made tea while Joe carefully rubbed Adam down with straw and sneaked him an extra scoop of oats.

Little Harry made a thick layer of straw against one of the walls while Sam and Joe stuffed up the worst of the cracks with old rags and bits of straw. Then, all their tasks completed, they bedded down together and were soon fast asleep.

They had been sleeping soundly for some time when Mary woke up with a start and a scream as some object landed on her body.

'Summat's on me!' she cried.

Sam was awake in a flash. He groped around and grabbed the offending creature. 'It's nobbut a cat,' he said.

'Chuck it out, Sam.'

'Don't be daft, wife, as long as he's here we're not going to be bothered wi' rats,' said Sam, stroking and calming the frightened animal.

Purring with contentment at its acceptance, the cat settled happily in the small of Mary's back, and they were all, very soon, sound asleep once more.

The next morning the cat, which turned out to be a tabby of

40

mixed origins, was still there. It condescended to share their breakfast and then returned to the still-warm straw. Sam had his thumb dressed again after another liberal application of Germolene. It was still painful, but he collected his gutting knife and started to leave.

'Does tha think thou ought to work today?' Mary called to him.

'I mun try,' he replied and set out through the stable door. Mary followed him.

'Sam, I don't think thou ought to go,' she pleaded.

'We need the money, wife.'

'There's money in the Tin Box.'

'Aye, and it'll stay there,' said Sam firmly. 'That's only for emergencies.'

'Sam Hardacre,' she said, barring his way, 'would tha mind telling me what this is if it is not an emergency? There's no reason why we can't live on what we've got for a few days until thy thumb's better.'

'Get out of my way, Mary; I'm going to try.'

She knew that it was pointless to argue with him. 'Sam,' she said, 'if thou's going to be a pigheaded fool and try to work, will thou at least make me a promise?'

'Tha knows I will if I can.'

'If that thumb starts to hurt thee bad, thou'll come straight home.'

'There'll be no need for that, but if it does, then I will.'

'Promise?'

'I promise.'

Satisfied, Mary watched him go, secure in the knowledge that he would keep his promise, even though his definition of 'hurt bad' might differ greatly from hers. Sam walked out into the town, where the cold grey November dawn was just breaking. His lodgings were nearly a mile from the harbour, and as he walked he turned up the collar of his coat and pulled it tight around him to try to combat the chill. In doing this he stubbed his thumb, and a sharp stab of pain warned him that it was more than likely that he was going to have to keep his promise to Mary. Stubbornly, however, he kept going, down the promenade and past the lines of shops that catered to the tourist trade, most of which were shuttered against the winter, not to open again until next Easter heralded the return of another holiday season. He was determined to try to work, even though he knew that the odds were that he would not be able to. He took some small comfort from the look of the angry sea on his left, the legacy of last night's storm. Most of the boats would have put in for shelter during the night, and there would not be much fish in that day.

Fifteen minutes after leaving his lodgings, he arrived at the harbour, only to find it devoid of any activity. If there were boats coming, they were not there yet. He looked out to sea towards where Flamborough Head was being pounded by heavy seas some three miles away across Bridlington Bay, but there was nothing in sight. He had no other choice but to wait. For a full half hour he hung around, stamping his feet and flapping his arms to keep warm. Finally he decided to go into the little wooden café at the end of the South Pier and get himself a cup of tea, a sit down and a warm. He could afford it, he had fourpence halfpenny in his pocket, and the rent for his gutting pitch was only threepence.

The café served the harbour workers during the winter and did duty as a sweet shop cum café for the visitors in the summer. Inside Sam found two or three men sitting about drinking tea and smoking their pipes. Sam got his cup of tea for a farthing and sat down at one end of the form flanking the plain scrubbed wooden table, which was the only other piece of furniture in the room.

'Hello, Sam,' said a voice; it belonged to one of the fish porters whom Sam had known for years. 'Tha's here early.'

'Aye,' said Sam. 'What's happened to boats, when are they coming?'

'There's not many out, and them as are'll be late. It were quite a night last night. Reckon we won't see the first boat for more than an hour yet.'

Something in the café caught Sam's eye; it was a pile of shining tin trays standing in a corner, and in front of them was a notice written on a slate.

'Can thee read?' Sam asked his acquaintance.

''Corse I can't, don't be daft. He can, though,' he indicated

42

a man dressed in a serge suit complete with collar and tie. 'He's clerk to t' Harbour Master.'

'Can I help?' asked the clerk.

'Aye, if tha wilt,' said Sam. 'Can tha tell me what them words on those trays says?'

'Toffee trays, going cheap, only one halfpenny each,' the man said.

'Ta,' said Sam. 'I'm beholding to thee.' He sat and thought for a moment and then walked over to the counter. A boy of about twelve or thirteen was serving. 'Where's boss?' demanded Sam.

'Me dad?' replied the boy. 'He's in back there, dost tha want him? Here there's nowt wrong wi' the tea, is there?'

'Nay, nay, I just want a word with thy dad.'

In a few moments a small wiry man emerged, wiping his hands on a greasy apron.

'Who wants me?' he demanded.

'How many toffee trays hast tha got there?' asked Sam.

'I don't rightly know, but I should think there's upwards of five hundred.'

'How much dost tha want for lot?'

'Oh, I doubt I could let them go under thirty bob.'

'Tha bloody well could or tha won't sell them, not to me any road. Fifteen bob.'

They haggled for a while and finally closed the deal at a pound and sixpence. They both spat on their hands, and with a handshake the bargain was made.

'I'll be back a'fore noon wi' t' brass and I'll take them then,' said Sam.

Sam had had an idea. It had been formulating for the last twenty-four hours. He had not talked it over with Mary, but gradually his mind was being made up. In a way those tin trays were Sam's Rubicon. He had committed himself to buying them, he had given his hand on it; it had been a very deliberate act, and he had forced himself into a position where he had to give his idea a try. Everything now depended on some boats arriving with at least some herrings.

He left the café and hurried back to the lodgings, where he found Mary and the boys busy moving their things into their, now-vacant, room.

'Where's landlord?' he asked.

'Downstairs,' said Mary. 'But Sam, what are thee doing back? Is tha thumb bad?'

'Never thee mind about my thumb and don't do any more unpacking. Happen we'll be leaving after dinner.'

'Sam, would thee mind telling me what's going on?'

'I've no time now,' said Sam, 'I'll tell thee when I get back. Tell landlord that we might be leaving this afternoon, but we'll pay for week and leave some of our stuff here. Now, where's Tin Box?'

'Here, Sam,' said Mary. She was worried now but determined not to show it. Here was her Sam demanding the Tin Box without any of the ritual of discussion which usually preceded even its mention.

'How much dost tha want?' she asked.

'Two and a half sovereigns.'

'Two and a half sovereigns?' It was a fortune; if they were careful they could live for a month on two and a half sovereigns.

'Don't thee worry, Mary, I haven't gone mad. Just give me brass and tell Joe to be at harbour wi' Adam and the cart by twelve o'clock.'

Without further explanation he took the money and left. Mary sat on their pile of blankets clutching the Tin Box.

'Was that Dad?' asked Joe, coming into the room with a pile of stuff.

'I think so, Joe,' said Mary. 'It looked like him but it didn't act like him.'

'Are thee all right, Ma?' asked Joe.

'I'm all right, Joe but I think thy father might have gone off his head.'

Harry came in. 'What's wrong wi' dad?' he asked.

'Nowt as tha's going to notice, but he's acting strange,' said Mary. 'Joe, he says that thou's to be at harbour at twelve o'clock wi' Adam and the cart.'

'What for?' asked Joe.

'I only wish I knew,' said Mary sadly.

Meanwhile, Sam was on his way back to the harbour. He

44

saw that there were now three boats in Bridling Bay; they were just inside Flamborough Head, pitching and rolling in the still-rough waters. The wind had backed northeast, and the stiff breeze was driving them lickety-spit towards the shelter of the harbour piers. Sam reckoned that he had about half an hour before the first boat tied up and started to unload.

He went down to the fish quay on the end of the pier. There were four tables for hire next to the cleared space where the fish would be auctioned. When Sam got there the quay manager came over to him.

'I heard that you were here, Sam,' he said. 'I'll keep a table for you.'

'I'm not gutting this day,' replied Sam. 'I'm going to t'auction, I'm buying. And by the by I'll need three fish boxes, the large ones.'

The manager looked after Sam astonished as he took his place among the comparatively well-dressed fish merchants who were already gathering as the first boat, *Girl Pat*, rounded the north pier. Sam watched her with an experienced eye. She was low in the water, but not too low. That indicated an average-to-good catch. She was a herring drifter, and Sam wanted herring. Her crew looked exhausted, which meant that she had probably fished well into the storm; it was doubtful if many of the other boats would have done so. So the odds were that the rest of the boats would have lower than average catches. It would therefore pay him to buy early, as the price would almost certainly rise as the day wore on and the rest of the boats berthed.

A couple of sample baskets of herring were winched on to the quay and put in front of the auctioneer's rostrum. The remainder of the catch was being loaded into boxes of half a cran, about five hundred herring each. The buyers grouped around the samples, examining the fish; then the auctioneer took his place, and the bidding began.

The bidding was brisk, and the price was rather high, but Sam was in a hurry and bought two cran off the *Girl Pat*, for which he paid ten shillings and nine shillings, respectively. He handed over the money, collected his fish, then sat on a bollard and gutted and split them into the boxes which the quay manager had produced.

Just before noon he was finished, and he walked down to the end of the pier, where he found Joe waiting for him.

'What tha been doing, Dad?' asked Joe casually.

'Buying fish,' said Sam equally casually.

They led Adam and the cart down the pier to the place where Sam had left his boxes. As they got near, Sam spotted a pinch-faced urchin taking a couple of fish out of the top box and stuffing them under his shirt. Joe saw the incident as well and leapt forward with an oath, only to be stopped by Sam's great hand descending on his shoulder.

'Hey, tha's hurting me!' yelled Joe.

'Where dost tha think tha's going?'

'There's a fella there pinching fish.'

'I saw him. They're my fish.'

'Well, let go of me, Dad. I'll get him. I'll break his bloody neck.'

'Leave him be,' said Sam, 'happen lad's hungry. He's welcome to a couple of herring.'

As the boy passed, Sam called out to him, 'Enjoy tha dinner, lad, them's my fish thou's got.'

The boy looked up startled and ran off. Sam laughed and turned back to Joe. 'But never let them think as they're getting away wi'it,' he said.

On their way back to the lodgings they collected and paid for the tin trays. Several times Joe tried to draw his father into telling what he had in mind, but without success.

When finally they arrived at the lodgings, Sam went in search of Mary. He found her getting the last of their things out of the stable.

'Come, lass,' he said, 'let's get packing. I want to be in Beverley tonight.'

'But what is all this, Sam?' she asked. 'What about thy work?'

'There's summat tells me, Mary, that this is going to be my work from this out. We're going into business. And Mary...'

'What is it, Sam?'

'Happen we'll have a holiday next year.'

46

CHAPTER FOUR

They were soon packed and on the road. Just as they were leaving, a small furry object leapt on to the cart and curled itself into a ball. It was the cat.

'I think he wants to come with us,' said Sam.

Joe offered to chase the animal away, but Sam would have none of it.

'Mebbe it's our luck,' he said. 'Tha wouldn't want to chase that away. If it wants to come wi' us it can.'

The cat, thus reprieved, sat on the cart next to the aspidistra, looking longingly at the boxes of fish. All through the journey Mary and the children tried to find out exactly what it was that Sam had in mind. However, he was still not to be drawn. To Mary it was a side of her husband that she had never seen before. Here he was, rough, tough Sam Hardacre, behaving like a mischievous child and keeping a secret from her. It would have been funny if she had not been worrying about the two pounds ten that he had taken out of their savings.

'When we get there, we'll set up camp, and tomorrow morning we'll look for a site, and if you'll all just do as I say, thou'll get that holiday, I promise thee that.'

It was nearly pitch dark when they arrived near the race-course, so they just pulled off the road and bedded down where they were for the night.

When they awoke the next morning, after a fairly uncomfortable night, they were surprised at the transformation that had taken place since they had left on Sunday. They had camped on a slight rise just off the road overlooking the course, and the whole place, as they looked around, seemed to have taken on a fairground aspect; the whole area of open ground outside the course now looked like a patchwork quilt. Dozens of multicoloured stalls and carousels flanked the outside of the tall grey stands which covered those parts of the course where one had to pay for admission. There was the Silver Ring, threepence, Tattersalls, one shilling, and the Enclosure at two shillings and sixpence, where one could mingle with the trainers and owners. The stands obscured the winning post and the last half furlong of the track, but beyond them and all the way down to the six-furlong starting gate was the free course, and it was here that one found all the colour and variety of a Victorian race meeting. Even the elite from the Enclosure would spend a little time wandering around the free course and tasting of its pleasures. Bookmakers' stands lined the track, thinning out as they got farther away from the stands. These were not like the bookmakers in the Enclosure, who would take a bet of £5000 from a belted earl at a nod of the head, but the little men who took their bets in pennies and prayed that the favourite would not win the last race. It was here, when they had had a bad day, that one might sometimes see the classic sight of a bookie who had been unable to pay out, with satchel under arm running for dear life, pursued by a crowd of angry punters.

Then there were the tipsters, men whose outrageous costumes could not fail to attract attention, who offered to 'mark your card' for twopence. Most of the stall holders were honest merchants trying to make a living and competing honourably with each other, but there was another side to the racecourse. Meetings swarmed with pickpockets, petty thieves, and the gangs of racecourse toughs who made a living by extortion and terrorized the weaker of the stall holders. Every now and then someone would produce a couple of bantam cocks, and an illicit cock fight would draw a big crowd and its inevitable profit in wagers; and of course there were the prostitutes, who plied their trade through the whole social strata of the course. They ranged from threepence a time behind a hedge on the free course to the exotic creatures in the Enclosure at fifty guineas and a champagne supper, for a night at the best hotel in the district.

There was at least one meeting every day except Sundays somewhere in England, and throngs of these people, good and bad, followed the horses, jockeys, and trainers from one location to another week in and week out.

Sam, still uncommunicative, sent Mary into the town to try to find them lodgings for the next few nights, telling her to look for him and the boys on the free course on her return. When she returned, she found them about a third of the way down the course. Sam had dug a shallow trench, Joe had staked out Adam, and the two boys were foraging around for wood.

'Did tha get a place?' asked Sam.

'Aye, and it'll cost us a shilling a night, and it's no better than our lodgings in Brid'.'

'Don't tha worry, we'll be able to afford it,' said Sam.

'Sam,' said Mary, firmly seating herself on one of the baskets, 'thou's going to tell me what we're on. I'll go mad if tha don't, and I'm not going to do another stroke until I know.' She looked at the pile of wood. 'What dost tha want all that for?'

'I'll tell thee over breakfast, lass, be patient till then,' Sam smiled at her. 'I'll get a small fire going, and thou can cook up some of the herrings and while us eats, I'll tell thee.'

Over breakfast, he at last told them his idea; he was going to build a wood fire, then roll the herrings, and bake them on the tin trays. He would sell them at a penny each or seven for sixpence. When he had finished, he sat back and waited for the compliments.

Mary had listened in silence. 'Is that all?' she asked.

'Aye,' said Sam smiling, 'that's all.'

'Sam Hardacre,' she said, 'thank thee very much for letting me know what's going on. It would have served thee a damned sight better to have told me last night.'

'What's wrong, it's a bloody good idea.' Sam was on the defensive now.

'It's a gradley idea,' replied Mary, 'but thou are nobbut a man and being a man thou can only think like a man.'

'Well?'

'Well, he says? Well, he says, how are thee going to serve herrings? Just hand them over to customers in their fingers so that they can get all greasy and burnt?'

'Oh ... well, I hadn't really thought about that part yet.'

'Of course thou hadn't. It's just like I said, thou's a man.

I reckon it's high time that I took a hand. And thee can thank tha lucky stars that thou didn't leave it any later to tell us. Joe! Harry! Come over here, I want thee.'

She stalked over to the cart and got the Tin Box out from its hiding place. Sam watched her, silent and astonished.

'Mary, what are thee doing?' he demanded at length.

'I'll tell thee that after I've done it, Sam Hardacre.' She turned to the boys, 'Joe, Harry, thee see this? It's half a crown – that's a lot of money, two whole shillings and six-pence.' She had fished the coin out of the Tin Box and was holding it up for the boys to inspect.

'What the hell's going on?' roared Sam.

'Thou'll find out all in good time,' replied Mary. 'Now, lads, I want thee to take this half crown into Beverley, there's a good secondhand shop there, I saw it this morning. Thou's to buy a big sheet. Get a good 'un, it shouldn't cost no more than eighteen pence, but make sure that it's white. After that spend the rest of the brass on white paper, get the biggest sheets thee can and as much as thee can.'

'Yes, Mum,' said Harry.

'Do thee understand, Joe?'

'Aye.'

'Well, I'm damned if I do,' roared Sam.

'Off thee goes then, boys, and no playing on the way. I want thee back as soon as thee can get.'

'Right, Mum,' said Joe, and they were off.

After the boys had left, Sam again tackled Mary, 'Woman, will thee tell me what thou's doing?'

'Aye, Sam, I'll tell thee now.' She was maddeningly calm. 'The sheet is to make thee a decent white apron, two in fact so that thou can allus have a clean one. The paper is to cover the cart with and to wrap the herring in as thou sells them. Do thou think for one moment that anybody's going to buy food from a man standing there in a filthy hessian guttie's apron?'

'It's clean, thou washed it.'

'Aye, but it's all stained and it looks mucky even if it isn't.'

Sam looked at her for a long time; suddenly he smiled, and the smile became a broad grin creasing his weather-beaten face, 'By gum, but thou's a wonderful woman,' he said. He laughed and put his arms around her.

'That's quite enough of that, Sam. There's work to be done,' she replied, evading his embrace but smiling. 'And thou'd better pray for fine weather, because we're going to be in a heap of trouble if it rains.'

'I'd never given that a thought.'

Mary was suddenly serious. 'Sam, there's a whole lot of things us won't have thought of, but I'm sure that the idea's right. Whatever we haven't got right we'll sort out as we goes along. This is no time to start to worry. I think there's still enough of that fire left to boil a kettle; come on, I'll make thee a cup of tea.'

About an hour before the first race the crowds started to gather. Sam had got the big fire going early, so that there was a good red heat for Mary to start baking the herrings. When the boys returned with their purchases, Joe petitioned his mother to cut out an apron for him too, so that he could help with the serving. Sam agreed, and Joe got his apron. Harry was detailed off to keep the supply of wood going. Joe and Sam covered the cart, with white paper; this done, their possessions neatly stacked behind the cart, they were ready for business. It was not without some trepidation that they waited the arrival of their first customer. They had not to wait long.

A man dressed in rough tweeds, knickerbockers, and gaiters – probably a local farmer – hesitated a short distance from their stall. Sam, standing behind the first two trays of steaming herrings, nervously ran his tongue over his lips as he watched him. Mary looked up from where she was loading trays. Oh, dear, she thought, what if he buys one, what if they're not cooked right? Harry cocked his head on one side and smiled in the general direction of the man.

'Like to try one, mister?' said Joe.

The man came over. 'That looks like a good idea,' he said. 'Yes, I'll try one, how much are they?'

'Penny,' said Joe before Sam could reply.

The man handed Joe a bright new penny, Sam gave him the fish on a piece of white paper, and four pair of eyes watched anxiously as he took his first bite.

'Good,' he said. 'I'll have another.'

The man walked away with his purchase, and the family breathed a quite audible sigh of relief.

Sam turned to Joe, 'Give that first penny to your mother,' he said.

'What do I want wi' it?' asked Mary.

'Yon's the first penny of our new business,' said Sam, 'and it's a new one at that. Keep it, happen it'll bring us luck.'

The farmer proved to be the first of many, and they were soon busy. It proved a good day, and they learned a lot. One thing was that business was heavy before the first race and very heavy after the last race, while in between time it slackened off considerably. They wasted a fair number of herrings during that middle period. Mary cooked too many, and they got too cold to sell, but when the rush was on, she found it impossible to keep up with demand. The cat was delighted with the slack period; he filled himself up with waste herring to such an extent that he spent the whole of the evening rush, bloated and content, lying on top of their pile of belongings.

When the day ended and they got back to their lodgings, they brought their things in, and then Sam counted the take.

'Four pounds, two shillings, and fourpence,' he announced with satisfaction. 'By gum, it ud take me a month to do that on fish quay.'

Sam handed the boys sixpence each; it was more money than either of them had ever had in the whole of their short lives.

'Thou's working, so thou gets paid wages,' he said. 'Nobody does owt for nowt in business, it wouldn't be right. Now, then, seeing that we're in this thing together, does anybody want a say?'

'Dad,' said Joe.

'Aye, lad, thou's got an idea?'

'A couple, Dad. I noticed, once or twice, that tha gave fish away when tha didn't have any change. I think that we should save all of our small change and take it wi' us so that it doesn't happen again.'

'Thou's right, Joe,' said Sam, 'we'll do that. What was

t'other thing?'

'Well, I wondered if Mum could half bake the fish when things were quiet, then we'd get them quicker when the rush was on.'

'What about it, Mary?'

'I could do that, all right,' said Mary. 'Aye, it's a good idea.'

'Dad,' said Harry, 'I think we should have a notice with the price on it, so that people don't have to ask.'

'It's a good idea, Harry, but who's going to write it?' asked Sam.

'I think that I might be able to if I had a piece of cardboard,' said Harry.

'Why not a slate?' said Mary. 'Tha knows, like a school slate.'

'We'll get one tomorrow morning first thing,' said Sam. 'Well done, Harry.'

'And I think that one of the first things we've got to do is to make a cover for the stall and the fire. If it rains, we won't be able to do owt,' said Mary.

'Thou's right there, lass,' said Sam, 'but that'll have to wait until weekend. We go on to Redcar then; we can get the stuff in Brid' and make them at weekend.'

They all went to bed that night happy and contented. As they settled down to sleep, Mary turned to Sam.

'I'm glad thee don't have to go to fish quay tomorrow, husband,' she said.

'So am I, wife, so am I.'

The following morning they bought the slate and a further supply of white paper, and well before noon they were on their way back to the racecourse.

When they arrived, they soon settled down into a routine which was to become familiar. Mary started preparing the stall, Joe staked out Adam and fed him, and then joined his father and Harry in a search for a supply of wood.

While they were away, two strangers began to hang around the stall where Mary was working. They were a rough, unpleasant-looking pair, and they stood watching Mary for some time. Mary, quite aware of their presence, ignored them.

Finally the bigger of the two came over and grinned at her, revealing a single yellow fang which protruded at an angle from his upper jaw.

'And just what might tha be doing here?' asked the tooth.

'Minding my own business, just like thou ought to be,' snapped Mary.

The other man, a small wiry creature with a ferret face, joined them. 'Happen this is our business,' he said.

'You get out of here and leave me alone,' said Mary.

'We couldn't do that,' said ferret face, 'we have to make sure that everything is nice and peaceful around here; besides, I don't think you've paid your rent.'

'And what does that mean?'

'We're reasonable folk,' he continued. 'You won't find us over-charging.'

'Thou'll get nowt here, so get off wi' the pair of you,' said Mary.

'That's foolish talk,' said the tooth. 'Accidents happen, you know, but we see that they don't happen to our customers.'

He walked over to the pile of tin trays and aimed a vicious kick at them, scattering them all over the place. His tone changed, and his voice became hard, 'Where's the money?'

'Get out of here,' yelled Mary.

'That might be it,' said ferret face, pointing to the Tin Box, 'Get it.'

'Aye, this is it,' said the tooth, picking it up and shaking it. 'We'll just hang on to this for today.'

'You put that back,' screamed Mary, rushing at him and trying to drag the Tin Box out of his hands. 'When my husband gets here ...'

'She has a husband,' said the tooth, pushing Mary out of the way. 'We'd like to meet him, wouldn't we?'

'Aye,' said ferret face, 'reckon we could come to an arrangement with him.'

'Then now's your chance,' growled a voice.

Sam had returned unnoticed by any of them. Slowly and deliberately he put down his pile of sticks. He sized up the pair as he walked over to them.

'Is this your stall?' said ferret face.

'Aye,' said Sam, 'and that looks like my box thy friend's got.'

'It was thine,' said the tooth, smiling, 'it's ours now.'

Before either of them could move, Sam hit the tooth full in the mouth. He went down screaming, writhing on the ground, blood streaming from his face as he tugged at his lower lip trying to pull it away from his solitary tooth which now protruded through it. Sam turned quickly and grabbed the little man.

'Pick up that box and put it back where tha found it.'

Ferret face struggled, and Sam hit him hard across the face with the back of his hand; the man screamed.

'Get on with it!' said Sam, raising his hand again.

'All right, all right,' he whimpered, 'there's no need to get nasty.'

Ferret face struggled free, and suddenly there was a knife in his hand. Sam did not wait, he kicked him hard in the crotch. Ferret face dropped the knife and doubled up, screaming in agony. Sam picked up the knife and booted him hard up the behind.

'I'll keep this,' said Sam, pocketing the knife. 'Now, tha little sod, put that box back.'

Ferret face hobbled to the cart and replaced the Tin Box. Sam turned to Mary, 'Did they do owt else?'

'They kicked trays over.'

'Reeght,' said Sam. 'Stack them trays and make sure that every one of them is clean.'

'I've got to go and get me face fixed up,' whined the tooth, spitting blood.

'I'll bloody well fix tha face if tha don't get on wi' it,' Sam said as he took a pace towards him and pulled his foot back.

'Don't kick me, mister, we'll do it.' he squealed.

Sam stood over them as they cleaned and stacked the trays. When it was finished to his satisfaction, he growled, 'Now get to hell out of here and don't come back if tha knows what's good for thee.'

'We'll get you for this,' snarled ferret face.

'No tha won't,' said Sam, 'because if anything else happens to my stall, and there's no matter who done it, I'll seek thee out and make thee feel that today was a picnic. Now on tha way, and if tha knows what's good for thee tha won't let me see either of thee again.'

The pair of would-be villains skulked off.

During the fight a small group had gathered around Sam's stall; one of the men – their friend from the previous Sunday – spoke to Sam.

'It's about time somebody taught those two a lesson,' he said.

'Them?' said Sam with massive contempt. 'They wouldn't last ten minutes on fish quay.'

The rest of the day passed off without incident, and by the middle of the following afternoon, the last day of the meeting, they had sold out. That evening in their lodgings they counted the take and found that the profit over the three days amounted to well over eight pounds. This was more than enough to allow them to buy the materials for their stall and still be left with over nine pounds in the Tin Box.

That Friday they moved back to their lodgings in Bridlington, and on the Saturday morning Sam and Mary went shopping. At the ships' chandler's between the piers they were lucky to find a piece of red and white striped canvas ten yards by two; then they went to the timber yard and bought planks and two-by-three timber. They loaded this on to the cart and took it all back to their lodgings. In the back yard, during the rest of Saturday, they built their stall. It finished up eight feet by six by four, covered top back and sides with the striped canvas and with a serving counter in front and storage rack to one side for the trays of partly cooked herrings. The whole had to be made to pack and stow easily on to their cart, and they also had to make an arrangement for the fire. They used the remaining scraps of material for this and made a windbreak and a cover to use in bad weather. They put the whole stall up and, after standing for a while admiring it, dismantled it and stowed it on the cart.

On Monday Sam bought herring at the quay, and then they set out for Redcar and the two-day meeting there. They again did well, and over the next month Sam earned more money than he had ever made in a whole year. They were living better than they had ever done before and at the same time managing to save.

That Christmas Sam and Mary spent some of their money on clothes. A sailor suit for Harry and navy-blue suits for Sam and Joe. Sam even persuaded Mary to have a dress made. It was quite a job; he had to get her a neat skirt and blouse from a secondhand shop before she would consent to enter the plushy emporium which advertised 'latest Paris fashions'. They changed their lodgings too. They rented a ground-floor, three-room apartment on Harbour Road in a middle-class district of Bridlington, which had become the base for their operations. Their new apartment was real luxury. There was a tap and running water in the kitchen and in the yard, just outside the back door, was their very own privy.

On Christmas Day, at Mary's insistence, they went to church. She insisted they should say thank you to somebody for their good fortune. It was the first time that Sam and Mary had been in a place of worship since their wedding at the Seamans' Mission, and for Joe and Harry it was their first time ever. They sat as near to the back of the church as they could so that they would not be observed when they did the wrong things, but they got by – it was not so difficult. After the service, as they were leaving the vicar greeted them.

The vicar was a round man, everything about him was round: his corporation, his eyes, his spectacles, and his almost-bald head. His hair, what there was of it, was snowy white, and it stuck out horizontally in two solitary tufts, one over each ear.

'I don't think we have met before,' he said, beaming a round smile at them. 'Are you new to the parish?'

'Well, it's first time we've been here,' said Sam uncomfortably, shifting from one foot to the other.

'But you do live in Bridlington?'

'On and off,' said Sam. 'We travel around in our work.'

'Perhaps I might call on you, Mr ... er?'

'Hardacre, Sam Hardacre. This is my wife, Mary, and these are our two lads, Joe and Harry.'

'And fine-looking boys they are too,' said the vicar, patting Joe on the head, much to his disgust and embarrassment.

'We live at sixteen Harbour Road,' said Mary, thrilled at

57

being noticed by a real 'gentleman'.

'We'll be off again next Monday,' said Sam, not sure whether he wanted the vicar to call or not.

'Then we must make it soon; how about Friday afternoon? My name is Cox, by the way.'

'Will you stay to tea?' asked Mary.

'I'm sure that a cup of tea would be most welcome,' replied the vicar.

'What did thou want to ask him to tea for?' demanded Sam as they left the church. 'Now we'll have to go and buy some fancy cups, tha can't serve vicar tea in mugs.'

The meeting with the vicar was to prove fortuitous. He came to tea as arranged, and Sam spent an uncomfortable half hour balancing a cup and saucer on his knee while trying to keep up a conversation. Mary, on the other hand, came through the ordeal with flying colours. She did not do everything right, of course, but neither did she do anything very wrong. In any case, Mr Cox was a kindly man who was well aware that his hosts were ill at ease. Gently and gradually he drew them out, and by the time he was ready to leave he had heard most of their life story. It was Sam who, as he was leaving, asked him to call again.

'Of course I shall,' was the reply, 'and for your part you must never hesitate to call on me, especially if you feel that I might be of some service to you. It's my job, you know.'

It was not until the following spring that Sam took the vicar up on his offer. In spite of the winter and the fact that the national hunt and point-to-point meetings were nowhere as well attended as the flat racing of the spring, summer, and autumn, their new business prospered. Mary soon gave up going to the meetings with them, and Joe was promoted to cook. Mary stayed home in Bridlington most of the time, while Sam and the boys travelled around the country.

It was May, and they had just returned from the first flat meeting of the year at Wetherby. As always when they got home, they sat around the table in the living room, opened the Tin Box, and solemnly counted its contents.

'One hundred and seven sovereigns, thirteen shillings, and fourpence,' said Sam, and paused for a moment, deep in thought. 'Mary,' he said, 'this is far too much brass to keep in t'house. I get real worried when I think of thee here all alone in this place wi'it.'

'I'm all right, Sam,' she replied. 'Any road, what else can us do wi' it? Thou doesn't want to carry it around wi' thee, dost tha?'

'No, I don't.'

'There thou art, then, there's nowt else to be done.'

'Us could put it in a bank,' said Joe.

'I suppose we could if I knew how,' said Sam.

'Go and see them,' said Joe, 'they'll tell thee how it's done.'

'Sam,' said Mary, 'I've got an idea.'

'Let's have it then, luv.'

'Why don't thee go and have a talk wi' Mr Cox, I reckon he'd put thee right.'

'Talk with the vicar?' said Joe scathingly. 'That's daft, what does he know about money except for trying to get it off folk?'

'Joe!' roared Sam, 'Don't thee talk to tha mother like that.'

'I'm talking sense.'

'Not that way tha's not. Remember thou's not too old for me to put thee over ma knee.'

'Now thou's being daft, Dad.'

'Mary,' said Sam, 'get me strap. Reeght, Joe, get thee sen over yon chair.'

'Don't strap Joe, Dad,' Harry pleaded.

Joe stood eyeing his father, his small face tense, his fists clenched, and his lips drawn into a thin tight line, as Sam wrapped the end of the strap around his hand.

'Please, Sam,' said Mary, 'let him off.'

Sam hesitated; he knew that he and Joe tended to pick fights. He always felt easy with Harry, but there was a tension between him and his eldest son. Joe had all of the belligerence and hardness that had made Sam a survivor on the fish quays but none of the gentleness which made him the man he was. Sam told himself that age would soften Joe, but it didn't seem to be working out that way. Maybe it was his own fault. He let the strap fall.

'Tell thy mother thou's sorry,' said Sam.

'Sorry, Mum,' said Joe.

'Now get thee out to tha room and stay there until I tell thee thou can come out.'

Sulkily Joe went off to his exile.

'Happen I'll go and see Mr Cox in t'morning,' said Sam.

The next morning found Sam ringing the bell at the vicarage. Mr Cox welcomed him warmly and soon had Sam at his ease. Sam explained his predicament, and the vicar listened carefully to all that he had to say.

'Well, now,' said Mr Cox when Sam had finished, 'I'm only a parson, you know, and these matters are somewhat outside of my sphere. But I think I have a friend who would be willing to advise you and whom I am sure that you can trust.'

'Who would that be?' asked Sam.

'His name is John Saunders; he is a solicitor.'

'What's that?' Sam wanted to know.

'A solicitor is a lawyer. They look after other people's affairs for them. Of course they make a charge for their services, but I do not think you would find Mr Saunders unreasonable. What do you think of the idea? I am afraid it is the best advice that I can suggest.'

'Well, if that is thy advice ...'

'It is.'

'Then whatever thou says.'

'Good. Well, as there is no time like the present, if you are willing, I shall be happy to take you round to meet him now.'

Together they left the vicarage, and Mr Cox led Sam to an office on the Promenade. They climbed up some dusty book-lined stairs and went into an outer office.

This was a long, narrow room with two doors leading from it. All the way down one wall was a high sloping desk on which were scattered piles of leather-bound books, inkwells, and steel pens. At the far end of the office was a massive pile of deed boxes, mostly dusty, and the lower ones rusting with age. Every other spare piece of wall was covered with book-shelves carrying large volumes with gilt-embossed titles. Perched on a high stool, scratching away with pen and ink in a large ledger, sat a thin old man. As he hunched over his work, the pen clutched in a scrawny claw, pince-nez perched right at the tip of a slender beaky nose, he looked like a frustrated bird of prey which had lost half its feathers.

'One moment, please,' said the clerk, his Adam's apple bobbing in and out of his high collar.

They stood in silence while he scratched a little more.

'Now, gentlemen, what can I do for you ... Ah, it's Mr Cox, I'm sorry I did not recognize you.'

'Is Mr Saunders in?' asked the vicar.

'Mr Saunders, junior? Yes,' replied the clerk, 'he is free at the moment if you wish to see him.'

They were ushered into an inner office, where a man rose to greet them. This office was much tidier and better furnished than the outer one. It was dominated by a huge leather-topped desk. A grey rug covered the centre of the polished wood floor. Behind the desk were two tall windows with brown velvet curtains, in front of it were two leather-seated oak chairs, and the walls to either side were filled with the inevitable books. A pile of documents bound with red tape lay on the desk; one of these was open, and the occupant of the office was annotating it in pencil in its margins.

The man was pleasant-looking, slim, about average height, with pale-blue eyes and an intense stare. His face was that of an intellectual, heralding, in its bone structure, a cragginess to come. He was wearing a dark-brown lounge suit, and his hands protruded from starched linen cuffs, long and slender, almost like a woman's. But there was nothing effeminate in the strong handshake he gave Sam when Mr Cox introduced them. John Saunders was about thirty-five, a graduate of Durham University, and a partner in his father's law firm, which he was gradually taking over.

'Glad to meet you, Mr Hardacre,' said Saunders as they shook hands. His tone was cultured and precise. 'I hope that you were not looking for my father, Mr Cox. I'm afraid he's not in.'

'No, no,' said Mr Cox. 'Actually Mr Hardacre has some problems about money that I thought you might be able to sort out for him.'

'We can but try,' said Saunders.

'He came to me this morning,' continued Mr Cox, 'asking for guidance, but not the sort of guidance that I am used to dealing in. So, feeling that you were very much better equipped to deal with these matters, I brought him along.'

'If I can help in any way I shall be delighted,' said Saunders, turning to Sam. 'I probably should not say this, but are you looking for someone to handle your affairs?'

'I can handle my affairs all right,' said Sam, 'it's just that I don't know what to do with my money.'

'Do I understand that you have too much money?' said Saunders, surprised.

'In a way, aye, I suppose I do.'

'And where is this money, Mr Hardacre?'

'You can tell Mr Saunders,' said the vicar as Sam hesitated. 'Anything you say in here is absolutely confidential.'

'Well,' said Sam, 'it's in t' Tin Box.'

'In the tin box?' said Saunders, raising his eyebrows.

'Aye,' said Sam, 'at home. I get a bit worried about Mary, that's ma wife, her being alone all day wi' it. I mean there's more than a hundred sovereigns in it.'

'Let me be sure I have this straight,' said Saunders, who was a great stickler for detail. 'You have one hundred sovereigns in cash in your home in a tin box?'

'Hundred and seven,' said Sam.

'That is a great deal of money,' said Saunders. 'It should certainly be in a bank at least; it should not be lying around in a tin box.'

'That's what my son Joe said. That's why I went round to see Mr Cox.'

'Your son Joe sounds a very sensible lad,' said Saunders. 'I think, Mr Hardacre, you had better go home, get your tin box, and bring it back here. The first thing we must do is to get that money into a bank where it will be safe. After that, if you want me to assist you, we can discuss our next move. What do you say?'

Sam looked at Mr Cox, who nodded. 'I'll do that right away,' he said. 'Tha'd better tell me how much I'm due thee for this.' He put his hand in his pocket.

'We can talk about that later,' said Saunders smiling. 'As of now you owe me nothing. You can put this consultation down as a favour to Mr Cox.'

Sam hurried back to Harbour Road, where he got down the Tin Box. Mary saw what he was doing, and it worried her. 'If tha takes that, we'll have nowt left,' she said.

Sam tried to explain to her that the money would be in a bank.

'What do they want wi' our brass?' she asked.

'But we'll be able to get it any time we want it.'

'But we won't have it, will we?'

'Of course we will,' he said, 'it'll just be in a different place. Dammit all, it was thee as wanted me to do this.'

'Aye,' said Mary, 'but I didn't think tha would, and now I'm not sure. What did Mr Cox say?'

'Same as Mr Saunders, put it in a bank.'

'Reckon thou'd better, then,' said Mary.

Sam was about to reply but thought better of it and left her still unconvinced of the wisdom of this course.

Saunders took Sam into Martin's Bank, only a couple of doors away. There they asked to see the manager and were shown into his office. Saunders explained the situation to the banker, and their business was soon completed. Sam was given a deposit slip for his money, and the manager explained how he could get any or all of it on demand. When they left, Sam was looking very worried; Saunders asked him if anything was wrong.

'Aye,' said Sam, 'I don't see how I'm going to get the money out if I need it.'

'But the manager explained all of that. All you have to do is sign for it.'

'That's just what I can't do,' said Sam, 'I can't even write me name.'

Saunders laughed, 'Is that all? Don't worry, we'll soon put that right. Come back to the office with me now, spend an hour with my clerk, and I'll wager that you'll be able to sign your name with the best of them.'

'Thou's taking a lot of bother over me,' said Sam.

'It's self-interest, Mr Hardacre; I think you are going to become a very valuable client. That is good business; how would you define good business?'

'I never gave it much thought. I suppose what it amounts to is buying three fish for twopence and selling 'em for a penny each,' he said. 'That's all there is to it as far as I can see.'

Saunders won his wager when an hour later Sam left his office with his bank receipt, the Tin Box, and the ability to sign his name. It all gave him a feeling of respectability. 'Dammit,' he said aloud, 'I'm going to get young Harry to learn me to read.'

When he got back to Harbour Road, Mary greeted him still worried.

'Didst tha do it?' she asked.

'Aye, it's done,' he said, starting for the back door.

'Where are thee going?' asked Mary.

'I'm going to chuck this old Tin Box out,' he said. 'We won't be needing it no more.'

'Sam Hardacre, don't you dare do any such thing,' she said with sudden spirit. 'That Tin Box has been wi' us since before us was wed. Thou's not going to chuck it out now.'

'But what use is it?'

'I don't know, nowt I suppose, but I like having it here, it makes me feel safe.' She was near to tears.

'All right, luv,' said Sam. 'Thou shall have thee Tin Box.'

He took it over to the mantelpiece and put it in its usual place; then he took two half sovereigns out of his pocket and put them in.

'There thee are, Mary, lass, it's never been empty before, and I promise that it'll never be empty again for as long as thou wants to keep it.'

CHAPTER FIVE

Shortly after Sam had opened his first bank account, he, with Joe, Harry, and on this occasion Mary, went to the two-day meeting at Market Weighton. The weather was beautiful. Mary had come along on account of not wanting to be left in town on such a lovely day. Monday, the day they travelled, was blazing hot; it seemed that the summer had decided to come a month early. They arrived in Market Weighton in the mid-afternoon and made a camp on the course. The two boys stayed with their gear and slept in a nice tent which Sam had bought for that purpose. Sam and Mary took a room at a small inn in the little town. Market Weighton is a market town some thirty miles inland from Bridlington, and it was a very hot and perspiring family that arrived there.

The following morning Sam and Mary rose early and made their way to the course. On arriving they were met by a despondent Joe.

'We might as well go home,' he said.

'What's up, Joe?' asked Sam.

'Fish. It's off.'

'Oh, my God,' said Mary. 'Here, let me see.'

She went over to inspect their stores. Before she got within ten yards she knew the truth of Joe's statement. The herring were most definitely off.

'Sam,' she said, 'it's no good, it's like Joe says, us might as well go home.'

Sam made no reply. He had a habit of tugging at his left ear when he was deep in thought. This seemed to switch off his outward consciousness and make his concentration complete.

'Sam,' repeated Mary, 'look, even cat's not interested, fish is off, we mun go home. Sam, we're not going to be able to come to meetings as far away from fish quay as this, not in summer, any road. Come on, let's pack up and get going.'

Sam reached a decision. 'We'll do no such thing,' he said.

'But, Sam, we can't sell rotten fish.'

'Who said we are going to?' said Sam. 'You lads get shovel and dig a bloody big hole and bury that fish; make sure that it's well covered. Mary, thee get Adam and cart and come wi' me.'

'What are we going to do, Sam?'

'We're going to buy up every bloody sausage in Market Weighton. We'll get loaves of bread, and we'll serve sausage on a half slice of bread, hot or cold. In this weather happen a lot of folk'll want them cold.'

By lunch time there was not a sausage to be had within five miles of Market Weighton. And by midday on Wednesday there was not a meat pie to be had in the same area. Sam Hardacre had begun to expand his interests.

With summer almost upon them, the holiday makers and day trippers were beginning to flock into Bridlington. The thought struck Sam that his stall might do as well on the beach as it did on the racecourse. He made up his mind to put this to the test, and so he set up at the foot of the north pier on the far side of the harbour from the fish quay. He ran it for a week, and the results were good. He did not take as much in a day as he did at a race meeting, but it was seven days a week, and at the end of the seven days he had taken as much or more than he would have taken in a four-day meeting. There was, of course, also the additional advantage that there was no travelling involved.

He realized also that if he did so well off the north beach, then he would do equally well off the south beach, and for that matter there were, within easy reach, Scarborough, Whitby, Filey to the north, and Hornsea to the south, all of which had a large influx of holiday makers.

He discussed the whole matter with Mary at the end of their week of experiment.

'Well, are thee going to carry on in Brid'?' she asked.

'Oh, aye,' he answered, 'and in half a dozen other places as well.'

'But tha can't do that, Sam; tha can only be in one place at a time.'

'I'll have to take on labour,' he said.

'Tha means?'

'Aye, us is going to be bosses.'

'Will tha be able to trust folk?'

'Aye, tha's got a point there. In t'first place I'll give jobs to folk that I know, folk on the fish quay and the like. I'll pay them well, and they'll have no reason to want to fiddle.'

'But suppose they do?'

'Then I'll knock the hell out of them, and they'll be looking for another job.'

'How long is it going to take to get this going?' asked Mary.

'I'm going to see if I can get somebody to take over the pier stall tomorrow; I could have four more stalls built during the week, and we could start them next week. I reckon that there's room for seven stalls between Hornsea and Whitby, and we can have them going in two weeks.'

Mary was frightened. She had everything she had ever dreamed of, especially an apartment of her own; they had plenty of money and lacked for nothing. She could not understand why her husband should want for anything more, but she realized that his mind was made up and that there was nothing she could do about it.

The following morning Mary and Joe went down to run the stall. Sam went down to the fish quay. The herring fleet was in Scotland, and only the local boats were operating out of Bridlington at this time. The migrant workers were gone, but there were of course the locals who worked the quay all the year round. He arrived at the quay mid-morning, when the day's activity was at its height. Wandering around the familiar scene, he found the man he was looking for, Bert Armitage. He had not seen Bert since the morning that he had bought the tin trays, but he knew him fairly well as a man who could be trusted.

'Hello, Bert,' he said.

'By gum,' said Bert, who was busy filleting and skinning codling, 'thou looks as if thou's come up in t'world.'

Sam compared his neat navy-blue suit and clean linen with the familiar hessian apron and fish-stained clothes. 'I'm doing all right, Bert,' he replied. 'Dost tha mind if we talk?'

'So long as I can keep working while we do, carry on.'

'I've got a job for thee if tha wants it,' said Sam.

'Oh, aye?'

'I've got a little stall on t'north side,' said Sam. 'I sell baked fish, sausages, and pies to the visitors.'

'I think I heard summat about that,' said Bert. 'What of it?'

'I'm looking for someone to work it; thou can have the job if tha wants.'

Bert was not enthusiastic. 'I don't like working for a wage, I can make more here.'

'No, thou can't,' said Sam, tugging at his ear; he had not allowed for the fierce independence of these people. 'I wouldn't be paying thee a wage.'

'I don't work for nowt.'

Sam had the idea now. 'Of course tha don't,' he said. 'Listen, that stall's been open for a week, it's been taking uppards of three pounds ten a day. The arrangement would work this way. I supply thee with everything, fish, sausages, pies, and the rest. Thou has the stall, and every three shillings thou takes thou keeps one.'

'Go on,' said Bert, 'what else is there?'

'Well, thou'd need a lad to help thee. Thou would have to pay him, but he wouldn't cost more than a shilling or two a day. The rest would be thy own. Thou'd need to wear clean white coats and straw hats, but I'd supply them and keep them laundered, and that's about all there is to it.'

'What about winter?' asked Bert.

'So far as I can see at moment, there'll be nowt in winter, but we can talk about that later. In any case thou'll earn more in the summer season than thou'll ever do here in a whole year. It's up to thee, what dost tha say?'

Bert skinned another fish in silence. Sam could see that he was thinking it over. Finally Bert said, 'Can I try it for a week?'

'That sounds fair,' said Sam. 'Aye, I'll agree to that.'

'When do I start?'

'Tomorrow morning, eight o'clock, I'll be there to show thee the ropes.'

'Right. I've got a lad of me own, he's thirteen, he'll do to help me. If what tha says is right, I'm tha man. Thanks, Mr Hardacre.'

So it was Mister Hardacre. Bert had never called him that before. It made Sam realize that everything had changed in those last few months. He was one of the bosses now, an employer. This was the watershed; he was no longer Sam the guttie, he was Mister Hardacre.

The next day, after he had shown Bert the ropes, he bought a large quantity of red and white canvas sailcloth, timber, nails, and new tools. With the help of Joe and Harry, working until late that night, they built three more stalls. The following day he had one of them up on the south beach, again staffed from the fish quay, then one at Sewerby and another at Filey, four miles to the north. Within the week he had the four stalls operating and within three weeks he had ten, reaching up as far as Whitby. He found his labour on the fish quays, mostly men he knew, and those he did not know were recommended by the ones he had already employed. Within a month his income had quadrupled, and by the time he had all of his stalls working, he could reckon on about fifty pounds a week nett. He was entering the realms of affluence.

It was Joe who produced the next idea – a white board, long and about a foot wide, and on it, in large red letters, the name HARDACRE. Sam hung one over every stall. Sam and Mary went around the stalls every week inspecting and collecting the cash. Mary looked to the cooking utensils and the general cleanliness of the stalls and woe betide the manager whose place was not spotless; he very soon received the sharp edge of her tongue. Halfway through the summer, the name Hardacre was becoming synonymous with good, fresh, clean food at a reasonable price.

Then their landlord died. He occupied the rest of the house at Harbour Road, and Sam instructed Saunders to see the executors and if possible to buy it. The acquisition of the rest of the house gave them a bathroom and a flush toilet on the first floor, a bedroom for each of the boys, and a dining room and sitting room downstairs on the ground floor. At last they had a real home of their own. They bought most of their erstwhile landlord's furniture, and the whole house was comfortable and neat. Mary's one regret was that they did not have a real garden. She planted roses and other flowers in the little patch under the sitting-room window, and of course the aspidistra had its place of honour in the middle of the table in the sitting room, but it was not a real garden.

Sam did not give up his racecourse venture, in spite of his new interests, though he did use managers, and of course he went around the courses where Hardacre stalls were operating.

During these trips Sam occasionally ran into Jim Atkinson, the man he had met on that first Sunday night at Beverley. Though their relationship fell short of friendship, they enjoyed each other's company, and whenever they met they would spend a little time talking together. Their talk was usually about business, and Atkinson was not a little envious of the manner in which Sam had prospered in less than a year. It was at one such meeting in the late summer that Sam found Jim very morose and asked him if anything was wrong.

'It's my woman,' replied Jim. 'She's not well. I wish I didn't have to travel around, reckon she'd be a lot better off if only we could stay in one place instead of living in lodgings all the time.'

'Well, why don't thee?' asked Sam.

'How can I?'

'There must be summat tha can do at Brid' or Scarborough; tha must have put a bit of brass aside,' said Sam.

'Nay, we saved nowt. We was allus going to, but it went on the holiday every year. Happen I'll just have to keep going somehow.'

Sam tugged at his ear; he was getting an idea, part philanthropic, part business. He knew of some premises on the sea front at Bridlington; they would be for sale at the end of the season, and he had been toying with the idea of buying them. They were well situated to catch the growing trade of trippers who flocked into the town throughout the summer, for a day at the seaside.

'Why not a tea shop in Brid'?' he said. 'Tha could manage that.'

'Oh, aye, I could manage it all right.'

'I know just the place, it's a little shop wi' two rooms over it. It would do thee fine; tha could live there and only go downstairs to work.' Sam waited for him to reply. 'I know that thee could do it,' he urged.

'Nay, Sam, not me, I'd never be able to get it. I'm not the sort as can save enough for a thing like that.'

Sam filled his pipe, slowly digesting this information. Atkinson had three qualities; he was honest, he was a good worker, and he could not save money. This last one meant that he would probably be a good employee, as he would never be able to afford to lose his job. On balance Sam was sure that his idea would work, and he knew that he could buy the place for under a hundred pounds.

'It would be just right for thee,' he said. 'Thou'd have to work real hard for about six months, then shut up shop and live on tha fat for t' winter.'

'Tha needs brass for that sort of thing, and even if I had it, how do I save up for winter? I know what I am, Sam.'

'I've got brass,' said Sam, 'and I'll tell thee what I'm prepared to do. For a start I'll buy the place and pay for the stuff tha needs to get going ...'

'But, Sam ...'

'I haven't finished yet. Like I said, this is business. I'm willing to pay thee fifteen shillings a week for six months in the winter, that way tha won't starve even if tha can't save. In the summer tha gives me three pounds a week and half of everything tha takes over a figure that we'll have to work out. The rest'll be thy own, and if tha don't make ten pound a week clear, there's summat wrong wi' thee.'

'I'm not afraid of work, tha knows that; but why shouldst tha do this for me?'

'If I do owt, I do it for me'sen. This is good business. I'll have me money back inside a twelvemonth, and after that it's all profit, and I've got bugger all to do for it. I'll do all right, don't thee fret.'

'How dost tha know tha can trust me?' asked Jim.

'I think I can, and if I ever found out that thou was robbing me, thou'd be out on t' street, and there'd be no second chance. Dost tha believe that?'

Atkinson looked up at Sam's unsmiling face. 'I believe thee, Sam.'

'I have a motto,' said Sam. 'Every time I step out of my house, I try to make a friend or make a profit. Happen today I've done both.'

'I hope so, Sam.'

'There's just one other thing,' said Sam.

'What's that?'

'Are thee and thy woman wed?'

'What dost tha want to know that for?'

'I thought tha wasn't. Thee'd better get wed, because I shall want to see thy marriage lines afore thou go into that house.'

By the following Easter, Jim Atkinson was lawfully wed and thoroughly respectable. He had spent the winter preparing the premises; and had opened the tea rooms for business. Over the window of the shop, in large red letters on a white ground, was the name HARDACRE.

During the months following his decision to set Atkinson up in business, Sam started to look around for other catering establishments, realizing the immense percentage profit that there was in a cup of tea. Even before Atkinson opened his tea shop in the spring of 1887, there were two more tea shops under the Hardacre banner, one in York and another in Malton. With these Sam was not dependent on season or weather. Both of these ventures provided a steady source of profit and gave every indication that they would, in less than a year, repay the capital invested. Sam had rapidly grasped the principle of the incentive provided by profit sharing with his managers. This was to be the basis on which, during the following eighteen months, Sam opened tea rooms over a wide area of East Yorkshire at the rate of just under one a month. Though at the outset Sam was borrowing from the banks, by the time that he had a dozen of these tea rooms going, he found that they became self-generating, their income providing the capital to open new establishments.

Mary meanwhile began to indulge herself and her family to a modest extent. Though she almost always wore serviceable clothes, grey woollen skirts and plain blouses, she was not above the occasional new dress, having got over some of the fears which she had had on that first visit to the fashion shop. She became so bold as to ask a dressmaker to call at Harbour Road and bought one or two modest items from her. Madame la Farge (her real name was Gummer) spent a long time trying to persuade Mary that she really ought to go in for at least one gown in the latest fashion. At first Mary balked at the idea; as she looked over Madame la Farge's sketches of Paris fashions, she could not help feeling that the bustle, at that time all the rage, was somehow immodest. However, vanity triumphed, and to Madame la Farge's delight she ordered a tight-bodiced, drape-fronted, green velvet gown complete with bustle. When this was delivered, she tried it on once and then hid it away in the back of the wardrobe.

One day, when Sam was out and the boys were away, she went up to her room and tried the green gown on again. She had difficulty in lacing her corsets tight enough but finally managed. She viewed herself in the long mirror, greatly pleased with the effect though feeling guilty that she was not shocked. It certainly enhanced her figure, but what would Sam say should he ever catch her in it. She did not have to wait long to find out.

'Mary!' It was Sam calling from the hall.

Without thinking she went out on to the landing, where she stopped suddenly, feeling guilty. Sam looked up at her, and a huge smile of genuine pleasure creased his face.

'By gum, tha looks champion, lass,' he said. 'Thou's a real lady now.'

'Thou don't think it's a bit too ... er ...' She dared not turn around and let him see the bustle.

'Too what?'

'Well, tha knows.'

'Nay, it's right gradely,' he said. 'Now come thee down, there's someone I want thee to meet.'

For the first time she noticed that Sam was not alone. He was accompanied by a small, neat man with long black sideboards and a grey lounge suit.

'This is Mr Horton, Mary,' said Sam. 'He's an inventor.'

73

'An inventor!' Mary was impressed; she came downstairs and shook hands with Mr Horton.

'Aye,' said Sam, 'but his inventions have more to do wi' women than men so I brought him along to show thee it.'

Mary was feeling uncomfortable in her new dress and tightly laved corsets, not to mention the bustle. She tried to show her interest, inviting Mr Horton into the sitting room.

'Now, Mr Horton,' she said, 'tha must tell me all about it.'

Mr Horton produced a piece of wire bent into a U shape. 'Do you know what that is, Mrs Hardacre?' he asked.

'It looks like a hairpin,' replied Mary. 'I use them by the dozen. Dost tha call a little thing like that an invention?'

'Mary,' said Sam, 'the things that do best in this world are the little things, and I think that Mr Horton might have sommat here.'

'Mrs Hardacre,' said Mr Horton, 'you use so many hairpins because they are always slipping out of your hair. This one is different, it won't slip out.'

'How come?' asked Mary.

'If you will observe, Mrs Hardacre,' Mr Horton assumed the manner of a lecturer, 'each leg of the hairpin contains several bends. These bends will serve to give it a much better grip on the lady's hair.'

'What dost tha think, Mary?' asked Sam.

'I really don't know, happen it might work.'

'I've asked Mr Horton if he'll leave a dozen of these hairpins with thee for a few days for thee to wear so we can find out if what he says is true.'

'That's all right wi' me,' said Mary. She was a little disappointed at the smallness of the invention.

'Thank you, Mrs Hardacre,' said Mr Horton.

'Well, Horton,' said Sam, 'come back in about four days, and if they work, I'll back thee.'

Horton gave a packet of hairpins to Mary and left.

'Well, luv,' said Sam, after Horton had gone, 'I think tha new dress is lovely, but why don't thee sit down now, tha stood all the time Horton was here.'

'I'd just as soon stand, Sam,' she said, biting her lip.

'Is there summat wrong, Mary?'

'Oh, Sam, it's this bloody bustle, I don't know how to sit down,' and she burst into tears.

Sam roared with laughter and pushed her down into a chair. 'Sit down and don't be daft,' he said.

A smile broke out on Mary's face. 'Sam,' she said, 'it works, it folds up, look.' She started bouncing up and down on her chair.

'Eeh, tha's a right one, there's no doubt about it,' said Sam. 'Now just thee get them pins into tha hair. I want to know if they work.'

Mr Horton returned a few days later to find that the experiment had been successful and that Sam was willing to back him. He asked Sam for fifty pounds.

'I'm going to give thee a hundred, Mr Horton,' said Sam, 'and I'll tell thee why. I don't want thee to get started, then run into a snag that tha can't cover or not have any brass left to do a bit of advertising or to buy enough stuff to make thy first orders. It'll be no profit to me if thou suddenly finds tha'sen broke. I don't wear hairpins.'

Sam had recognized a good simple idea for what it was; he took one quarter of the profits, and inside the first year his guess had been proved right and he had netted over two hundred pounds. Horton was just a beginning; there would be others with ideas, some good, some bad, but they would always find a ready listener in Sam, and when he thought the idea was a good one, he was always willing to put his money where his mouth was.

The Collingwood Hotel, built a few years after the battle of Trafalgar and named after Nelson's gallant second-in-command, was the grandest of the hotels in the area. It was built in the grand style of the day with all the Gothic flamboyance that architects were beginning to find irresistible. It was spared the sheer parody of elegance that was coming in the next decades and still had a certain dignity about its grey stone front and steep blue-slate roofs and gables. However, it was already too tall for necessity, too narrow for grace, and the windows were ridiculously elongated by the sheer height of each storey. It suited its high, sea-backed setting, however, looking fittingly bleak against wet North Sea skies.

It dominated Filey. By sheer bulk and by its height it gave the impression of having drawn itself up on haughty feline haunches to look down on the Sams and Marys who passed by its grey granite feet.

It catered to an upper-middle-class clientele, business and professional men. The Collingwood was certainly popular; there were some who said that the railway came through Filey because the directors were so partial to the hotel and wanted easy access to it.

It was the spring of 1887; Sam had gone to see John Saunders on some routine matter when, in casual conversation, Saunders mentioned that the Collingwood was on the market.

'I can't believe it,' said Sam. 'Yon's making a mint there.'

'And spending it,' said Saunders.

'Does Leyland own the place?' asked Sam.

Mr Leyland, who was the manager of the hotel, was known to Sam by sight only. He frequented the Enclosure at most race meetings. Sam had seen him often in his grey frock coat and top hat, always wearing a fresh red carnation in his lapel.

'Oh, yes,' said Saunders, 'he owns the place lock, stock, and barrel.'

'Why is he selling?'

'Debts, I'm afraid, personal debts. Our Mr Leyland has a fondness for the horses which far outweighs his good judgment, and it is now a case of sell up or a debtor's jail.'

Sam tugged at his ear, thinking hard. The Collingwood was way above the class of catering that he was used to, but it might be worth a shot.

'Can tha get Leyland here?' he asked.

'I could, but you're surely not ...'

'I'm thinking about it,' said Sam.

The following afternoon Sam was again sitting in Saunders' office, opposite a tall aristocratic-looking man. He was lean, cadaverous, and grey-haired; he wore a grey frock coat, a red carnation, and a silk cravat tied with that intriguing careless-ness that is achieved only by long hours of practice.

Sam wasted no time; there was little time in his nature for verbal pleasantries.

'Well, Leyland,' he said, 'I hear the Collingwood is on t' market.'

'I might be prepared to part with it, provided the right offer came along,' said the other coolly.

'How much?' said Sam.

'Really, Mr Hardacre!'

'Listen, Leyland, we both know why thou's here. Thou's a gambling man and thou's lost. I'm a gambling man as well, but the gambles I take are all odds on. I'm thinking of taking one now.'

'You mean you wish to make an offer.' Leyland could not conceal the excitement he felt.

'I'll tell thee what I mean in a minute, first I want to know how much tha owes. Don't look offended, happen I might help thee. I know thou's in deep and I want to know how much. Thou can trust me, anything thou says here will never go outside of this room.'

'About five thousand pounds.'

'Does that mean six?'

'Well, nearer six than five.'

Sam did some ear tugging. 'Mr Leyland, I'll make a bargain with thee. Thou gift me the Collingwood, and I'll pay all thy debts up to seven thousand.'

'Seven?' said Leyland.

'Anybody who's in as deep as thee are is going to under-estimate how bad things really are.'

'But the Collingwood is worth more than seven thousand.'

'I'm well aware of that, but if tha does it my way no one will ever know, and thou'll not be out of a job.'

'A job?'

'Mr Leyland, thou may be a fool about the horses, but tha runs a good hotel, thee are one of the Collingwood's best assets. Now, I know bugger all about the hotel trade, but I shall bloody soon learn, so don't think thou'll be able to do me cos tha won't. What I'm offering is this, tha can carry on doing the job tha knows well and does well; thou'll have thee own flat in the hotel, two hundred a year, a small share in the

77

profits, no debts, and the certain knowledge that the next time thou sets foot on a racecourse thou'll be out on t' street wi'out a penny.'

An hour later Sam owned the Collingwood.

CHAPTER SIX

George Smeaton was a self-made man. He exuded an air of affluence from the diamond pin which adorned his cravat, through the heavy gold chain which hung across his ample middle, to his tailormade, elastic-sided patent-leather boots. Smeaton always stayed at the Collingwood and would on occasions bring with him a group of business associates. This was one such occasion. He made cotton; so did Dinsdale. The other three men in his party ran stores which retailed, in a large way, cotton and cotton manufactured goods.

At Smeaton's instigation, they had got together to discuss the possibility of drawing within their orbit one or two factories which turned Smeaton's and Dinsdale's cotton into consumer goods, thus forging the final link in the chain from raw cotton, imported from India and the United States, to the customer.

It had been a day of agreement and hope – hope, that is, that they might be able to find sufficient investment to go ahead with their plans. At the end of the day their wives had joined them for dinner, and Smeaton was just in the process of carving the saddle of mutton which they had ordered when a man and a woman came into the dining room and sat at the next table. The couple were well dressed; the woman was smart and well groomed, her dark hair piled on top of her head, pleasant-faced, and with a mature but attractive figure. The man was big, keen-eyed, and solemn-lipped. Their hands, however – and Smeaton was a very observant man – were the hands of labourers, calloused and gnarled with years of manual work. When they spoke it was with the thees and thous of the working class; they didn't quite fit in the lush surroundings of the Collingwood.

It had been a tricky day for Mary. She had had to entertain Mr and Mrs Deacon for lunch. Sam had become aware that an education was going to be necessary for his sons. He knew that little could be served by sending them to the parish school; they would be too far behind in what he referred to as 'school learning'. He did not want them to have to suffer the embarrassment of having to sit in a class along with children who were both younger and further advanced than they themselves. His solution was a simple one – he would engage the services of a private teacher.

Lunch had been a trial for Mary. She now possessed a cook general and a maid, and she had acquired the trappings of the middle class but was not yet at ease with them. As for the Deacons, they lacked the working-class ignorance and the establishment casualness about the 'right way it should be done', and poor Mary, who had ordered a meal of soup followed by Yorkshire pudding, then roast beef, and ending with apple pie, had been most uncomfortable. She had watched Mrs Deacon barely pick at the contents of her plate, unaware that Mrs Deacon's corsets were laced so tightly that she was unable to do otherwise. Mrs Deacon was one of those people who had risen in social standing as a result of her marriage to a teacher and wanted to make sure that everyone realized that she was a lady. Mary, who tended to accept everyone at their face value, was impressed and felt even more uncomfortable when Sam and Mr Deacon left the ladies in order to go to meet the boys. The conversation in the sitting room ran along the lines of fashion, about which Mary knew little; jewellery, about which she knew less; and the latest Bridlington scandals, in which she was not interested.

Meanwhile Sam had discovered that Deacon – who had been recommended by the Reverend Cox – once he was removed from his wife's presence, was a very pleasant person, and it was agreed that he should come to Harbour Road three afternoons a week to try to instill into Harry and Joe the rudiments of the three 'R's'.

· 'He seems all right,' said Sam to Mary later. 'He only did one daft thing in his life and that was to marry yon bitch. Mary, luv, go and put on thee best frock and we'll go to t'Collingwood tonight.'

Mr Leyland came into the dining room and nodded

deferentially in Sam's direction. This intrigued Smeaton, and he called Leyland over.

'Who is that fellow?' he whispered. 'He doesn't look the type of chappie we usually get here.'

'That is Mr Hardacre,' whispered Leyland. 'He owns the hotel.'

'I thought you did,' said Smeaton.

'Only a very small piece. Mr Hardacre bought it a few months ago.'

Smeaton was impressed. 'Can you tell me how he paid for it?' A surreptitious five-pound note found its way into Leyland's palm.

'He paid cash.'

'Ask him if he and his lady would care to join us for liqueurs after dinner.'

Leyland conveyed this request to Sam, who nodded his acceptance.

'Sam,' said Mary, 'must we?'

'Why, what's wrong?'

'Well, they look ever so grand; I'd rather go home.'

Sam glanced at the occupants of the other table. Like Smeaton they looked wealthy. The women especially were bejewelled and expensively gowned, but Sam was not impressed. These people were not the aristocracy; they were just that little bit too ostentatious for that. They were much nearer his own kind. Besides, he was curious as to the reason for being asked over.

'Mary, thou's got to mix wi' folk. Thou can take a drink, and there's nowt very posh about that lot. I don't know who they are, but happen they know me and they're after summat.'

'But, Sam,' said Mary, 'that chap said liqueurs, and I wouldn't know what to ask for. In any case, I'd rather have a glass of stout.'

Sam laughed. 'If that's all that's worrying thee, have a glass of stout, and I'll have a beer to keep thee company.'

It proved much less of a trial than Mary had feared. The men dominated the conversation, probing to try to find out about each other. Smeaton, who had a little of Sam in his makeup, put his scheme to Sam straight. Sam, as always on these occasions, listened intently. He was impressed but not convinced. Smeaton had, however, succeeded in stimulating sufficient interest for Sam to spend the next few weeks doing a lot of homework on the possibilities of the idea. Finally he decided that the scheme was sound. He also decided he didn't need Smeaton.

It were a right rum go, Oliver Ramshead decided, shifting his cold hands on the wet tiller, it were that. The canal barge slid, smooth and silent, making a quiet ripple on the still water. Albert's heavy, muddy hooves plopped softly on the towpath, but the bare feet of the child beside him made no sound at all.

Not that passengers were all that rare on the barge, though paying ones were an exception, and one who came across with half a sovereign unheard of. Oliver wasn't complaining. That was a good half a week's wage, come like a gift. And he could use it. He could certainly use it.

But this Mr Hardacre did not fit into any picture. To begin with, he dressed like a proper gentleman, with his velvet-collared overcoat and all, and still he talked like one of Oliver's own folk. And friendly enough, not above having Oliver's bairn on his knee and taking a mug of tea from Lil through the painted cabin door. So what was he doing, then, riding a cotton barge down the Macclesfield canal? It were odd, all right, but Oliver Ramshead was not one to question good fortune too closely. Not with a wife and two bairns to feed on a bargee's wage.

Oliver would have found it even odder if he had known that the same Sam Hardacre who now glided quietly into Macclesfield on Ramshead's boat had only that morning arrived in that town off the train from Manchester and then walked four miles out of town for the doubtful pleasure of riding back in on a barge. But Sam had his own reasons.

Higgs Cotton Mill stood on the bank of the Macclesfield canal, and it so happened that Sam Hardacre was due to meet with the owner that afternoon. Sam knew exactly how the meeting would go, he had seen it all before. He would be met by an elegant secretary who spoke better English than he did and would be ushered into a wainscotted board room. There sherry would be drunk from crystal glasses by a number of dignified gentlemen who would talk about the weather until obliged, in the final ten minutes, to discuss, with some distaste, money. He would learn damn-all about cotton, cotton mills, or the viability of the Higgs enterprise. All of this would no doubt please Higgs no end, but not Sam.

So Sam decided to have a look through the back door; and the back door of Higgs Mill – where the loading and unloading and the stock were evident, and where the men who worked there could be seen – was the Macclesfield canal.

'She'll be just around bend through tunnel,' said Oliver Ramshead.

Sam could already see the red-brick, smoke-blackened top of the tall chimney. 'Higgs' was lettered in white, vertically down the brick. If he liked the place, he could use the 'H' and save a bit of paint. Sam grinned. Oliver Ramshead grinned back, instinctively and nervously, not sure that he was included in whatever joke had pleased his passenger.

'Happen tha might want to walk round wi' lad.' Ramshead gestured to the tunnel mouth and to the towpath, where his six-year-old son was unhooking the towrope from Albert's harness. The tiny child clawed his way up the harness on to the broad piebald back, and the horse, without breaking its pace, ambled on over the top of the tunnel, jumping the stile on its way.

'Nay, I'll help thee leg her through,' Sam answered easily as the boat slipped into the tunnel mouth. Oliver did not argue. It was hard work, and usually Lil had to help. It seemed that Sam Hardacre knew about canal boats, then, for he stretched out on the deck on his back, like Oliver, and with his feet braced against the curved brick tunnel wall, walked the boat through. Oliver heard the scrape of his passenger's fashionable leather boots on the wet brick and shook his head in the darkness. Canals, like the rest of the world, were not what they used to be.

Sam stood up as the boat slipped into the daylight at the end of the tunnel. The child, waiting beside the piebald horse, now on the opposite bank, caught the towrope thrown him by his father.

The canal turned sharply around a wooded hillside, a hundred yards farther, and suddenly the four brick storeys of Higgs Cotton Mill hung huge and dark over them. The canal water lay coldly black in its shadow. The narrow towpath broadened into a stone quay below the massive walls. Dark entranceways, wide enough for horse and cart, opened on to the canal sides. Barges – some family boats like the Ramsheads', gaily painted, others black utilitarian company boats – were tied up the length of the quayside. Horses waited, at towropes, in wagon shafts; the air was full of the smell of them and of coal smoke from the chimney. Iron-shod hooves clashed and thudded on the stones, and the stomp of men's work boots and voices shouting above the thundering clatter of the looms within added to the noise. The place looked busy and well ordered; the men seemed active and interested, and the high piles of bales of cotton going in and hessian-wrapped bolts of cloth coming out showed there was work enough going on. On either side coal barges were steadily unloading on to mountains of coal, and just as steadily men with wheelbarrows shifted the coal to feed the vast steam engines which were the mill's heart. Sam smiled as Oliver Ramshead leapt ashore, securing his boat aft with a heavy line. The place was full of the stench and sounds of hard work, and hard work meant prosperity. He'd have it, all right, whatever Higgs said.

Sam stood aside, watching as Oliver's boat was unloaded quickly and expertly by the Higgs Mill workers. He noticed too that Oliver cast off and moved on behind his piebald horse with no new load from the mill.

'Don't thee carry that lot?' Sam asked, nodding towards the processed cloth on the quayside.

'Nay, there's little on that now, it all goes on bloody train,' Oliver said. He looked ahead at his son's small back and the black-and-white rump of the horse. He sounded more weary than bitter.

'So what's for thee now?' Sam asked, gesturing forward over the low cabin roof.

'Stockport,' Oliver shrugged. 'Maybe pick up some cattle feed if we're lucky. Have to be lucky nowadays. Lucky to get owt. Time was there was a living to be made off canals. Me and Lil, we mind on the time we had a house of ourn own, down Cheadle way, afore the bairns, mind. Nowt like that now for canal folk. Can't pay rent and feed two bairns on a bargee's wage no more. Houses is for better folk these days. Gypsies, that's what we are, bloody gypsies.'

Sam nodded. He had seen that. The cabin was a home; the painted windows and the flower boxes showed where a woman was using all her ingenuity to make a place to live out of what was intended as a place to carry coal. It reminded him of Adam and the cart and the fish-quay road, as endless and circling as the canals.

The horse plodded on into the afternoon. Sam would be leaving soon, off on to the towpath and back into the town. Ahead, a black iron trestle bridge swept smoothly over the canal, on either side the railway embankment curving off through the green hilly countryside. As they approached, the shriek of a whistle cut through the pastureland. Black-and-white cows raised their heads from the canal water; Albert shook his mane nervously, his ears twitching. The rumble and clatter drew closer, and the bridge began to vibrate, the rails humming across it. The shriek sounded again, furiously loud, and the locomotive roared around the corner, shaking the earth and trailing a curling plume of smoke. Albert half reared, and the canal-man's son caught at the bridle. Lil opened the cabin door and peered out, with narrow, slightly frightened eyes beneath her tousled brown hair. Sam stood by the tiller with Oliver Ramshead as the train crashed across the iron bridge – shaking the earth, making the canal waters tremble, pouring coal smoke and steam over land and animals and people and the little boat in its narrow ditch.

It passed, the noise eased and receded. In the sharp stillness left behind Oliver Ramshead said quietly, 'That's the bastard.'

Sam glanced across at the pinched, tired face, feeling sad for Oliver and his wife and his son, and even for the horse, but within still wildly elated with the beauty of it.

'No,' he said softly, 'that's tomorrow.'

It was not tomorrow, it was three weeks later. And it was not all of it; Sam bought Higgs Mill outright, and also picked up a shirt factory at Leeds to go with it. He had had to buy shares, bits of it; Saunders explained how that was done and how to borrow the money to do it with. Just as well, too, because he certainly couldn't buy a whole railway right off. Not yet, anyhow. But he had already bought a bit of one, a share. It amused him to wonder which bits he could call his own. A few carriages, or a line of goods wagons? Or maybe all the wheels? (What would they say if he fancied taking all of his wheels away somewhere?) But no, he got the point. A little bit, a share, of each and every working part and the coal that ran it and the men that worked it – even a small share of the glorious white mane of steam trailing its thunder round the countryside. Sam Hardacre was 'in railways' now, as they said. He was 'in cotton' as well, and now he had things nicely tied up, even the railway to shift his cotton around. There was more yet, of course, to be had. A shirt factory was not the clothing industry. There was more to it than that. And more at the other end. Why stop at raw cotton? What about the land out in India that grew that cotton? And the ships, the fast clippers and the modern steamers that carried it to England. Sam had the idea – shares, little shares, all tying up, linking up, like the wagons on a goods train. His goods train. Sam was right happy with himself.

Sam bought something else that winter. He bought another tea-shop. An empty storefront further down the Promenade from the one Jim Atkinson occupied. There would be trade enough in the summer for two; he wasn't doing Jim out of anything. But it was not summer he was thinking of. Right now it was winter and Jim was not doing any business at all. For all that, it was Jim who had given him the idea; though he would have been surprised to realize it.

Sam had been in seeing Jim, having a cup of tea, asking after the wife, seeing how things were going. It had been a cold day with a mean wind out of the north east, and the place was warm, inviting and empty. Jim was in his element.

His feet were up in front of a glowing coal fire. The sturdy windows rattled with the rain outside; but inside all was comfort. Jim's wife was at hand supplying endless cups of tea for her lord and master and only customer. It was a good life; a long way from the winter race-tracks; and Jim was utterly content.

Too damned content, Sam realized quickly. A fact that was underlined a moment later when a family of rare winter visitors arrived out of the storm. They had asked for lunch, and Jim stirred himself only to point to a table and inform them cheerily that lunch was beyond his scope. Tea scones and muffins they would get here; and nowt else.

They settled for that, in bad humour, but with little choice, and Sam watched, somewhat astounded, as Jim whistled for his wife, passed on the order, and settled himself back at the fire, feet on the footstool and back to his customers.

It was apparent that here was a man settled happily for life, in a perfect niche. Enough work in the summer to make ends meet year round. And eight months' holiday with a warm roof over his head. Courtesy of Sam Hardacre. Who needed a winter trade?

Sam did. And he was not getting it from Jim Atkinson. He could have thrown Jim out and put someone in there who would serve lunches, make a better profit and get on in the world. But that was not Sam's way. He'd find another site and another man who'd run it right. He was going far, now, and fast. He could afford to carry a little dead weight. For old times' sake.

There were fortunes to be made in the world just now, but not for fools like Jim Atkinson, or for the visionless losers like Oliver Ramshead. They would be passed by. And the man who would pass them by was Sam Hardacre.

At home with Mr Deacon, Harry was proving an apt and attentive pupil. His early fascination with letters had developed into a great love of books, and every stage of his learning opened up new horizons and new delights. Sam indulged him in this. Harry had only to express a slight interest in any work, and Sam would produce it the next day with the result that, within a very short time, Harry had the foundation of a fine, but not expensive, library of poetry and minor classics. On the other hand, if Joe showed any interest in learning at all, it was in mathematics and acquiring sufficient reading ability to be able to study the financial column of *The Times*. Joe was happy where the action was and, in spite of their differences, liked most of all to be with his father, keeping a watchful eye on their various businesses.

They ate well, and never a Sunday passed without a great sirloin of beef on the table. Mary still followed the traditional working-class custom of serving the Yorkshire pudding first as a separate course. Food was never wasted; Mary was too conscious of her past and the horror of hunger ever to permit food to be thrown away. If the bread or the cakes were stale, they had to be eaten anyway. She was lucky in this, for Sam was never one to worry much about food as long as there was plenty, and the boys were never given the chance to develop a fastidious appetite.

They lacked for nothing. The children were dressed smartly, they always got new clothes at Easter and Christmas, but always hard-wearing and 'sensible'. As for Sam, Mary saw to it that her husband was always neatly dressed with pure-white starched linen. For business he wore a lounge suit in a dark worsted, with a cutaway jacket, and a stiff winged collar with a spotted cravat. His footwear had changed too, now; he almost always wore elastic-sided boots and sometimes even spats. Mary, who loved her husband to look smart, had her greatest triumph when she persuaded him to buy a frock coat and top hat to wear on Sundays at church.

Sam could not persuade Mary to take on more staff for the house. She admitted quite readily that they could afford it, but, to tell the truth, she was a little afraid of servants. The two she had she tended to treat as social equals and would often sit with them and gossip over a cup of tea in the kitchen. She always insisted to Sam that she really wanted to do a share of the housework – otherwise she would not know what to do with herself – and, as usual in domestic matters, she had her own way.

Adam had been provided with a shining new dog cart to

give them transport for shopping and visiting. Their home was warm and comfortable, and they continued to entertain occasionally such people as the vicar, and the Deacons. Mrs Deacon turned out to be not too bad — just out of her depth, like Mary. And of course there was always Saunders. Though Mary was still a little self-conscious when she found herself cast in the role of hostess, she was beginning to 'get the hang of the thing'.

The only thing that Mary still yearned for was a garden.

CHAPTER SEVEN

In the autumn of 1889, Sam Hardacre was looking for a house. It was not any house that he was looking for; this was to be something very special. The house he wanted was to be the dwelling place of the Hardacres for generations to come. In one way the house was to be the end of the road; everything else had been a staging post, but this house would be different. He knew exactly what he wanted. For some time now he had been able to sit back, close his eyes, and visualize just what it had to be. Of course there was nothing stopping him from building a home, but somehow that would not have character, for character in a building took many years to develop, and Sam was in a hurry. He was quite sure that somewhere the home he wanted stood waiting for him.

The idea of owning his own home was not new. He had lived with it since it had first come to him on the day he realized that he had made his first hundred sovereigns. He owned the whole property in Harbour Road, but it was merely a stage on the way. Mary had for some time been trying to get him to move; she had no aspiration to a larger place, but she did want some land around her.

Sam had finally decided to take action. He had gone to his office one day at half past eight and had spent an hour sitting at his desk thinking about his idea. Saunders, now fully employed by Sam, occupied the next office; he was sitting at his desk reading through some files when Sam came in.

'Something I can do for you, Sam?' he asked.

'Aye, John,' replied Sam, plunking himself in the chair across the desk from Saunders, 'I've got an idea, and I want to know how much cash us could raise inside of, say, forty-eight hours.'

'Difficult to say off hand, Sam, though I doubt if we'd have much trouble in finding ten thousand. And certainly, if we wanted more, the banks would help out.' Saunders waited for a reply and then went on, 'I could let you know definitely by this afternoon.'

'Happen ten thousand might be enough,' said Sam.

'What exactly have you in mind?' asked Saunders. 'Some new investment?'

'Aye, but there's no brass in this one; I want to buy an estate.'

Saunders was not surprised; he had given up being surprised at anything Sam did a long time ago. He had not expected it, but Sam had a habit of doing the unexpected.

'Had you anything particular in mind?' he asked.

'Nowt,' replied Sam, 'but when I see it, I'll know it.'

'How?'

'Because in a strange way, it'll speak to me: it'll say, "Sam Hardacre, thou's home."'

Saunders smiled.

'I've never done this sort of thing before,' said Sam, practical again. 'How do we start?'

'If you can give me a picture of what you are looking for,' said Saunders, 'we can start right away.'

Two weeks and three estates later, Saunders came to see Sam in his office.

'Another one?' said Sam without enthusiasm.

'I think this one might be it,' replied Saunders. 'Certainly the location is right – it's five miles the other side of Driffield. There are two hundred acres of home farm, kitchen gardens, orchards, and the rest, and there are three other farms, all over a hundred acres and all with good tenants.'

'What's the house like?'

'Old – it's early seventeenth century. Red brick, which is unusual for these parts.'

'How big?' asked Sam.

'I'm not sure, but big enough.'

'Tha sounds like a house agent's catalogue, John,' said Sam, 'but it might be worth looking at. When can us go?'

'I thought that you'd want to see it, so I've arranged for the estate agent to meet us at the station tomorrow morning. We can take the eight o'clock from Bridlington and then go by carriage from Driffield.'

'I'll be bringing Mary.'

'Naturally.'

'Only one other question – why are they selling?'

'Not a bad reason. The owner died recently. The heir lives in India and has no use for the estate. He has ordered his agents to sell it and buy him a town house in London.'

'More fool him,' said Sam.

The next morning Joe got out the dogcart and drove his mother and father to Bridlington station. They arrived at ten minutes to eight, to find Saunders already waiting for them with their tickets.

'Where's t'other chap?' asked Sam.

'I think that is him standing by the barrier,' said Saunders, indicating a tall, willowy individual dressed in formal frock coat and shining top hat. 'I have not yet met the gentleman, but I believe he is a junior partner and his name is Smythe ... with an "e".'

'He looks like a bloody parson,' said Sam in high good humour.

'Sam!' said Mary.

'All right, a bloody undertaker then. Come on, us had better introduce our sen.'

'Delighted to be sure,' said Smythe as the introductions were made, offering a limp hand.

'How do,' said Sam, taking the proffered hand and grinning as the other winced at his grasp.

They boarded the train, and Mr Smythe launched himself into a long eulogy, describing the property which they were about to view.

'Don't waste thy breath,' said Sam.

'But I understood that you were interested in this property.'

'That will be decided after I've seen it. There's nowt tha can say what'll make a ha'porth of difference.'

After that the conversation lapsed until they arrived at Driffield and set out in a hired landau along the Beverley Road.

'Dost tha remember the last time us came along here?' Sam asked Mary.

'I do that,' said Mary. 'It were just before our first race meeting, nigh on four years ago.'

They drove on past neat fields and hedgerows for about three quarters of an hour; then the fields gave way to a high brick wall.

'This is the boundary to the house proper,' explained Mr Smythe.

'Aye,' said Sam, 'I've seen it before.'

'Then you know the property?' asked Smythe, his interest quickening.

'No,' said Sam, 'only gates.'

'That's right,' said Mary, 'aren't they the ones ...'

'Aye, lass, they're the ones.'

They arrived at the gatehouse, with its neat green tiled roof and scalloped wooden porch, standing behind the same wrought-iron gates which had closed on them four years ago. It was the same servant who came out of the house and opened the gates.

'Dost tha remember me?' asked Sam.

'No, sir, I can't say that I do,' replied the servant.

'I remember thee, and tha didn't call me sir last time we met,' said Sam. 'Drive on.'

Their carriage wheels made a delicious crunching sound as they turned on to the raked gravel drive. The tall elms were still there, in their long lines on either side. Beyond was open woodland, a beechwood with the clear barren brown light which only lies beneath beech trees, where nothing else will grow. The high branches were rust-orange now, and falling leaves drifted down the shafts of clear sunlight. A cluster of fallow deer lifted their heads and watched, undisturbed, as the carriage rolled on.

'Look, Sam,' said Mary, fascinated. She had never seen deer before. 'Are yon wild?'

'Sir John always maintained a herd,' Smythe said smoothly. 'He thought they added dignity.'

'Oh, aye?' said Sam, unimpressed.

Sunlight flooded down on them, warm for the time of year, as they slipped out of the shadowy wood and left both elms and beech behind. The wide lawns were natural and rolling, highlighted occasionally with a carefully tended tree. Some were ornamental – red Japanese maples and hollies rich with berries – but the English oaks were older, older indeed than the house itself. Beneath one, huge and twisted and still dark with summer green, Mary saw strange beautiful birds and grasped Sam's hand, shouting, 'Oh, look, look!'

Smythe cleared his throat and said conversationally, 'Ah, yes, the peacocks.' He sounded as if peacocks were a boring familiarity.

'Peacocks!' Mary gasped. She had thought such creatures utterly alien and tropical, perhaps even mythical like griffins and unicorns. They trailed their glorious, shining trains about the leaf-strewn lawn like rainbows. Amidst them was one of pure, shining white, its tail like a snowy veil.

'Like a bride,' said Mary.

'Nay, lass,' said Sam, 'yon's a chap.'

She giggled and then went silent as the carriage approached a line of dark, sculpted yew hedges. Behind were others, in stiff, immaculate lines, making shapes – squares and circles and dark curving patterns – against the rich green lawns. At corners and central points elaborate forms had been cut and coaxed out of the living leaf and wood.

Mary thought them huge, dark, and ominous. The higher ones would be over her head. She could get lost among them, she was sure, but she had to see first.

'Sam,' she said, 'I want to get out and walk the rest of the way.'

'All right, luv,' said Sam, and he ordered the driver to stop. 'How much farther to the house?'

'About quarter of a mile,' said Smythe. 'We can walk from here if you wish.'

'Not we. Just Mary and me,' said Sam. 'John, we'll meet thee and Mr Smythe at the house.'

Sam stepped from the carriage and handed Mary down. It was an unconsciously elegant gesture, and it surprised Saunders, who was immediately ashamed of his surprise.

'Come on then, luv,' Sam said, taking Mary's hand. His voice was suddenly loud in the stillness. Mary felt inclined to whisper, as if in church. They stepped off the drive and on to the soft grass, still wet with the night's heavy fall of dew. Mary lifted her skirts to save the hems from a soaking.

'Wait, Sam,' she called, but he was pulling her along, and she had to follow. The hedges made a corridor which twisted and suddenly opened into another corridor and then another. Sam could see over them, but Mary could not, and she was frightened by the dark closeness. Sam grinned, let go her hand, and ran ahead of her. He slipped through a gap and then another, and when Mary reached the second, he had gone, and she could not see him.

'Sam,' she called, her voice small and trembling, 'Sam, where art thee?' He did not answer, and she called his name again, knowing that he was laughing at her somewhere, but too frightened to be angry. She wanted to cry, and he heard that in her voice and came hurrying back through the hedge-rows, sorry now to have teased her.

When, half laughing, half crying, she saw him, he put his arms around her, which she liked. Then, because he was feeling young and excited, he began to kiss her, which she did not like at all. It was shocking – like kissing in a stranger's house or in church, which was not done. She pulled away, and he let her go.

He took her hand again, and they walked through the rest of the complicated maze and then under a complete archway of yew into the rose garden. The dark, turned earth under the plants was freshly tended and had been heaped with manure against the winter. There were again geometric patterns, this time cut neatly out of the green lawn, each shape containing a different colour or variety of rose. The flowers were fading now, and the blooms were heavy with wetness; there had been a slight frost, and the petals were damaged and translucent. Still, the remains of summer were there – reds and golds, pale yellows, perfect whites. Brick walls enclosed the whole garden, and trellised arches carried rambler and climbing roses over the walkways. A long, dramatic row of standard roses stood like sentries down to the far flank of the garden.

'Oh, Sam,' said Mary, unable to say anything else.

'Well, is that enough roses for thee?' Sam said, laughing.

He went to one of the bushes and plucked a yellow rose.

'Nay, Sam, it were happy where it were.'

'That's for thee, lass, pin it on thy frock, it'll be happier there. Look yonder.'

The arched walk led them to yet another garden.

'Tha wants it, then?' he asked, shocking her again.

'This? Why, Sam, how could I look after this? How could anybody? It's so big, there's so much ...'

'Thou'll have gardeners, lass,' he explained, surprised that he had to explain. 'Tell them what tha wants. They'll do it, they'll do t'work.'

'I see,' said Mary quietly, scared of the gardeners she would have to supervise and sad that she would not have a garden of her own. She wondered if there might not be a little bit she could have to herself, but she was too worried to ask.

Beyond was one last bank of yew, tall and dark. The brick path on which they stood wound its way through a black gap in it. Sam said, 'Shall us see what's through there?'

Mary stood for a moment, looking down at her buttoned leather shoes and the little area of moss-grown red bricks around them. The sun was warming the spot, and it seemed suddenly safe and gentle among the flowerbeds. With an effort she said, 'All right, Sam.' They walked down the path and out through the gap.

The lawn beyond was broad, perfect, and two hundred yards wide. It all rolled up and up and away from them, and on the height of the hill it made stood the house, foursquare and solid, ruling lawns and gardens, woodland and farmland, and even the wide moors beyond.

An architectural parallel to Sam Hardacre himself, it was uncompromising in its strength, but was still looking youthful in spite of its years. The broad red-brick oblong of the front was raised behind a balcony, reaching the full length of the house and bordered with a grey sandstone balustrade. High on the flat roof another identical balustrade echoed it, outlined against the crisp blue sky. The twin rows of tall rectangular windows, their sandstone surrounds set out against the red of the brick, marched with military precision along the face. Sam could see, from the slight angle at which they faced the structure, the march of windows continuing on down the west wall amidst the climbing green ivy. That side wall seemed to go on for ever, as if the house was as deep as it was broad.

'Eeh, it's big,' said Sam, almost under his breath, and there was awe in his voice; it was out of character, and it frightened Mary.

The gravelled drive swept through the green lawns in a wide graceful curve that carried it right up on to the wide flagstone balcony. Their landau now stood behind the balustrade and before the pillared sandstone portico. Mary could see Saunders and Smythe conversing on the far side of it and she didn't want to face them just yet. More than that, she didn't want to face the massive front door behind the grey pillars.

'Let's walk round, Sam,' she said. 'Let's walk right round first.'

'Aye, lass,' said Sam. He was pleased to see as much as he could without Smythe's attentions, and besides he was curious about the long ivy-hung wall and what lay beyond and behind. They passed the wide, expanding semicircle of shallow stone steps which swept down to the lawn from the centre of the balcony, and Sam nodded to Saunders, indicating where they were going. There was a rockery on either side of the steps, and Mary hurried to it instinctively, but then suddenly stopped short. The odd curved stones were not stones at all.

'Eeh, Sam, what are them? They don't look right for stones.' Sam prodded one – grey-white and porous, among the rock plants – with his boot.

'Nay, lass, them's not stones, them's bones, big'uns.'

Mary withdrew a step. 'What are they, Sam?' she asked in a small voice.

Sam shook his head and then saw the anchor, ornamentally embedded in the bone rockery.

'That's it,' he said, 'yon's whale bones. Somebody's been to sea from here, then.'

'And brought them things back to put in flower garden?' Mary was incredulous and vaguely disapproving. 'I don't like it,' she added, with such boldness that she glanced nervously across her shoulder as she said it.

'Then they'll come out,' Sam said. 'If'n they don't please thee.'

'Oh, no, Sam,' Mary said quickly, 'we couldn't do that.'

'And why not?' Sam asked mildly. 'Happen I'll buy the place. We'll do what we like with it when it's ours.'

Mary turned away, frightened at the very thought of the whalebones and of the ghost of the seaman who had put them there.

The building faced south, and the sun had not yet reached the west wall. Sam and Mary walked a distance out from it to keep clear of the long frosty shadow. Sam looked up. The red brick stood high above them, and the grey balustrade continued beyond. At the corner it was ornamented by a weathered and anonymous female statue in long robes, looking out on the green moorland away in the distance. Sam could just see the sunlit, elaborate buff tops of the confused cluster of clay chimney pots, their random assortment the single break in the precision of the architecture.

Another sandstone statue, this time a griffin, highlighted the next corner. Sam liked it better than the lady and wondered what might be on the other corners. He hoped for a dragon.

The long autumn shadow fell far back behind the house, covering the cluster of smaller buildings which all reflected it in architecture, though not in size. They were work buildings – laundry and carriage houses, tackroom and mews – all in the same red brick, and Sam was fascinated by the care which had gone into the building of them. No less thought in design, no skimping of the ornamental brickwork beneath the eaves or the wide sandstone door frames. The doors themselves were elaborate and polished, though none but working folk would use them. He liked that. It showed a thoroughness and no stinginess. That he knew would hold true through the rest, in the bits he could not see. The place had been built in a generous frame of mind and heart – and it had been built to last.

Mary pointed to the long line of brick arches down the near side of the longest building.

'What's that, Sam?' she asked. It was pretty, and she liked it.

'Stables,' replied Sam. He went towards them, and she followed.

'What, all of that?' she asked. 'It's so big.'

He led her through one arch, and they peered into the darkness. The place was empty and swept clean, but the rich horsey smell was permanent. Along the back wall was a solid line of loose boxes. Sam had a quick vision of the beautiful beasts that had been there and would be there again.

'Fancy Adam in there, lass,' he said, smiling.

'Adam? He'd never find hisself in there; happen us wouldn't find him either,' she laughed. She felt better now. The rear of the house pleased her, with its look of utility rather than ominous grandeur. They stepped back into the cobbled yard. They were now at the rear of the house. Sam saw that the structure was a square 'U' shape, and this slight suggestion of vulnerability in the massive bulk pleased him. The hollow of the 'U' was the cobbled courtyard behind the kitchens. It was softened by two ash trees whose branches drifted over the mews. The grey, rounded stones beneath Mary's feet were covered with rustling, delicate brown and yellow ash leaves. A streak of sunlight came from behind two high chimney pots and lit a small patch of ivy on the red brick.

'I like it, Sam, it's bonny,' she said, never thinking that this was the one part of the house the mistress would never see.

'Come, lass,' said Sam, and they left the courtyard and walked behind the rear of the east wing. The east corner did indeed have a dragon. Sam laughed softly and considered it a good omen. They came into the sunlight, which baked the east wall and turned the day back to summer.

'Sam, Sam, look,' Mary cried out in sheer delight, 'a glass house.'

The conservatory stood two thirds the length of the east wall; it was a high, white-wood-framed glass structure with a delicate arching roof. Mary ran over to it and pressed her face against the glass, like a child. Inside were plants she had never seen, never dreamed of. Some were bushy with fat scaly trunks and huge spiked leaves; others, delicate with tiny pink and purple flowers trailing along the walls. At the centre, beneath the highest arch of the roof, was a tall, thin tree, spread out like a vine against the brick wall; it had odd dark-green leaves and strangely shaped green fruit. It was un-imaginable and beautiful. Mary reached out her hand as if to touch it and was stopped by the glass. Sam saw the gesture, and he went searching along the glass front for an open door until he found one. Had he not, he realized with a shock, he would have broken the glass to let Mary in.

'Sam, we mustn't,' she protested as he stepped through the open door, but she followed. He watched her as she walked with slow, solemn grace all around the glass enclosure, her small feet deliberate and careful on the Italian mosaic floor. Mary was conscious of the thick, warm air, which was stifling to breathe and heavy with dampness. She felt she was in another world. She reached out again and again, to a flower, a broad leaf, a delicate green fruit. Only after they had gone out and shut the glass door behind them did Sam realize she had never actually touched anything.

The east corner facing front had another robed lady of stone, high up on the balustraded roof, facing the morning sun. Sam and Mary walked, briskly now, up the carriage ramp and on to the flagstone balcony in front of the house. Smythe and Saunders were still waiting by the landau. Smythe said, with a pointed glance at his watch, 'Shall we go in now? We have kept the senior staff on, and we are ex-pected.'

'I mun see what'is like,' said Mary, almost dutifully.

'I also left instructions that the fires be lit, so that we might view the establishment in comfort. Shall we?'

The oak doors – massive, multipanelled, and intricately carved – were standing open to the entrance hall. Mary fol-lowed Sam, who strode through the doorway side by side with Smythe. Saunders instinctively slipped his hand under Mary's elbow as she stepped over the low stone threshold. She found the gesture funny but gentle. Over her head the vaulted stone roof was dark. On either side black oak monks' seats guarded the doorway. The floor beneath them was again of Italian tiles, black and white and delicately patterned. The effect was cold rather than welcoming.

The half-glass inner doors were also open, and within them stood a middle-aged man dressed in formal black.

'How do,' said Sam, greeting him.

'This is Wilson,' said Smythe. 'He was butler to the late Sir John Wildebore and agreed to stay on, at least until the estate has found a new owner.'

'That were nice of thee,' said Sam.

'Thank you, sir,' replied Wilson.

Wilson stood aside as they passed through the second doors and into what Smythe described as the great hall. Mary could find no sense in the name. To her a hall was a corridor between two rooms. And this was a room, a bigger and grander room than she had ever seen. It was, she realized, unnerved, bigger than their whole house on Harbour Road. It stood the full two tall storeys of the house, climbing away to an ornamental ceiling into which were set two glass domes. Between them hung a heavy, highly polished brass chandelier, now converted to gas. The walls were half panelled in black oak, carved in the Tudor linenfold pattern. Taken with the leather chairs and settees and the dark-red carpet, they would perhaps have given a sombre aspect to the room, had not so much rich light flooded through the two glass domes and the four large postcard windows. Sunlight, reflected from the white painted plaster of the upper walls, gleamed on the deep gilt frames of the portraits that looked down on them from all sides. Mary's eyes went from one to another as she turned slowly. Gentlemen and ladies, beautifully dressed in costumes which, she only faintly realized, were from another era, stood impassive and serene. Besides them, also framed and frozen, were their pretty children, their horses, even their favoured pets – a little golden dog painted with large eyes, a small anonymous cat, and even the children's toys. She knew that all of them, even the children, had long since grown old and died.

Sam's eyes swept the paintings quickly, a little wary of the grim-faced gentlemen and prim-mouthed ladies. He fancied that they were not approving of the present company.

'That lot don't look too happy to see us,' he said, gesturing to the portraits.

Mr Smythe laughed professionally. 'The portraits in this room are the only things which are not being offered for sale. Sir Eustace, the son of Sir John, intends removing them within the week.'

'Can't say as I'll miss them,' said Sam.

Mary stopped before a portrait of a young girl, dark and slim like herself, but coquettish and beautiful, with soft dimpled hands and lace cuffs with many jewelled rings. As she glanced at her own rough hands and the plain gold band on her wedding finger, she was glad that the portraits were going.

A broad, shallow staircase, red-carpeted like the floor, swept up from the centre of the room, narrowing until it joined a gallery. The carved oak banisters curved up and became the gallery railing. On either side at the foot of the stairs stood burnished suits of armour. Mary did not know what to think of those at all.

Smythe waited for the hall to make an impression on them and then went into what was obviously a prepared speech, learned by heart, with the sole purpose of impressing his potential clients.

'To our left we have the west wing, containing three principal rooms – morning, withdrawing, and dining; beyond these is the staircase leading to the kitchens, steward's room, and servants' hall. The east wing, to our right, contains the master's study, library, and music room. Both of the latter give access to the conservatory. Upstairs, on the first floor are four suites, eight bedrooms, nursery, schoolroom, and the usual offices. The servants' accommodation is above these and is approached from the back stairs.'

'Tha sounds like a catalogue,' said Sam, unimpressed. 'Come on, we'll have a look round for our sen. Mr Wilson?'

'Yes, sir?'

'Will thee come wi' us?'

'With pleasure, sir,' said Wilson.

Sam did not reveal that they had seen the conservatory

already, and he and Mary exchanged a smile as they entered the library through the glass doors. Sam grinned again as Smythe explained young Sir John's deep regret at the necessity of leaving the family books behind. Smaller accommodations had apparently forced the hard decision. Smythe was sure that Sam would find the library a most valuable inheritance. Sam let his eyes rove down the rows and rows of dark-green, maroon, and brown gilded leather bindings. What use would they ever be to him and Mary? But there was Harry of course. He stepped closer to the shelves and noticed a certain regularity in the lines of the dust, an untouched permanency. He had a feeling that, for all Sir John's regret, the Wildebores had made hardly more use of them than he would.

Mary was worrying more about the music room, with its grand piano and that great thing Smythe had called a harpsichord. What would the likes of them do with such things? There was none of them could use them, and she couldn't bear the thought of them sitting there unused.

In the west wing Smythe took them through the morning room, explaining as he did how her late Ladyship, having an abhorrence for sunlight, had decreed that the morning room should be established in the opposite wing from the usual, so that it would be sun-free until afternoon. Mary, unable to understand why her late Ladyship could not have sat elsewhere in the morning, or why anyone should not like sunlight, shook her head in tired confusion.

Room followed room. The withdrawing room, with brocaded curtains, heavy carpets, and layers of velvet and organza curtains looked feminine and warm. She could be comfortable there. If only it had not been so big. Everything was so big. The dining room table *needed* eight people to sit around it. And Smythe said that it could be made bigger with leaves. Where would the four of them eat? Scattered at far points around it? The vast stretch of shining mahogany frightened her. Where would the food come from to fill it?

Mary followed behind them all as Smythe led them upstairs. Their backs were to her, and for a moment she reached out a hand to the banister rail and let her rough fingers trail up the polished wood. Then she remembered the portraits looking down on her, and she took her hand away.

Upstairs the house became like the yew maze – tall corridors with many identical white-painted and gilt-trimmed doors, rows of gleaming brass doorknobs. She would get lost, she knew, and the children? How would she find them if Harry woke in the night, crying, as he still sometimes did, frightened by a dream of being left alone on a dark and sinister road.

There were bathrooms too, and she, who had not yet become used to the luxury of having one, would be able to choose from four separate, gleaming, copper baths. There were carpets in the bathrooms and the dressing rooms attached, which even had paintings on the walls. It was unimaginable. Mary thought of Sam and the tin tub in front of the fire and for a brief moment saw the humour of it. It gave her strength, and she faced three more bedrooms with calm. Then Smythe showed them the schoolroom, with little desks and a blackboard. She thought proudly of Harry; he would love that. Beside the schoolroom was the nursery, and though it had probably been long, long unused, there remained a carved rosewood cradle and a glorious dappled rocking horse. Mary went down on her knees beside the cradle, forgetting everyone in the room, stroked the wood, and thought something she had not dared to think about for years.

Smythe had saved the master bedroom for last. It was the pièce de résistance, the grand finale, and he knew it. He stepped back from the door so that they could all enter with the view unimpeded. There were two doors, of course, off the corridor, but he had chosen to take them directly into the bedroom itself, rather than its adjoining sitting room, so that they might enjoy the full impact of the cherrywood four-poster, with its royal-blue canopy matching the blue, gold-tasselled draperies and the elegant Adam fireplace. To his personal taste, the elaborate maroon, blue, and gold wallpaper was just the slightest bit extravagant, but then again, it was in the very latest mode and he could scarcely question the Wildebores' taste. This Mrs Hardacre was another matter entirely. If only she would say something. She must be impressed. How could she fail to be? Still, she remained silent, almost displeased, if he could judge by her expresion. Not that one could, of course, with these people. Heaven alone knew what they were thinking. Smythe thought resentfully, the woman should be grateful for the mere sight of such a place. It was an odd world indeed when properties of this calibre fell to people like the Hardacres. He dreaded to think what they might do to it. Still, that was not his affair. His affair was to sell the place.

'It's right pretty, Sam,' Mary Hardacre said finally, still standing in the same spot on the rich Persian carpet.

Smythe turned his face away. Right pretty. Indeed. Probably the bright colours had appealed to her. These people were like children.

'Shall we return to the morning room?' he asked in his smoothest and most gracious tone.

Sam Hardacre nodded, and they all turned to go, but Mary hung back. Saunders and Smythe had already started down the corridor, but Sam realizing that Mary was not following, turned back.

'Sam,' she spoke solemnly, 'could you let them go and hang on, just for a minute?' She nodded towards the doorway.

'What is it, lass?'

She did not answer but stepped, for the first time, properly into the room, walking carefully across the deep pile carpet until she stood beside the sumptuous bed. Then, gravely, she eased herself down on to the royal-blue bedspread, smoothing her grey skirt and carefully keeping her booted feet clear of the satin flounce. Then she lay back across the bed, looking up at the canopy and for a moment closing her eyes. She never said a word, and Sam watched, silent and wondering.

'I had to do that once,' she said, 'just once.'

'Tha can do it every day of tha life if tha wants,' he said laughing. 'Tha can bloody live on that bed, if tha wants. Tha need never come off of it.'

He was laughing but she said, 'Aye, Sam, I can,' so solemnly that he suddenly realized that she didn't believe him. Not about the bed. Not about the house. Not about any of it. He knew then that he had to have that house if it cost every penny he had and if he had to throw his soul into the bargain.

Just now, however, he would go downstairs, meet Smythe in the morning room, and announce with a faint air of dissatisfaction that he would, probably, consider the place.

On their way through the great hall Sam noticed Wilson, and a thought struck him.

'Mary, luv,' he said, 'would tha mind telling the others I won't be long?'

'If tha wants me to,' replied Mary. 'Where are they?'

'In the morning room, madam,' replied Wilson. 'Can I show you?'

'Aye, do that,' said Sam, 'then come along to study if tha don't mind, happen I'd like a word in private wi' thee.'

'Certainly, sir,' replied Wilson, and he led Mary towards the morning room.

In the study, Sam offered Wilson a seat.

'I should prefer to stand, sir, if you don't mind,' he replied.

'Just as tha pleases,' said Sam. 'Well, now, as I said, I want to have a talk wi' thee.'

'Yes, sir.'

'I own factories, and I'll tell thee something about them. I allus wait until I've found a manager before I even start to look for the factory,' said Sam. 'Dost tha see what I'm driving at?'

'Frankly, sir, no.'

'Tha will in a minute. No place is worth having unless it's run proper. Now, happen I'm going to buy this place; what would thee have to say about that?'

'Really, sir, I'm not in any position to have an opinion.'

Sam paused; what he had in mind was not going to be easy. 'Listen,' he said, 'I'm going to be frank wi' thee and I'm going to expect thee to be as frank wi' me. Dost tha understand?'

'I'll try to, sir,' said Wilson.

There was a sincerity about the reply. That was better, thought Sam; he was getting somewhere. He sat down at the desk.

'Are tha sure tha won't sit down?'

'It is not done, sir.'

'As tha wants,' Sam said. 'Let me get to the point; if I buy this place, would thee be willing to carry on?'

'Well, sir, that would depend on a number of factors, but it is possible that we could come to some arrangement.'

'I think I know what's on tha mind,' said Sam, seeing his hesitation. 'Tha's been looking after quality folk, and we're not quality.'

'I wouldn't say that, sir,' said Wilson.

'Tha doesn't have to, it's obvious. But we're going to *be* quality, I'll tell thee that. Only now there's none of us as would know what knife to use if tha set us down at one of them posh dinners.'

'It's really quite simple, sir.'

'When tha knows how, anything's simple. We don't know how. Let me ask thee something.'

'Yes, sir?'

'How much wages dost tha get?'

'My present remuneration is seventy pounds per year, sir.'

'If tha stays with me, that'll never be less than a hundred, happen it might be a damned sight more. The only thing is thou'll have to earn it.'

'Of course, sir, but how should I do that? I mean, apart from my normal duties of running your household?'

'I'll tell thee how,' said Sam. 'As I said, us knows nowt about the right way to do things. All of us has got to learn. We don't even talk proper, as thou'll have noticed. If thou stays, thou'll have a lot of teaching to do. Thou'll need to tell us when we're wrong, keep us right on who's who and who does what and see that we aren't cheated just because we didn't know summat.'

'I think I am beginning to understand, sir.'

'Thou can say anything tha wants to the family, and I'll back thee up and see that things are done thy way. We'll all make mistakes, dozens of them; it'll be up to thee to tell us when we do and to be sure that we never make the same mistake twice. Thou'll not find me ungenerous if tha does thy share, but thou'll find me a right bastard if tha don't.' Sam paused. 'That's about all there is, then; what has thou to say?'

There was a long silence as Wilson thought it over. He was approaching fifty, and positions were none too easy to find for a man of his age, even though he knew that his references were impecable. Also, Sam had impressed him. He had found the down-to-earth, gruff honesty of the man quite appealing.

'Come on, now,' said Sam, 'I'm asking for thy help. As I told thee, thou can say what tha wants.'

'Sir,' said Wilson, 'thank you for being so frank with me. I must admit that your proposition is unusual, and it will take some time to complete your plan. It will not be easy to ... to ...'

'Turn a sow's ear into a silk purse?' Sam smiled.

'I wouldn't have said that, sir,' said Wilson.

'Of course tha wouldn't. But it's true.'

'I shall be honoured to try,' said Wilson. 'I shall do all that I can to the absolute limit of my ability.'

'Tha can't say more than that,' said Sam, rising and offering his hand. 'That's settled, then.'

Wilson looked at the proffered hand, and for the first time the flicker of a smile crossed his impassive face. 'We do not shake hands with our servants, sir, except in the most exceptional circumstances.'

'Lesson number one,' said Sam. 'Thou's getting the idea already. But where I come from, where most folk can't read or write, we always make a bargain wi' a handshake and thee and me's just made a bargain, so what do thou say?'

'I understand, sir.' Wilson took Sam's hand. 'Will that be all, sir?'

'For this trip, Mr Wilson,' said Sam.

'It's Wilson, sir, no mister.'

'Thank thee, Wilson, that's all.'

Sam came out of the study and found Mary, Saunders, and Smythe waiting for him. As soon as she saw him, Mary rushed towards him.

'Sam, I'm scared. I ...'

'There's nowt to be scared of, luv. Just thee come along of me a minute,' he said, and then, turning to the others, 'I shan't be long.'

He took Mary into the study and closed the door. 'Mary,' he said, 'tha likes it, don't tha?'

'It's beautiful,' she said, 'and I've never seen owt like the gardens. But, Sam, it's not for the likes of us. Us just don't belong here. This sort of place is for grand folk.'

Sam grinned.

'All right, luv, don't thee fret about that. I'll tell thee now that I'm going to buy it, but don't let on to the others. I don't want tha saying how much tha wants it in front of Smythe. That's the best way I know to put price up.'

'I'm sorry, Sam.'

'There's nowt to be sorry about, Mary. I'll buy it, whatever the cost. But if thou says anything on the way home, try and think of some of the things tha'll want to have done to it before we can move in. When we gets home and we's alone, thou can tell me how wonderful it is.'

'But what about thee? Do thee like it?'

'Lass, it's what I've been looking for, it's right gradely.'

They left the study and rejoined the others.

'Are we ready for off?' asked Sam.

'If you are quite sure that there is nothing else I can show you,' said Mr Smythe.

'I've seen enough,' said Sam. 'How about thee, Mary?'

'Oh, yes, thank you, you've all been very kind.'

During the journey back to Bridlington, Sam refused to be drawn into giving any sort of opinion, insisting that he had to think it over. Eventually he responded to Smythe's entreaties by agreeing to see him in his office at five that afternoon, after he had had a chance to have a bite to eat and a private talk with Saunders. Mindful of Sam's remarks in the study, and not being able to think of anything to criticize, Mary remained silent throughout the journey. When they reached Bridlington, they left Saunders, who declined Mary's offer of a late lunch. Smythe went about his business, and Mary and Sam went back to Harbour Road.

Over a lunch of cold ham, the boys plied Sam and Mary with questions. Sam was enthusiastic and forthcoming in his replies, but Mary, quite suddenly, became strangely silent. Sam became, during the meal, very conscious of his wife's reticence and as soon as lunch was over, he sent the two boys out.

'Lass, there's summat wrong,' he said when they were alone.

'There's nowt wrong, Sam,' she replied, chewing at her bottom lip.

'There is, Mary, and I want to know what it is. Hast thou decided that tha don't like the place, after all?' His tone was kind but firm.

'Nay, Sam,' said Mary. 'It's lovely; I think it's the most beautiful place I've ever seen in my whole life. Them gardens were like heaven, it's like a palace, and I love it, but ...' she stopped.

'But what? If it's all thou says it is, then there's nowt to worry about.'

'There is, Sam. Sam, can't thee see it's not for the likes of us? Us living in a place like that, a guttie and a fish-quay tart, it isn't right.'

'Mary,' Sam's voice was stern. 'Don't thee ever say owt like that again. Thou can call me a guttie as often as tha likes, it's true enough. But never talk about thee sen as a tart. It's not true, and it never was.'

'I'm sorry, Sam, I didn't mean it.'

'All right, then we'll forget it. Is that all that's worrying thee? Or is it summat real?'

'Sam, how am I going to manage a house like that? It's that big, I won't know where to go or what to do, or ... or ... well, anything.'

'Don't worry tha head about that,' said Sam. 'We'll be learned. I've already had a talk with yon butler chap. He's going to help us. He seems a decent enough fellow, and he wants to stay on.'

'Tha means we'll have servants?'

'Dozens of them, we'll have to.'

'But then I'll have nowt to do.'

Sam roared with laughter. 'Now there's not enough for thee. Eeh, Mary, thou's a real woman. Don't fret, lass, there'll be plenty to do. For a start, thou'll have to learn how to be a great lady.'

'But I don't want to be a great lady. All I want is to be Mrs Sam Hardacre.'

'Thou is a great lady, thou allus was, and thou allus will be.'

*   *   *

Sam left the house and walked briskly to his office. When he arrived, he found Saunders waiting for him.

'Well, John,' he said, 'Mary likes it, so I reckon we'll buy it.'

'I'm not surprised, Sam,' replied Saunders. 'I expected you to say that.'

'How are us going to go on about paying for it? Banks are closed now.'

'Assuming you were going to buy, I went to the bank and had the necessary document drawn up.'

'Good lad,' said Sam. 'I suppose we might as well walk over and see him and get this over with. Come on, John, we can talk on the way.'

Mr Smythe greeted them cordially and offered them chairs, then seated himself on the other side of his large desk and made washing motions with his hands.

'Now, then, gentlemen,' he said, 'you wish to discuss the purchase of one of our properties? That is correct, is it not?'

Sam snorted; he was not one for verbal fencing. 'Tha knows damned well it's right.'

'Quite so, Mr Hardacre.' Smythe's hands had now assumed a gesture of prayer. 'Watton Manor by Great Driffield, the property of the late Sir John Wildebore,' he sighed professionally, 'and now offered for sale by his son and heir Sir Eustace Wildebore.' Smythe cleared his throat. 'The house, a fine red-brick Elizabethan mansion standing in two hundred acres of home farm and . . .'

'How much?' said Sam.

'I beg your pardon, Mr Hardacre, did you say something?' Smythe was not used to having his eulogy interrupted.

Saunders permitted himself a smile; he knew what was coming.

'How much?' repeated Sam. 'Don't fret, I'll buy it if price is right.'

'Oh, er . . . yes, I see. Forgive me if I find your directness in this matter a little abrupt.'

'I don't see that there's owt else to discuss,' said Sam. 'Let me put it as I see it. Thou's selling, perhaps I'm buying. If we agree on a price, that's all there is to it. If we don't agree, then *that's* all there is to it.'

'Very well, Mr Hardacre, let us do it your way,' said Smythe.

'It's the only way I ever do business.'

'In that case, perhaps you would care to make an offer?'

'A thousand,' said Sam, sitting back in his chair.

'But that is ridiculous.'

'Right,' said Sam. 'It's up to thee to put a price tag on it. How much?'

'Hum,' said Mr Smythe, and then reassuming his official manner, 'I do not think that my client would consider any offer under fifteen thousand. There are others who are interested.'

'Like hell there are,' said Sam, 'but we're getting somewhere. Thou don't expect fifteen, or it wouldn't have been thy first figure. I'll give thee ten.'

Smythe put on his hurt expression. 'Really, Mr Hardacre, you cannot be serious. I might be able to drop a thousand.' And then as Sam made a move as if he was going to leave the office, 'Please do not go. I could possibly get it for you for as little as thirteen and a half, but ten . . .' He made a deprecating gesture with his hands.

'John,' said Sam, returning to the desk and speaking to Saunders, 'let's have it on t' table.'

Saunders laid a document on the desk.

'Dost tha know what that is?' asked Sam, though it was quite obvious that Smythe was well aware of the significance of the document. 'That is a BILL OF EXCHANGE IN BLANK,' he said in capital letters. 'It's cash in anybody's language. Now, Mr Smythe, thou's only got to say yes, and Mr Saunders here will make it payable to thy firm to the sum of twelve thousand pounds. I shall sign it, and the property will be mine. That, Mr Smythe, is my last word. 'Tis for thee to say, thou has one word left, yes or no.'

'But . . .'

'Yes or no.'

There was a long pause as Smythe weighed up the chances that Sam might be bluffing. Finally he decided not to risk it. 'Yes,' he murmured.

'Good,' said Sam, 'it's a bargain, then.' He signed the bill. 'Mr Saunders will fill in the rest; I want to get back and tell Mary. All right, John?'

'All right, Sam,' said Saunders, 'I'll fill in the details.'

'Thank you, Mr Hardacre,' said Smythe, coming around his desk doing his hand washing again. 'And might I take this opportunity of wishing you and your family many happy years in Watton Manor.'

'And that's the first thing I'm going to change,' said Sam.

'Surely not the name,' said Smythe horrified. 'It has been Watton Manor for three hundred years.'

'Until today,' replied Sam. 'From this out it's going to be called HARDACRES.'

CHAPTER EIGHT

It had almost been a white Christmas. On Boxing Day morning there was a crisp stillness over Hardacres. It had started snowing during the night, and the household awakened to a silent, white world, as the large flakes fell lazily to the white carpet beneath. The snow stopped at around ten o'clock, and Harry and Joe were out and on to the lawn, constructing a large grotesque snowman.

They had been at Hardacres for two months and were, as Sam put it, beginning to get the hang of things. Most of the things that happened they liked. Wilson had engaged a full staff before they took up residence, and they had moved into a house which ran smoothly and efficiently. Their first breakfast was quite an occasion. For the first time Mary had not got out frying pans and kettles and cooked it for them. She might have tried, had not the excitement of the previous evening and their move kept them awake long into the night, the first in their new home, with the result that they had all slept late.

They had come downstairs and into the dining room to find the large mahogany dining table laid for four and on the heavy oak sideboard a row of dishes, all of silver plate, being kept warm over small spirit lamps. There had been eggs, sausages, bacon, kidneys, kippers; and even, much to Sam's amusement, baked herring. Wilson had been there and had explained that they should help themselves, that breakfast was put out at eight and removed at half past nine to the servants' hall, where the staff then had their breakfast. This relieved Mary, who, suddenly confronted with all this food, imagined that what they did not eat might be thrown away. At eleven Wilson brought a tray containing a decanter of Madeira wine and a cherry cake into the morning room; lunch provided few problems, nor did afternoon tea, but dinner was a different matter. Sam liked his high tea and then a snack before he went to bed. The idea of a formal dinner at eight o'clock every evening was alien to him. He tried it a couple of times, so that he could practise and get the host business right for him and Mary, but after that he went back to his high tea. This also allowed Sam and Mary to have their evening meal with the boys. So, every evening at six, except on the rare occasions when there were guests (apart from Saunders, there had been only two to date, and they were businessmen who were much more interested in doing deals than having dinner), the four of them sat down to a fry or a grill, bread and butter, jam and cakes, and a pot of tea, served with all ceremony in the dining room. Boxing Day was going to be a little different, for they were going to have their first house guest; Saunders, having spent Christmas Day with his mother, was coming to stay for a few days.

Mary had moved into the house with a great deal of trepidation. Her first hurdle had been the domestic staff. The day they had moved in, Wilson had had the servants lined up in the great hall to greet them.

As Mary walked down the line, being introduced to each one by name – names she forgot as soon as they were spoken, she tried very hard to smile a welcome as each woman made her little bob and each man his little bow. By the time she had reached the end of the line, her knees felt like jelly; all she wanted was to hide away somewhere, but there was still one person left.

Standing a little apart from the others, at the centre of the foot of the stairs, as though to indicate that hers was a higher station, stood a tall, formidable, bosomy woman. She wore a long, black, fine woollen gown, with a tiny starched ruffle at her throat; the only ornament in her dress was a row of shiny black buttons running down the middle of the bodice. Her gown was belted at the waist, and from this hung a black reticule and a large bunch of keys. She wore gold-rimmed pince-nez, attached to a gold chain that was secured to her dress by a tiny gold safety pin. Her face was grey, her lips thin, her eyes dark and piercing. Her dark, greying hair was pulled straight back from her face into a tight bun at the nape of her neck. She was the only female member of the staff who wore no head covering. She stood impassive as

Wilson escorted Mary down the line of servants. Finally they approached her.

'And finally may I present Mrs Ellis. Mrs Ellis is your housekeeper, madam.'

Mary was terrified of the august figure before her.

'Welcome home, Mrs Hardacre,' said Mrs Ellis formally.

Mary started to offer her hand, then glanced appealingly in the direction of Wilson, who shook his head ever so slightly. She dropped her hand.

'I'm pleased to meet thee, Mrs Ellis,' said Mary in a small voice.

'Mrs Hardacre, I should like to meet you as soon as possible in order to . . .' Mrs Ellis started.

'Mr and Mrs Hardacre wish to see both of us tomorrow. I shall let you know the time later,' said Wilson. 'Everything will have to wait until then.'

Sam and Mary had made no such arrangement but were both grateful for Wilson's interruption, and Mary felt her heart warming towards him.

Looking back on it, Mary realized that things had not been nearly as frightening as they had at first appeared. She and Sam soon found themselves getting into the way of things. Mary was never quite at ease with Mrs Ellis, who she felt was her social superior. She did, however, get on famously with Basset, the head gardener. At first she was hesitant about asking him for a piece of garden, but when she broached the subject she found him most enthusiastic. She decided that she would, for a start, look after part of the rose garden and spent many happy hours forking in manure and, when the frost came, pruning the bushes ready for the next season. She enjoyed Basset's company, and among the many things he told her and taught her was how to bud a rose. He brought her a briar root, and she attempted the delicate task, and then planted it and waited anxiously to find out if it had taken. Basset even helped her with her aspidistra, telling her to rub the leaves with a little olive oil. The result was most gratifying; the spiky leaves shone as they had never shone before from the plant's place of honour in the morning room.

Probably even more than Basset she enjoyed the company

of Mrs Grey, the cook, who was a motherly soul and sensed her mistress was ill at ease. Many times Mary would slip down to the kitchen in order to discuss some completely trivial point, and Mrs Grey would make a cup of strong tea for her and, after much persuading from Mary, join her. Also, in the kitchen Mrs Grey was Mary's champion, and woe betide the girl who made a deprecating remark about the mistress.

Apart from Adam, who was beginning to show his years, the mews also contained a pair of matched hackneys and, as of Christmas, three saddle horses. These three horses were the Christmas presents of Sam and the boys. Mary would never sit on a horse, and Sam had bought her some silver-fox furs. They had also acquired two carriages in addition to the dogcart, a brougham, and a landau. For several weeks Mary had held out and insisted on driving herself into Driffield whenever she wanted to go shopping, until at last, persuaded by Sam backed up by Wilson, she consented to Grey, cook's husband and head coachman, driving her in, in the brougham.

Mrs Ellis had proved a problem and a blessing. She was, as Wilson had assured both Sam and Mary, thoroughly efficient and completely honest. But she lacked warmth, and Mary was always a little afraid of her. Mary did, however, accept Sam's argument that it would be most unfair to rob her of her livelihood by dismissing her when she was so obviously good at her job. Mary avoided her as much as she could and let her get on with the running of the house while she pottered about in the garden. Sam became very aware of this.

'I think tha should do more with Mrs Ellis,' he said to her one day.

'Oh, Sam, I know I should.'

'Then why don't thee? Tha ought to know what's going on around here.'

'She frightens me, Sam; I don't like being with her.'

'If that's true she'll just have to go,' said Sam.

'Nay, Sam, tha can't do that; it's not her fault, it's mine.'

All of this was very true, and it was a pity, because there was a great deal that Mary could have learned from Mrs Ellis.

Another problem which had beset them since they had

arrived at Hardacres was to prove much more potent. Sam had made several attempts to have Joe and Harry accepted by a public school. St Peter's at York was one obvious choice, and Oundle was not too far away. Sam had applied to both of these and also to a couple of lesser schools. The reaction to this correspondence, conducted by Saunders, had been most favourable in every case. It was when he took the boys for an interview that attitudes changed; invariably, within a few days, he would receive a letter bemoaning the fact that they had discovered the school full or giving some other, equally dubious, reason for not being able to accept his sons.

Sam was no fool. He knew the reason for their nonacceptance, and so did Mary. The Hardacres were not good enough; it was as simple as that. Money they had in plenty, but it was breeding that counted. Mary quite naturally resented this attitude, but strangely Sam did not. He knew that his time would come, and he was not worried, but for the boys it was different; they needed a good school, and they needed it now.

Both Sam and Mary were pleased that Saunders was coming to stay a while, for there was much to discuss in this matter of schools.

Wilson came in with the decanter and the cherry cake. He set them down on an occasional table and poured out two glasses, handing one to Mary and one to Sam.

'Excuse me, sir,' he said, 'but the young masters want to know if they may have permission to ride their ponies in the snow.'

'Damned if I know,' said Sam. 'Isn't Grey around?'

'I do not think so, sir.'

'Do you know if it's all right?' Sam was beginning to lose his 'thees' and 'thous'.

'I am no expert, sir, but old Sir John often went hunting in the snow.'

'Well, tell them to go ahead,' said Sam.

Armed with their father's permission, the two boys ran around to the mews.

'I'm going to ride bareback,' called Joe, 'are you?'

'No, I don't think so,' replied Harry.

'Coward,' said Joe.

'I'm not a coward,' said Harry.

'Yes, you are, you're scared to ride bareback.'

'No, I'm not; Mr Grey said we shouldn't, not until we knew the ponies better.'

'You're scared of Mr Grey, then,' taunted Joe. 'Cowardy custard.'

Little Harry flew at him. Joe easily held him at arm's length and laughed as Harry's fist flailed at the empty air.

'All right, Harry, take it easy,' said Joe laughing. 'I were only joking; come on, I'll help thee saddle up.'

Peace having been established, they got the saddle and their bridles, tacked up their ponies, mounted, and trotted off around the house. They rode up the ramp on to the raised terrace, stopping outside the windows of the morning room and waving to their parents.

Sam and Mary, sipping their Madeira, looked up at the boys and smiled.

'Them's fine lads, Sam,' said Mary.

'They'll do,' said Sam, 'though I wish that Joe would take more interest in book learning.'

'Joe hasn't got a saddle,' said Mary, concerned.

'So I see; he's a bit of a show-off, thee know.'

The boys trotted down on to the lawn, and Sam and Mary watched them as they cantered in a wide circle around their snowman. There was little question about their separate abilities; Joe, even without his saddle, seemed part of his mount. He was really riding his pony, like a natural horseman, whereas Harry merely sat on his, content to let Joe give him a lead.

Joe pulled up his pony underneath the stone balcony. 'Come on, Harry,' he called, 'I'll race thee to the woods.'

He was away almost as soon as he had spoken, and he arrived at the line of trees well before his brother. Harry pulled up beside him, arms and legs flapping all over the place.

'That's not fair,' said Harry. 'You should have given me a start, your horse is bigger than mine. Here, what's that?'

'What?'

'Listen,' said Harry.

In the distance they heard the plaintive note of a hunting horn.

'Reckon it must be the hunt,' said Joe. 'Wilson told me that they allus meet the day after Christmas.' The horn sounded again. 'Aye, it's them all right; I wonder if we'll see them.'

'They're getting nearer,' said Harry.

'Happen they're coming this way; let's follow them,' said Joe.

'I can hear the dogs,' said Harry.

'Hounds,' corrected Joe. 'Harry, look!' Across the lawn in front of them streaked a brown furry creature. 'It's fox.'

As they were talking, Harry's pony, freed from restrictions, had started to walk towards the centre of the lawn in the direction of the mews.

Away to their right, upwards of a dozen couples of hounds broke through the tree line, flanked by the huntsman and whippers-in. The hounds, their noses to the ground, were running across the lawn at a fair pace straight towards Harry.

'Harry, come back,' called Joe.

But Joe called too late. Harry was already surrounded by the hounds, which frightened his pony, who started to shy and buck, causing the boy to hang on to its mane in a desperate attempt to stay on.

The hunt was now coming through the woods – twenty or more of the local aristocracy, the men in hunting pink, the women in fine broadcloth riding habits, top hats, and mud-spattered veils. All of them seemed to be calling some form of abuse at the frightened Harry.

One large red-faced man, riding a heavy Irish cob, was bearing down on Harry. Harry looked up in near panic.

'Get out of the bloody way, you young pup!' yelled the man.

Harry was too frightened and confused to do anything, even if he had had the ability to. His pony shied again, right across the path of the big man, who had to rein in suddenly to avoid a collision.

'You bloody little idiot,' he roared and brought his riding crop hard down on Harry's back.

Joe had not been idle. Seeing what was happening, he had

ridden across the line of the hunt towards Harry, and as the big man raised his crop to strike again, Joe flung himself at him, grabbing for his arm.

Several things happened at once. Harry's pony suddenly dashed off towards the mews. The hunt passed them by in the direction of the far line of trees, and Joe, wrenching at the big man's arm, succeeded in pulling him out of the saddle and, in doing so, fell on top of him. Sam Hardacre, having seen the start of the fracas from the morning-room window, was hurrying through the house towards them.

The big man scrambled to his feet and grabbed Joe. 'You blasted little whippersnapper, I'm going to teach you a lesson you'll remember as long as you live,' he snarled.

The big man started laying into Joe just as Sam arrived on the scene. Joe was screaming as the crop fell across his back. Sam, his eyes blazing, ran to them and snatched the crop from the big man's grasp. The big man whipped around on him.

'Who the devil are you, sir?' demanded the big man. 'Keep out of this, I warn you.'

'I'm lad's father, and someone tha's not going to forget in a hurry,' said Sam. 'Thou's very good wi' lads. Let's see how tha stands up to a man.'

'Do you know to whom you are speaking?'

'I don't gi' a bugger if tha's Prince of Wales,' said Sam. 'Tha's going to get a bloody good hiding. Put 'em up.'

The by-now thoroughly frightened Joe scrambled to his feet and started off towards the house.

'Come here, Joe!' roared Sam, peeling off his jacket. 'Here, grab hold of that.'

Joe took the jacket and stood there in tearful anticipation of what was to follow.

'Very well,' said the big man, 'if this is the way you want it. I shall deal with you first, and then I shall give that young devil the thrashing he deserves.'

'Tha's not going to be fit to thrash the skin off a rice pudding by the time I've done with thee,' said Sam, and he broke the other's crop across his knee. 'Happen we won't be needing that,' he said, tossing it aside.

'Very well,' the big man spoke grimly and started to take

off his hunting pink.

'Joe,' called Sam, 'take this fella's coat, there's no sense in messing up good clothes.'

The two men squared up to each other. The big man was obviously no stranger to the art of boxing, but it served him little. The fight was short and bloody. The big man found that he was no match for Sam, who followed no rules because no one had ever taught him any; his vicious fighting, gleaned from long years of survival on the fish quays, soon took its toll. The big man lay on the ground in front of Sam trying hard to regain his feet.

'There's no point in going on wi' this,' said Sam. 'Tha's had enough. I'll say this for thee, thou's got spunk.'

The big man staggered to his feet, took his coat from Joe, painfully mounted his horse, and rode off without another word.

'I say, you certainly taught him a lesson. I bet you don't know who he is.'

Sam turned, surprised to find that the fight had been observed. A tall elegant man with fine aristocratic features, dressed in hunting pink and smoking a slim black cigar, stood watching him.

'He's a bloody great bully whoever he is, that's all I know,' said Sam.

'That chappie you nearly pummelled to death is Lord Bainton.'

'So?' said Sam, unimpressed.

'He happens to be the Lord Lieutenant.'

'Well?' said Sam.

'No reason. As you half killed the fellow, I thought you might like to know who he is.'

'I don't give a bugger who he is.'

'That's obvious. I'm not complaining, mark you; the chap's been asking for it for years, Mr ... ?'

'Hardacre,' said Sam.

'Glad to meet you, Hardacre, Middleton's the name. We march with you.'

'March?' said Sam, not understanding.

'You know, we're neighbours.'

'March, I see.'

'Well,' said Middleton, 'how about asking a fellow in for a drink? My damned horse seems to have wandered off, gone home I suppose; can't say I blame him.'

Sam laughed. 'Come into the house and meet the wife. This is Joe, my eldest.'

'How do you do, sir,' said Joe.

Sam took his coat from Joe, and they started towards the house. Half-way there they met Mary. She was very worried.

'Oh, Sam, are thee all right?' she said.

' 'Course I'm all right, lass,' he replied. 'A bit puffed, that's all. Mary, this is Mr Middleton, he's coming in for a drink. He marches with us.' And smiling at the puzzled look on Mary's face, 'That means he's our neighbour.'

Mary was impressed. Middleton was all of six feet tall, slimly built, with that elegance of manner and ability to wear clothes which would always ensure him a second glance from the ladies.

'Charmed,' he said, bowing low over Mary's hand. 'Forgive me, Mrs Hardacre, for not having made your acquaintance before.'

'Come on in, then,' said Sam, and to Mary, 'You'll catch thy death coming out without a coat.'

They sent Joe off to find Harry to make sure that he was all right and then went into the morning room.

'Madeira all right, Middleton?' asked Sam. 'Or would you like something a bit stronger?'

'Madeira will be fine,' said Middleton. 'Well, Hardacre, after what I've seen I certainly shouldn't like to cross you. Tell me, where did you learn to fight like that?'

'On the fish quays,' said Sam. 'There you either fought or starved. It's not so long since.'

'You've come a long way since then,' said Middleton.

'Reckon we have, but there's still a long way yet,' said Sam.

They talked pleasantly enough for a while, and Middleton assured Mary that Mrs Middleton would call on her. Their conversation ranged over various subjects and finally got on to the question of a school for Joe and Harry. Sam explained, without rancour, how he had tried a number of schools and in every case failed to get the boys accepted.

'I'm not holding it against them,' he said. 'I don't talk right, and I'm not their usual class. But I'm going to be. Before I die, Hardacre is going to be one of the most respected names in the country.'

Middleton did not comment but returned to the matter of education. 'As far as schools are concerned, have you given a thought to Barlow's?'

'Barlow's?' Sam had not heard of it.

'Yes, it's at Seamer, not far from Scarborough. It's small, but they have a pretty good academic standard; not so good at games, mark you.'

'Have you got lads of your own, Middleton?' asked Sam.

'Yes, one boy and two daughters.'

'Is the lad at Barlow's?'

'Oh, no,' Middleton smiled slightly. 'He's at Harrow.'

Sam understood. He would never get his boys into Harrow. 'What makes you think that I could get them into Barlow's?' he asked. 'Happen it would be just the same as the rest of them.'

'Not necessarily. Barlow's is owned by the daughter of the founder, but it is administered by a board of governors; she never interferes. I happen to be one of the governors. Only one among seven, though ...'

'So there's not much you'd be able to do?'

'Frankly, no. But there is something else. I am speaking out of school, if you'll forgive the pun, but I know that the place is in some financial difficulty. Now, if it suits you and you offered to help out, I doubt if you'd have much trouble.'

Sam got paper and pencil, and Middleton wrote down the details of the school. Sam had an idea. That evening after Middleton had left and Saunders had arrived, he talked it over at length with him and instructed Saunders to find out all he could about the school, including the extent of its debt.

Saunders retired early, and later that night Sam and Mary were sitting together by the fire in the withdrawing room. The dark wine-coloured velvet curtains were drawn, and the gas light lent a yellow warmth to the flowered chintzes of the furniture.

Promptly at a quarter to eleven Wilson appeared, carrying a tray of hot chocolate and biscuits. He handed a cup and saucer to Sam and the Victoria and Albert mug to Mary.

'Will there be anything else, sir?' he asked, putting his tray down within easy reach of Mary.

'Nothing else, Wilson, good night,' said Sam.

'Good night, Wilson,' said Mary.

It happened every night. Mary poured the chocolate as soon as Wilson had left, and then they sat for a while in silence, sipping the hot steaming liquid and gazing into the fire, just as they had done with a cup of tea every night in their lodgings by the fish quays.

'What did you think of Middleton?' asked Sam at length.

'Ever so nice, a real gentleman.'

'That's because he kissed tha hand,' said Sam laughing, 'but you'll notice that Barlow's wasn't good enough for his lad.'

'He didn't mean that, Sam.'

'He didn't say it, but he thought it all the same,' said Sam. 'Still, I'm going to look into it, happen it might do.'

There was another long silence.

'Sam,' Mary spoke very quietly.

'What is it, lass?'

'I've got summat to tell thee.'

'Aye?'

'It's important, Sam.'

'Go on, then.'

'Sam, it's not very easy.'

'There's nowt wrong, is there?'

'Oh no, there's nowt wrong,' Mary stopped. Her embarrassment was obvious.

Sam smiled. 'Then out wi'it, love.'

'Well . . .' she stopped again.

Sam smiled. She didn't really have to explain to him. He knew the news that she had. It had happened before, and it was the same each time. He knew what it was that she wanted to tell him, and he knew that she could not. She never had been able to do it. So, as always, Sam helped her out.

Very gently he said, 'I'm glad, Mary love; happen it'll be a girl this time.'

CHAPTER NINE

If Barlow's Academy for the Sons of Gentlemen had stood upon a hill it would have been imposing, but, standing as it did in a slight depression in the North Yorkshire moors, it rarely drew a second glance. Had the school been a little better, it would have been well on the way to becoming, if not an Eton or a Harrow, then certainly a St Peter's or an Oundle. It had been founded some forty years ago by Joshua Barlow when he found himself in the situation of possessing an academic degree in the arts, a large country mansion of mixed antecedents, and very little money. His reply to this situation was to found a school, and, until a few years before his death, he ran it with vigour and enthusiasm, churning out a steady stream of reasonable professional men, most of whom went on to take degrees at universities other than Oxford or Cambridge.

The building itself had proved ideal for Joshua's purpose. It was constructed in the shape of an 'H'. The central bar became School House, presided over by the headmaster himself, and the east and west wings became Peabody's and Armstrong's, respectively, being named after their first housemasters.

The entire ground floor became classrooms and halls. The first floor was studies, masters' accommodation, and the housemasters' flats, while the attic was converted to long dormitories for the inhabitants of lower and middle school. The classrooms still possessed the original furniture which Joshua Barlow had put there forty years ago, and among the names and initials carved into the now-pitted and scarred desks could be found a few minor celebrities, including a Rear Admiral of the Blue and a lesser politician.

The halls' corridors and rooms were all painted dark brown to a height of four feet, six inches, and then, after a black line one inch wide, green for the remainder of their height, making strange contrast with the ornate plaster work of the ceilings. Outside, what had once been lawns and flower gardens, had become playing fields and an extended kitchen garden which managed to supply all of the vegetables served on the school tables.

Joshua Barlow had died about eight years ago, and his place had been taken by the Reverend Peter Davies, a grim-faced clergyman whose self-imposed task of turning about one hundred and forty savages into young gentlemen had brought with it frustration and satisfaction in equal amounts. Davies wore a high clerical collar under his scholastic gown, which had once been black but had now assumed a dingy, mottled appearance liberally spotted with patches of in-grained chalk. He had a lean, hawk-like face and a beaky nose from the end of which, when the weather was cold, hung an almost permanent globule of moisture which was responsible for the fact that, throughout the school, he was irreverently referred to, always out of earshot, as 'dewdrop'.

His large pale eyes blinked constantly behind his steel-rimmed spectacles. He was married to a woman some twenty years his junior, who was a great favourite with the senior boys of School House. At first sight Davies did not inspire confidence as either an educator or anything else, but this was a false impression. During the last years of his reign Barlow had become quite senile and had let the school slide into debt and inefficiency. It had been a slow process, but Davies was beginning to restore its reputation as a seat of learning and even to make some slight inroads into the debt.

It was about three weeks after Middleton's visit that Sam Hardacre stood in the Reverend Peter Davies' study for the second time. Sam had received his letter that same morning. It had been the usual polite note expressing deep regret that, since Mr Hardacre's visit, it had been discovered that the Academy had a serious problem of overcrowding and that, sadly, they would be unable to find places for either Joseph or Harold Hardacre.

Mr Davies had been about to consume a digestive biscuit and drink his mid-morning cup of tea, when, much to his surprise, Sam had, unannounced, walked into his study.

'Mr Hardacre,' said Davies carefully, brushing a crumb from his academic gown, 'I hardly expected to see you here.'

'Happen you didn't,' replied Sam.

'Surely you received my letter.'

'Oh, I got that all right, it came today,' said Sam, 'but I'm going to do thee a favour and ignore it.'

'Mr Hardacre, if you received my letter, you must realize that there is nothing further to discuss.'

'Damned right there isn't,' said Sam pleasantly. 'Harry and Joe are starting here tomorrow.'

'I am sorry, Mr Hardacre, but that will not be possible,' said the Reverend Davies. 'I thought that I had made that perfectly clear.'

'You like your job here, don't you?' asked Sam.

Davies blinked several times in quick succession. 'Very much, though I hardly see what liking my position here has to do with this.'

'It has a hell of a lot to do with it, Mr Davies. I'd be the last person to want to interfere with thy work; I've no desire or any expectation of any special privileges for my sons, but, that apart, they start here tomorrow.' Sam wagged his finger at Davies. 'Or there'll be a new man sitting in that chair the day after.'

The Reverend Davies rose to his feet; he was becoming quite angry. 'Mr Hardacre, you forget yourself. I shall be obliged if you will leave my study immediately. Now, if you will be good enough to excuse me, I have a great number of things to attend to.'

'All right,' said Sam, 'I'll go. But there's just one thing you ought to know before I do. Three days ago I saw Sally Barlow, Joshua's daughter. I anticipated your letter, so I bought this place from her lock, stock, and barrel.'

Davies did not reply. He slumped back into his chair and sat with his mouth open as Sam continued.

'I gave her a good price for it, probably more than it's worth. Don't fret, I'm not going to interfere with the running of the school; the governors and you will carry on just as before. I'm not looking for a profit; happen I'll give it to the governors after my lads leave. Thou's got to understand my point of view; I had to get my lads schooled. I'm not a gentleman and never will be, I know that, but those boys are going to be different, they are going to be gentlemen.'

Davies sat for a long time drumming his fingers on the desk. 'I see,' he said.

'I know this is a shock for you, and thee needn't say owt now. I'm bringing my lads tomorrow; happen you'll let me know your decision then.'

'Mr Hardacre,' said Davies.

'Well?'

'Mr Hardacre, I will not deny that this has been a shock. I suppose I should feel offended at your actions, but I am surprised to find that I do not. I think that your boys are very fortunate in having a father like you. What time will they be arriving?'

Sam turned back to the desk and smiled. 'No hard feelings; I've had a hell of a job finding a school. I'd rather you hadn't known about me buying it, but now you do, there'll be no special treatment? No favours?'

'Mr Hardacre, rather than do that, I *would* resign my position here.'

'I think we understand each other, Mr Davies,' said Sam. 'Those boys are never to know what I've done. I'll have them here on the afternoon train tomorrow. Their mother's packing now.' Sam held out his hand.

'You are very sure of yourself, Mr Hardacre.' Davies' tone was one of grudging admiration as he took the proffered hand. 'And I think you are quite right. About us understanding each other, I mean.'

Back at Hardacres, Mary had summoned up enough courage to ask the formidable Mrs Ellis to help in preparing the boys for school. Together they had searched the attic and come up with a couple of suitable lined wicker hampers. These they had packed with all the clothes and sports gear that Mary and Sam had bought after the abortive attempt to have their sons accepted by St Peters at York.

Mary was still somewhat overawed by her housekeeper. Mrs Ellis, for her part, was always formal and correct in her manner and never forgot her place in the presence of Sam and Mary, treating them with all the respect due to the master and mistress of the household. Nevertheless, Mary felt somewhat inadequate in the big house and could not get used to others doing all the household tasks which had always been so much a part of her life. Always she had scrubbed and sewn, cooked and mended for her menfolk. Now, with all of that lost and it being that season when there was little to do in the garden, she spent a lot of the time, when Sam was away, looking for something to do.

This was no easy matter. The things at which she was competent were all menial tasks, and she discovered that trying to perform them only gave offence to the servants. On one occasion she was sweeping up the hearth in her private sitting room when Brigit, the upstairs maid, came in. The poor girl was horror-struck, fearing that she had failed to complete her tasks, and begged Mary not to report her to Mrs Ellis. Mary was afraid of horses, so that riding as a relaxation was denied her. She was learning to read, but it was proving a slow process, and she could not really manage anything more advanced than the simplest of children's literature. She longed for the spring so that she could really get to work on her garden.

Shortly after the visit of Mr Middleton, a visiting card had arrived at Hardacres; it was inscribed 'Jennifer Middleton', and on it was written 'Second and third Thursdays'. It was while they were packing the boys' things that Mary decided to raise the matter.

'Mrs Ellis,' she asked, 'did anyone call last Thursday?'

'Not to my knowledge, madam,' was the reply. 'Was there someone you were expecting?'

'Well, yes, as a matter of fact there was,' said Mary. 'I had a card from Mrs Middleton saying that she would call, but she never came.'

'I think I remember that card, madam,' said Mrs Ellis, 'but surely it was a calling card.'

'A calling card?' said Mary. 'But I don't understand. It said second and third Thursdays, but she never came, and last Thursday was the second Thursday in January.'

Mrs Ellis suddenly realized that her mistress really did not understand. 'Madam,' she said, 'that card meant that Mrs Middleton would be at home on the second and third Thursdays. It was an invitation for you to call on her.'

'Oh, dear,' said Mary, 'tha must think I'm very stupid, Mrs Ellis, but I didn't understand, really I didn't.'

'Not at all,' said Mrs Ellis primly, 'there is no harm done. The day after tomorrow is the third Thursday; why not call on Mrs Middleton then?'

Mary sat down on the hamper, biting her lip. 'I think I'd be scared to.'

'Madam,' said Mrs Ellis coldly, 'do you mind if I speak frankly?'

'No, say what thee like.'

'I think that it would be rude if you failed to call. It is your duty to mix socially with your fellow ladies, especially your neighbours.'

Mary was not sure, but had there been the slightest note of sarcasm in the word 'ladies'?

'Very well, Mrs Ellis, I shall go. Now let's get on with this job.'

'One other thing, Mrs Hardacre; I feel that you really must engage the services of a ladies' maid.'

'What for?'

'To look after you, to attend to your bodily needs. One cannot be a lady without a ladies' maid.'

Mary was aware of the veiled insult. 'I think tha's said enough, Mrs Ellis. Shall we finish the packing?'

Mary was glad when it was over and she could get away to the kitchen and her cup of tea with cook while she discussed Sam's evening meal.

On her way back from the kitchen she had to pass the servants' hall. As she passed she heard raised voices; Wilson was speaking. She knew that she should not have done so, but she stopped and listened.

'I don't care what you think,' Wilson was angry. 'I will not have anyone refer to the mistress in those terms.'

'Don't try to give me orders, Mr Wilson,' it was Mrs Ellis' voice. 'I called her a fishwife because she is a fishwife. A slut like that pretending to be a lady ...'

Mary did not wait to hear more; choking back her tears, she ran to her bedroom and flung herself on the bed, sobbing her heart out. An hour later Sam found her there.

'Mary, love, what is it? What's happened?'

Little by little, between sobs, Sam got it out of her. Grim-faced, he went down to the study and summoned Wilson.

'Wilson,' he said, 'I want all of the staff in the servants' hall at once. Come back here and tell me when they're there.'

Five minutes later Wilson returned.

'They're waiting for you, sir,' he announced.

Sam marched down to the servants' hall, followed by Wilson. As he entered, the buzz of conversation stopped. He stood for a moment glaring at all of them.

'I've got summat to say to you, all of you,' he started. 'First of all, I'm not a fool; I know full well that every one of you is being paid over the odds. That's not important. You get it because we are probably not the sort of family you've been used to, and it's a way of us showing our appreciation of the little bits of help that most of you give us.

'Before I bought this place, I told Wilson here that we had a lot to learn about how things should be done and all of that sort of thing, and I'm grateful for what he's done to put us on the right road. Now I'm going to tell thee all a thing or two about us Hardacres.

'Both me and Mrs Hardacre was born poor. She's known times when she's had to pawn her shoes to get a crust of bread. I've been hungry me sen. I don't know how many of you have ever been hungry, but I can tell you this, it's not funny; if tha thinks it is, just ask them as have known it.

'A house like this isn't a dozen or more people looking after one family. I've learned that much in three months. When you get right down to it, we all look after each other. For instance, cook's job is to feed us, not just the family but all of us, while my job is to pay the bills and keep a roof over our heads. We all depend on each other.

'Now, all of you know where we came from. I'm a guttie who got lucky. I'm not ashamed of it; I worked hard, and it were an honest living. If anybody calls me a guttie, I don't get

132

hurt. If they mean it as an insult, I might punch their nose, but I wouldn't be offended. Mrs Hardacre is another matter; she is a lady. She doesn't talk posh, and she doesn't know what a calling card is, but she's a bloody sight more lady than a hell of a lot I've met around here, for all their airs and graces. There's just one thing I want you to remember, all of you. Nobody hurts my wife and continues to live under my roof. Is that clear? Do you all understand?' Sam paused, but nobody made a sound. 'All right, that's all, you can go now.'

As they started to move away, Sam turned to Wilson. 'Bring Mrs Ellis here, I'm not quite finished.'

Mrs Ellis stood before him, tight-lipped and silent. Sam waited until the others had gone and only he, Wilson, and Mrs Ellis were left in the room.

'Mrs Ellis,' said Sam, 'this evening you called my wife a fishwife.'

Mrs Ellis glared at Wilson.

'No, Mrs Ellis, Mr Wilson did not tell me. Mary heard you.' Sam was in a state of controlled fury. 'You also called her a slut. Mrs Ellis, you will be out of this house within the hour. You will be given five pounds instead of notice, and Wilson will arrange to have you taken into Driffield, where he will pay for one night's lodging at the inn. Good-bye, Mrs Ellis.'

Sam turned on his heel and was out of the room before she could utter a word.

Sam gave Wilson the money for Mrs Ellis and then went straight back to Mary. He found her sitting on the edge of her bed. She looked better but still worried.

'Well, that's done,' he said. 'You won't be seeing her again.'

'Oh, Sam, you didn't?'

'I did. How do you think you'd ever be able to face her again after hearing her say a thing like that?'

'But the poor woman, whatever will she do?'

'Don't worry yourself about her. That one'll be all right. I gave her five pounds and sent her packing. Come on now, I want my supper.'

'Dinner,' she corrected.

'Supper, dinner, tea, what the hell does it matter what tha

calls it. I'm hungry. Are lads in?'

'They should be; we're late.'

They went to the dining room together. Harry and Joe were waiting for them. They sat down and ate in silence, the boys sensing the tenseness of their parents, and it was not until the sweet had been served that Sam spoke, and everyone relaxed.

'Well, lads,' he said, 'school tomorrow.'

'Great,' said Harry.

'Oh, no,' said Joe.

CHAPTER TEN

The Reverend Davies gazed over the top of his spectacles at the two boys standing before him. After a somewhat tearful farewell from Mary, Sam had taken them by train to Seamer and, then on, by hired carriage to Barlow's Academy. He had dumped the boys in the headmaster's study and left. Harry and Joe, silent and a little uneasy at being away from their parents for the first time, stood on the other side of the desk from Mr Davies.

'Ahem,' the Reverend Davies cleared his throat, 'it is my duty to welcome you two boys to Barlow's. Whether that duty will prove a pleasure or not is entirely up to you. *Venite, filii, audite me.*'

'Eh?' said Joe.

'"Eh" is not a word with which I am familiar,' said the Reverend Davies, 'and when you address me you say "sir".'

'What did tha say, sir?'

'*Venite, filii, audite me.*'

'Is that a foreign language, er ... sir?' asked Harry.

'That, Harold, is Latin. *Venite*, come; *filii*, children; *audite*, listen to; *me*, me. That, however, is beside the point. Soon you will be speaking Latin with a greater fluency than that with which you now prostitute the English language. Harold, you will be known in this school as Hardacre Minor; we do not use Christian names. You are eleven years old, approaching twelve. Your form will be the lower third, and there you will join eight other boys in your house; they will be of like age and of equal incompetence. You will, until attaining the ripe old age of thirteen, be required to fag.'

'What's that, sir?' asked Harry.

'Fagging is service. A fag is a boy who is appointed as a servant to one of the seniors in his house. Incidentally, we have three houses here, and you two will both be in School House, my house. A fag serves his master by performing a series of menial tasks such as polishing his shoes, pressing his trousers, cleaning his study, making his toast – in short, any legitimate work which he may choose to delegate. Should you displease him, he will beat you; should you not, you will be spared.'

'That's not fair, sir,' said Joe.

'Of course not. But it instils discipline, and discipline is one of the greatest qualities of man. However, you may have observed that I was addressing Hardacre Minor.'

'Yes, sir,' said Joe.

'Then you will remain silent until I have finished. I shall then address you.' The Reverend Davies rang a small handbell on his desk.

A woman of average height tending to stoutness, with white hair and the suspicion of a moustache, entered. She was wearing an immaculate light-blue linen dress with a starched white apron.

'Matron,' said the Reverend Davies, 'this is Hardacre Minor. I am placing him in the lower third, School House.' Then, speaking to Harry, 'Matron will take you to the lower-third dormitory, where you will unpack and store your things neatly in your locker. After that you will report to Barker in the prefects' common room. Do you understand?'

'Who's Barker, sir?' asked Harry in a small voice.

'Barker is head boy of School House; he will give you whatever further instructions are necessary. *Quis est sapiens, qui observet haec.*'

'Yes, sir,' said Harry.

'Dismiss,' said the Reverend Davies.

'Come with me, boy,' said Matron.

'And now, Master Hardacre,' said the Reverend Davies, 'we can give you our undivided attention provided you will do me the courtesy of standing still.' Joe was moving nervously from foot to foot. 'Thank you, that is much more agreeable. I have here a report written by Mr Wilkins, your tutor. I did not mention this in front of your brother, as it would appear that his progress has been slow but diligent. You, on the other hand, I am assured, have, with the exception of mathematics, little devotion to learning. I wish it clearly understood that, here at Barlow's, we do not tolerate specialization. We are determined to produce the complete man, preferably a gentleman. Persuasion and example are the easiest methods, but there are others which can sometimes prove extremely painful. At your age you are to be placed in the Remove.' The Reverend Davies held up a hand as Joe was about to speak. 'I shall explain – the Remove is that limbo which exists between lower and upper school, populated by a higher proportion of pimples than the rest of the school together. But remember this, Hardacre, I shall not hesitate to move you down to lower school if at any time I find that you are failing to apply yourself to your studies.'

'Do I 'ave to be a fag, sir?' asked Joe.

'The word "have" is aspirated thus: "have". Say it, boy.'

'Have,' said Joe.

'That is better. No, you are spared the degradation of fagging, not by merit but on account of age, and remember that if you succeed in your work, you may be given a study at the commencement of the autumn term when you should enter the lower fifth. Now you may make your exit through that door there and await Matron's return. Tell her you are for the Remove and then, after unpacking, go and see Barker. Dismiss.'

Matron led Harry out of the headmaster's study and down the main corridor on the ground floor.

'That's the prefects' room, Hardacre,' she said, indicating a door which bore the legend: 'Prefects only, Vermin will knock, wait, and tremble.'

They went up a staircase and then another and then another. The entire school seemed to be painted in dull greens and browns. The staircases were devoid of any covering; the first was polished and the others plain wood. Everything seemed clean and functional.

At last they entered a large room containing a dozen iron beds, nine of which were made up in identical fashion with rough, brown blankets and coarse linen sheets; the other three contained bare mattresses and pillows. Beside each stood a wooden locker and a small table on which was a candle in a candlestick. The slope of the ceiling indicated that this room had started life as the attic. The floor consisted of bare wooden boards, apart from a small square of matting which lay at the foot of each bed.

Harry's basket was lying beside one of the beds on the side of the room opposite the two dormer windows.

'Is that your hamper?' asked Matron.

'Yes, miss.'

'You say "Matron" when you address me, boy.'

'Yes, Matron, sorry.'

'Right. You can unpack now and put everything neatly into your locker. Leave your hamper where it is; it will be removed and returned to you at the end of term.'

'Please, Matron,' said Harry, 'where do we ...'

'At the end of the corridor. During the night you will use the chamber pot which is under your bed, and at seven every morning water is placed outside the dormitory. You wash in the basin which you will find in your locker, and once every two weeks you will have a bath. Remember to keep clean, Hardacre; a gentleman is always clean.'

'Yes, Matron.'

'Very well, I shall leave you now. When you have unpacked, go to the prefects' room,' and she swept out of the room.

Harry felt miserable; he sat down on the edge of his bed, choking back the tears, but he did not sit for long – it was cold in the dormitory. He unpacked his things as he had been instructed and then made his way downstairs to the prefects' room. He stood outside the door for a while and then, summoning up his courage, tapped gingerly on the door.

'Come,' said a voice.

Timorously he opened the door. He found himself in a large, comfortable room furnished with old armchairs, a table spread with magazines and books, and a blazing log fire in the grate. There were three or four youths in the room, their ages about seventeen. One tall, well-built youth was standing with his back to the fire; he gazed expressionlessly at Harry.

'Please ...' said Harry.

'Silence.' The voice came from someone sitting at the table.

'What do you want?' asked the youth with his back to the fire.

138

'Please, sir ...'

'Don't "sir" me. My name is Barker, and you address me as "Barker".'

'Please, Barker, I'm looking for you. The headmaster sent me.'

'Ah!' said Barker, 'you must be one of the Hardacres; Minor, I presume?'

'Yes, Barker.'

'Well, young Hardacre, I want you to know that I am sacrificing a fully trained fag, one Smith Minimus, in order to break you in myself. But first I must introduce you to the pleasures of the classroom in this noble seat of learning. According to the latest intelligence reports, the lower third are at this moment incarcerated with their form master, Mr Brooks, more familiarly known as "Boko". Come with me, young Hardacre, and I shall hand you over to his tender mercies.'

Barker led Harry back along the corridor. 'After class, come to my study,' he said.

Barker opened the door to a classroom, and they went in. Eight boys were sitting in varying degrees of disinterest as a tall, gangling man, with a large dome-like head and a great deal of chalk dust on his person, droned on.

'... during part of the year 1585 and the whole of 1586, Drake was actively employed against Philip on the coasts of Spain and ... yes, Barker, what is it?'

'I've brought the new boy, sir,' said Barker.

'Ah!' said Mr Brooks, 'you must be Hardacre. Thank you, Barker. Come here, boy.'

Barker left, and Harry stood nervously before the formidable Mr Brooks.

'Now, then, boy,' said Mr Brooks, 'you may sit there' – he pointed to one of the unoccupied, battered wooden desks at the front of the class – 'where we will be able to keep you under close observation.'

'Now, sir?' asked Harry.

'Now, Hardacre.' Harry took his place. 'We are studying the history of this great nation of ours. Here is a textbook to which I trust you will apply yourself with enthusiasm until you have caught up with the rest of your form. Are you aware of the activities of one Sir Francis Drake?'

'Oh, yes, sir,' said Harry, 'I read about him.'

'Indeed, it is a relief to know that you can read. We were discussing his exploits in the year 1585 *et sequentia*.'

'Please, sir, what does that mean, sir?' asked Harry.

'I trust your history is more advanced than your Latin. It means "and onwards"; perhaps you can tell us a little more about him ... Gillis, come here.'

A boy of about Harry's height and twice his girth came to the front of the class.

'Gillis, you are eating one of your filthy confections in class.'

'Oh, no, sir, not me, sir,' protested Gillis.

'And now you are lying, Gillis,' said Mr Brooks, picking up a cane which lay beside the blackboard. 'Over.'

Slowly Gillis bent his portly body over the desk next to Harry. Mr Brooks took careful aim and delivered two hefty swipes across Gillis' buttocks.

'Two for eating in class,' said Mr Brooks and, as Gillis started to move, 'stay there, boy.' Twice more the cane descended on to the seat of Gillis' trousers. 'And two more for lying. Back to your desk.'

White-faced, Gillis went back to his place, where he sat down gingerly. Harry watched horrified.

'Now, Hardacre, you were about to tell us a little about Sir Francis Drake's activities after 1585.'

'Well, sir,' said Harry, glancing back at the suffering Gillis, 'he spent two years on the coasts of Spain and Portugal and in 1587 he burned a lot of Spanish ships at Cádiz.'

'Excellent, and what did he call that episode?' Mr Brooks was impressed.

'Singeing the King of Spain's beard, sir,' said Harry.

'That will do, Hardacre. Gentlemen, I see that we have a great historian in our midst.' The class sniggered. 'Silence, now to continue ...'

Matron had taken Joe to his dormitory on the floor below Harry's, and after he had finished his unpacking he had wandered off in search of Barker. Classes were coming out, and Barker escorted Joe to the masters' common room. He left Joe outside and went in. In a few moments he emerged accompanied by a youngish man — well-built, square-jawed, red-headed, and with a pleasant, friendly face.

Mr Searl was form master of the Remove; he taught mathematics and also did duty as the school sports master. He was a man who had not yet suffered the disillusion of his profession, as had so many of his seniors. He was respected by the senior school, held in affection by his own form, and worshipped by the juniors. He came out of the common room and greeted Joe brightly.

'You're Hardacre Major, eh?'

'I suppose so, sir,' replied Joe.

'Welcome to the Remove. We'll cut along to my study and have a little chat. After that I'll take you and introduce you to your classmates.'

Searl's study was a small, sparsely furnished but comfortable room around which hung an aroma of linseed oil and dubbin. It was littered with cricket bats, footballs, a pile of boxing gloves, and several daguerreo-types of Mr Searl in various sporting poses. Along the mantelpiece over the fireplace was a row of somewhat tarnished silver sports trophies.

'Well, Hardacre,' said Searl, seating himself behind a desk piled high with exercise books, 'I hear that your maths are good, which will please me, but that you do not work hard at any other subject, which will probably anger the rest of your masters. If you will take a tip, I should get down to a spot of serious study, especially of English, Latin, and penmanship. It would appear, from your tutor's report, that you are bent on a business career. In this I can assure you that the subjects that I have mentioned are every bit as important as mathematics. Do you take my point?'

'Eh. Oh, aye,' said Joe, who had been much more interested in his surroundings than what was being said to him.

'And, Hardacre, that is not the way to address your form master, or any master for that matter.'

'Sorry, sir,' said Joe.

'All right, we'll let it pass. Now, then, what about sports?

What games do you play?'

'I haven't played many games, sir,' said Joe; 'I like riding, though.'

'Unfortunately, we do not ride here, and pupils are not allowed to have a mount here during term time. Is there anything else?'

'I don't know, sir.'

'How about boxing?'

'Tha means fighting, sir?'

'In a way I suppose I do.'

'I'm good at that,' said Joe; 'I haven't met anybody of my size as I couldn't lick, and that goes for some a lot bigger than me, sir.'

'Well, that's a start. We'll have to get you into the gym and see what you can do. We have sports on Thursday and Saturday afternoons, so we'll try you out then; I must say you look sturdy enough. How about your brother?'

'Harry? He's interested in nothing but books.'

'I see,' said Searl. 'Is there anything you want to ask me?'

'Not yet, sir,' replied Joe. 'So far I don't know enough to know what I don't know.'

Searl smiled at the boy's logic. 'Very well,' he said. 'Oh, there is just one other thing. You must write a letter home every week, and this must be done by call-over on Sundays.'

'What for, sir?' asked Joe.

'To let your parents know how you are getting on.' Searl was surprised at the question.

'Can't see how that's going to do any good.'

'Whyever not? I presume that your parents are fond of you and would like to know how things are going.'

'Aye, sir,' said Joe, 'but I can't see any use in writing to 'em, except for a few words; neither my mum nor dad can read.'

'Oh.' Searl paused while he digested this piece of information. 'Nevertheless, you will write to them every week; no doubt they will be able to get your letters read for them. Now, if you'll come along with me, I shall introduce you to the rest of your form.'

Without waiting for a reply, Searl swept out of the study at such a pace that Joe had to trot to keep up with him. He took

Joe up to the first floor. There was activity now in the corridors; classes being over, the building had somehow come alive. Joe noticed, to his amusement, that all the boys touched their foreheads with their right index finger as Mr Searl passed them. Searl, for his part, acknowledged each boy by name. At last they arrived at a door from which a great deal of noise was emanating.

'That bedlam, Hardacre,' said Searl, 'is being provided by your fellow Removers.' He flung the door open.

'*Cave*, beaks,' called a voice.

There was instant silence.

'Martin,' called Searl.

'Sir?' A tall, good-looking youth about the same age as Joe came over to them.

'Martin, I want you to meet a new boy who has had the doubtful fortune of being placed in the Remove. Hardacre, this is Martin, your form captain. Martin is a man of many virtues; not only does he play an excellent game of football, but he manages to combine it with a reasonable academic achievement.'

'Thank you, sir,' said Martin grinning. 'Hello, Hardacre.'

'Hello,' said Joe.

'Hardacre has just arrived at the school and knows nothing of our routine, so I shall leave him with you for instruction. His errors and omissions, over the next few days, will be upon your head. Good-bye, Hardacre, I wish you well; I shall see you at call-over.'

Mr Searl left to a chorus of good-byes from the boys. There were about a dozen of them in the room, and as soon as the master had gone, they all crowded around Joe, plying him with questions.

'Cut it out chaps,' called Martin, 'I shall question our new boy and see if he is a fit person to be initiated into our society.'

'What dost tha mean by that?' demanded Joe.

'What dost tha mean by that?' mimicked a big, burly boy who sported a thick mop of black curly hair. 'Wherever did it learn to talk like that?'

'Leave him alone, Tarrant,' said Martin.

'Don't thee bother, Tarrant,' said Joe, pushing past Martin

and going to him, 'now, what did thee say?'

'I say, fellows, he does it all the time,' said Tarrant, 'I wonder what stone he crawled out from under.' Tarrant turned towards the others as he spoke.

Joe grabbed him by the shoulders and swung him around to face him. 'I think thee had better say "sorry".'

'Are your hands clean? You're touching me, you know.' Tarrant pointedly brushed the shoulder of his jacket.

The rest of the boys had withdrawn to the sides of the room, leaving Joe, Tarrant, and Martin the centre.

'Put 'em up,' said Joe, squaring up to Tarrant.

'Cut that out,' said Martin, standing between them. 'If you two must fight, it's going to be done properly. Tarrant, I think you ought to apologize.'

Tarrant merely grinned. 'I'd rather teach him a lesson,' he said.

'Hardacre,' Martin asked, 'do you want to fight?'

'I'm bloody well going to,' said Joe.

'Right,' said Martin. 'Faulkener, get the gloves.'

'What do we want gloves for?' demanded Joe.

'It happens to be a school rule,' explained Martin. 'You can get yourself sacked for fighting without gloves.'

'Sacked?'

'Expelled.'

Faulkener, a small, weedy youth with steel-rimmed spectacles, handed two pairs of boxing gloves to Martin. The two belligerents put them on.

'Now, then, for your benefit, Hardacre,' said Martin, 'you fight three-minute rounds with one minute between rounds until one of you calls enough. Faulkener, keep time, right? Box on.'

Tarrant adopted the classic boxing guard; he obviously had some technique and was strong. Joe rushed at him, arms flailing, and brought his knee up into Tarrant's stomach. Tarrant doubled up gasping. Martin separated the two contestants.

'Cut that out, Hardacre,' he commanded. 'I don't know where you learned to fight, but you don't fight like that here. You fight with your fists only, and you don't hit below the belt. All right, get on with it.'

Tarrant hit Joe often enough but with little effect, apart from one blow which bloodied Joe's nose. In spite of Tarrant's boxing ability, within a couple of rounds Joe had unscientifically reduced him to a bruised and bleeding mass. Fit though Tarrant undoubtedly was, he was no match for the brute strength of his opponent. It was just after the start of the third round that Joe finally floored Tarrant, and before Joe could dive on to his beaten adversary, Martin stepped between them.

'That's enough,' said Martin.

'I haven't finished wi' yon yet,' snarled Joe.

'Oh, yes, you have,' said Martin, 'get the gloves off.'

And such was the authority in Martin's voice that Joe obeyed him. Painfully Tarrant clambered to his feet and came over to Joe.

'Sorry, Hardacre,' he said, offering his hand.

Joe looked down at the proffered hand.

'Shake hands, Hardacre,' said Martin. 'Tarrant's apologized, so it's over.'

Reluctantly Joe took Tarrant's hand.

'You can fight, I'll say that for you,' said Tarrant. 'We'd better cut off to the dorm and clean up before call-over. I've got some cake up there; like a bit?'

As Harry came out of class, someone tugged at his sleeve. He looked around and found that he was being accosted by one of the smallest boys, of his own age, he had ever seen.

'I say, Hardacre,' said the small one, 'I'm Smith Minimus; you've got Barker, haven't you?'

'I reckon,' said Harry.

'You're frightfully jammy,' said Smith; there was more than a touch of envy in his voice. 'Barker's super.'

'How?' asked Harry, unimpressed.

'Well, for one thing, he only beats you with a slipper; it doesn't hurt nearly as much as a cane, and he won't beat you at all for the first week, unless you do something absolutely awful.'

'Oh?' said Harry.

'But you'd better cut along to his study now,' said Smith.

Disconsolately Harry wandered off in the direction of the prefects' studies. On his way he passed Joe and Tarrant.

'Joe,' he said, concerned, 'are you all right? Your nose is bleeding.'

'I'm all right,' said Joe, 'I've been fighting, that's all. This is Tarrant, a friend of mine.'

'How do you do,' said Harry.

Tarrant grunted.

'My brother,' said Joe, by way of explanation.

'Come on, Hardacre,' said Tarrant, ignoring Harry. 'We've got to get cleaned up; can't spend all day with these scruffy little urchins.'

'He's my brother,' said Harry defensively.

'He's also a Remove man,' said Tarrant, 'so just be careful, youngster; come on, Hardacre.'

'I'll see thee, Harry,' said Joe, and he followed Tarrant off along the corridor.

Harry was left alone. He suddenly realized that, for the first time in his life, he really was alone. Swallowing hard and chewing at his lower lip, he went off in search of Barker and his slipper.

Jane was born in the July of that year, and at last Sam had the daughter he had always longed for. For the first time in her life Mary was attended by a doctor and a midwife. But when Jane was born, the doctor had been at lunch at his own house, and Mary had sent the midwife off to Driffield on an errand. Thus she was able to produce her daughter as she had produced her sons – alone, without fuss and without inconvenience to anyone.

Both the doctor and the midwife had been horrified and filled with remorse when they realized what had happened, but Sam had understood. It was not just Mary's desire to do it herself, alone; she did not want anyone, not even a midwife or a doctor, to share the secrets of the most intimate moments of her life.

Sam was of course overjoyed, too happy even to remonstrate with Mary over the risk that she had taken. At last he had a girl child to spoil, and he was determined to make, what he called, 'a right job of it'.

The boys would soon be home for the long summer vacation. Sam was looking forward to that, too. They had settled down at Barlow's, each in his own way. Harry loved school because he loved learning, and he accepted the extracurricular activities, such as compulsory sport and the discipline, as a price that had to be paid for the instruction he received in class. Mr Davies was extremely impressed with Harry; a classical scholar himself, he found a great affinity with the boy and spent many hours discussing the relative merits of the Victorian poets and the older classics. This was reflected in Harry's reports, which constantly lauded his learning and application to work.

Joe was quite the reverse; only the sports master and, to a lesser extent, his mathematics master ever seemed to have any praise for him. School bored him, but he was rapidly making a name for himself as a sportsman. Ever since his first day he had been grudgingly admired, if not respected, as 'that new fellow who whipped Tarrant'.

Apart from Tarrant, who became quite close to Joe, neither of the boys made many friends; Harry, because he was by instinct a loner, preferring his books, and Joe, because of his aggression. Joe always had to be the leader, whatever the activity. Each week they dutifully wrote their letters home, and by the end of the summer term Sam was able to read them without assistance. He had managed this by keeping Mr Deacon on as his own tutor after the boys had left for school.

'Tha learn me to read writing and to talk proper,' he had said to Deacon. Mary would have none of it. It was part of her inherent shyness that she would not let Deacon teach her. So her reading never progressed very far beyond the nursery-rhyme stage.

Joe and Harry duly arrived, and everything seemed set for a wonderful summer. They had been home for about three days, when a brougham pulled up at the main entrance, and Mr Higgs hurried into the house.

Sam had left the Higgs Mill under the management of the nephew of the founder and had been very satisfied with his performance. Higgs had proved a very reasonable sort of boss. The mill workers had a twelve-hour day and all of Sunday off. They were paid sixpence an hour from the age of fourteen and twopence an hour if they were younger than that, and as a result competition for jobs was high. As for Higgs himself, he knew the trade and seemed to get on well with the men. He was a bustling little man who sported mutton chops terminating in a large moustache, which made his small face seem too large for his slim body and gave him an air of being top-heavy.

When Higgs arrived, Wilson showed him into the study and went in search of Sam.

'What brings thee here?' asked Sam, somewhat surprised at seeing him.

'There's trouble at the mill,' said Higgs.

'Trouble?' asked Sam. 'What sort of trouble?'

This was something that Sam could well do without, especially just now. He was overextended, he knew that. The purchase of Hardacres had been just the beginning of his commitment to the house. Several more thousands of pounds had disappeared in all the necessary extras which the move had entailed. The farms were in a neglected state and needed re-equipping and restocking. There had been horses and carriages to buy and a hundred and one other items which had all bitten into his credit. While the banks still regarded him as a good risk, he was aware that right now his empire was poised on a knife edge. If all went well for the next year or two, he would be able to look to the future with confident ease. But he needed that time, and a major crisis could, just now, send him backsliding down the slope to the poverty from which he had emerged.

'Come on, man, out with it,' he said. That mill was probably his largest single investment, and it was important, bloody important. It was the first link in the chain which ended in better, cheaper shirts and cotton goods in the shops through the length and breadth of the land.

'They're going on strike,' said Higgs.

'Strike!' roared Sam. 'We'll bloody soon see about that. Wilson!' He flung open the study door as he shouted.

'Yes, sir?' said Wilson, appearing in the hall.

'Find out what time's the next train to Manchester and pack me a bag.'

On the journey Higgs explained to Sam that the workers at the mill were demanding an extra threepence an hour, a ten-hour day with an hour off for lunch, and double pay for extra time. Sam realized that to do this would turn a profitable empire into a white elephant. It would double the price of the finished goods in the shops and destroy the whole fabric of the business which he had so carefully built up.

'Who's behind it?' he asked.

'His name is Harry Stubbs.'

'And who the hell's Harry Stubbs?'

'He's the one who was at the centre of the troubles at Whiteheads.'

Sam was grave. Whiteheads had been one of his competitors, which had been crippled by a two-month strike that had forced it to close its doors. 'What's he after?' he asked.

'You know how it is,' said Higgs, 'stirring up hatred of the bosses. Why shouldn't he have what you've got? All that socialist stuff.'

'Socialism's got its points,' said Sam. 'There's far too many factory owners who don't give a damn about their men.'

'Try and convince this lot that you do.'

'I'll do it,' said Sam. 'Never forget that I'm one of them.'

It was the next morning before they got to the mill, and when they arrived, it was obvious that the situation had worsened since Higgs had left. The plant was silent, and when they arrived, it was to find the work force gathered in front of the loading bay, where they were being harangued by a burly individual who wore an open, striped, cotton shirt revealing a hairy chest, two-days' growth of beard, and thick serge trousers held in place by a wide leather belt.

'... and they'll bleed thee,' he was shouting, 'they'll bleed thee. They'll drink their wine and eat beef and ride in fine carriages while thy women and kids go hungry. And why will they go hungry? Because the bosses don't give thee enough brass to feed them for seven days a week. We can do wi'out bosses. What's to stop us smashing this factory up and letting them feel the pinch?'

'Where are we going to work if us smashes up mill?' shouted a voice from the crowd.

'Who needs to work? Take it from the bosses, they've got plenty. They're too soft to stop us. If they don't give in to our just demands, we'll watch them rot. Do thee want more pay?'

'Yes,' shouted the men.

'Is that Stubbs?' asked Sam, and Higgs nodded.

'Dost tha want shorter hours?'

'Yes,' came the answering roar.

'Then follow me, brothers, we'll show them bastards with their fine ways. We'll show them what us workers are made of. Yon idle buggers don't know what work is,' he leaned forward. 'I'll tell thee summat. I know this Hardacre, him as owns this mill. I've seen his fancy house and his fine horses and expensive women. And I'll tell thee this, brothers, he never did a day's work in his whole life.'

'Thou's a bloody liar!' Sam was stripping off his coat and handing it to Higgs as he shouted.

'Who said that?' growled Stubbs. 'Whoever it was just come up here and say it again if tha dares.'

'Don't thee worry, I'm coming,' shouted Sam.

'Shall I call the police?' said Higgs.

'No,' said Sam, 'I'll handle this,' and he started towards the loading bay as the men moved aside to let him through, some of them recognizing him as he passed.

Sam was now over forty and not as fit as he had been when on the fish quay. As he approached the loading bay he sized his man up. He would have to lick him, he knew that. That was the sort of language that the men would understand. Stubbs waited for him, a sneer on his face. Sam clambered on to the loading bay.

'You're a liar,' said Sam.

'And who's calling Harry Stubbs a liar?' Stubbs shouted so that everyone would hear.

'Hardacre's the name, Sam Hardacre.'

Stubbs' eyes widened. 'That's him, that's the man who's taking the bread out of tha kids' mouths. Look at him, with his posh clothes and his belly full of the food that thee worked for ...'

It was at that moment that Sam hit him. Stubbs turned on Sam, wiping his mouth with a grimy paw and squaring up. 'Now tha's asked for it, Mr bloody Hardacre, and now tha's going to get it.'

A few years ago the fight would have been over in seconds, but this time it took several minutes before a battered and bleeding Harry Stubbs lay on the loading bay at Sam's feet and refused to get up again. Sam, too, had not escaped un-scathed. There was blood pouring from a cut under his eye, and his left jaw was all puffy and swollen. He took out his handkerchief and staunched the flow of blood, then turned to the men.

'If tha didn't know before, tha knows now who I am. Yon's

a bad lot, and thee should know it. A few months ago, what he is trying to do here he did at Whiteheads. Today Whiteheads is shut, and there are about three hundred men out of a job. Some of them are here today. They're here because I took on as many of them wi' families as I could afford to. Now, I'm not going to try and tell thee that tha's rich. I know that it's not true. But tha's getting twice the brass that them as go down pit gets. I've never lied in my life, and I don't lie now when I tell thee that thou's getting as high a wage as this business'll afford. If tha wants more tha can have it, but only if tha make more cloth. If tha does that, I'll see that each one of thee gets his fair share of the extra. What dost tha say, lads? Are thee going back to work?'

'Aye, Sam, we'll go back,' shouted a voice.

'Thanks, lad, but us can't run a mill on one; what do the rest of thee say?' Sam paused. 'Talk it over if tha wants to.'

Sam waited for half an hour while there were low-voiced conversations around the yard, and finally one of the men came forward.

'Hang on a minute,' said Sam, 'I know thee.'

'Last time I saw thee, tha was on my barge,' said Oliver Ramshead; 'I sold it and bought a house and came to work here.'

'I remember,' said Sam. 'Are thee speaking for the men?'

'Aye,' said Ramshead, 'we'm going back.'

'Good,' said Sam. 'Now, just before thee get looms going, I'm going to see that tha gets a decent dinner break in t'middle of the day. I can't promise more, but we'll look into things. And remember, any man that's sick gets half pay, and any man as wants to see me has only got to ask.' Sam looked at Stubbs. 'I'll leave this un to thee.'

Sam got down from the loading bay and, accompanied by a cheer from the men, made his way back to Higgs.

That night, when he got back to Hardacres, Mary greeted him. 'Sam, what's happened, what's the matter with thy face?' she exclaimed, worried.

'Tha ought to see t'other chap,' said Sam, grinning.

For the next three years Hardacres was a happy place.

Mary would not hear of a nanny and devoted herself to the management of her baby whenever she managed to get the child away from Sam. It was a great happiness to her to be able to devote time to little Jane with nothing else to worry about. She would spend whole afternoons in her rose garden with the child in the pram nearby, while she collected blooms for the house. The boys enjoyed their vacations, each in his own way. For Harry it was an extension of school; he found his pleasures in books, and there were books aplenty in the library in Hardacres. Joe spent his time riding and bringing himself up to date in the firm's business activities; he made it obvious that he had no desire to 'waste another three years' by going to university. Sam accepted the fact that Joe would end his formal education at eighteen and enter the business, while Harry would almost certainly go to university, where he would undoubtedly read Greats.

It was the early summer of 1893, just before the end of Joe's last term at Barlow's. Sam and Mary had come in from the garden and were in the morning room sipping their Madeira. Jane was asleep in her pram, encased in mosquito netting, outside the open window. It was one of those perfect English summer days, that absolute perfection of nature which can only occur in a climate as variegated as Britain's in the setting of the 'English country house', of which Hardacres was no mean example. There was the buzzing of the bees, the scent of the flowers carried in on the warm gentle breeze, the nearly cloudless sky, the green, green lawns, and the profusion of colour in the flower beds. Everything was at peace – the world, Sam, Mary, and baby Jane.

A large, black open landau came crunching down the drive and swung around in front of the house. Sam did not recognize the livery of the coachmen nor the lady who sat bolt upright and alone in the carriage. She was dressed entirely in black and was carrying a black lace parasol which concealed her face.

'Who's that?' said Mary.

'Damned if I know,' said Sam; 'maybe she's just leaving her card.'

'There's not many that do that,' Mary spoke wryly but without rancour; 'she does look important, though. I think I'd better go and see.' She started towards the door.

'Stay where you are, Mary,' called Sam, 'Wilson'll tell us. You don't want to let them think that tha's too keen, you know.'

Wilson came in, carrying a silver salver on which was a visiting card.

'Who is it, Wilson?' asked Mary.

'It is the Countess of Lewiston, madam,' he said.

'Is she a real countess?' asked Mary, a little overawed.

'Oh, yes, madam,' replied Wilson.

'Oh, Sam, what are we going to do?'

'Seems to me that we can either ask her in or tell her to go away,' said Sam with a grin.

'Shall I show Her Ladyship in, madam?' asked Wilson.

'Ought one of us to go and meet her?' Sam asked.

Wilson was about to reply when the subject of their conversation swept into the room.

'Quite unnecessary, Mr Hardacre. I always said that this was a delightful house, except for the fact that nobody could ever find anybody in it. Hello, there.' She spotted Mary and went over and took her hand. 'Harriet Lewiston, at your service.'

'Pleased to meet you, my lady,' said Mary.

My Lady then went to Sam. 'Well, Mr Hardacre, is no one going to offer me a glass of Madeira? I see that you keep up the custom – quaint, but very nice. Madeira wine and cherry cake at eleven – civilized, don't you agree?'

Sam watched his guest as she peeled off her gloves while Wilson poured the wine. She was tall and angular but with more than a hint of the slim beauty that she must have been. Approaching sixty, Sam guessed, but magnificently preserved and beautifully turned out with just the merest suggestion of overdressing, if it is overdressing to wear mourning like a ball gown. Her gown was tight-waisted satin, drawn tightly over the bosom to a high-standing ruffed collar; her arms were enfolded in the large balloon sleeves which had become all the rage; twirls and lines of black velvet decorated her bodice and full flowing skirt; she wore a large hat decorated with black flowers, over which she had pushed her travelling veil.

'I am very pleased to meet you, countess,' said Sam in response to her greeting. 'Do you mind telling me why you called on us? I don't want to seem rude, but there are not many who call on us, and those that do usually want something.'

The countess sat down on a settee. She sat right in the centre of it, spreading her skirt. From her reticule she produced a pair of lorgnettes, which she flicked open as she proceeded to scan Sam.

'Mr Hardacre,' she said sternly, 'that is an unpleasant suggestion, made infinitely more unpleasant because it is most certainly true. Of course I am after something, and I can assure you that anyone who knows me will tell you that I always am.'

'Well, you're straight enough, anyway,' said Sam. 'What is it you want?'

Wilson cleared his throat. 'Excuse me, sir, but will Her Ladyship be staying to lunch?'

'Is that lovely Mrs Grey still the cook here?' asked the countess.

'Yes, madam,' said Wilson.

'Then I shall most certainly stay to lunch,' she said, turning back to Sam and Mary. 'There, now, don't you think that was rude?'

'Oh, no, my lady,' murmured Mary.

'Yes it was,' said Sam. 'It was bloody rude, but I think I'm going to like you all the same; come on, Lady Lewiston, what is it you want?'

'Don't rush me, Mr Hardacre, all in good time. I've got something to sell, something which I believe you want to buy.'

'If that's true, all we've got to do is to fix a price,' said Sam.

'What is it that we want that you've got?' asked Mary.

'Social position, Mrs Hardacre. You want to be accepted. Not because you're rich but because you're you. You won't do it, you know, not without me, not in a thousand years.'

' 'Ere now ...' Sam started.

'It's quite true,' said the countess, 'why bother to deny it? I can put you on to the ladder; I wouldn't be able to get you to the top, but with luck and good will on all sides about halfway. Don't start an argument about that, because I know it's what you want. Mind you, whether you're going to like what you find when you get there is quite another matter.' She paused. 'Well, then, what do you say?'

'I go and see Mrs Middleton sometimes,' said Mary.

'I know you do, Mrs Hardacre,' said the countess. 'That is something that must stop.'

'But she's my friend,' protested Mary, 'and she's an "Honourable"!'

'Bertha Middleton is nobody's friend, believe you me. She is a tittle-tattle, and if there is one kind of person I cannot bear, it is a tittle-tattle, don't you agree, Mr Hardacre?'

'That's quite right, of course,' said Sam vaguely.

'I'm glad we see eye to eye, and I suggest that we find out if Mrs Middleton is as keen to let people know that Mrs Hardacre has struck her from her visiting list as she is to recount the more lurid details of Mrs Hardacre's conversation in other women's withdrawing rooms.'

'Oh, she wouldn't do that, I'm sure,' said Mary.

'Of course she would; she's not much different from practically every woman you'll meet in the next six months; an idle lot with damned little to do except to be catty about one another. You have a baby, I believe.'

'Well, hardly a baby; Jane is nearly three.'

'And no nanny?'

'No nanny,' said Mary. 'We have a nursery maid.'

'Quite enough,' said the countess. 'Every woman should have something to occupy her, and raising a child is as amusing a way as any. Well, now, are we all agreed?'

'Agreed?' asked Sam.

'Agreed that I move in here and take immediate charge of all your social activities.'

'You intend moving in?' said Sam, wondering if he had heard right.

'But of course. How can I possibly achieve anything unless I am here on the premises?'

'I'm not so sure,' said Sam. 'You may be a countess and all that, but what do we know about you?'

'Ask Wilson, he'll tell you. It's not an unusual story. I was an actress . . .'

'An actress?' Mary was pleasantly shocked.

'And Earl Lewiston asked me to marry him, so I did and got a title; then, rather thoughtlessly, he went and died on me. The old duke, his father, disapproved of me and kicked me out when Rodney died. I found myself right back where I'd started except for my title. I didn't realize it at the time, but I'd managed to get hold of one of the most valuable possessions a woman can own. For a year or two I studied my trade.'

'What was that?' asked Sam, now thoroughly interested in what he was hearing.

'Well, first of all I thought I was going to become a professional guest. I wandered from house to house, staying a while at each one, and I thought for a time that this could go on for ever. Then I realized that though I could eat and sleep free of charge, I also had to have money, because if my clothes wore out and I could not replace them, I would not be able to go guesting.'

'What did you do?' asked Mary.

'I knew that I had all the necessary qualifications to become a professional hostess or social organizer and that there were many establishments where the family had become newly or suddenly rich. I realized also that the people who needed my services most would never come and ask for them, so I had to seek them out and sell myself before I could sell them.'

'Well, I never!' said Mary.

'We're going to need a little while to think this over,' said Sam. 'Where are you staying, in case we want to get in touch with you?'

'I shall stay here,' replied the countess. 'Where else should I stay?'

'That's just what we haven't decided yet,' said Sam.

'Mr Hardacre,' said the countess, 'did you happen to notice my carriage when I arrived here?'

'I did, and a very nice carriage it is,' said Sam.

'That carriage and its contents are all that I possess in the world. I normally drive it myself. The coachmen were hired in Driffield; they cost me my last half sovereign. But that is no business of yours. I give value for money. Mr Hardacre, I am sure that is something that you will appreciate.'

'I would if you could prove it to me,' said Sam, 'but what does the likes of thee know about the likes of us?'

'Aye,' said Mary, 'how can a countess ever understand folk as 'ave worked on fish quay?'

'I probably understand you a great deal more than you realize. I am not unacquainted with the type of life you must have led before your fortunes changed ... aw, cum orf it, mister, spare a copper for a starvin' girl; git aht of it yer nellie.'

Sam and Mary listened in amazement as the countess broke into a broad cockney accent.

'Thou is one of us,' said Sam.

'Straight up, matey, not the fish quay though, the coster-monger's barra',' said the countess.

'Will somebody please tell me what is happening?' said Mary.

And so it was that Harriet, Countess of Lewiston, moved into Hardacres. She got down to her self-imposed task with a will and a drive which even Sam admired. The ever-faithful Wilson had been true to his promise and corrected error when-ever it was observed; the countess started off right away in drilling Sam and Mary in the finer points of social etiquette and how to become a successful host and hostess.

'You will never be a welcome guest until people want you to return their invitation,' she would say.

She initiated Mary into the art of protocol, and they gave mock dinner parties so that Mary could seat her imaginary guests in the right order.

'I imagine you would start a war if you placed the Italian ambassador's wife below the French ambassador's wife,' said the countess, replying to a question from Mary.

'Then what should I do?'

'Avoid politicians and career diplomats like the plague,' she said, 'and never have more than one at your table.'

At the beginning of July they made the great decision:

they would give a house party. In the second week in July Joe and Harry came down from Barlow's, Joe for the last time. When they met the countess, Joe was unimpressed. He had finished with school, he was not interested in the social round, and all he wanted was to get into the business.

Harry, on the other hand, was delighted. The theatrical background of the countess proved fascinating to him, especially when she talked personally of such theatrical giants as Garrick, Bernhardt, and Macready.

Neither of the boys showed any enthusiasm towards the coming house party. This did not go unnoticed by the countess, and she asked them both to take tea with her in her sitting room.

'I want to talk to you two, because I feel that both of you are being most unfair to your parents.' The countess then proceeded to give the pair of them a long lecture about their filial duties and how she felt that the least they could do would be to show a little enthusiasm for the whole idea.

'You cannot,' she concluded, 'try and live this style of life alone and without support, support that can only come from friends. You never meet people here, so how can you expect to make friends? All I am doing is inviting a selection of your nearest neighbours to come and visit you. Some of them you will like, some you will loathe. It is more than likely that those sorts of feelings will be mutual. If you manage to find one friend, and the exercise broadens your horizon a little beyond the boundaries of Hardacres, it will have achieved its purpose, and if it does the same for your mother and father, it will all have been worthwhile.'

Having dealt firmly and effectively with the opposition, the countess called the family together for the task of drawing up the guest list.

They all sat around the dining table – Sam, Mary, Joe, Harry, and the countess, with Wilson in attendance.

'Why is Wilson here?' asked Joe.

'Because he is probably much better acquainted with the local families than any of us,' said the countess. 'Now to begin, house guests.' She turned to Wilson, 'Wilson, how many can we accommodate?'

'We have three bedrooms with sitting rooms and four plain guest rooms, my lady.'

'And servants?'

'We could manage three or four valets or ladies' maids without much trouble after allowing for the extra staff we would need ourselves.'

'Thank you, Wilson. So then we can invite four or five families as house guests; they will have to be chosen according to rank and distance. We can assume three acceptances out of five invitations.'

'What happens if they all come?' asked Mary.

'Then they would be very overcrowded,' said the countess. 'First, we must invite the Lord Lieutenant.'

'No,' said Sam.

'Whyever not? He almost certainly will not come, but invited he must be.'

'Harriet,' said Sam, 'we can't have him because I've met him. It were three years ago last Boxing Day; we fought.'

'Fisticuffs?' demanded the countess, disapproving.

'I just about knocked his block off,' said Sam.

'I never knew that,' said Mary.

'You saw it happen,' said Sam; 'he were laying into Joe.'

'Him?' said Mary, horrified.

'I remember,' said Joe. 'Nasty piece of work.'

'Fiddle faddle,' said the countess. 'Nevertheless, he must be invited. It is quite possible that he has forgotten the incident, and he is such a bad-tempered man that if he never returned to any place where he had had a row, he would never go anywhere.'

So it was decided, and the guest list was headed with the Lord and Lady Bainton and their daughter, the Honourable Judith Winstanley.

'I feel we need a duke,' said the countess.

'Why not the Prince of Wales?' said Sam with a touch of sarcasm.

'Next time,' said the countess. 'I wonder if Bunny is free?'

'Who's Bunny?' asked Mary.

'He's my tame duke. Absolutely broke, poor darling. The only time he gets a decent meal is when he's a guest in somebody else's house.'

'Why doesn't he get a job like everybody else?' Sam spoke with limited sympathy.

'What could he do? He's sixty-four and has never done a day's work in his life. Still, we ought to have someone to out-rank the Baintons just in case they come.'

At last the guest list was drawn up, and plans were discussed for the party. Here the countess proved a most competent organizer, taking charge of everything to do with the forward planning.

The invitations went out, the croquet lawn was prepared, the marquee was ordered, the band was arranged, the wine, the food, the extra staff; all that was left was to wait to collect the replies.

CHAPTER TWELVE

The countess arranged for the party to start on the first Friday in August, so as not to clash with the exodus to Scotland for the Glorious Twelfth. She had chosen her guests with care and managed about two thirds acceptances. She had made a point of picking families who might be attracted by Sam's wealth but not too greedy for it. Quite a few accepted out of curiosity and a desire to meet this family which had lived in their midst for approaching four years without ever socializing. Among the acceptors as house guests were, much to Sam's embarrassment, Lord Bainton, his wife, and daughter, and the countess' friend, the impoverished Bunny.

Mary enjoyed the preparations. She had never engaged a housekeeper since Sam had summarily dismissed Mrs Ellis, not out of any fear of repeating her experience with that lady, but because she genuinely wanted to do the work herself. She was much happier that way. She spent the last couple of weeks before the party arranging beds and linen, interviewing temporary staff, doing all the jobs that her housekeeper would have done, looking after her three-year-old daughter, and keeping an eye on her rose garden. With three years of house management behind her, she was finding what had once appeared an awesome task mere routine.

The countess' lecture had had its effect on the boys, and Harry, at least, now accepted that the idea might be a good one. Joe wanted to get the whole thing over and done with. Now that he had left school, Sam had promised that he would be given a chance to take over a small factory near Leeds. Joe did not want to waste time socializing; he had a career to get on with. However, nothing could be served by not cooperating, so he pitched in with the rest.

After they had laid out the croquet lawn, the countess gave Mary and Harry a crash course in the game, though Sam and Joe would have none of it.

It was at eleven o'clock on the Friday morning of the party that the countess gathered the family in the morning room for a final briefing.

'Our guests will start arriving after lunch,' she said. 'Sam and Mary, you will have to be ready to greet them as they arrive.'

'What about their baggage?' asked Sam.

'Wilson has arranged all of that,' replied the countess. 'The guests' personal servants will deal with their own unpacking, but Wilson will have a man available at the back stairs to help with the handling.'

'And you don't think anybody will be here till after lunch?' said Sam.

'That's what I said,' replied the countess, 'unless of course Bunny.'

'What's he likely to do?' asked Mary.

'If he arrived at Driffield early, he might just arrive before lunch.'

'But the carriages won't be at the station until the afternoon train,' said Joe.

'Oh, that's all right,' said the countess. 'If he's early, he'll either hire a cab or have lunch in Driffield, whichever is cheaper.'

'Then we won't see him early,' said Sam. 'You can get a good lunch at the Bell for tenpence, and a hansom out here would cost one and threepence. What do we do with them once they arrive?'

'We have afternoon tea on the lawn, or, if it rains, in the conservatory,' said Mary. 'And, Sam, please don't ask for thy Victoria and Albert mug.'

Sam laughed. 'All right, love, I'll not embarrass you.'

They decided against lunch, and Wilson laid a cold table in the morning room. They were picking at this when they heard the sound of a coach on the drive.

'Who'll that be?' asked Sam.

'Bunny, of course,' said the countess. 'You forgot, Sam, he would have to buy his man lunch, and that would have made it one shilling and eightpence, more than a cab.'

'Hadn't we better go and meet him?' asked Mary.

'I suppose so,' said the countess, 'though he doesn't really deserve it.'

They trooped out of the morning room just as Wilson was opening the inner hall door; the main doors were standing open, to reveal His Grace himself: a white-haired, pink-faced, slightly tubby man wearing white trousers and red-and-yellow-striped M.C.C. blazer, busily mopping his brow with a red-spotted handkerchief.

'Glad to meet you, Hardacre,' said His Grace, shaking Wilson warmly by the hand.

'Bunny,' called the countess firmly.

'Harriet, me dear, how absolutely spiffing.' He came over to the countess and embraced her. 'Just greetin' me host.'

'That's your host's butler, Bunny.'

'No harm done. At least he knows where the port's kept. Where the devil is Hardacre? He is my host, isn't he?'

'He is,' said the countess, 'and you'd better come and meet him before you say another word.' She pointed His Grace at Sam and turned to Wilson. 'Wilson, you'd better make sure that there's someone to help his man; he's twenty years older than His Grace.'

'So you're Hardacre,' said Bunny. 'Have to forgive me. I'm always putting my foot in it. Got to apologize; damned train was early, don'cher know. Ah,' he said, as he caught sight of Mary, 'this must be your lady, you lucky devil; charmed to meet you, ma'am.' His Grace bowed low over Mary's hand.

'I'm sure that Your Grace must be very hungry after your long journey.' Mary was enjoying the attention. 'You come along with me, we have a cold table laid out in the morning room.'

'Jolly decent of you, ma'am; by the by, Bunny's what I'm known as, be honoured if you'd use it.'

'That's real nice of thee, Bunny; come on, let me feed you.'

Mary's natural instinct to look after anyone who crossed her path ensured her instant success with Bunny. He wolfed down vast quantities of cold boiled ham, chicken, and mutton pie in an incredibly short space of time.

Satisfied at last and sitting over a glass-bottomed pewter

tankard of ale, he turned to the countess. 'Why wasn't I sent a guest list, Harriet?' he demanded.

'It's Mary's party, you know.'

'Yes, but you organized it, it's got your mark on it. You're not going to try and marry me off to some rich widow again, I hope.'

'No, Bunny, I'm afraid that you're going to be the last of your line.'

'Damned good job too,' he turned to Mary. 'Begging your pardon, ma'am, but my family was a mistake from the word go. Anyway, who's coming? Anyone I know?'

'Do you know the Baintons?' asked Sam.

'Now I know why I didn't get a guest list; can't stand the fellah, nor her for that matter; mind you, his daughter's a little topper, can't think how they managed it. Must be some sort of a throwback, believe the grandparents were all right. When do they get here?'

'They should arrive just before dinner,' said the countess.

'Ah, well, might as well enjoy ourselves till then.' He turned to Mary. 'Care for a turn round the garden, ma'am?' And then to Sam, 'At my age, husbands don't object, more's the pity.'

'Sam?' asked Mary.

'Go on if thee'd like to, love,' said Sam.

'Your servant, ma'am,' said Bunny, offering his arm.

They went off together with a slight blush rising on Mary's cheek.

Sam laughed as he watched them go. 'That's the first time she's gone out with another man since I wed her.'

Mary got on famously with Bunny and was quite sorry when, later in the afternoon, she was called away to greet her other guests.

The Hendersons, from Market Weighton, arrived next. Henderson's father had started under circumstances similar to Sam's: he had managed to get a little capital together and then invested in cotton early and made a killing. Now his son was – typical of the second-generation industrialists – trying to get back to the rural life.

The Macdonalds arrived from Scarborough with their son and daughter. Macdonald was becoming quite eminent in surgery; a disciple of Joseph Lister, he had created an enviable reputation for his hospital in Scarborough. It was no surprise to hear that his son was studying medicine, but when it became known that his daughter was also going to be a doctor, the tongues were really set a-wagging.

Joe had been given permission to invite Tarrant. They had become firm friends at school, and Joe had wanted Tarrant to come into the business with him, but to the disgust of both of them Tarrant's parents would hear of no such thing, and so he was destined for Cambridge in September.

When he arrived, Joe rushed to him. 'Tarrant, you old blighter, thank God you could make it,' he cried.

Tarrant greeted Joe's parents, and then they shot off to Joe's room, which they were to share during his stay, and smoked a forbidden cigar.

The arrival of the Reverend Peter Davies, accompanied by his wife, tended to subdue Harry who, for all his life, would feel a small boy when confronted by his old schoolmasters.

Pre-dinner drinks were already being served in the hall when Wilson announced the arrival of Lord and Lady Bainton and their daughter, the Honourable Judith Winstanley.

Everything that Bunny had said about Judith was only an understatement. She was small and slender, half girl, half woman, with soft brown hair cascading in gentle ringlets down against her pale cheeks. She possessed the delicacy of a piece of fine porcelain, contrasting with the poise and assurance which go with the onset of womanhood. And yet, her large brown eyes had a frightened fawn-like quality that seemed to say 'I have much to learn.' But a beauty she undoubtedly was, and at the moment she stepped into the hall at Hardacres, there was not a man in the room who was not aware of her presence.

Sam greeted Lord Bainton with some apprehension, but the Lord Lieutenant had either forgotten or had chosen to ignore their previous encounter. Harry, in common with every other young and not-so-young male present, made for Judith. Casting dignity aside, Harry practically ran in order to be the first to greet her.

'I'm Harry Hardacre, Miss Winstanley, I wonder if I might get you a glass of sherry wine. I'm allowed one before dinner, are you?' he blurted out all in one breath.

'I assure you I am quite adult, Mr Hardacre,' she replied. Then, seeing the hurt look come into his eyes, 'But I would love to join you in a glass of sherry.'

Harry went off in search of the sherry, making a slight detour so as to be able to speak to Wilson en route.

'Wilson,' he pleaded, 'could you be a brick and arrange ...'

'I have already done so, Master Harry,' replied Wilson.

'What have you done? You don't know what it was that I was going to ask.'

'It would be a matter concerning which lady was seated next to you at dinner?'

'How did you guess?'

'I have eyes, Master Harry,' said Wilson, making a signal in the air. A waitress appeared at his elbow, carrying a tray of drinks. 'I should take Miss Winstanley's sherry before Mr Tarrant beats you to it.'

'Thanks, Wilson,' said Harry, and he grabbed a couple of glasses and made it back to Judith just in time to cut off Tarrant's advance.

'Here's your sherry, Miss Winstanley,' he said, edging around so as to stand between her and the approaching Tarrant.

'Hello, Hardacre,' said Tarrant, recognizing Harry's existence for the first time since his arrival. 'Well, aren't you going to introduce me?'

'Oh, er ... yes, of course, this is Mr Tarrant, Miss Winstanley.' His voice trailed away.

'Charmed, Miss Winstanley; may I get you something?' said Tarrant.

'Thank you, no. I am taking sherry with Mr Hardacre,' she said, smiling sweetly, though her tone was quite firm.

'Some other time, perhaps,' said Tarrant, accepting defeat and moving on.

Harry felt a flood of gratitude as his goddess brushed aside the opposition. 'I say, would you care to sit down?' he asked.

'There's a rather pleasant little corner over there by the window.'

'I think that would be most agreeable; would you be a dear, kind man and carry my drink?'

She led him to the corner and sat down. Harry set the sherry on a small table which stood beside the only chair. He waited, silent, trying desperately to think of something to say other than 'I think you are the most beautiful creature that I have ever seen and I am so desperately in love with you.' Somehow he had to admit that that sort of announcement would be a little premature. Judith smiled encouragingly at him. He had been on the point of saying something, but the smile bereft him of words. Harry at fifteen found himself completely overawed by this tiny creature who was certainly no older than he was.

'Do you . . . ,' 'Did you . . . ,' they started together.

'I'm so sorry,' said Harry, 'you were going to say something?'

'I was wondering if you read a lot, Mr Hardacre,' said Judith, who had been wondering no such thing.

'Oh, yes,' replied Harry, 'an awful lot. Do you like poetry?'

'I love it, though it does depend on the poet,' she replied. 'Have you read any of Lord Tennyson?'

'Well, yes, some,' replied Harry.

'What do you think of him?'

'Well, he's er . . . er . . .' '

'Well, I think he's stodgy,' said Judith. 'Otherwise the Queen wouldn't like him.'

Harry was suitably shocked by this display of lese majesty and in return demanded, 'How about Byron?'

'Young ladies never read Byron.' Her tone was scandalized.

'Oh, yes, of course not, I only . . .'

'He is far, far too wicked.'

'Yes, of course, I should never have mentioned him.' Harry was suitably chastened.

'I keep a copy of his poems hidden away at the bottom of my school trunk.'

'You do!' Harry's eyes opened wide.

'So we'll go no more a-roving
So late into the night,
Though the heart be still as loving,
And the moon be still as bright,' she quoted.
'Though the night was made for loving,
And the day returns too soon ... ,' continued Harry.

'Really, Mr Hardacre,' she said. 'Besides, you missed a verse.'

They both laughed; their sherry lay untouched where Harry had put it when the dinner gong sounded.

'My lords, ladies, and gentlemen,' announced Wilson, 'dinner is served.'

'Do you know where we are sitting?' asked Judith.

'There are place cards,' said Harry, 'but you will be next to me.'

'How do you know?'

'I've got influence with the butler. May I take you in?' he said, offering his arm with all due reverence.

The Reverend Davies said grace, and the meal started. Dinner was neither a success nor a failure. Sam, seated between the countess and Lady Bainton, had to suffer a long dissertation on the latest fashions, while at the other end of the table Mary was trapped between a garrulous Bunny and an almost silent Lord Bainton. Towards the centre of the table the younger contingent was taking matters with considerably less seriousness than their elders, with the notable exception of Harry, who was very serious indeed.

When the meal was finished and the ladies had retired, Harry drew his chair up to the top of the table, where he found himself sitting next to the duke.

'Damned nice filly you've found there, eh?' said His Grace.

'I'm afraid I don't understand, sir,' replied Harry.

Bunny glanced around to make sure that Bainton would not overhear him and then continued in a conspiratorial tone, 'The Winstanley girl.'

'Oh, yes, she's charming isn't she,' Harry responded weakly.

'Take a tip from me,' said the duke, 'beware of women, my boy; they're born fourteen years older than you are, and you'll never catch up.'

Having delivered this piece of wisdom, the Duke wandered off in search of the brandy decanter, leaving Harry alone with his one permitted glass of port and happy in his solitude.

Sam was aware that, before and after the meal, Lord Bainton had been, if not actually avoiding him, at least not seeking his company. Sam guessed, quite rightly, that Bainton had come to Hardacres without ever connecting it in his mind with the incident of three and a half years ago, but that he had since remembered. Never one to avoid an awkward situation, Sam took the direct approach.

'More brandy, Lord Bainton?' he asked.

'Thank you, no.'

'Thou's remembered, hasn't thee?' said Sam, deliberately slipping into his broadest brogue.

'Yes,' said Bainton, and his lips snapped shut like a steel trap as he started to turn away.

'Don't go,' said Sam, 'give me your hand instead. I don't like hatred, especially when I can feel it under my own roof. Can I say something?'

'Carry on.'

'There's little profit in bearing a grudge. When Harriet wanted to invite you, I wanted to say no. But then I realized that I had probably only made one enemy since I came here. I don't like having enemies, there's no profit in them.'

'Why don't you get to the point, Hardacre?'

'I'd like for us to be friends. We are likely, both of us, too hot-headed to be real friends, but that's no reason why we can't get on. My lad and your lass seem to be doing all right.'

'Yes, I had noticed. I don't think I altogether approve of that. But I'll shake hands with you, Hardacre. I was going to leave immediately after dinner, but we'll stay the night anyhow. Mark you, I'll probably never like you, but you're quite right, there's no profit in grudges.'

'You'll not be staying for the party tomorrow, then?' said Sam.

'I doubt it,' replied Bainton, 'but we'll see.'

Sam left it at that and suggested to his guests that it was about time that they joined the ladies. They all trooped into the withdrawing room, where, to Harry's horror, Judith was nowhere to be seen. After a few minutes he managed to summon up his courage to approach Lady Bainton.

'I see that Miss Winstanley is no longer with us, ma'am,' he said, trying hard to make his voice sound casual. 'I trust she is not unwell.'

'Thank you for your solicitude,' replied Her Ladyship. 'Judith is perfectly well, I am happy to say, but she is still very young and has retired for the night.'

A crestfallen Harry mooned around for another half hour or so and finally took himself off to his own bed. He went the long way round, as that way he passed the door of Judith's room. Outside the door he paused and gazed resentfully at the two inches of oak which stood between them. He did not have any intention of knocking, and he knew that there was absolutely no chance of Judith coming out, but he stood there for quite some time fantasizing until the sound of approaching footsteps made him hurry away to his room.

On the other side of the door Judith sat and waited, hoping for the tap which she knew would not come.

After the return to the ladies, Joe had been buttonholed by the Reverend Davies, who apparently felt it incumbent upon himself to preach Joe a homily on the dangers of the wicked world that he was now entering. Joe, who had the ability of appearing to listen to a conversation while being totally occupied with something else, heard not a word of the Reverend Davies' good advice. His concentration was directed to the curvaceous Mrs Davies. They had caught each other's eye during dinner and had both felt a chemical reaction which demanded further exploration.

Emma Davies loved her work as the wife of the headmaster. Some twenty years his junior, she was a woman who exuded a warm, sensuous charm which, according to rumour, she made little attempt to control. Her love for her work expressed itself in the entertainment of senior boys before they left Barlow's for university and in making sure that they were fully cognizant of the facts of life before they did so. Whether or not her husband was aware of these happenings was a subject of whispered conjecture among those who had been initiated. Those who had not received her favours had little or no knowledge of what went on, as Emma chose well – only the young men of the highest integrity were permitted to know her fully. But Emma loved the young and the passionate, and when she looked at a man as she had looked at Joe Hardacre that evening – with his cold eyes and mouth, his slim lithe hips encased in tight breeches – she had to have him. She could think of little else except his body and his crude, clumsy inexperience. It would hurt, but Emma loved being hurt like that. Thank God she had a predictable husband.

'Peter,' she said, 'it is so warm in here, would you be so kind as to take me for a turn around the garden?'

'It's almost ten o'clock, Emma,' he replied; 'I would like to go to bed soon, please forgive me. Perhaps Mr Hardacre?'

'Would you?' she asked, turning to Joe and looking hard into his eyes.

Again he felt that weakness in his loins. 'Of course,' he managed to blurt out. After all, Emma Davies was a damned attractive woman, and it was a warm summer's night.

They went out through the open French windows and were soon lost from view. The pungent smell of the newly mowed lawn, the velvet blackness of the moonless sky seemed to give the stars an extra brilliance; a silence grew up as they moved away from the house towards the heady sweetness of the honeysuckle near the edge of the wood.

Joe's mouth was parched as he asked, 'Where shall we go?'

'Where can we go?' she asked. 'Your room?'

'I share it with Tarrant.'

'Come here, Joe,' she said; they stood facing each other. She took his hand and placed it inside the décolleté of her bodice. He felt the softness of her large breast, the nipple hardening under his touch; then she pulled his hand away. He made to embrace her.

'Not yet,' she said, 'just put your hand here.' She put his hand on her stomach – it was soft to his touch, with no corsets. 'There's only me underneath.'

He gasped aloud as she ran her hand up his leg and on to his crotch.

'Now you must take me somewhere,' she breathed.

'The summer house,' said Joe.

'Darling boy, everybody always goes to the summer house, and I don't like sharing, not this anyway. What about the mews?'

Joe's throat was so dry by this time that he could not speak. Silently he led her to the mews; they went through the stables and up into the hayloft. As soon as they were there, she lay down in the straw and raised her skirts. She dragged him down on top of her and took him with a ferocity which frightened him. As soon as it was over, she threw him off her.

'Oh, my darling,' said Joe, 'oh, my darling.'

'Just relax, and in half an hour we'll do it again, slowly. And, Joe, don't be silly. I love it, but I don't love you any more than you love me. Just relax, and when you're ready we'll play some more.'

'But I'll see you again,' said Joe.

'No,' she replied, 'not like this, anyway. I'm not saying that it won't happen again, but it'll never be the same; you see, neither of us would be a virgin next time.'

An hour later he took her back to the house. She did not go back into the drawing room but went straight up to bed; it was only when she had left him that he realized that he had not kissed her.

Joe went back into the withdrawing room, where he found his father, the countess, and the duke deep in conversation. Everyone else appeared to have retired.

'Come in, Joe,' said Sam, 'we were just talking about you.'

Joe felt immediately guilty and found-out; he flushed to the roots of his hair. It was the countess who sprang to his rescue.

'Yes, Joseph, we have been discussing your future,' she said. 'I think that what your father has to tell you, if I know anything about you, you're going to find very pleasing. So why don't you just go and help yourself to a drink and come and sit down with us?'

She spoke at length in order to give the boy a chance to pull himself together, and as he went to the decanters she smiled. I suppose it was his first, she thought.

Joe came back and joined them.

'Well, Harriet,' said Sam, 'I think you're jumping the gun a bit; he wasn't supposed to know until his birthday, to-morrow.'

'As it is now ten minutes past midnight,' said Bunny March, 'no one has jumped the gun, and congratulations and all of that damned nonsense are the order of the day. As I'm feeling generous, as I usually do when it isn't my cellar, why don't we have a bottle of bubbly to celebrate?'

Sam laughed. 'Good idea, I'll go and get one. I told Wilson to turn in an hour ago.'

'I'll come with you,' said Bunny. 'Not that I don't trust you, but I want to make sure that in this bad light you don't pick a poor year by mistake.'

After they had left, there was a silence for a little while. The countess smiled at Joe.

'You've guessed, haven't you?' said Joe. The countess did not reply, but Joe knew that she knew.

Sam and Bunny returned with the bottle of champagne. Sam opened it while Bunny managed to find four clean tumblers.

'These seem to be the only clean glasses left,' he said.

'They'll be right,' said Sam, and he divided the wine equally into the four tumblers.

'Happy birthday, son,' said Sam.

'Happy birthday,' echoed the others, and they all drank.

'Thanks,' said Joe, and he went to the countess and kissed her. 'Thanks a lot.'

'Well, now, what about the news?' said Bunny. 'Are you going to tell him, Sam?'

'I seem to have no option.' replied Sam. 'Well, Joe, it's quite simple, really. You wanted to go into the business, and I think you're probably right. There's no use in asking you to start at the bottom; you've done it all. And there's no use asking you to go on to university, 'cos you wouldn't. So I'm going to give you a start. Tha knows Welbeck Shirts?'

'Yes,' said Joe, 'I know them, Dad! I remember when you bought them.'

'They've been losing money – not much but a little – and they need a new boss; well, they've just got one, it's thine. You own Welbeck Shirts.'

CHAPTER THIRTEEN

Over two years had passed since the party, and Harry was sitting in Betty's Café in Oxford sipping his fourth cup of coffee. He had gone out that evening with Hughes and Grant, two other undergraduates who had rooms on the same floor at Balliol College. It was getting late; they had spent the evening at the Oxford Playhouse, and after the show his two companions had struck up the acquaintanceship of some of the actresses from the company. Harry had left them to it and gone on alone to Betty's for a bite to eat before returning to college. Harry had very little time for women, other than Judith Winstanley.

'Big Tom' started to chime the hour. Idly toying with his cup, Harry counted the notes – nine, ten, eleven! Curfew! If he failed to get back to his room unobserved, it would be the proctor's office the next morning, a dressing-down, and a fine. He paid his bill and went to the door of the café. The street seemed deserted; no sign of the Bulldogs, those servants of the proctor who spent their time apprehending undergraduates committing misdemeanours in the town.

Harry pulled on his short undergraduate gown and started off at a brisk trot in the direction of Balliol.

'One moment, sir,' called a voice.

It had to be a Bulldog; there was nothing for it now but to run. He tore down the street and reached the college wall. The gate would be locked, and entrance could be gained only by an admission of guilt. Harry leapt for the top of the wall and had just managed to get one leg over when a brawny hand seized his other foot.

'Sir,' said the Bulldog, politely raising his bowler hat with his free hand, 'may I have your name and college?'

'Hardacre, Balliol,' replied Harry, obeying the unwritten rule that if a Bulldog succeeded in touching you, you had lost. Ah, well, it would cost him a fine, probably six shillings and eightpence, but it had been a good evening.

Harry had left Barlow's that summer and to his utter delight he had managed to secure a place at Oxford, and not only Oxford but Balliol, usually regarded as the preserve of the establishment public schools such as Eton and Harrow.

He lived in college in one of the sixteenth-century halls of residence. On his first day he arrived early, having travelled to London the previous day and caught an early morning train out of Paddington to Oxford. He went into the quadrangle, carpeted with a magnificent lawn upon which undergraduates must never tread, and through a heavy stone arch where a man sitting behind a window took his name and gave him directions to his room.

The room was approached by a winding stone staircase worn and polished by generations of undergraduates who had used it. His room was very little larger than the study he had occupied during his last year at Barlow's. A cubicle about twelve feet square, it contained the bare minimum of furnishings – bed, desk, drawers, washstand, cupboard, bookshelves, and a couple of chairs. A coal fire had been laid in the grate but not yet lit. Standing there for the first time, looking out through the narrow arched window and touching those stones so saturated with history, Harry was a very happy young man. There was a tap on the door.

'Come in.'

A small, greying man entered the room; he was wearing a green baize apron and carrying a paper.

'Mr Hardacre, sir?'

'Yes?'

'Good morning, Mr Hardacre; I'm Gibbs, your scout.'

'Scout?' Harry had been briefed on what to expect, but scout was something that had not been mentioned.

'Yes, sir, scout; I do for all the young gentlemen on this floor,' said Gibbs. 'I suppose you'll be taking commons for lunch?'

'Commons?' asked Harry.

'Bread, cheese, and a pint of beer, sir; most of the young gentlemen seem to prefer it. It costs threepence. Of course you have to dine in hall.'

'Thank you, that sounds a good idea.'

'And your tutor would like to see you at two o'clock. If you give me a shout – I'm in the little room at the bottom of the stairs – I'll take you over.'

After his first interview with Doctor Parkinson, who was to be his guide and mentor during his undergraduate years, Harry felt that at last all he had ever wished for had come true. All, that is, except for one thing.

After the party two years ago, Harry had immediately written to the Baintons, asking for permission to call on their daughter. His request had met with a blunt refusal: 'Judith was much too young'; 'No such permission could be contemplated until after she had been presented'. In spite of this, they had managed to keep in touch. By an enormous stroke of good fortune, Judith had been given her first ladies' maid, who turned out to be none other than the niece of Mrs Grey, the Hardacres' cook. So an underground correspondence was set up, most of which consisted of references to various of the Victorian Romantic poets. But this was a slender thread on which to hold their romance, for neither of them dared, at that stage, to risk parental wrath by a discovered meeting.

Harry's hopes had risen when he heard that Judith would be coming out that autumn, before he went to Oxford, but they had soon been dashed; he was not included in any of the guest lists, and it began to filter through to Harry that the Baintons did not consider the Hardacres suitable company for their daughter. Be that as it may, Harry never gave up hope, and when he heard that the Baintons were taking the Middletons' shoot that summer he realized that an opportunity was almost upon him. He had never doubted that he was in love with Judith; the brevity of their one meeting at Hardacres two years ago made no difference at all. The coming summer would decide his fate, regardless of parental objections; he intended to see her and make known to her his feelings.

Joe, on the other hand, was not bothered by any of Harry's romantic notions of love and devotion. To Joe, women were a matter of sex. After his first experience with Mrs Davies, he tried again a few days later. Not with Mrs Davies, of course;

she indulged only in virgin boys, so Joe had to look elsewhere. It did not prove difficult, and within the year there were few attractive girls on the estate who had not had a roll in the hay with the young master; in fact, it became a sort of status symbol among them. But sex was not important to Joe; whenever it bothered him, he did something about it, but most of the time it did not worry him. Joe had developed into one of those people who are able to keep sex locked away in a separate compartment of their lives.

It was strange but true that neither Sam nor Mary knew anything about Joe's liaisons. They had retained a simple innocence ever since the day that Sam had refused to share Mary's bed until they were married.

Joe's real interest lay in the business, and he was for ever pestering his father to allow him a more active part in it. This seemed utterly reasonable to him, as Sam's attentions seemed to focus more and more on Hardacres. Joe felt that his father was getting soft. His approach was harder than Sam's. The affair at Higgs Mill was all right up to a point, but Joe could not agree with the concessions which Sam had made to his workers when it was all over. Sam had personally investigated the conditions of the work force, and the result was that he had managed to make life in the mill a great deal more pleasant. Joe was much more a product of his age than Sam, and it was difficult, if not impossible, for him to see that better working conditions and rewards could result in higher production, which more than compensated for the increased outlay.

Joe believed that the boss should remain an anonymous 'them' and not be a person who the man on the shop floor could confide in or who bothered about families and homes.

But it was more than that. Recently Sam had seemed to be taking a less active part in his various enterprises. As his circle of friends increased, so was he, more and more, drawn to the life of a country squire. Not that he neglected his businesses or that the old magic touch had become dulled – he was well aware of how they were doing, and every now and then he and Saunders would take off on a trip, which might take anything up to a month, to keep an eye on his ever-increasing empire.

Though a late starter, he had learned to handle a horse well. Never a stylist he managed to keep up with most and of course he never lacked courage. On his third application and on the receipt of one hundred guineas (and on the occasion of Lord Bainton being absent from a committee meeting), the Middleton East Hunt had elected him a member. Sam was never sure whether he had joined because he wanted to or because he knew that Bainton didn't want him. His relations with the rest of his neighbours had changed. He was fully accepted by the professional classes, and though the establishment may not have encouraged him, he felt that he could now meet them on equal terms.

The countess had stayed on at Hardacres. She had more or less taken upon herself the duties of housekeeper, and this pleased and relieved Mary. She was now free of the awesome morning ritual of directing staff. Now it was the countess who could go to Mrs Grey to arrange the day's menu, and Mary, who could create a hearty meal from a few potatoes, a turnip, and a soup bone but found the fanciful planning of a dinner on a piece of paper nearly impossible, could gratefully nod approval at the result. The expressionless row of faces awaiting comment on the freshly polished silver, the newly turned out second guest bedroom, or the floral arrangements for the afternoon visit of the vicar, could now be left to the countess. Tradesmen, dressmakers, staff, and food were her problems now, and, perhaps for the first time at Hardacres, Mary was able to relax.

Relaxation brought its own problems, however. She was naturally and by force of habit a hard-working person whose body demanded activity, whose hands needed action. The finer arts that occupied ladies born were both beyond her and beneath her. Her hands had known too much sheer hard work ever to adapt to the refined delicacies of needlework, other than darning a sock or watercolour painting. And her mind, which knew too well the necessity of work, could not respect pretence at work.

One rainy afternoon she found her inactivity so irksome that, while Jane slept in the pram in the morning room, Mary took herself below the stairs to the kitchen. Without speaking to any of the astonished staff, she began gathering flour and butter, currants, and glacé fruit on to the kitchen table.

Her scones were cut out and she was setting them out on the big tin baking trays when Mrs Grey, back from arguing with the butcher, arrived at her kitchen door. Sally, the scullery maid – a local girl, heavily built, and bold-natured – giggled aloud. Mary realized that she had hurt Mrs Grey; she had stepped out of her place and implied criticism. It was no good telling Mrs Grey that she was working only for pleasure and not because she needed scones.

She left them on the table for Sally to finish. As she climbed back up the steps, she knew that she would likely never bake, or knead bread, or make up a stock pot again. She wiped her floury hands against her good skirt and sighed, then she slipped them into her pockets for want of anything to do with them.

But she did not give up looking for work.

It was a late summer afternoon, and Mary had taken the pram, with baby Jane – who was fretful with the rare heat of the day – along the cobbled, shaded drive behind the house and down to the brick wall which surrounded the kitchen garden. She often came here with Jane, partly for the sheltered sunlight and partly because the long neat rows of cabbages, cauliflower, pale-green lettuce, and neatly staked pea vines pleased her eye. The earth was always freshly hoed and black between the rows, and the rich greens of the salad plants, the feathery carrot tops, and the white butterfly flowers among the pea tendrils had a beauty as satisfying as the rich herbaceous borders of the ornamental gardens. To Mary they had the added pleasure of being useful. They were food, and that gave her confidence. Mary knew that if things somehow got bad again – poverty always remained to her a possibility – she could live off this garden. Soon Basset and his undergardeners would be lifting the potatoes and carrots, the turnips and parsnips and dark-red beetroot, and storing them away in the low, brick root cellar. Mary Hardacre could feed her whole household all winter from that root cellar, if she had to.

But within its high walls, the kitchen garden had its luxuries too. Basset had put in big, thistly artichoke plants and

181

tall Jerusalem artichokes. There were rows of raspberry canes and blackberry brambles and leafy gooseberry bushes. With those and the fruit from the orchard, Mrs Grey kept the family well supplied with jams, jellies, and fruit butters.

And Basset had added, purely for his own pleasure, a row of bright tall sunflowers along the north wall. But along the east wall was Basset's pride and Hardacres' treasure: an old and splendid grapevine, spreading from a vast, gnarled, grey trunk, up on to its white wood trellis which roofed all of the east wall.

Mary stood now, gently rocking the pram back and forth, watching the dappled patterns of the sunlight through the vine on to the mottled old brick walk. After a while the baby went to sleep, and Mary, leaving the pram where it was, began walking slowly up and down the grape arbour and around the brick walls in the dreamy sunlight.

One of the gardeners had left a hoe leaning against the wall, and Mary stopped beside it, running her fingers up and down the work-polished wood. Between two rows of carrots the ground had been freshly tilled, halfway down. Beyond remained a hard, flat section, with tiny weedlings still growing. Mary stood, her fingers still on the handle of the hoe, looking at the spot where the gardener had stopped. There was no one in sight; Jane was silent and sleeping.

Mary lifted the hoe and walked down the row to the unfinished portion. She turned the metal edge against the ground and slid it into the soil. The thrust felt good and smooth, and the black earth curled up over the edge of the hoe, as if over a ploughshare. The sight pleased her, and she continued, experimentally, careful of the growing plants on either side. Within a few steps she realized that her good leather shoes were gathering soil and would be damaged by the damp earth. She laid the hoe aside and returned to the brick walk, where she unlaced her shoes and slipped them off.

Glancing carefully the length of the garden and still seeing no one, she reached up under her skirts and slipped off her garters and stockings, which she carefully rolled and placed inside the shoes. Then, she caught up the hem of her skirt and petticoat, drew them up underneath and tucked them into the drawstring of her pantalets, leaving her legs bare, halfway up the calves, to the sun. She smiled and stepped back on to the earth. It felt soft and good. She picked up the hoe again and set to work with confidence.

Basset saw her there some fifteeen minutes later, absorbed in her work. He was surprised, of course, at the sight of his mistress, barefoot, hoeing his garden. But he was surprised at how beautiful she looked with the sun shining on her black hair, slipping loosely out of its bun, and her thin, graceful, bare legs.

He had always liked Mary Hardacre. She was honest. He liked the way she looked right at him with those straightforward, rather beautiful, blue-grey eyes. She didn't look around him when she discussed the garden, or over his head as his former mistress had done. She admired his garden, and she meant it. He could tell the difference between formality and sincerity, though most gentlefolk seemed to think they were one and the same.

She whirled around when she heard his boots on the brick walk and in one quick gesture tugged her skirts loose so that they covered her feet again. She looked younger than she must be, Basset thought. He himself was nearly sixty, and the fact that he could have been her father probably helped him in the situation; it certainly helped her.

'That's nicely done,' he said, gesturing to the neatly hoed row.

'I'm sorry for interfering,' Mary said quickly.

Basset could have been patronizing and have said that the mistress was free to do what she wanted in his garden. But he was not; it would not have been true.

'Anyone who cares about the soil is welcome in my garden,' he said.

Mary was glad that he said 'my garden', because it was his in her eyes too and that made his welcome all the more real. She thanked him and asked if she might come to do some more work. Basset was delighted. She promised never to do anything without first asking his advice. He offered to teach her how to prune the fruit trees and her roses in front of the house. Their relationship quietly turned their respective social positions upside down, and they were both equally pleased.

It had been a great day for Joe when he had been given Welbeck Shirts. Joe was possessed of no romantic notions of starting from the bottom, as his parents had done. If he had any feelings towards the establishment, they were feelings of contempt; he certainly did not envy them, nor did he wish, as his father, to be one of them. His attitude towards the poor was similar – they were weak; and though he would give a starving man a crust, he would never give a weak man a job. Even pride in achievement did not concern Joe; he had no desire to make good shirts at Welbeck, only profitable ones, and if the two things happened to be synonymous, that was all right, but it was not important.

What Joe really wanted was power, real power; and as Joe saw it, power could be bought, it had to be bought. It was not an easy commodity to buy – you didn't go to the power shop and purchase five pounds' worth of influence. That was not the way. What you had to do was to amass a fortune, a fortune so large that it would make Sam Hardacre look like a pauper. When you had that, you retired into anonymity and started collecting.

The second echelon of power seekers – the public figures, the politicians, the philanthropists – all came to you. They needed your capital, your help, and you gave it freely; then they were in your pocket. They became your creatures, and a man called Joseph Hardacre, of whom no one had ever heard, pulled the strings and watched his puppets dance.

All of these thoughts were already in Joe's mind when he stepped on to the platform at Leeds station and took a hansom cab to Welbeck Shirts for the first time.

The cab took him out of the city centre and through a series of dismal streets of back-to-back houses with the inevitable little shop on the corner. Occasionally there would be a boy playing with a whipping top or a hoop, or a group of girls hopping from square to square in some complex geometric design chalked on the pavement. The hansom rattled on over the cobbles and at last came to King William Street, home

184

of Welbeck Shirts.

King William Street could loosely be described as an industrial road. There were gaps between the mean little houses, gaps walled in by high wooden palisades with double gates to allow the passage of horse and cart. There was a coal merchant, a cooper, a wheelwright, a dairy complete with its own cows, and finally Welbeck Shirts.

Joe was not very pleased with what he saw. It did little to further his ideas of wealth and power, but he took courage in the old Yorkshire adage, 'Where there's muck there's money'; he paid off his cab and went through the gates. Inside the cobbled yard he found himself facing a long, low brick building with a gabled roof. He went in through the door in the gable end and found himself in a dismal hallway. Opposite him was a pair of double doors which obviously led to the workshop; to his right was a door marked 'Manager' and to his left another marked 'Office, Enquiries'.

He pushed open the centre doors and went into the workroom. There were four parallel lines of tables; at each table sat a woman. Her age would be anything from twelve to about fifty, though it was certain that all of them looked more than their years, with their uniformly grey complexions, bedraggled hair, and lacklustre eyes, as they bent to their tasks with needle and thread or with the hand-operated sewing machine which stood on each table.

They were producing striped, flannel, collarless shirts of the type most favoured by the working man of the day. At the far end of the room was a long table on which lay the bales of flannel; these were being attacked by two men armed with long tailors' shears – they were cutting the material, using wooden patterns. A couple of ten-year-old boys were collating the cloth as it was cut out, and when one of them had a complete set, he would hand it to a woman, who in her turn took the material to one of the seamstresses who had a completed shirt. The woman, who seemed to be a sort of overseer, would examine the shirt and then take it away, leaving the fresh material and a red tally with the seamstress, who immediately applied herself, with listless concentration, to the next shirt.

The finished garments were taken through a door at the

far end of the room, presumably for pressing and packing. Joe stood watching the scene for some time, and though they must have been aware of his presence, no one, not even the ones nearest him, looked up. They worked on as if their lives depended on their efforts, which was more than likely true. Pervading the entire set-up was a smell of stale sweat and unwashed bodies.

A man wearing a suit walked slowly up and down the rows of women, occasionally sniffing at his handkerchief; scented, thought Joe, who was beginning to find the stench of the place a bit nauseating. The man had been aware of Joe since he had arrived, but he had not changed his route. He had continued up and down the rows, inspecting the work until he finally arrived face to face with Joe.

'And what can I do for you, sir?' he asked politely enough.

'Who are you?' demanded Joe, ignoring the question.

'I am the undermanager, sir,' was the reply. 'I am Mr Smithers' assistant.'

'I see, and what's your name?'

'As a matter of fact, it also happens to be Smithers, if that is of any concern to you, sir.'

'It might be. You're no relation, of course.' This with heavy sarcasm.

'Mr Smithers is my uncle.'

'We'll go and see him,' said Joe.

Joe turned, walked out of the workroom, and, much to the consternation of the younger Mr Smithers, made to open the door to the manager's office.

'Look here, sir, you can't ...' he cried, running towards Joe.

But he was too late. Joe had already opened the door, revealing a very startled elder Smithers. Mr Smithers hastily withdrew his hand from under the skirt of the not-unattractive young woman who was sitting on his lap and sprang to his feet in an abortive attempt at dignity.

'Who the devil are you, sir?' he demanded in a tone of outrage, 'and how dare you come barging into my office? I demand an explanation at once.'

'Thou'll get it,' said Joe. 'I'm Joe Hardacre.'

The effect was instantaneous; Smithers' jaw dropped, and

he started to splutter. 'Mr Hardacre, sir, you didn't tell me . . .'

'That's right, I didn't,' said Joe, 'but I'm telling you now. You want to know who I am? Well, I was your boss. You're sacked. You've got two minutes to get out before I have you done for trespass.' Joe pulled out his watch. 'Two minutes, and then I'll throw you out on the street.'

The unfortunate Mr Smithers did not argue, and Joe felt, for the first time, the thrill of power as he watched a man broken at his command. Smithers gathered together his few personal bits and pieces and went without another word.

'You wait,' said Joe, this directed to the remaining Mr Smithers. 'I've got some questions I want to ask you.'

'Yes, sir,' said Smithers.

'That place out there, why does it stink like that? Get out there and open some of the windows.'

'Open the windows, sir?' Smithers sounded surprised.

'You're not deaf, are you? Is there any reason why they shouldn't be open?'

'The dust, sir.'

'Dust?'

'If you open the windows, you get a lot more dust in the workroom, and the shirts would almost certainly become soiled.'

'I see,' said Joe.

'Do you still want the windows open, sir?'

'No,' said Joe 'let them sweat.'

'You really are despicable, aren't you?' said the girl who had been standing there practically unnoticed.

'Do you work here? Or are you . . . ?' said Joe.

'I did, and I'm not,' she snapped back at him and walked out.

Joe watched her as she left. She carried herself proudly, and her voice was educated – not the type one would have expected to find in a place like this. 'Who is she?' he asked Smithers.

'Helen somebody-or-other,' he answered. 'My uncle found her.'

'You don't seem very worried about your uncle,' said Joe.

'I'm not,' was the reply. 'With a bit of luck I'll get his job.'

'Well, let's see if we can make this barn show a profit first,' said Joe. He understood just what sort of man Smithers was.

Two years later, with Harry starting at Oxford, Welbeck Shirts was making a respectable profit. Joe was an innovator. When he first got to Welbeck, the women each made a complete shirt and were paid one and a halfpence for each one that was accepted. Each woman was provided with a table and a sewing machine, and the sewing machine was standing idle for most of the day while the seamstress made button holes and sewed on buttons by hand. Joe changed all that. He divided the women up into teams – one machinist, one hand sewer, one finisher. That way all of the machines were working all the time; output doubled, and Joe managed to cut the piecework rate by a third. There were a few mutterings when this happened, but a few selected sackings took care of that. In all of this Joe found a willing ally in Smithers, who had inherited his uncle's job and was being considered for a partnership.

It was just about then that Sam happened to visit Leeds.

With no little pride, Joe showed his father around his factory. Sam walked in silence through the foul-smelling atmosphere, watched unmoved as Smithers warned a woman and fined her a penny for allowing sweat to drip on to her work. He walked past the hungry faces, each turned away and into its work. He could feel the resentment and the hopelessness. Once he almost spoke, when he saw a weeping child being sent away because she had run a needle through her thumb. After his tour of inspection, Joe took him into the office, where he got out a decanter of sherry and poured out glasses for himself, Sam, and Smithers.

'Well, Dad,' said Joe, 'you haven't said much; after all, there isn't much to say.'

'No, Joe, there isn't,' said Sam, sipping his sherry.

'It's the books that count. I'm clearing over thirty pounds a week net in this one shed. How's that for a start?'

'It'll make you rich, Joe,' said Sam, 'and it'll make Mr Smithers here rich as well, I shouldn't wonder. Did you notice there was a little girl in there hurt her thumb?'

'They're always doing something stupid, what of it?' said Smithers.

'Happen they are,' said Sam, 'but I were talking to Joe.'

'Sorry, sir,' said Smithers.

'Did you notice that, Joe?'

'Yes. I don't understand what you're driving at.'

'Dost tha remember how we started?'

'Of course I do; you got the idea about the baked herring.'

'No, it wasn't that, that came later; that came because me thumb kept me off the fish quay. I wonder if that lassie's hurt thumb'll do her any good.'

'What does it matter,' said Joe, 'who cares?'

'I care,' said Sam, still in the same quiet tone. 'Mr Smithers, I wonder if you would be so kind as to leave me alone with my son here?'

'Certainly, sir; I shall be in the other office if you want me, Mr Hardacre.'

Smithers left them. Sam got up and put his glass down. He walked slowly over to Joe and hit him hard across the face with the back of his hand.

'You bastard,' said Sam, 'thou money-grubbing little runt.'

'What's the idea? What have I done?'

'Joe, them's people out there. They might not be all that bright, but they've got feelings, they hurt, and when they get into the hands of the Joe Hardacres and the Smitherses of this world, they hurt a lot. I'm ashamed of me sen for giving thee this place. I want it back. I want it back now.'

'It's mine, Father; I've seen the deeds, you gave it to me, and you gave it to me legally. If you want it back you can buy it, and I want a bloody good price for it.'

'I'm having it, Joe, because if I don't get it I shall beat you into a pulp; I'll make thee so that thy mother won't recognize thee. When I look at this place and think that a son of mine could have done the things that thou's done ... it makes me sick.'

'There's laws about this sort of thing, you know. If you lay another finger on me ...'

'Tha wouldn't jail thy own father, tha haven't got the guts. Thou'll be in Saunders' office in Bridlington at eleven o'clock tomorrow morning to sign the transfers.'

'And supposing that I'm not there?'

'Then I'll come looking for thee.'

Sam walked out of the office without another word. Joe sat there white-faced and tight-lipped. After a moment or two Smithers poked his head around the door.

'I say, has he gone?'

'Get the hell out of here!' roared Joe.

Joe caught the night train to Driffield and stayed at the inn. He hated himself for not having the courage to defy his father. Early next morning he ordered a cab and set out for Hardacres, where he met Wilson in the hall.

'Master Joe, we have not seen you for some time,' said Wilson.

'Is my father in?' asked Joe.

'He is not returning until tonight so far as I am aware,' said Wilson. 'Mrs Hardacre is in the morning room.'

Joe went straight into the morning room, where Mary greeted him warmly.

'Joe, what a lovely surprise; it's good to see thee, lad,' she said. 'Tha dad's not home.'

'I know, Wilson told me.'

'Still, he'll be here after lunch. Hast tha had thy breakfast? Is there anything thou wants?'

'Yes, Mother, I've had breakfast, and please don't fuss.'

'There's summat wrong,' said Mary, suddenly serious. 'Thou'd better tell me.'

'I expect Father will tell you all about it when he comes home,' replied Joe. 'I've only come here to say good-bye.'

'Good-bye?' Mary sat on the sofa. 'Joe, what are you saying? I want to know what this is all about, Joe. We don't have secrets, not thee and me; thou's always told me everything, ever since thou was a little lad, so let's be having it now.'

'I'm leaving, Mum, that's all there is to it. It'll be a long time before I'm back.'

'But where are thee going and why? It's tha father, isn't it?'

'Mother, I'm going to America. The *Majestic* sails from Liverpool on the afternoon tide tomorrow, and I shall be on board. Mum, we're getting soft over here; as far as I'm concerned, this country's finished.'

'When did thou see thy father, Joe?'

'Yesterday.'

'What was the row about?'

'Never mind about the row. I want to get away from the name of Sam Hardacre. I can make it on my own, and when I have I'll come back, but not until then.'

Mary knew her son; she knew better than to try to argue with him, but being Mary she was ever-practical. 'I know thou'll do it thy way, Joe, but how are thee for brass?'

'I've got my ticket and ten pounds.'

'Aye, well, we can do better than that, come along o' me.'

Mary led Joe upstairs to her sitting room. She opened a glass-fronted silver cabinet and from the middle shelf, where it was displayed as if it were the Crown Jewels, she took the Tin Box.

'There's the best part of a hundred sovereigns here,' she said, tipping the contents on to the table. 'Thou'd better take that.'

She picked out two half sovereigns and put them back in the Tin Box. 'I never let it get empty,' she said, carefully returning it to its place. 'Take what's there, Joe, happen thou'll need it.'

Joe picked up the pile of gold and put it in his pocket. He embraced his mother.

'Be seeing you, Mum,' he said.

'Take care, boy,' and it was not until the door had closed behind him that she allowed the tears to come.

Joe went straight back to Driffield, where he caught the train for Bridlington. On his arrival he made his way to his father's offices, where he found Sam and Saunders waiting for him. The atmosphere in Saunders' office was tense, and throughout the entire meeting Sam stood gazing out of a window with his back to Joe.

'Well, Joe,' said Saunders, obviously embarrassed by the situation in which he found himself, 'I have the transfer deeds here; all I need is your signature.'

'I'm not signing,' said Joe.

'But your father told me ...'

191

'I don't give a damn what my father told you. I want two thousand pounds for that business. I'm willing to give you first refusal, but if you don't buy it, I know someone who will.'

'Who's that?' Sam spoke without turning.

'Smithers. I'm leaving the country tomorrow, so I want the money today; that's why I'm letting it go so cheap.'

'What am I to do?' asked Saunders.

'Pay him and be done wi' it,' said Sam.

'Well, Joe, you heard your father. How do you want the money?'

'I'll take a bill of exchange as long as it's negotiable in New York.'

The few formalities were soon completed, and Joe, without having said another word to his father and two thousand pounds the richer, started to leave.

'Joe,' Sam called. Joe paused. 'I just want thee to know that I know thou was lying about Smithers being able to buy.'

Joe caught the next train out of Bridlington, spent the night in Manchester, and caught the boat train to Liverpool the next morning.

It was quite late that evening when Sam got back to Hardacres. He found Mary waiting for him, tense and angry.

'Hast tha seen Joe?' she demanded.

'Aye, I've seen him,' replied Sam grimly.

'So have I. Sam, what have thee done to him?'

'Owt that's been done to Joe, he's done himself.' And then as Mary was about to protest, 'There's no use arguing with me, Mary, that young man has no respect for anything in life except brass.'

'Tha knows where he's gone?'

'He says he's going to America.'

'And how are thee going to learn him respect in America, Sam Hardacre, that's summat I'd like to know.'

'He'll be back,' said Sam.

'Happen he will and then happen he won't,' said Mary. 'And him wi' nobbut a hundred sovereigns I gave him out of Tin Box.'

'And he took it?' Sam was astonished.

'Of course he took it, the poor lad had nowt.'

Sam did not mind Joe getting the two thousand out of him, but to take his mother's pin money, it made Sam want to vomit. 'That lad's a wrong un if ever I saw one. You know, Mary, if it was anybody else but our lad it ud be funny.'

'What would?' she demanded.

But he could not tell her; she was hurt enough, and it would only hurt her more to know the rest.

'Sam,' she pleaded, 'go after him. Bring him back. Tell him we're sorry.'

'Sorry?' Sam looked at her in amazement. 'And just what is it that we are supposed to be sorry for?'

'Does it matter?' She was near to tears. 'There might still be time if tha goes now, Sam, for my sake.'

'Mary, lass,' he said, 'there's damned little I wouldn't do for thee, but this I can't do and even if I could, I wouldn't, it would be wrong.'

'But, Sam, he's our lad, we love him.'

'Do we, Mary?'

'Tha knows we do; please, Sam.'

'No son of mine behaves the way that man did.' Sam's voice was hard.

'Sam Hardacre, thou'll take that back.'

'No, Mary.'

'Take it back, Sam.'

'I can't.'

'Then there's nowt more to be said.' She left the room, and that night for the first time since their marriage, Mary slept behind a locked door.

CHAPTER FOURTEEN

Helen Peterson, an attractive woman in her early twenties, stood on the Liverpool dockside and gazed at the great ship. She was wearing a dark-blue travelling skirt and blouse, such as might have been worn by any off-duty ladies' maid. Her bonnet, a plain straw, concealed most of her dark brown hair and was held under her chin by a bow of broad, blue ribbon.

R.M.S. *Majestic*, pride of the White Star fleet of ocean liners, was coaling in preparation for her departure on the afternoon tide. A constant chain of sweating stevedores were heaving coal from the collier alongside and into her bunkers. Already a wisp of smoke was coming from the forward of the twin black-and-yellow funnels, as she commenced to build up steam for the start of the six-day journey which would take her over three thousand miles of ocean, to New York and a new and better world; at least, that was how Helen saw it.

At twenty-two, Helen already possessed a jaded view of life in Victorian England in general and of Victorian Englishmen in particular. Born of middle-class parents who had died by the time she was thirteen, she had spent the last seven years earning a living as best she could. She soon discovered that her background qualified her as a prospective mistress to most of the men who became her employers. Mr Smithers, Senior, of Welbeck Shirts, had proved no exception. She had no moral objection to such an arrangement; Helen's morals were dictated by her needs, but the price had to be right. It was a strange thing, but as soon as she got down to the nitty-gritty of the business, she would almost invariably find her suitors stricken by acute attacks of conjugal remorse and morals. It all made her sick. The facts were simple; she was for sale to the highest bidder, she was certainly attractive enough to be able to pick and choose, and she would choose only a man and not a hypocrite who would make a pretence of undying love to save having to open his wallet. She had finally come to the conclusion that the Englishman's morals would always cost her money, so, as there was no reason why she should not, she decided to try her luck in America.

There was only one thing that prevented her getting aboard the *Majestic* there and then – the fare. To travel steerage – sleeping in communal cabins, living on porridge, soup, and bread, and sharing one toilet and washbasin with fifty others – would cost six pounds. Either Helen had been misinformed, or the fare had gone up, but she only possessed five pounds, and that was not enough. A single gold sovereign stood between her and the United States, but there was no way of raising it, except to steal it. Helen would not have minded stealing, had she believed she could get away with it, but she knew that, if she tried, she would more likely end up in jail. There were too many professionals on the docks for the amateur to stand a chance. She thought about begging for it, but there was not much chance there; four hundred and eighty halfpence would take a long time to collect. She would willingly have sold her body for it, but that would have meant all night for a pound, and the ship sailed in a few hours.

It was noon, and the ship was due to sail at four. The wealthy first-class passengers had not yet arrived to take possession of their fifty-guinea staterooms on the promenade and main decks, but their luggage had. Lying around the quayside in great profusion, it was being carried on to the ship by a number of men and women porters, each of whom wore an armband with a white star on it. This gave Helen an idea. Helen reckoned that she had a couple of hours to do what she had in mind. First, she went to one of the many little souvenir shops that abounded around the quay. There she bought a White Star pennant. Then, at a baker's she bought three loaves of bread and three bottles of lemonade. She drank a little of the lemonade and threw the rest away; then she filled the bottles with water from a public tap. She had with her a small bundle of clothes done up with a leather strap. She opened this and put the bread and water inside. The pennant she rubbed in the dirt and then wrapped it around her arm so that the white star was showing. She would pass as a porter if no one looked too hard.

She tucked her own bundle under her arm, walked to the middle of the stacks of luggage, picked up a couple of leather suitcases, and joined the line of porters passing up the gangway, through an iron hole, and into the ship. It was all so easy. Now that she was on board, she knew that, as long as she could stay there undetected until after the pilot cutter had taken off the pilot and returned to Liverpool, there was no way to get her off the ship until they arrived in New York. Once inside the ship, she found herself in a large lounge strewn with luggage. Everyone was very busy, and no one was in the least interested in the very ordinary young woman who walked out of the room carrying a cloth bundle and a suitcase.

Helen found herself in a long corridor; halfway down it she noticed an arrow pointing up some stairs to the 'Promenade Deck'. She went up and dumped the suitcase on the top landing near a cabin door. The open promenade was practically deserted, so she hurried around to the seaward side, where there was only the collier and no one to observe her.

There was another companionway on the promenade deck, and here the arrow indicated the 'Boat Deck'. There was no point in Helen hanging around on the promenade, where she would be bound to be seen, so she went up.

On each side of the ship there were eight lifeboats, all swung inboard on their davits. It was the obvious and only thing she could do; there was nowhere else to go, other than back the way she had come, so after a quick look around to make sure that she was unobserved she slacked off the corner of one of the tarpaulin covers, pushed her bundle into the lifeboat, and squeezed in after it.

Helen lay there in her hiding place, hardly daring to breathe as the ship completed its preparations before getting under way. The chattering and calling of voices grew in intensity as the moment for departure grew nearer. At last there was a long, low blast on the ship's siren, followed by much banging of gongs.

'The ship is about to sail,' called a voice, 'all visitors ashore.'

Then the engines started to pulsate through the whole vessel as power increased and her screws started to turn. Then that, ever-so-slight, motion that told her that they were away from the quay and must now be moving down the Mersey Estuary and towards the Western approaches. In an hour they would be on the high seas, the pilot would leave, the last link with England would be broken, and Helen would be safe.

Two days outward-bound from Liverpool, the great ship rose and fell gently on the long Atlantic swell. The warm summer day had given way to the chill of evening, which always came with the setting sun. The first-class passengers, having gorged their way through the seven courses provided for their dinner, had dispersed to the ballroom or the bars or the decks – some of them towards the stern to watch the steerage passengers giving their nightly show of song and dance in the tiny well of deck reserved for them. Joe had gone to his cabin after dinner to get a cigar and his coat.

He stood on the open promenade deck, midships, leaning over the rail and watching the white spume, illuminated by the lights of the liner, as it sped past the iron hull. The faint vibration of the engines as they drove her through the ocean at about twenty knots turned the ship into a living, pulsating world, detached and isolated from the two real worlds between which she now stood.

A round, well-groomed jowly individual joined Joe at the rail.

'Hardacre, isn't it?' he said.

'Yes,' replied Joe tonelessly. He did not want to get into a conversation; he was enjoying his solitude. Two days on board had brought a new man out in Joe. He found himself without bitterness towards his father, more a sense of relief that, at last, he was free of parental discipline and morals. He accepted the fact that there was absolutely nothing he could do until he arrived in New York; that much, at least, he had inherited from Sam. Whenever anything was inevitable, he never argued; he just waited for it to go away or do what it inevitably must. Come New York, the harsh business of the world would start all over again, but for the next four days there was nothing to do, so he might as well enjoy them.

'Got your name from the passenger list,' said the other man

by way of explanation. 'I'm Hardy, in the next cabin to yours, what?'

'Oh,' said Joe.

'Jolly nice night, what?' said his companion.

'Yes,' said Joe, wishing the fellow would go away and stop 'whatting' at him.

'Care for a turn around the deck, what?'

'No,' said Joe, by now being deliberately rude.

His companion, however, was the true bore, the type who only asked the questions and never listened to the answers.

'Must take a turn around the deck every night after dinner; helps the digestion and keeps the waist line down, what?' He paused. 'Aren't you coming?'

'No,' said Joe, looking pointedly down at the water, 'I'm not.'

'Oh! All right, see you when I get back; have a drink together, what?'

The man left him, bustling away towards the stern. As soon as he rounded the cabins at the end of the promenade deck, Joe practically sprinted to the for'ard companionway which led to the boat deck.

Once on the boat deck – with the wind and the mixed tang of the salt sea, the smoke and the steam from the two huge funnels – Joe sat himself on a life raft facing the stern and finished his cigar. It was getting quite late, and there were not more than two or three couples on the deck; and they, one by one, drifted off until by about midnight he was, as far as he could tell, the only occupant of the boat deck – alone with the moon, the stars, and the sea.

Still, in spite of the hour, he was not tired and had no desire to go to bed. Perhaps in an hour or two he would return to his stateroom and order a bottle of champagne from the night steward, but for the moment he was content to enjoy the air and the smell of the sea.

Besides, he was curious; the deck represented a whole new playground. He walked to the leeside and threw the remains of his cigar overboard; then he went to one of the giant ventilators and put his ear to it – he heard through it the roar of the engines. He played games with himself, and so his first game was guessing where each ventilator went; then, there was the stars. Joe had but the most elementary knowledge of astronomy, but he managed to find the plough and work out the position of the North Star, and, having decided that the ship was sailing in the right direction, he then found Orion, the only other constellation he could recognize.

He then went to examine the life raft on which he had been sitting. He did not find that very encouraging – a sort of square box, covered with wooden slats with lots of rows of rope around it, presumably for you to hang on to. The lifeboats looked very much more substantial. He made a mental resolve that, should the worst happen and the ship founder, he would make every effort to get into a lifeboat.

He wandered over to one of them and stroked its gleaming white paint. They had not looked big when he had boarded the ship, but they really were quite large when you got close to them. Joe smiled as he realized how one spent a time like this voyage acquiring useless bits of knowledge. He examined the davits and quickly saw how they worked, how they would swing the boat out clear of the side of the ship; then it would be lowered by its own weight into the sea. The oars, he supposed, were stowed away inside the boats under the tarpaulin covers, and he wondered what else was carried in these boats; were they provisioned for the emergency, if and when it arose?

His curiosity led him to one of the boats, where he noticed that the tarpaulin was not as tightly drawn as on the others. Well, he thought, there was certainly no harm in looking, so he lifted up a corner of the canvas and found himself looking into a beautiful, frightened face.

'Hello,' he said. He raised his eyebrows a little but showed no other sign of surprise.

The girl gasped.

'My name's Joe,' he said. 'Who are you?'

'Helen.'

'Well, Helen, either you live here or you're a stowaway, am I right?'

'What are you going to do?' she asked. 'Hand me over?'

'I shall have to make my mind up about that, won't I?'

'Shall we get one thing straight first?' she said, 'You can

hand me over if you want to, I can't stop you. But there are certain things that I'm not willing to do in order to buy you off. I think you understand what I mean.'

'Perfectly.'

'Good. Now, if you wish, we can talk.'

'In that case, I think you'd better get out of there,' said Joe. 'We can walk around while we discuss the situation. You're certain to get picked up if you carry on talking to me from inside a lifeboat.'

'I suppose you're right,' she said.

He watched her admiringly as she scrambled out of the lifeboat. Her clothes were wrinkled and a little grubby, but she had really not made a bad job of looking after herself during her incarceration.

'Do you think we'll be safe?' she asked.

'I certainly shall be,' said Joe. 'I've paid for my stateroom and, as for you, I think I shall be able to hold off the wolves while we decide what's going to be done about you. Incidentally, I've got a feeling that I've seen you before. I'm not trying to make conversation – that would be quite pointless. Why don't we sit down while we consider the alternatives?'

'I'm cold,' said Helen.

'We can go to my cabin if you wish.'

'I've already told you.'

'All right, if you won't trust me, you'll just have to shiver,' said Joe. 'Tell me, what did you intend doing when they finally caught you?'

'I hadn't made any plans.'

'Have you got any money?'

'Four pounds, eighteen shillings.'

'Why didn't you use it to pay your passage?'

'Because it wasn't enough; it costs six pounds, steerage.'

'I see; well, then that's our first alternative. I could advance you one pound, two shillings, and you could go to the purser and become all legal.'

'No,' she said, 'I would have done it if I'd had it in Liverpool, but now I'm going to need something when I get to New York.'

'True,' said Joe. 'I could increase the loan by, say, two

pounds or, as a second alternative, I could hand you over to the captain, who would probably clap you in irons and make you scrub decks all the way to New York and then all the way back to Liverpool.'

'You could leave me where you found me,' she said. 'Anyhow, I know that you're not going to hand me over.' She smiled for the first time.

'What makes you so sure?'

'Because,' she said, 'if you were going to you would have done it right away.'

Joe laughed. 'What do you do for a living?' he asked, and then suddenly, 'good lord, I remember you now – Smithers, Welbeck Shirts, you were the secretary!'

A look of recognition crossed Helen's face. 'You're that bastard Hardacre,' she said without rancour.

'That's right,' said Joe smiling. 'Whatever happened to you?'

'I walked out after you took over. Not because you were a bad boss – you were, but then practically everybody is. I didn't mind old Smithers either; I let him have a bit of a fumble every now and then, usually just before pay day, and there'd be an extra half crown in my pay packet. But when you gave him the boot, the young one really made me want to vomit, so I left. Anyway, what happened to you? What are you doing here?'

'Pretty much the same. My father kicked me out, or, rather, he bought me out.'

'That would be Sam Hardacre?'

'Yes.'

'I've heard about him; most of the girls liked him,' she said. 'Anyway, go on.'

'Well, that's all there is to it. I thought that I'd go and try my luck in the U.S.A.,' said Joe. 'But let's get back to you; what are you going to do when you get there?'

'Find a job, I suppose; there's little else I can do.'

'There are other ways a girl can earn a living.'

'I've tried it – it makes me sick and it gets you nowhere,' she said. 'If I ever do it again, it'll be for big stakes, so, Mr Hardacre, if you want me it will cost you a diamond, a large diamond.'

'Do you think you're worth it?' asked Joe, laughing.

'No,' she replied, 'but what the hell does that matter if I can find a man who does?'

'Have you thought about a job?'

'Doing what?'

'Well, you're a lady typewriter, you could work as a secretary.'

'Yours?'

'Yes.'

'No strings?'

'I will pay handsomely for anything I want, other than your services as a secretary.'

'And what will you pay for the secretary?'

'A pound a week. That would be five dollars American money,' he said.

'All right,' she said. 'It's a deal, it'll do for a start, but if I get a better offer I'll take it.'

'Unless I meet it.'

'That will depend on how we get on,' she smiled at him.

'Then the first thing to do is to go and see the purser,' said Joe.

Joe had never been spoken to like that by a woman. He realized that he had, in Helen, found a quite remarkable self-willed and independent person who was not going to allow her sex to be a barrier to her advancement; rather, she would use it as a weapon if need be. At first the purser wanted to report the whole business to the first officer, but a five-pound note slid unobtrusively across his desk produced a remarkable change of attitude.

Joe had Helen installed in one of the lower-priced cabin-class cabins. Since theirs was to be a business arrangement, he was not going to go to the expense of first class. Also, he pointed out that the shipboard social barriers were such that, while she would not be able to visit him, he would, at any time, be able to visit her.

By the time their business had been completed it was approaching three A.M., and after Helen once again refused to go to Joe's cabin, they settled for sandwiches and a bottle of wine in the lounge.

The wine was a mistake. Helen had had nothing but bread and water for two days, and the effect of a full-blooded claret on an almost-empty stomach was catastrophic; Helen was violently sick. She managed to reach her cabin before Joe realized what was happening, and she spent the rest of the night in a comfortable berth regretting the loss of the fresh sea air in the lifeboat.

Joe went to his cabin, puzzled by his own feelings. He could not have explained his actions at all rationally. Helen was a good secretary, he knew that, but he didn't know if he was going to need one in New York, and yet he had done this stupid, unbusinesslike thing. It annoyed him, and to top everything he found that he wanted Helen Peterson; he did not just want a woman – that would not have been difficult to understand or to deal with – what he wanted was Helen, and that annoyed him even more.

CHAPTER FIFTEEN

Harry Hardacre was no great horseman, but he had taken to riding every morning during his summer vacation from Oxford. He had inherited Joe's mare, a black beast of about fifteen and a half hands and irreverently named Victoria. Every morning he would collect Victoria from the mews at about ten o'clock and ride out over the ample moorland which surrounded the estate, returning usually just in time for lunch, around one.

There were two reasons for Harry's sudden interest in riding and the outdoor life. First of all, life at Hardacres was not what it had been. There was a coolness between Sam and Mary which Harry always found much more embarrassing than the open display of affection which used to mark their relationship. A barrier had grown up since Joe left the country. Mary, without ever saying it, made it obvious that, in spite of what Joe had done at the factory, she held Sam responsible for the virtual loss of her son. Mary occupied her time almost exclusively in the garden and at her needlework, whereas Sam spent more and more time away on business, and when he was at home, he devoted all of his spare moments to little Jane, who was now an attractive if somewhat precocious six-year-old.

There was certainly something lacking at Hardacres; gone was the gay informality that had been such a feature of life there: it was as if it had stopped being a home and had become just a place where people lived. Everyone behaved absolutely correctly, nobody ever used the wrong knife or fork any more, but somehow the fun seemed to have gone out of it.

Harry would have regarded this state of affairs as all rather sad, had he not been very preoccupied with matters of much greater importance to him.

The Baintons had taken the Middletons' shoot, and Judith

Winstanley was a very keen horsewoman and, now that she had come out, a very independent young lady as well.

It had been the discovery that Judith rode most mornings and that occasionally she rode alone; that was the real reason for Harry's equestrian interests. He had subjugated his dislike of horses and had gone to see Grey at the stables.

'Grey,' he said, 'I want to learn to ride.'

'But tha can ride, Master Harry,' had been the reply.

'No, I can't, Grey,' he said. 'I can sit on a horse, and that's about all. Everybody knows it, including you.'

'Well, it takes time to make a horseman, tha knows,' said Grey.

'That's another thing; I haven't got a lot of time. Oh, I don't expect to be able to ride in the Grand National. All I want is to be able to control a horse and persuade it to go where I want it to go when I'm on my own, with no one to give me a lead.'

'Well, that shouldn't be too difficult, Master Harry. It's mostly a question of the right horse. Them's like women; some'll do owt for thee, and others'll do nowt. Reckon we've got one horse here that might do for thee.'

'Which one's that?'

'Master Joseph's black mare.'

'Not Victoria!'

The mare was a full blood, a magnificent-looking creature. Joe had always looked the picture of the complete horseman when he was up on her; Harry could not see himself riding her, now or ever. Joe had always been full of stories of how difficult she was, giving the impression that it required a really superb horseman to control her.

'Not Victoria,' Harry repeated, 'I'd be scared to death.'

'Now why, Master Harry?' asked Grey. 'Because of all those stories that yon brother o' thine used to put about ofen her?'

'Well ... er ...'

'Master Harry, as long as she were Master Joe's horse, there weren't much I could say. He wanted to cut a fine figure and he did; Victoria's a right good-looker, but that didn't mean that she were difficult. Bless your soul, she's the gentlest-natured beast that I've ever known; I've even had little Miss

Jane up on her.'

'Jane?'

'Aye, and she's dead easy in traffic. I promise thee, if there was ever a horse without any vice, it's Victoria.'

'Would I be able to jump her?' he asked. 'Small jumps, of course.'

'Oh, aye,' said Grey. 'And little ditches?'

They both laughed, and Harry started a crash course on his brother's mare.

'I say, Grey,' he said two or three mornings later, 'Joe was a bit of a fraud, wasn't he?'

'No,' was the reply, 'Master Joe was a gradely horseman, and Victoria's the horse she is today because of him, but he liked to keep up the illusion. Nobody's ever all honest about a horse or a woman; I expect thou'll lie about her sooner or later.'

So it was that after his few days of hard learning, every morning he rode out in search of Judith Winstanley. Though he had hardly spoken to her since that house party all that time ago, she had never been very far from his mind. There had been the spasmodic clandestine correspondence carried out by the below-stairs underground.

When he read great verse, he applied it to her; when he saw a beautiful setting, its beauty sprang from the fact that she fitted into it, and when he lay alone in his room at Oxford and thought about her, he knew that he had to see her again soon, if for no other reason than to destroy the illusion which he had created and to substitute for it a reality worthy of it, or to expurgate the memory.

In spite of his careful planning, the manner of the renewal of their acquaintance was not by any means what he had expected. One morning he finally saw her, riding alone about two or three miles from Hardacres.

He put his mare into a canter and was overhauling her rapidly when she spotted him. Harry's heart sang within him as he drew closer. She looked wonderful on a horse in her grey broadcloth habit. The horse was a big Irish cob, a heavy animal of about sixteen hands, which she was probably going to hunt, come the autumn; he was the type of animal well suited to the heavy going of the East Yorkshire moor, but he made Judith look even smaller than she really was.

Judith had obviously regarded Harry's approach as a challenge, and when she spotted him she put her horse into a gallop. It was no contest; her cob may have been built for the terrain, but he was no match for Harry's thoroughbred when it came to speed. He had almost overtaken her when she jumped a hedge – it was no more than three and a half feet – and went streaking away across an open field.

Not to be outdone, Harry put his mare at the jump. As the animal made to jump, Harry remembered something awful; he had, in strict disobedience to Grey's instruction, omitted to tighten his girth after he had mounted. He now paid the penalty. Horse and rider both took the jump: separately. That in itself might not have been too bad but for the fact that Harry landed face down in a muddy ditch which ran along the far side of the hedge. He lay there, feeling frustrated and impotent.

'Why, it's Mr Hardacre. What are you doing down there?'

He looked up. Judith had pushed back her veil and was smiling down at him.

'In case you had not noticed, I'm sitting in a ditch up to my eyeballs in mud,' he replied, somewhat crossly.

She laughed. 'I'm sorry, but you do look ridiculous. I know I shouldn't laugh; come, let me help you.' She slid out of the saddle and came over to him.

'No!' he shouted.

'Oh,' she said, stopping abruptly. 'I'm sorry.'

'I didn't mean that, really I didn't. What I meant was that you'd get muddy and you mustn't, it wouldn't be right.' He had already decided that the reality was every bit as beautiful as his dream.

'I clean easily, you know,' she replied. 'Come on, let me help.'

'No, no, really I'm all right.' He scrambled out of the ditch. 'Where's my horse? I'd better get back home and change.'

'Your horse is over ...' she stopped and laughed. The mare was grazing peacefully with its saddle hanging down under its belly. 'Slack girth?'

'Yes, I know, Grey will play hell with ... I'm sorry, I mean he'll be angry if he finds out.'

'Who is Grey?'

'He is my father's head groom, and my father is a great believer in the delegation of authority.'

'Meaning?'

'Grey is responsible for horses and riding, and disciplinary powers go with the responsibility.'

'I say, what fun,' said Judith. 'It's just like the socialists.'

Harry went over to his mare and, with some little difficulty, managed to catch her.

'You don't know very much about horses,' said Judith, smiling and leading her cob over to him.

'I'm afraid not, I don't even really like them; would you mind holding her head while I try and do something about the tack?'

Judith held the mare while Harry sorted out the saddle; when it was done and she had checked it for him, he gave her a leg up on to her cob and then mounted himself. It was an awful moment, because he knew that, according to the rules, they should now ride off in opposite directions.

'You wouldn't care to come and take sherry wine with me, I suppose ... would you?' his voice trailed away.

'Why, Mr Hardacre, I do not believe you have permission to call on me, and as you see I am without a chaperone.' There was a slightly mocking note to her voice. 'And you are so bold as to ask me to sherry?'

'Well, Madeira, actually, and I did ask your parents for permission to call.'

'I know, my father was furious.' Her tone was more serious now. 'I'm sorry.'

'You won't come? I suppose you can't, really?' Harry was very dejected. 'Would it do any good if I was to try again?'

'I shouldn't think it would do any good at all.' And then, smiling at his dejected face, 'Well, are you going to take me for that Madeira or not?'

'But you said ...'

'I said that I was sorry that my father would not give you permission to call on me; he never said anything about me

208

calling on you.'

'Well, let's go.'

A jubilant Harry rode along for about five or six minutes in absolute silence

'Miss Winstanley,' he said at length, 'I have got to see you again, you know, whatever your parents say about me.'

'Well?'

That wasn't much help, he thought, and finally he blurted out, 'But I must know if that is also your desire. I would not wish to try and force my presence upon you if it were to cause you any embarrassment.'

'I shall have to consider this at length,' she said, and then a couple of seconds later, 'what about your people?'

'They won't mind; whether they would help us I don't know. My father doesn't like your father, but he wouldn't regard that as having anything to do with us.'

'Hardacres looks nice, doesn't it?' said Judith.

They had breasted a rise, and the house and grounds were spread out before them in the summer sunshine. Judith was right, Hardacres did look nice with its gardens a blaze of colour, the greens and browns of the kitchen gardens, the neat orchards, the green, green lawns, and beyond the great square house itself.

'I suppose it does,' said Harry, 'I'd never thought about it before. It's home, and you tend to take home for granted, don't you?'

'But you haven't always lived here, have you?'

'Heavens, no; I can remember when I was about seven when we all lived in one room and we used to move every week or two to follow the herring.'

'I heard about that,' said Judith. 'Your father must be a remarkable man.'

'I suppose he is, I'd never really thought about that either. Please, what am I to do about seeing you?'

'Is it very important to you?'

'Very.'

'Then we'll find a way.'

They had reached the mews, and Harry handed over the horses to Grey. 'Miss Winstanley will want her mount in a little while, and I shall need the mare again,' he said.

'Yes, Master Harry,' said Grey. 'Have you taken a fall, sir?'

'Yes.'

'Not too hard, I hope, sir?'

'It might have been fatal,' said Harry, smiling down at Judith. 'Come on, the Madeira should be in the morning room.'

When they got there, they found that Mary was alone, sitting beside an untouched glass of wine.

Mary rose as they came in. 'Hello,' she said.

'Don't you remember me, Mrs Hardacre?' said Judith.

'Is it? Eeh, I do believe it's Judith, Judith Winstanley. Come in, love, have a glass of Madeira.'

Harry poured out a glass for Judith. 'I had a fall, Mother.'

'Them horses,' said Mary, 'dangerous things, don't thou think so, Miss Winstanley?'

'Miss Winstanley was riding too; she helped me, and I invited her to come home and have a glass of wine,' explained Harry. 'Where's Father?'

'He's in study, he's not often in here in t'morning any more. Won't thee sit down, Miss Winstanley?'

Judith looked up at Harry, who said, 'I think I'll just go and ask him to join us, if you'll excuse me.'

He hurried across the hall and into his father's study. Sam looked up as he entered. 'Hello, Harry, lad, I thought that you were riding; did you want something?'

'Dad, I haven't got time to explain now; I've got Judith Winstanley with me, and I want you to ...'

'Hang on, hang on, did you say Judith Winstanley?'

'Yes.'

'By gum, I'll bet her old man doesn't know.'

'Father, will you come and talk to her? I'm ever so much in love with her, and I want to marry her.'

'Easy, lad,' said Sam, 'you've only met the lass a couple of times in over two years.'

'But we've been writing to each other.'

'Well, I'll be damned, how did you manage that, or had I better not ask?'

'It's probably better if you didn't know. But I really am serious about her, and I think she's fond of me.'

'Have thee asked her?' said Sam.

'Well, not yet.'

'Well, tha'd better bloody well ask her; it's the only way tha'll find out.'

'I can't, not yet anyway, not until I come down from Oxford. Besides, her father doesn't approve.'

'You didn't need to tell me that,' said Sam, 'but it's damn all to do with him. If you want the lass, go ahead and grab her. Allus assuming she'll have you. From what I've seen of her, she's a nice girl, though how she managed it with them for parents I'll never know.'

'Dad,' said Harry, interrupting his father's speech, 'will you please come over to the morning room? She's waiting, and she can't stay long.'

Together they returned to the ladies; Judith was just finishing her glass of wine and preparing to leave.

'I thought you were not coming back,' she said to Harry as he entered.

'I'm terribly sorry ...' he began.

'It's my fault, Miss Winstanley; dost tha mind if I call you Judith?' said Sam.

'Not at all, I wish you all would,' she replied, looking straight at Harry.

'Well,' said Sam, 'I kept the lad, Judith. He were jumping up and down trying to get back to you.'

'I really must be getting off home,' she said. 'They'll be sending out search parties if I don't.'

'Please may I accompany you?' asked Harry.

'Do you think it wise?'

'There are highwaymen between here and the Middletons' Lodge,' said Harry darkly, 'but I'll leave you before we get there if you'd rather.'

Harry and Judith collected their horses from the mews and started out over the open moorland in the direction of the Middletons' Lodge. It was a glorious day, full of the scents and sounds of summer. For a while they rode in silence, Judith occasionally glancing at Harry and wishing he would say something, and Harry occasionally glancing at Judith and wondering if he dared.

'Judith?'

'Yes, Harry?'

He felt a thrill of pleasure; they had never before called each other by their first names. 'I think Judith is a lovely name.'

'So is Harry; it's friendly.'

'It suits you.'

'Harry does?' said Judith.

'Of course not; Judith, I meant.' They both laughed.

'I suppose,' he said, 'it would be useless for me to approach your father again?'

'Worse than useless. I think it is much better that he doesn't know. Not yet, anyway.'

'Do you want to meet me again, Judith?'

'Very much, Harry.'

'Then how?'

'We could meet riding. I tell you what. Every Monday and Wednesday that I can manage, I'll be at Nerdwell Beck at ten o'clock in the morning, until the family moves to London for the season.'

'But that's wonderful,' said the exultant Harry.

'After that we'll make other arrangements ... dear Harry.' She held out her hand.

Harry took the proffered hand, and together, holding hands, they rode for several silent minutes.

'I think it is time for you to turn back,' said Judith. The Lodge was now visible about a half mile away. 'Please don't hang about and get recognized. Till Monday.'

She tapped her horse with her crop and was away before he had time to reply.

Back at Hardacres Mary and Sam stood and watched them go from the morning-room windows.

'She seems a nice girl, Sam,' said Mary, 'though I can't say as I'd want to lose my other lad as well.'

'How do you mean?'

'If folk try to keep them two apart, they'll be off and away,

212

just like Joe.'

'Mary, will you never get Joe out of your mind? Can't you understand I never drove him away, and if I'd known that it was going to do this to thee, I'd have run after him like you wanted me to. It's never been quite the same since, has it?'

'Nay, Sam, I suppose I'm nobbut a stupid woman. Principles are much more important to men, aren't they?'

'Happen they are, Mary, but thou's got to have principles if you're going to live a decent life.'

'You know, I think that love is so much more important than principles. You've got to love thy own, even when they're right rotten, 'cause that's when they need love more than owt else,' said Mary. 'It's the same the world over. Principles cause more trouble and grief than anything. Look at what's going on in South Africa now; mark my words, Sam Hardacre, but there's going to be fighting there soon. Then what's going to be the use of principles to the mothers and wives who'll lose their sons and husbands?'

'But the Boers are ...' said Sam.

'Are people just like thee and me.'

'Mary,' said Sam after a long silence.

'What is it, Sam?'

'Us. We've been like strangers lately. I'm sorry about Joe, more sorry than you know. But I don't worry about him, and I don't want you to. Joe will never want for anything; he'll see to that, and he'll never care for anybody the way I care for thee.'

'Well, Sam,' Mary walked over to him and took his hand, 'we've summat else to worry about now.'

'How do you mean, Mary?' Sam put his hand on top of hers.

'I said I didn't want to lose Harry, and if we're to keep him, then we've got to help him with that lass.'

'And that is not going to be easy. Yon Bainton would see his daughter in a nunnery before he'd see him wed to one of my lads.'

'If you don't mind, Sam, you'd better leave this lot to me. Just don't put tha big foot in it, this is a job for a woman.'

Mary was right. Over the next months Harry and Judith saw quite a lot of each other, and not only on Monday and Wednesday mornings. The below-stairs underground functioned well through Mrs Grey, her niece, Judith's lady's maid, and occasionally Mrs Grey's son, all superintended by Mary, who also took it upon herself to chaperone the meetings.

But while ordinary people worried about matters of loving and living, events were moving towards what appeared to be an inevitable showdown in South Africa. Even Sam was getting himself worked up about the attitude of the Boers, and it was a matter of some surprise and not a little concern to Mary to find that her husband had become so wrapped up in the imperial dream.

One evening Sam brought a certain Henry Butler to dinner. After Mary and Mrs Butler had retired, Sam revealed to Harry that Mr Butler was the adjutant of the East Yorks Imperial Yeomanry and that they had been discussing for some time the possibility of Harry taking a commission in that regiment. The majority of Harry's contemporaries had done similar things, and as Harry was to come down from Oxford at the end of the current term, Sam had decided that it would be a good idea if he had something active to do, especially if he was going to spend most of his time with his books.

Harry could see the logic of the arguments that they put forward. Whether, left to make his own choice, he would have picked the militia was a matter of some considerable doubt. But his father's advice was sound; there was no denying that, and in the absence of any positive objection that he could see, he went along with Sam and became Second Lieutenant Hardacre of the East Yorks Imperial Yeomanry.

He kept the decision from Judith, for he wanted to surprise her with his uniform after it had been made. He did. Judith was furious.

CHAPTER SIXTEEN

On 9 October 1899, a dispatch was handed to the British Agent at Pretoria by the Transvaal government. It demanded 'the immediate withdrawal of British troops from the Transvaal border, the removal from South Africa of all British reinforcements, and an assurance by the British government that British troops now en route for the Cape shall not be landed in any part of South Africa.' The dispatch went on to state that 'should these conditions not be complied with by five o'clock on the afternoon of the eleventh, the government at Pretoria would be obliged to regard the noncompliance as a tacit declaration of war.'

On 12 October the East Yorks Imperial Yeomanry was embodied into the regular army. They received sailing orders to embark at Liverpool on R.M.S. *Britannia* for the Cape. Officers were to deliver their chargers to the dock six hours before sailing.

Sam and Mary travelled north with Harry on the thirteenth. Sam had managed to book rooms at the Adelphi by pulling every string that he could lay his hands upon. They had arrived late in the afternoon and gone straight to the hotel. Harry had shown no desire to go to the docks to see the ship or the loading. His orders were to report there at ten the next morning, and he had no intention of being a moment early.

He dressed for dinner and went along to his parents' room. Sam was sitting there in his shirt sleeves having a drink; Mary was nowhere to be seen.

'Aren't you coming down to dinner?' he asked.

'Aye, I shan't be long,' said Sam, 'just you go down and wait for us. The table's booked in your name.'

Thinking all of this was a little strange, Harry left his father and went down to the dining room. He gave his name to the head waiter.

'Mr Harry Hardacre?' asked the waiter.

'Yes,' replied Harry.

'This way, sir,' said the waiter and led him to a secluded alcove in a far corner of the huge dining room.

'Are you sure that my table's over here?' he asked.

'This is it, sir.'

'Well, you'd better lay another place,' said Harry, 'there are three of us.'

'Can I bring you an aperitif?'

'No thank you, I'll ...'

Harry rose to his feet with his mouth open as a second waiter led Judith Winstanley to the table and seated her opposite him.

'Surprised?' she said.

'Judith, this is wonderful.'

'The meal has been ordered, sir,' said the waiter. 'Do you wish me to start serving?'

'You had better bring us some sherry first, and please don't hurry,' said Harry.

They sat in silence for a while, their fingertips touching across the snow-white linen of the table.

'How?' said Harry.

'I don't know,' she replied. 'Your mother arranged it.'

'Do your people know?'

'No.'

After the soup he told her he loved her, after the fish she said she loved him, over the roast beef he asked her to marry him, and over the crepe suzettes she said yes.

'But we will probably have to wait till February,' she said. 'I shall be twenty-one, and then I shall marry you with or without my father's consent.'

Naturally their talk drifted to the war, and Harry told her how much he hated the idea of killing. He had even thought of resigning his commission until he realized what effect such an action might have on his father. For her part, Judith agreed with him. She had never really accepted his association with the army. They were two very gentle people who hated violence but suddenly found themselves in a situation which demanded it and from which escape was impossible.

'But what if I am still in South Africa in February?' asked Harry, bringing her back to the subject of their marriage.

'You'd better be,' she said. 'I have joined the V.A.D., and I shall be sailing for the Cape in five days. I expect we'll have to get married out there.'

'You're going nursing?' said Harry. 'But it will be horrifying, Judith. You don't know what war is like.'

'Do you? Really, Harry,' she said, 'men do make me laugh. They seem to think of certain women, and only certain ones, mind you, as if they were pieces of fine porcelain, and we're not, you know. One day the world's going to wake up to the fact that we're much tougher than men. Anyhow, I shall look for you over there. Good-bye, Harry. Dearest Harry ...'

'You're not going,' he said.

'I'm afraid I must. I don't want to do anything to upset the apple cart until I'm over there in the Cape. And my father is expecting me now.'

Harry could not persuade her to stay, and she begged him not to accompany her to the station; his parents, she insisted, deserved a share in his last evening before sailing.

When she had gone, Harry went in search of his mother and father. There was little he was able to say to them; the whole business had been too emotional for words to come easy. He just tried to thank them for arranging the meeting and left it at that.

The next day he sailed. Sam and Mary stood at the dock-side, watching the gap widen between ship and quay as the liner drew away; they were left feeling so alone, though surrounded by many people. There was nothing left to do, save to return to Hardacres and little Jane, the last of the brood. They caught their train and sat together in an almost empty first-class compartment. Somehow this experience had drawn them closer than they had ever been since the day that Joe left for the United States.

The only other occupant of their carriage got out of the train at Leeds, and for the rest of the journey they had a compartment to themselves.

'Sam,' asked Mary, 'dost tha think our Harry'll make a good

soldier?'

'Funny you should ask that,' said Sam. 'I don't rightly know, Mary. I never thought, when I suggested the militia to him, that he might have to go to war. To me it were just good exercise. I don't think that Harry really likes soldiering. You know, I always thought that Joe might have gone into the army or the navy; he seemed to have the right sort of aggression.' He paused. 'I wonder what Joe's doing now.'

'Sam?'

'What is it, lass?'

'Would you really like to know?'

' 'Corse I would.'

'Sam, promise me you won't get mad.'

'What's going on, Mary?'

'Promise me, Sam.'

'All right, I promise,' he said.

'Joe's doing all right,' she told him.

'How the hell dost thou know?' roared Sam.

'Sam, thou promised.'

'I'm sorry; go on, tell me.'

'I hear from Joe every month; the letters come to Mrs Grey. Now remember that promise and don't lose thy temper. I know how tha felt about it, but I've got feelings too. He's my boy, and I had to do it.'

'Mary, love, I'm glad you did. Happen mebbe I were hasty when I threw him out at Leeds, but there are some things that just stick in my craw.'

They were both silent for a long time.

'Sam,' said Mary.

'Aye?'

'Joe's wed.'

'Wed? And I knew nowt about it. Who's he wed?' he asked.

'She's an English girl, Sam. He met her on boat going over. But that's not all; thou's a grandfather.'

'A grandfather?'

'Twice.'

'Why wasn't I told?' he roared. 'Thou should have told me. Imagine, me a grandfather and knowing nowt about it.'

'I were scared to tell thee, Sam. Tha knows how tha was about talking about Joe. The first one were a lad – Arnold they called him – and now they've had another one, a lass. They've called her Emily.'

'Mary, is there owt they need, money or anything like that?'

'So far as I can tell, our Joe's a very rich man. He were never one to let grass grow under his feet, and as soon as he got to America, he took an office in a place called Wall Street. There all he seems to do is to sit at a desk and make money.'

'What's his wife called?' asked Sam, who was much more interested in Joe's domestic affairs.

'Helen.'

'Happen we ought to go over and see them.'

'Not yet, Sam, not as long as war's on. We'll have to stay here for Harry.'

'Reckon you're right,' he replied. 'We could go and look up her folk, though.'

'She doesn't seem to have any, or if she has, Joe's never mentioned them.'

'Mebbe she's one of us. Do you think I should write to him?'

'No, Sam, I wouldn't if I were thee. I'll tell him that I've told thee and that tha wants to let bygones be bygones. I think us should wait and see what he says afore thou writes.'

It was late evening when Mary and a very thoughtful Sam arrived back at Hardacres. Wilson met them in the hall.

'Excuse me, Mrs Hardacre,' he said, 'Miss Winstanley is in the withdrawing room, and madam, she appears to be in a state of considerable distress.'

Mary started towards the drawing room.

'I'll come with thee,' said Sam.

'No, Sam,' she said, 'I can guess what this is about. It'll be better if I handle it alone.'

Mary had barely left him when there was a loud hammering at the front door. Wilson went to answer it, and a second later a red-faced and furious Lord Bainton stormed into the hall.

'What the devil have you done with her, Hardacre?' he demanded.

'I don't know what you're talking about,' replied Sam calmly, 'and I don't allow people to come into my house yelling their heads off. So you can either talk decent or get out.'

'I want my daughter.'

'Then why come here?'

'I have reason to believe she is here.'

'I haven't seen thy daughter,' said Sam, 'and even if I had, I doubt if I'd tell thee where she was. Not the way you're carrying on.'

'She was with you last night, she told me so.' Lord Bainton was becoming a little calmer.

'Last night's not today. Happen she was with us, and she were welcome,' said Sam. 'Her's got a mind to wed our Harry if thou asks me.'

'That's laughable. Judith is a Winstanley.'

'And what's so precious about that? She's a woman, and she'll be a Hardacre once she's wed. There's nowt wrong with being a Hardacre, Lord Bainton.'

'I did not suggest that there was. It's only ...' Bainton realized that he had gone too far.

'It's only that Harry's father happens to be a guttie?' said Sam. 'Come off it, Bainton. Come into the study and have a drink. I give you my word that I have not seen your daughter since last night. If she has walked out on you, and I suppose that's what's happened, maybe talking it over will help. I'm sure that she's not in any danger, and she's not with Harry unless she's a damned good swimmer. Is there nowhere else she might have gone?'

'Her aunt, possibly. She lives in Scarborough.' Lord Bainton was obviously at a loss. 'Look here, Hardacre, I think I owe you an apology. I'll accept that drink, if I may.'

'That's better,' said Sam, leading him towards the study.

'Will there be anything else, sir?' asked Wilson.

'No,' said Sam, 'we can look after ourselves, but,' he said pointedly, 'if you happen to run into Mrs Hardacre, you might mention that Lord Bainton is here.'

'Please do not trouble Mrs Hardacre,' said His Lordship as Sam led him into the study.

Wilson went straight to the withdrawing room. There Mary was sitting on the settee, still trying to comfort a very unhappy Judith.

'What is it, Wilson?' asked Mary, looking up.

'Mr Hardacre told me to tell you that Lord Bainton is here, madam.'

'Father!' said Judith, jumping to her feet, 'What am I to do?'

'For a start tha can take it easy,' said Mary. 'Wilson, does Lord Bainton know that Miss Winstanley is here?'

'No, madam,' said Wilson, 'the master went to great pains to assure His Lordship that he had not seen Miss Bainton since last night.'

'What are they doing now?'

'They're having a drink in the master's study. After that, I got the impression that Lord Bainton might be going to Scarborough.'

'That's where my favourite aunt lives,' said Judith.

'All right, Wilson,' said Mary, 'not a word to anybody about Miss Winstanley being here. Thee take her up to my sitting room. Wait for me there, Judith. I think it's about time I gave them men a bit of a talking to.'

'Are you going to tell him that I'm here?' asked Judith.

'I might,' said Mary, 'but that depends on how he behaves himself. Off you go wi' Wilson now.'

Mary waited until they were out of the room and then started off towards the study.

'Come in,' called Sam as she tapped on the door.

'I'm sorry, Mrs Hardacre,' said Lord Bainton as he saw Mary, 'I asked Wilson not to disturb you.'

'I know tha did, and I know why tha's here, and tha'd better know there's summat I want to say to thee. Today, up in Liverpool, we said good-bye to our lad. He holds the Queen's commission in the army; that means that he's as good as any man in this land. Sam and me, we love our Harry, maybe in a way that you posh folks cannot understand. Thee never lived as close to thine as we did with ours. But all of that's beside the point; Harry's gone off to do summat he hates. He's gone to fight a war. Hopefully, he'll come back safe and sound. If he does, thy Judith is going to be waiting for him, because, Lord Bainton, those two young folk are in love. I'm proud that we was able to bring them together last night, because they're right for each other. There's nowt remarkable about either of them, they're just an ordinary lad and lass who love each other and who feel that they have a duty to do for their country, and to my reckoning, it's up to us as stay at home to remember that and to do what we can for their happiness and to hell wi' who's good enough for who.'

'Mrs Hardacre, I ...'

'No, Lord Bainton, I'm not quite finished yet,' said Mary. 'You see, I know where your daughter is, and I know why.'

Bainton stiffened. 'Then you must tell me at once. I demand to know.'

'Thou's in no position to demand anything,' said Mary. 'I'll tell thee this, though; thy lass is quite safe, and she's not going to come to any harm.'

'But where is she?' Bainton pleaded. 'She's my only child – please tell me where she is.'

'Not so fast, Lord Bainton,' said Mary. 'I'll tell thee only if thee promise not to interfere.'

'You leave me no option, Mrs Hardacre, apart from calling in the law.'

'And tha don't want to do that, because that'll take time. I have thy promise, then?'

'You do.'

'She's here, in this house. And it's no good thee glaring at Sam, he never lied to thee. He told thee that he hadn't seen her, and that were the truth. I've been with her, and I know what yon's going through. Lord Bainton, can't thee see, whatever airs and graces tha tries to gi' her, Judith's nobbut a lass in love who's just said good-bye to the man as means more to her than her mother or thee or anybody. Tonight she's going to stay with me because that is what she wants. Tomorrow, if it is her wish, she can go back home or she can stay on here. As for thee, if thou wants to stay to dinner tonight, thou'll be most welcome, but I don't promise that she'll come down. Can thee understand that? It's all up to her.'

Lord Bainton thought hard for a long moment. 'With your permission, ma'am, I shall leave now. I shall call again to-morrow morning; perhaps Lady Bainton will accompany me. I would appreciate then the chance to talk to Judith privately.'

'I'll put it to her, Lord Bainton. But understand, it'll be up to her.'

'I understand,' he said. 'Good night, Mrs Hardacre.' He turned to Sam. 'Good night, Hardacre; I don't suppose I'll ever like you, but damned if I'm not beginning to respect you.'

They walked to the door with him and then came back into the hall together.

'Mary,' said Sam, 'I'm right proud of thee, lass. I didn't know that thee had it in thee.'

'Eeh, Sam, but I were scared.'

'Never.'

'I were. Me, talking to a lord like that. But I had to do it. Sam, them two's just got to wed, they're that much in love.'

'Aye,' said Sam. 'Well, dost you think you could forget love for a minute? How about summat to eat?'

'Tha's right, that poor lass'll be starved. Tell Wilson that Judith and me'll have supper in my sitting room. Thou can scratch for thee sen.'

Mary kissed him lightly on the cheek and went upstairs.

CHAPTER SEVENTEEN

On Wednesday, 22 November 1899, General Lord Methuen camped south of Belmont, a small town about eighty miles south of Kimberley. Kimberley lay inside an iron ring of Boer commandos, and though the garrison there was in no immediate danger, the town was under siege.

Methuen, with a force of Guards, the Ninth Lancers, the Yorkshire Light Infantry, the Northamptons, the Northumberland Fusiliers, and three companies of the East Yorks Imperial Yeomanry, had been ordered to open the road from the south. One of the reasons for the concern about Kimberley was that it contained the most distinguished Englishman at that time in South Africa. Cecil Rhodes would have been a great prize if the Boers had managed to take him. This apart, Rhodes was a great embarrassment to the local commanders; opinionated and convinced of his own infallibility, he was interfering greatly with the military operations conducted by the garrison.

Lieutenant Harry Hardacre was Orderly Officer that night. After the camp had turned in, in company with the Orderly Sergeant – Sergeant White, a regular from the Guards – he was making the rounds of the sentries. These had been posted at intervals around the perimeter; they stood guard for periods of two hours on and four off until reveille at three thirty. There was no moon, and the stars shone brightly from the tropical black velvet of the sky. The silence could almost be felt, broken only by the sound of their breathing and the soft tread of their footfalls on the broken ground.

''Alt, who goes there?' the voice was little more than a whisper.

'Orderly Officer and Sergeant,' hissed White.

'Advance one and give the password,' whispered the voice. Sergeant White went forward. 'Little Bobs,' he murmured. 'All right, sir.'

Harry joined them. 'Everything all right, sentry?' he asked.

'Keep your voice down, sir,' said Sergeant White. 'I don't like it, I don't like it at all, it's far too quiet.'

'But that's all right, surely?' said Harry.

'No, sir,' said White, 'out here on the veldt you get most of the animals moving around at night. There's always something, but just you listen now, sir, there's not a sound.'

'What does that mean to you?'

'Boers, sir. They're around here somewhere. Have you seen anything, lad?'

'No, Serg',' said the sentry, 'I haven't seen or heard nothing.'

'It's the Boers all right, sir,' said White.

'What do we do, Sergeant?'

'With respect, sir, I think we should call out the duty field officer and suggest we double the guard.'

'How will that help?'

''Aven't been here long, 'ave you, sir?'

'Just over a week.'

'I've been here since it started. I was here in eighty-one an' all. It's like this, sir; if we double the guard, and the Boer attacks a post, he's got to kill two men before they can raise the alarm, and that's bloody difficult, sir.'

'I'll take your advice, Sergeant; do you suggest that we finish the rounds or go straight back?'

'Only one more post to do, sir. We might as well check that first,' said White, 'but we'd better keep our heads down from now on, and that goes for you too, lad,' he said to the sentry. 'Keep under cover, and if anything doesn't answer your challenge, open fire.'

'Yes, Serg',' said the sentry. 'Should I keep behind that rock?' He pointed to a large boulder dimly visible.

'All right, lad, but keep your eyes and ears skinned.'

The soldier, who was little more than a boy, moved off to behind his rock. As he disappeared from view, there was a slight sound. Before Harry could realize what was happening, Sergeant White had rushed around the rock, rifle at the ready. There were two shots. Harry was still tugging at his Webley revolver and not really aware of what was happening when White called to him.

'I've got him, sir; he got our lad, though.'

Behind the rock Harry saw the young private, grotesque with his throat slit, lying in a huge pool of blood. Beside him lay a bearded man. Sergeant White had shot the top of his head off, and blood and little bits of grey stuff were still pumping from the wound as the corpse twitched in its final agony.

'We'd better get straight back, sir; there's sure to be more of them around. I 'spect the major will want to send a patrol out.'

'Just a minute,' said Harry. It had all been a bit too much; he leaned on the rock and was violently sick.

'Your first one, sir?' said White, and Harry nodded. 'You'll get used to it, sir; took me the same way first time.'

'I'm sorry, Sergeant.'

'Don't be afraid of being sorry, sir, but don't let it get you.'

They crawled back to the guard tent, and, as Sergeant White had predicted, a punitive patrol was sent out. Harry tried to grab a few hours' sleep and not be distracted by the spasmodic firing, but no sooner had he closed his eyes, it seemed, than the bugler was sounding reveille.

'Mr Hardacre, sir,' the Company Sergeant-Major stood rigidly to attention as he barked at Harry's recumbent figure, 'Major Wilkins' compliments, and will you report to him immediately.'

Wilkins was the divisional adjutant, so it had to be important. Harry pulled on his field boots and went over to the Major's tent.

'Ah, Hardacre,' he said, when Harry arrived, 'that was a good show last night.'

'Good show, sir?' Harry was puzzled. 'But I didn't do anything; it was all Sergeant White.'

'Yes, I know it was,' said Wilkins, 'but there's many a damned young fool would have tried to take command when he should have been taking advice. Good man, White, he can out-track a Boer, and there's not many in the British army can do that. Anyhow, that's beside the point; the General wants to see you.'

Feeling nervous, as any young subaltern would on receiving such a summons, Harry accompanied the Major to the General's bivouac.

'I'll go in first,' said Wilkins. He returned a moment later. 'Come in, Hardacre.'

Harry went in and saluted the tall, moustached man who was sitting in his shirt sleeves, apparently in the middle of breakfast.

'This is the officer, sir,' said Wilkins.

'Ah, yes,' said Lord Methuen. 'Hardacre, isn't it? That was a good show last night, Hardacre.'

Harry wished everyone would stop complimenting him for doing nothing and being sick. 'Thank you, sir,' he replied, 'but I do feel that any credit is due to my sergeant.'

'Quite so, Hardacre, but you were in command; you made the decision to follow the right advice, regardless of where it came from, and that was what was good. Out here, you know, it is much more important for a man to know when he doesn't know than it is to know when he does know.'

'Yes, sir,' said Harry.

'And last night you proved the point. Showed you had common sense. Well, sit down, boy, I want to talk to you; all right, Major.'

'Sir,' said Major Wilkins, saluting and leaving them.

'Now then, Hardacre,' said the General, 'you will have guessed that this is no social call. I've got a job for you.'

'Yes, sir,' said Harry.

'In just over one hour we are going to make a frontal attack on the Boer positions around Belmont to try to force them into a set-piece battle. The aim of this is to destroy the potential of the units he has deployed around here. It's not going to be easy and might take us a couple of days. The Boer holds three important ridges between here and the town. However, we should be able to open the road to Kimberley if, and this is the big if, the Kimberley garrison breaks out in our support as soon as we have taken Belmont. Do you understand?'

'I think so, sir.'

'It's quite simple, really; if we can open the road north and

227

garrison it before Cronge and his lot – there are about three thousand of them – can be brought up for a counter-attack, then I believe we can hold the road by adopting a defensive posture, and the siege of Kimberley will be raised.'

'Please, sir,' said Harry, 'what has all of this to do with me? I'm a very junior officer and not even a regular soldier.'

'Quite true, Hardacre, but I think, and Major Wilkins agrees with me, that you are the man for the job.' The General held up two packages wrapped in oilcloth. 'Do you know what these are?'

'I suppose they're dispatches, sir.'

'You could call them that. One of them is for the garrison commander at Kimberley, informing him of our intentions and asking him to attack three days from now and to establish a series of heliograph stations.'

'And the other, sir?'

'Ah, yes. That is addressed to Cecil Rhodes and must be delivered to him personally. And look out for squalls when you do it.'

'Why, sir?'

'Because it tells him that the great empire builder is not a soldier, and it orders him in the name of the Queen to keep his damned nose out of military matters and let the army get on with the job.'

'Not very nice for him, sir.'

'No. And a damned sight less nice for the poor devil who has to deliver that dispatch; I don't envy you, my boy. Now, I'm giving you Sergeant White and four men. White knows the ground between here and Kimberley and will be able to get you there if anyone can. Obviously an officer must go, if for no other reason than that Rhodes will be bloody insulted that I didn't go myself. There's just one other point; if you can persuade Rhodes to come back with you, do so. He'll be a blasted nuisance here, but at least we might be able to ship him off to the Cape and get him out of the way. Any questions?'

'When do we start, sir?'

'As soon as you hear our attack get under way. Get well out beyond our left flank and start from there. Remember, no heroics; you've got a job to do, and you can tell Sergeant White that he's been promoted; he's Sergeant-Major with effect from today.'

Harry took the two dispatches and left the General. He found Major Wilkins waiting for him.

'Well, we'd better go and find Sergeant White and your men,' he said.

'Do you mind, sir?' said Harry. 'I haven't eaten.'

'I'll send something to your bivouac,' said the Major. 'I'll tell White to report to you there.'

It seemed that Harry had barely time to down a couple of sausages before the sound of artillery fire told him that the seven-pounders were in action and the attack was under way.

Together with Sergeant-Major White and the four others, they made their way to the west until White, returning from a forward reconnaissance, told them that they were clear to start heading north. They had three days to do nearly eighty miles.

The Yeomanry were mounted infantry, and each man owned the horse he rode. Harry was riding Joe's black mare.

The little squad had discarded their pith helmets in favour of broadbrimmed hats, hoping that this slight deception would fool any Boers who happened to see them at a distance. The country they were travelling was hot and dusty, with numerous rocky outcrops and hills or kops, any of which would provide cover for an enemy.

They had been travelling for most of the morning when Sergeant-Major White called to Harry.

'Sir,' he said, 'I reckon we should hole up for a while.'

'We haven't been going long, Sergeant-Major; why stop now?'

'We'll not make much distance in the heat of the day, sir; we'll do much better if we take our rest now and press on this evening.'

'Very good, White, we'll see if we can find some suitable cover.'

They stopped on the south side of a fairly high kop, dismounted, and rigged their khaki ground sheets to provide shade.

'The Boers are using the railway as far south as Spyfontien. We won't be able to work our way any further west. We'll have to work north and come into Kimberley from the east. There's not much water that way, sir, so if you have no objection, I'll take James and Rogers and see what we can find now.'

'But the canteens are full, Sergeant-Major,' said Harry.

'That's right, sir,' said White. 'We want to know where the water is before we start emptying them.'

Twenty minutes later White returned. 'I've found water, sir, and there's no sign of the Boers. I think they'll all be down at Belmont; our chaps seem to be giving them stick over there.'

'That all seems very satisfactory, Sergeant Major,' said Harry. 'Now we'll rest up here, then eat and fill the canteens at about five o'clock, and move on.'

'Yes, sir,' said White, 'that sounds about right; it'll be cooler then, and. we'll start making better time.'

Harry ordered sentries to be posted and the rest of the men to get as much rest as they could, since he intended to keep going for as long as possible during the evening before having to build fires to discourage the attention of the large nocturnal predators.

The balance of the day passed without incident. Promptly at five they started northward, keeping one man about a quarter of a mile ahead of their little force. They made good time and by midnight had left the sounds of the battle, still raging around Belmont, far behind. They must have covered about twenty-five or thirty miles when Harry decided to call a halt.

By this time they were well behind the Boer forward positions and in fairly open veldt, which was covered with patches of dry scrub and grass.

The tropical dawn was soon upon them; it was as if within a minute or so they had passed from velvety black night to red daylight. The great crimson orb of the sun rose rapidly in the sky, yellowing as it went and driving the temperature up to herald another day of steamy heat and the ministrations of the bugs and insects which abounded.

They located a water hole, and Sergeant-Major White went forward to inspect it; he found no trace of human beings though there were plenty of fresh animal spoor. With the caution which he was gradually learning from his Sergeant-Major, Harry decided to make camp in a thicket of tall grass about half a mile from the water hole after their horses had been given their fill.

The horses were staked out; the morning rations were allocated and eaten; and the canteens were refilled. Private Gerrard was detailed off for first watch while the others slept.

Harry had no idea how long he had been sleeping when he was brought to sudden wakefulness by a fusillade of shots. He scrambled quickly to where he knew Private Gerrard to be, tugging at his Webley as he went. White and the others were already there; a couple of shots were fired by his men as he got to them.

'Stop that, James,' hissed White, 'this isn't Woolwich Arsenal; if you're going to use a round of ammo' I want a dead Boer for it.'

'Sorry, sir,' said James.

'Where are they?' asked Harry.

'Oh, hello, sir,' said White. 'They're over there beside the water hole, and Mr bloody James has just told them where we are.'

'How many are there?'

'A dozen or so.'

'What were they shooting at?'

'The horses; they've done the bloody lot.'

The situation was serious, but all Harry could think of when he got this piece of information was how angry Joe would have been at the loss of his mare. The problem was, what to do? They were still more than forty miles from Kimberley and over thirty from General Methuen. They were outnumbered by at least two to one, by people who almost certainly knew the terrain a damned sight better than they did. Their chances did not look very bright.

Harry considered the options that were open to him. He could burn the dispatches and surrender; that way there would be no lives lost. The enlisted men and Sergeant-Major

White would be taken to prisoner-of-war camps, and he could give his parole to take no further part in the war and in return be given a safe conduct to the Cape. The second option was to slog it out with the Boers. They would probably kill a few of the enemy before being killed or wounded themselves, and if they were wounded, the odds were they would be left there to rot; anyway, if they did that, there was a fair chance of the dispatches falling into the Boer's hands. There was one other way. If they made a fight of it, then it was just possible that one man might get through to Kimberley if the rest of them could hold the Boers' attention long enough for him to get clear. The chances were not good, but it was the only way that gave any hope at all of getting the dispatches through to Kimberley.

White had to be the one to go. If anyone of the little party was going to get through to Kimberley, it would be White, so it was best to get him moving and then hold out as long as there was ammunition.

'White,' he hissed.

'Sir?'

'Take these and give me your rifle.' Harry took the dispatch case from his Sam Browne and handed it to White. 'We'll hold them as long as we can. You get round behind them and get these to Kimberley.'

'Why me, sir?' asked White. 'You should be the one to go; we can hold these bastards.'

'No, Sergeant-Major; you were sent on this mission because you know the country. Besides, you are a real soldier, I'm not. If any one of us can get through to Kimberley, it has got to be you. Take my revolver, and off you go.'

'But sir?'

'That is an order, Sergeant-Major.'

As White got ready, Harry told the other four what was going to happen. 'If anyone wants to surrender, he has my permission, but he must do it now.'

'Gerrard's been hit, sir,' said Private James.

'I didn't know that; is it bad, Gerrard?'

'Not really, sir, it's just in me arm; I'll be all right.'

Harry got an idea. A wounded man was not going to help

them much, but there was a way he could give them a little more time. 'Gerrard,' he said, 'I want you to leave your ammunition here and then go over to the Boers and surrender. Stand up with your hands over your head and walk over to them.'

'But I don't mind staying, sir,' said Gerrard, 'really, I don't.'

'I know that,' said Harry, 'but we need time for White to get away, so if you go over to them and tell them anything that they want to know except about the dispatches, it will give us time. Now off you go; you too, Sergeant-Major, and good luck to both of you.'

'Good luck, sir,' murmured White and started away through the tall grass.

Gerrard stood up with his hands up.

'Remember, tell them anything except about the dispatches,' whispered Harry.

'What you want, Englander?' called a voice.

'I've been hit and my officer says I can surrender,' called Gerrard.

'You got a nice, friendly officer, Englander?' called the Boer. 'Suppose he stands up and tells me himself.'

'The man's hit, and we have no dressings,' called Harry.

'Why don't all of you come over, Englander?' called the Boer.

'It's only me that wants to surrender,' said Gerrard, and then, whispering to Harry, 'I don't think this will work, sir.'

'It is working,' said Harry, and then he shouted, 'are you going to let this man give himself up?'

'I don't think so, Englander; prisoners are a bloody nuisance. All of you or nothing doing; I'll give you ten seconds, and then I'll open fire.'

'Get down, Gerrard,' said Harry. 'All right, men, fix bayonets.'

As Sergeant-Major White made good his escape, he heard the sound of the firing as it began again.

Two weeks later Sam Hardacre stood holding a scrap of

buff paper; he was near to tears.

THE WAR OFFICE REGRETS TO INFORM YOU THAT FIRST
LIEUTENANT HAROLD HARDACRE HAS BEEN POSTED MISSING
ON ACTIVE SERVICE. ANY INFORMATION AS TO HIS WHERE-
ABOUTS AND SAFETY WILL BE COMMUNICATED TO YOU
IMMEDIATELY.

Mary was sitting watching him as he read the telegram.
'Sam,' she said, 'it's Harry?'
'Aye.'
'Is he . . . ?'
'The lad's missing, Mary.' He sat down beside her and
took her hand. 'We mun pray that he's going to be all right.'

CHAPTER EIGHTEEN

Sam and Mary found a new bond in their mutual grief about Harry. As the days rolled by, they never discussed either of their sons, their life regained its old simplicity, and they started having tea with Jane in the schoolroom instead of dinner in the long, empty oak dining room. And though they never spoke of the boys, they each knew that the other's thoughts were constantly with Harry and Joe. Every time the door bell rang, every morning at post time, a tension would rise until the 'no news' of the day would leave them only tomorrow to hope for.

In all of this their one constant source of happiness was Jane. She was a lovely child, showing all the portents of turning into a very beautiful lady. Gentle and attentive to the moods of her parents, she shared their worry without letting that destroy her own zest for life.

Christmas was a subdued affair at Hardacres. Their only guest was Saunders, who was now quite alone in the world and more a member of the family than either friend or employee. So the century dragged to its close; it was 31 December 1899.

The whole country was preparing to celebrate the coming of the twentieth century. Even at Hardacres they intended to stay up until midnight and open a bottle of champagne. That was the morning that Judith's letter arrived.

She told them that there was still hope that Harry was alive. Sergeant-Major White had returned, and she had met him in hospital. He had told their story, praising Harry's gallantry, which had enabled him to complete their mission. But the important part of the letter was the fact that Sergeant-Major White, on his return, had passed the scene of the action. He told Judith what he had found. The letter concluded:

Apparently there were eleven graves. Seven were Boers, and the other four were White's comrades. Some kind soul had written their names on the crude crosses which surmounted the graves, and Harry was not among them.

I write to you now because I am being transferred to the base hospital at Pietermaritzburg in the near future and may not be able to get any more news. Please let me know if you hear anything. I don't want to raise your hopes too much, nor indeed my own, but it is possible that Harry is still alive. Let us pray that we hear soon.

With much love and affection, dear Mr and Mrs Hardacre,

I remain
Ever yours most sincerely
Judith Winstanley.

Sam read the letter through to Mary and then handed it to her. They sat together wordless, Mary staring at the sheets of paper in her hands. Jane came into the room and went out again unseen; a robin that Mary had been feeding all winter perched on the window ledge and tapped its request on the windowpane only to be ignored.

'Read it to me again, Sam.'

He did so.

'Sam.'

'Yes, Mary?'

'He's alive.'

'What?'

'Our Harry's alive.'

'How can you say that, Mary? This letter changes nowt.'

'I don't know, I never was one for this sort of business, I allus thought it daft. But I know that our Harry's alive as sure as I know that we're sitting here. So tha can stop worrying about him, Sam Hardacre; we'll see him again, thou mark my words. Don't ask me how I know, 'cos I couldn't tell thee. I just know, and that's all there is to it.'

For Sam, of course, nothing had changed. He wanted to but could not share Mary's confidence, and in a way he resented Judith's letter for raising what he could only regard as false hope. He felt that they had come to terms with the loss of Harry, and now this — they were back where they had been when they got the telegram. If only they could know one way or the other.

As soon as Private Gerrard was down, Harry hissed to his men, 'Try not to waste ammunition, but fire at any target you get.'

They had held out for a long time, several hours. Poor Gerrard had been the first to go, shot through the head, and then Harry had got one that had cracked the bone in his right leg. He was angry; it was all so stupid. He watched the other three of his men die with no knowledge of how many casualties they had inflicted on the enemy. He wanted it to be over, but for some reason which he could not name he was still keeping under cover, still firing at each blade of grass that moved, still playing at soldiers.

'Englander,' it was one of the Boers calling, 'have you had enough?'

'Have you?' called Harry.

'We want to get back to our farm while we've still got enough to look after it.'

'Why don't you go?' called Harry.

'There's dead to bury; it'll be dark in a couple of hours.'

Harry thought this over for a couple of moments. 'You want a truce?' he called.

'Right,' called the other. 'We bury our dead and go our separate ways. Agreed?'

'Agreed,' called Harry. 'You'll have to come and get me, I'm hit.'

'What about the rest, Englander?'

'There's only me.'

A huge, bearded figure rose from the cover of the grass not more than fifty yards from Harry. He was followed by four more, one of whom had his arm in an improvised sling. They approached Harry.

'You've got guts, Englander, I'll say that for you,' said the big man. 'Otto, come and see what you can do for him.'

Otto provided Harry with a dressing for his wound and

put his fractured leg in a crude splint.

The big man came over to Harry. 'Write down the names of your dead, Englander, and get on your way; you're going to need all the luck you can get.'

They gave him a makeshift crutch and let him hobble off.

Three days later a cavalry patrol of the Eleventh Lancers found an unidentifiable man, still wearing the shreds of a British uniform and only just alive. After being shunted around from hospital to hospital for several weeks, the still critically ill soldier was moved to the hospital at Pietermaritz-burg on the last day of the century.

At eleven o'clock that night Sam, Mary, Jane, and John Saunders were sitting in the withdrawing room at Hardacres. A bottle of champagne stood in a bucket of ice waiting for midnight. Sam had told the servants that they would look after themselves so as not to interfere with their celebration. There was little that any one of them wanted. The evening had become a mere formality, there was hardly any conversation, and any of them would have welcomed the suggestion that tomorrow was just another day and why didn't they all go to bed. But they had made the decision to see in the new century, and see it in they would.

In honour of the occasion they had had dinner in the dining room, and Sam and John Saunders had smoked a cigar together. Afterwards, they had joined the ladies and were sitting with them in fidgety silence as the minutes ticked by.

It was at precisely fifteen minutes past eleven, when the quarter hour had just finished chiming, that Joe walked into the drawing room.

On his arm, dripping with silver fox, pearls, and diamonds, was the most expensively dressed woman that Sam had ever seen.

For a moment no one spoke, and then Mary let out a little gasp and rushed to her son.

'Joe, Joe,' she cried, 'tha's come home.'

Sam could not take his eyes off Helen, his lips set in a grim line. 'And who's this?' he asked.

'This is my wife, Helen,' replied Joe.

'How do,' said Sam. His manner was strained and awkward.

'Helen, welcome home,' said Mary, going to her and kissing her.

'So tha's come back,' said Sam, turning to Joe. 'And what sort of welcome did you expect?'

'Just a minute, Father,' said Joe. 'I came home because mother asked me. She wrote and told me about Harry. I'm sorry.'

Sam's manner softened. 'All right, lad,' he said. 'It was nice of thee to think of thy mother in this.' Suddenly he brightened. 'Where are they?'

'Where are who?' asked Mary.

'Me bloody grandchildren, of course. Don't dare say tha's left them in America; I want to see them.'

'I told nanny to take them straight up to bed; they have had a most exhausting journey,' Helen spoke frigidly.

'Oh, aye, I suppose they have.' Sam tightened his lips; he knew that whatever happened he must not lose his temper tonight. He turned to Saunders. 'Come on, John, let's see if we can find some more champagne.'

Nurse Judith Winstanley took her candle and went to have a last walk around her ward before joining a small gathering of V.A.D.s and convalescing officers to drink a glass of wine at midnight. She had not been on duty since noon and knew that there were a couple of new admissions; these she would have a good look at.

She paused for a moment at the foot of each bed and raised her candle so that she could see the face of the occupant, who was, one hoped, sleeping. Twice there was a murmured 'Good night, nurse' from the bed, to which she replied with a 'Hush.' She arrived at the bed of one of the new admissions; here she went up the side of the bed to get a better look at the man. His eyes flickered open as she held up the candle.

'Hello, Judith,' he murmured, 'how nice of you to come.'

'Harry!' she almost shouted the name. 'Harry, my darling.' She put the candle on the locker beside his bed and cradled his head in her arms.

'Judith,' he whispered again, and smiled a little smile at her, and went back to sleep.

The clocks started to chime the hour; there was a glass of water by the bedside, and Judith raised it to Harry.

'Happy new century, darling.'

As the last stroke of midnight died away, a grim-faced Sam Hardacre raised his glass. 'This will be the first toast of the year, nineteen hundred,' he announced. 'To Harry Hardacre, wherever thou may be, happy new century.'

He drained his glass, flung it into the fire, and walked out of the room.

Book Two

The Establishment

CHAPTER ONE

Miss Jane Hardacre stood at the top of the steps outside her parents' house in Grosvenor Square, London, with Sarah, her lady's maid. She had been shopping, and they had just returned in a hansom cab. Jane was ringing the doorbell awkwardly through a profusion of packages, hoping that Wilson would answer before she and Sarah dropped everything.

She was a tall girl, whose height emphasized her slimness and added to her apparent age. Though she was barely eighteen, she was about to come out and embark on her first London season as an adult. Over the summer and under the guidance of 'Aunt Harriet', she had progressed through the rapid, almost ritualized, transformation from schoolgirl to young lady. Her hair, after years in the same schoolgirlish style, loosely tied down her back with an outlandish velvet bow, was now piled high and forward on her head and topped with an equally outlandish, but far more womanly, small tulle-trimmed hat. Her day dress – a green, neatly tailored skirt with a high-collared, tight-sleeved bolero jacket – was slimly fitted to her figure, and her skirts now covered all but the tips of the toes of her high, buttoned boots. Jane was not beautiful, but she had good strong features, and the masses of heavy black hair were definitely an asset. She had the ability, with style and training, to look extremely attractive, and her height and a certain confidence in her carriage made her stand out in a roomful of more conventionally beautiful women. Jane was aware of this, and after an adolescent awkwardness was learning to use her stature and her honest blue eyes to advantage. People talked to Jane; her manner was open and friendly, inviting intelligent communication.

As Wilson opened the door, Jane stepped quickly inside,

across the hall, and into the morning room, with Sarah trailing after her. She set her packages down on her mother's Sheraton writing desk and turned to Wilson, who was waiting in the doorway.

'Thank you, Wilson,' she said. 'Would you ask the countess if she would join me for tea?'

Wilson left, and Jane crossed to the mirror over the Adam fireplace to remove her hat. She slipped the long hat pin out of its anchorage in her thick black hair and then, carefully slipping it back into the green fluff of tulle, handed the hat to Sarah.

'Just take that box upstairs,' she said, indicating one of the packages. 'You can leave the others here.'

'The one from Madame Dupré, Miss Jane?' said Sarah, smiling slightly.

'Thank you, Sarah,' said Jane as Sarah left with the box. Jane always showed all of her purchases to Aunt Harriet; it was expected, and it was sensible. Aunt Harriet knew about such things, and Jane's mother did not. But Jane had ideas of her own, and her instincts told her that certain of her ideas, among them a particular new hat from a particular French milliner, who was patronized mainly by actresses, would not be considered suitable. She would have to wear it only on occasions when Aunt Harriet was not in evidence. Mama, Jane thought gently, would not know the difference.

The countess swept into the room, trailing yards of the inevitable black chiffon and the scent of white lilac.

'Jane, dear, what have you been up to?' Her eyebrows rose more with interest than disapproval, as she began poking about among the paper-wrapped packages on the desk. 'Spending your father's money again?'

'No, Aunt Harriet,' Jane replied proudly, 'just my allowance. I have my own money now.' It was true, even if she had only received the first instalment ever, yesterday.

'Spent all of it? Did you?' the countess said, arching her eyebrows again.

Jane nodded with slight remorse. 'The shops were so lovely, I couldn't resist,' she confessed. Anyhow, there would be more next month, she reminded herself secretly.

'We shall have to find a very rich young man for you, young lady, I can see that,' the countess replied, 'but have no fear, we will.'

Jane could not really imagine marrying anyone who was not rich. Not because she preferred rich young men, but because she did not know any others – with the exception of servants, of course, and some of the people who worked for her father. But she was not likely to marry any of those.

If her father had his way, Jane thought ruefully, she would marry some minor titled country squire from Yorkshire and spend all her days stalking about in tweed suits and riding to hounds. It was not the worst life in the world, she admitted – she liked the old place in Yorkshire, and, as a child, growing up in its vast gardens, she had truly loved it. In those days the house in Grosvenor Square, with its minuscule town-house garden, had seemed tight and repressive. But now, after her first summer of county social events, Grosvenor Square was a symbol of new freedom. Jane knew logically that it was not possible that every afternoon garden party at Hardacres had ended in a cricket match on the lawn, or that all of the gentlemen farmers had worn riding boots all of the time, even to dances. But that was the impression; that and red-faced farm boys, hopelessly eager to please and with a lingering smell of horses and tobacco. Not that she despised horses or the country life; she could ride with the best of them. Better than her brother Harry, though she admitted she could not match her eldest brother, Joe, on the rare occasions that he chose to join them at Hardacres. But then, few could.

Summer had left Jane with a definite suntan – which appalled Aunt Harriet; an athletic bounce in her stride – which also appalled Aunt Harriet; and a conviction that there must be more to life than galloping over the Yorkshire moors. And, as Aunt Harriet was the first to point out, London was the place for that wide, new life.

'Where's Mama?' Jane asked, glancing to the countess, who was unwrapping and carefully appraising her purchases.

'Upstairs getting that room ready for Judith.'

'By herself?'

'She's determined to. You know your mother.'

Jane smiled. The countess crossed to the tall window to study a lace blouse. The grey London daylight was kinder to the fabric than to Harriet's face. Jane saw, with sudden shock, the crapy skin of her throat above the stiff black lace collar, and the deep lines about her eyes and the corners of her mouth. There was a new stoop to her shoulders. Or at least Jane thought that it was new. Perhaps she was just beginning to notice such things. She wondered. The countess had always seemed perpetual and unchanging, rather like Hardacres.

'Anyhow, Judith isn't coming until the week after next.'

'No, dear, but your mother likes to be ready, and you know how she is about babies.'

'But it's not due for another six weeks.'

'Of course it's not. But just try and tell your mother that. It's her nesting instinct, and she's up there preparing the nest. Anyhow, we will all be in Glasgow next week, so perhaps she's just being sensible.'

Harriet began packing Jane's things away as the maid brought in the tea. 'Thank you, Millie,' she said, settling herself in a cloud of black lace on the flowered chintz of the sofa. Jane started to pour tea, suddenly thinking that Aunt Harriet had probably not changed her style of dress for twenty years. Anything different would not be the countess.

'I do wish that there was some way we could avoid Glasgow,' said Jane.

'So do I,' replied Harriet, and then firmly, 'but we can't, so you can stop wishing.' Jane lowered her eyes to the teapot. There was no arguing with Harriet.

'It's all right for Papa,' she said with a trace of girlish peevishness. 'And for Joe. They're both mad about machinery and engines and anything oily and smelly and clanky. Such a dreary bore.' She added, 'If they start going on again about their new marine engine, I shall positively curl up and die.'

'You may curl up if you wish, young lady,' Harriet spoke sharply, 'but it might be as well if you were to remind yourself that, boring or not, marine engines and railway locomotives and nasty, noisy cotton mills pay your keep, my dear.' Harriet was lightly mimicking her tone. She was rather good at that, and Jane sometimes wondered if the rumour, firmly unconfirmed by the family, that she had been on the stage was really true.

'Yes, Aunt Harriet,' she said in a small voice. Harriet could be very blunt, even for a countess.

'That's better, dear,' said Harriet, satisfied. 'Anyhow, console yourself. As soon as we have Glasgow out of the way, we can prepare for your presentation. Besides, you might even enjoy Glasgow. It is rather exciting commissioning a new cruiser.' Harriet did not sound excited. 'And we'll be surrounded with young naval officers; some of them come from the best families in the land. You can never tell what might happen.'

'Aunt Harriet!' Jane was shocked. 'You'd think I was on offer, like one of Harry's beloved prize Jersey cows.'

'Yes, dear?' said Harriet with a grim smile. 'And what precisely do you think that your presentation at court is? Come, come, my dear, we must all be honest like good little heifers. It doesn't do to lie to ourselves, even if we must all lie to each other.'

Aunt Harriet sipped her tea, nibbled at a biscuit, and leaned back mellowly. 'Still, my dear, it will be quite magnificent. You are to be my swansong. I'm getting too old for all of this, but you shall be my greatest triumph, and I shall go out in a blaze of social glory.' She sighed contentedly. 'Another cup, Jane, please.'

Jane leaned forward and poured from the silver teapot. She said, 'Has Harry decided to come down, do you know?'

'Well, he hasn't said, but you know as well as I do that he will find it impossible when the time comes. He'll never be separated from his heifers.'

'But Judith?'

'Rest assured that Judith will be far happier with your mother and no silly husband getting in the way. Men are definitely not welcome at times like this,' she added firmly.

'Aunt Harriet?' Jane said quietly. 'I think it's odd.'

'What's odd, dear?' the countess sounded sleepy and yawned.

'The Winstanleys. I mean Judith not wanting to be with

her own mother when the baby's born.'

'Would you want to be with Lady Bainton for a fortnight and have to have a baby at the same time?' the countess replied sharply.

'But she is Judith's mother.'

'More's the pity,' the countess replied, unyielding. 'Besides, as I recall, Her Ladyship did not deign to visit her first grandchild until he was at least three months old, and I think she has seen him on just two occasions since then.'

'Poor Noel,' said Jane, 'and he's such a nice little boy. I suppose he'll stay up at Hardacres.'

'I doubt if Lady Bainton finds any little boy nice,' said the countess, 'but I assure you that that is in every way in his favour. He is saved the dear lady's attentions, for one thing. I have no doubt that he will stay at Hardacres. His grandfather will hardly let him out of his sight. And he is a far better influence than the Baintons. Besides, I hear that Harry has engaged a nanny.'

'He has?' said Jane, interested. 'I don't think that Mama will approve. She didn't believe in nannies for us.'

'For you, my dear,' the countess replied. 'For your brothers nannies were not precisely part of the picture.'

'Oh,' said Jane with a little laugh, 'of course not, I forgot.'

'Then you are probably the only person who has,' said the countess, quietly thinking of the Baintons.

Jane found her parents' past a little mystifying. She knew it had all happened and where they had come from, but it was so far back in time – it was before she had been born. It was past history and hard to imagine.

'Anyhow,' the countess continued, 'Harry's situation is different. He's bound to need somebody for the child while Judith is in London, and she won't be rushing straight back; she'll need time to recover before she returns to Hardacres. A nanny is going to be an absolute necessity.'

'Who is she?' Jane asked. 'Will I know her?'

'Probably; she's a local girl, a farmer's daughter, I believe. A Miss Henrietta Cavandish.'

Jane thought carefully and placed the Cavandishes as a solidly respectable if slightly dull family whose farm bordered part of Hardacres. She remembered Henrietta, a plainish young woman some years her senior, with dark-brown hair pulled smoothly away from a full, pleasant face. She had a penchant for dark colours, and that, added to a slight heaviness of figure, made her appear older, more matronly than she was. She would do well as a nanny, Jane thought, and it would be a good job for her, because quiet and homely as she was, without title or much money, her chances of marriage were pretty slim. 'Oh, yes,' Jane said, 'I do recall her. I'm sure that she will do admirably.'

'Indeed?' said the countess. After all these years she still found the ringing self-assurance of the upper-class young disturbing.

'But I'm sorry that Harry won't be down for my presentation.' She thought of Harry, in his tweed knickerbockers and leather leggings, his tweed cap rammed hard down over his unruly black hair, making his way across a broad ploughed field with his odd, lurching gait. It was strange to think of him fighting in the Boer war and being decorated for gallantry. He was such a gentle soul, with his slow, wide smile, like their father's. She often wondered which Harry really loved best, Hardacres or Judith. Certainly, between them they were his whole life. Not that he did not love the rest of the family, but his love for his wife and his land bordered on the obsessive. Jane loved Harry. He was by far her favourite brother, and most times her favourite person anywhere. But at times she could not understand him. Why he should be content to spend his days out in the fields, doing a hard, unrewarding job, when he could so easily have paid a factor to do it for him, was quite beyond her.

Jane wondered if, sometimes, Judith did not resent Harry's total lack of interest in the social life of London or even Yorkshire. A sale of prize cattle or pigs was of much more interest to him than a house party. But Judith really did not seem to mind; she was here now only because Mary had had to come down, and Harry had insisted that she would be better off with his mother than with anyone else. There was no question but that Judith adored Harry; after all, she went halfway around the world to be near him during the war. Jane smiled as she thought of Judith; she was such a gay, pretty creature, with her pink cheeks and her honey-brown curls. She had been one of Jane's adolescent ideals, and now that she was older, they were as close as sisters. And yet, Judith must have great strength of character. The way she had, against the wishes of her family, married Harry in Durban the moment she was twenty-one had taken courage, but it had been worth it; it was a good marriage.

Jane glanced over to Aunt Harriet. A small snoring sound was coming from the sofa. The countess was nodding, asleep over her tea cup. Jane suddenly saw her as some odd, exotic blackbird dozing on a nest. She smiled as she carefully removed the tea cup from where it was balanced on the black lace skirt.

Mary looked around the room. She straightened the anti-macassar on the back of one of the armchairs, and she carefully and quite unnecessarily straightened the lace canopy over the cot for the fifth time. She stood back, thinking of the old drawer which had served as a cradle for the father of the child who would sleep there. She smiled at her efforts; they had come a long way since those days. It had been a bit of a nuisance, but it had been important to get everything done before they went to Glasgow. On their return she would bring Judith down here with her and await the arrival of the baby. She smiled when she thought of the fight she had had with Harry over engaging a nanny. He had no objections to Judith being with Mary when the child was born, but a nanny ...

'I can look after my own, Mother,' he had said.

'Don't be daft,' she replied.

'What's wrong with you?' he had asked.

She had loved him for that, but her mind had been made up. 'I brought up my own kids, Harry, and I brought them up my way with no help from anybody. But our ways have changed a lot since then, and I don't want any rows about how to bring up thine. It's better to pay someone to do the job, and if they don't do it right tha can allus get somebody else.' And when he protested, she continued, 'Why don't thee ask Judith? She's going to have her work cut out with the new bairn. And as for being able to look after Noel thee sen, that's just stupid. Looking after kids is a full-time job, so it's a case of a nanny or a factor. Besides,' she added with contempt, 'there isn't a man alive as knows how to look after kids; they're built wrong, for a start.'

And there the argument had ended. Mary sought out and engaged Henrietta Cavandish; Judith approved, and in company with Wilson Mary left for London to get the house ready for the two great events.

Mary turned around in front of the tall dresser mirror before leaving the room. She tucked her silk print blouse more firmly into her skirt and straightened the small simple bow at the throat. It was not a stylish costume, though it suited her well enough. Mary had to look hard to find clothing that did suit. Today blouses were all flounced up in ruffles and lace down the front, and though Sam was for ever encouraging her to wear such outfits, Mary knew better. When people got to be fifty, they were as well to be their age in plain clothes, rather than be foolish in fancy outfits. Mary had seen enough mutton dressed as lamb in the withdrawing rooms of the wealthy. She had no intention of adding to their number.

Mary's skirt was grey wool, and aside from a pleat at the hem and a bow above it, it was as plain as a ladies' maid's. She could never have lived with the fluffy creations that fashionable ladies wore. How would she have been able to do anything – bend or stretch, or get down on her knees to look for dust under a bed? At times she wished she could tie a big linen apron around herself, like the kitchen maids wore, but that, she acknowledged, would be too much.

So she favoured dark, practical colours that did not show dirt – greys and browns and dull blues. Besides, they flattered her, because her skin was still clear and quite fair. What lines she had were of laughter and lines of strength, pleasant enough, though here and there was a line of suffering. The heavy streaks of grey spreading through her hair softened the once-hard effect of the blackness of it and made her eyes seem almost violet. Mary would have nothing to do with the current elaborate hair styles. She couldn't abide the need for a ladies' maid to do her hair. She still got up at six, as she had done all her life, and she could not be bothered with a sleepy girl at that hour. So she styled her hair herself, in the way all the women she had known in her youth had styled theirs – pulled straight back from a centre parting and tied in a plain round bun at the nape of her neck. It was severe, but it also had a way of pulling loose and softening itself, and the few strands that always fell loose within an hour pleased Sam.

She had a girl's figure still; being thin helped, and refusing to wear the padded, pigeon-shaped corset of the day also helped. Sam thought she looked light and fragile beside the wives of his friends and laughed to himself to think that she was stronger than any of them and tougher than most men.

She smiled as she left the room and started to make her way downstairs. She was looking forward to Glasgow. For one thing, she would see Joe again. She had seen so little of him since that awful day at Hardacres, when Sam had found that he was investing heavily in the German armament firm of Krupp. They had gone on at each other for hours – Sam raging on about the German menace and Joe laughing and telling his father that if imperial Germany could show him a profit he was going to have it. He hardly ever came to Hardacres after that.

She sighed as she thought of Joe. He had bought a house just outside of London in 1901 and settled there with Helen and their son and daughter. A year later they had a third child, Maud. Mary had gone for the birth, but apart from that had seen very little of her grandchildren. Joe and Helen did not leave London often. Apart from the constant quarrels which Joe always had with Sam, he now had an office in the City, from where he dealt with his wide-ranging interests; and Helen, once she had delegated total responsibility for her children to her staff, could endure no other life than the constant round of fashionable London café-society events.

Even when Sam had bought the house in Grosvenor Square, she saw little enough of them. But Joe was coming to Glasgow, and she would see him there. Everything was ready here, so they could go back to Hardacres tomorrow, then to Scotland and the commissioning. Back then to Hardacres to pick up Judith and on to London again for the presentation and the baby. Mary was looking forward to her second visit to the palace. The first had been when Harry had been awarded his medal for the action in South Africa. It had been presented by the Prince of Wales, now Edward VII, and it had made Sam the proudest man in the country. Even if the whole idea of Jane's coming out was a little frightening, it would be quite an experience.

H.M.S. *Monmouth* was lying in the Firth of Clyde. Both Sam and Joe had interests in the firm which had built the engines which powered her. Joe had arrived in Glasgow two days earlier, so as to be able to be on board for the last of her sea trials before she was handed over to the Royal Navy. He was taking a more and more practical interest in engineering and had spent most of the trials sweating it out with the stokers in the engine room. This had surprised Sam, who had long ago decided that his eldest son was only interested in the mechanics of turning money into more money.

The official commissioning ceremony had been held in the morning, and that evening the captain and officers held a reception on board for their, and their Lordships of the Admiralty's, guests.

The ship was anchored fore and aft and the captain's pinnace and two liberty boats ferried the guests aboard from the quay at Greenock. There was not much sea running, but to Jane the little pinnace seemed to bob about on top of the waves in a most thrilling fashion, and when they came alongside the huge, grey motionless hull of the armoured cruiser, it was as if they had reached the shore again.

There was a companionway leading from the deck down to a flat grating, on to which, it soon became apparent, Jane was expected to step. It became equally apparent that Jane was not going to make it until a tall, young sub-lieutenant jumped ahead of her and lifted her on to the grating.

'Thank you, sir,' she murmured.

'A pleasure, ma'am,' he replied, and Jane thought she

detected just the slightest trace of a soft Scottish accent in his voice. 'Perhaps if I were to precede you up the companionway? Just in case there is no one on deck to help you aboard.'

'How kind,' replied Jane.

The officer ran nimbly up the companionway on to the deck and leaned over to assist her. She grabbed at his hand as soon as she could, for in spite of its seeming steadiness when viewed from the pinnace, the ship was moving slightly. As she stepped on to the deck, she looked up at him, smiled her thanks, let go of his hand, and lurched against him.

'Please forgive me,' she said. 'I do not know what you must think of me.'

'I don't think I had better answer that,' he said, releasing her. 'Do you think you can manage to stand up now?'

He grinned, and she laughed.

'Let me introduce myself,' he continued, 'just in case you want to avoid me in the future. My name is Ian Macgregor, and I come from Scotland.'

'Why should I want to avoid you?' she replied. 'I'm Jane Hardacre, and I come from Yorkshire.' She stopped, not knowing what she should say next.

He smiled. 'Then, Miss Hardacre, may I take you to the wardroom and get you a glass of sherry? Just in case you are suffering the after-effects of your rough crossing.'

'I wish you'd take her somewhere and let the rest of us come aboard,' growled Sam from somewhere down the companionway.

'I'm awfully sorry, sir,' called Macgregor over the side, and then to Jane, 'Who's that? Do you know him?'

'That's my papa,' she replied, as he steered her away from the companionway.

'Good.'

'Why good?'

'He told me to take you away. You cannot disobey your father; come on.'

Sam clambered on to the deck and helped Mary up.

'She gets a handsome lieutenant, I have to make do wi' thee,' said Mary, looking after her daughter.

'Aye, he's a right-enough-looking chap,' said Sam. 'He's

tall enough for her, any road.'

'Sam, tha mustn't say things like that.'

'Anybody can see he fancies her,' replied Sam. 'He must have good taste.'

Actually Sam was quite impressed by the tall red-headed young man who was escorting Jane. Later in the wardroom he discovered that the gentleman in question was Sir Ian Macgregor, heir to The Macgregor of Connon in the Scottish Highlands; he was delighted to give him permission to call on Jane in London.

The party itself was nothing out of the ordinary. It consisted mainly of people standing around discussing things naval and talking of the new type of battleship, 'dreadnought', which was soon to come into service. However, Ian proved a fine host, even if, when he took the Hardacres around the ship, most of what he said fell on uncomprehending ears. At about eight the boats were alongside, and they all said goodbye. They took a cab to their hotel in Glasgow, had a late supper, and went to bed early.

The next morning they were up at five thirty and took a coach to Greenock, where they stood on the pier to watch *Monmouth*, under the white ensign, sail from the Clyde to join the fleet.

On the way back to Glasgow Jane assured them all that it was the sea spray which made her eyes red.

CHAPTER TWO

They had hired a landau for the occasion, and as it was a warm September day they were able to leave it open for the drive from Grosvenor Square to the palace, where Jane was to be received by the King and Queen. She was being chaperoned by Mary and the countess, though Mary's presence was a little unwilling.

'I allus feel so out of place among all of them swells,' she had said.

'Don't let that worry you,' the countess had replied, 'Sam Hardacre's daughter is a prize catch this season; there'll be more than a few impoverished matrons with instructions to get to know her so that their sons may be invited to her party.'

'Do people really behave like that about their own?' Mary asked.

'Indeed they do,' the countess replied. 'Some do it better than others, and I do it better than any of them.' She gave a satisfied smile.

The preparations had been going on for what had seemed months to Jane. The main item had of course been the Dress. It had been chosen with care and much deliberation. The countess had listened to everyone's suggestions and then discarded them all, relying solely on her own judgement. The Dress had to be of plain white silk, with an absolute mimimum of adornment. Tight-waisted of course, and Jane would have to suffer that instrument of torture, the body corset laced to maximum tightness, for at least the one day. It would have a plain apron front and an equally plain train, unrelieved even by a row of stitching. The mandatory fan of ostrich feathers was also plain and simple. The countess had decided that since the whole of London would be decorated to look like 'the display window of a Covent Garden flower shop, the way to make your mark, my dear, is to be as plain as a pike-staff. So no frills, no lace, no flowers, no decorations.'

As for the rest of the family, with commendable lack of courage Sam had managed to find an unbreakable business engagement for the day; Harry was up at Hardacres; Judith, who was getting very near her time, was at Grosvenor Square with a nurse in attendance; while Joe and his family, much to Helen's disgust, had not been included in the invitations.

The streets of London were crowded as they drove down Park Lane to Hyde Park Corner, narrowly missing a horse bus as they turned into Constitution Hill, where one of the new, noisy, smelly horseless carriages made one of their horses shy.

'Disgusting things,' said the countess.

'You don't really think so, Aunt Harriet,' said Jane. 'I've been trying to get Daddy to buy one for ages.'

'Joe's got two,' said Mary.

'I know,' replied Jane, 'but he won't let me learn to drive them.'

'And I should certainly hope not,' said the countess. 'That is no fitting pastime for a young lady of good breeding.'

Jane was already showing signs of an independence beyond that which was expected of a young lady of her station in life. She had, only a couple of days ago, to her mother's horror and to the delight of the countess, referred to the London season as 'that cattle market'.

'The girl's right you know,' the countess had said. 'Everyone there has a price tag, and everyone there knows exactly what it is.'

'I'm sure that I don't,' Mary replied.

'That's because you're a lady, and there's damned few of those about today,' replied the countess. 'I'm not a lady, I'm one of them. I can tell you every matron who wants her child to marry money, and those who don't want that want a title, and everybody is rated and graded according to how much they have of each.'

As for Jane, she did not care. It had come to her ears that a certain very junior officer in the Royal Navy would be at the presentation, and that was all that mattered as far as she was concerned.

Mary was naturally a little worried about leaving Judith.

255

Only that morning the doctor had told her that the birth was not imminent, but in her own mind she had decided otherwise; after all, what could any man, even if he was a doctor, know about such things? But the nurse was most competent, and the telephone was there to summon any help that would be needed and of course to inform Harry. And apart from all of that, Judith herself had threatened to go into hospital and have the baby there if Mary refused to go to court.

Their coach drove in through the palace gates and into the inner courtyard. Mary stared around her.

'By gum, it's right grand, isn't it,' she said, 'but I don't know as I'd like to live here.'

'I can assure you that their Majesties do not,' said the countess. 'Did you know that they never get a hot meal here? The kitchens are so far away from everywhere.'

The carriage door was opened for them and the step put into place by a footman in purple livery with gold-braid facings and a white periwig. They were ushered into a large anteroom whose tall windows looked out on to the gardens at the rear of the palace. The anteroom was buzzing with conversation; Jane handed her cloak to a servant and wondered how amidst all of this confusion she would ever get it back.

Mary and the countess watched her proudly as she walked assuredly around the room, greeting people whom she recognized and admiring some of the paintings which decorated the walls. A Major-domo came in and tapped with his mace on the floor; immediately all was silent.

'Ladies,' he announced, 'their Majesties will soon be entering the throne room. Will the debutantes please line up facing this door in the following order.' Here followed a list of names in strict order of precedence and, where that did not apply, in alphabetical order.

The countess ran a practised eye over the line and pursed her lips with satisfaction. She had been absolutely right; the plain severity of Jane's gown made her by far the most outstanding of all the debutantes.

Another pair of double doors opened, and the remaining ladies were invited into the throne room, where they formed

256

a wide semicircle around the low dais where the King and Queen would stand. A few moments later their Majesties arrived, the King wearing the uniform of an Admiral of the Fleet and the Queen in white with the blue Garter ribbon across her breast. The royal couple passed fairly slowly around the semicircle, pausing for a word here and there. They passed not two feet from where Mary was standing, but to her great relief did not speak to her. Then they took their station on the dais, and the presentations began.

For the first time Jane began to feel the butterflies in her tummy as the moment for her own presentation approached, but practically before she was aware of what was happening it was all over. A name spoken, hers and a touch of the royal hand.

'Charming,' murmured the King, and Queen Alexandra gave her a little smile.

Then she was out of their presence and into another room, which seemed to be overflowing with young men in military and naval mess kits, all looking very smart and all looking very predatory.

He must have been staring at the door since the first debutante had emerged, because she was barely two paces inside the room when Ian Macgregor was by her side, heading off two Lancers, a Guardsman, a Dragoon and a Hussar.

'Hello, Miss Hardacre,' he said, 'what can I get you?'

'First a chair and then, if you can find it, some tea,' she replied calmly, suppressing the excitement she felt at seeing him again.

Ian soon found her a seat and brought her tea.

'You will be at the ball?' he said.

'Of course.'

'You wouldn't by any chance have your dance card with you?' There was a note of entreaty in his voice.

Jane produced the item from her reticule.

'How many may I have?' he asked, taking the gold-tasselled card from her.

'Three.'

'Only?' he was disappointed.

'Well,' she said, 'how about ...'

257

'All of them?'

'Every other one.'

'Including the first and last waltz?'

'Agreed.'

They both laughed, and he wrote his name opposite the appropriate dances.

As soon as the last presentation had been made, Mary and the countess joined them. Mary asked Ian to call, and the conversation was going its pleasant, inconsequential way when a footman came over to their table.

'Mrs Hardacre?' he enquired.

'Aye, that's me,' replied Mary.

'There is a message for you, madam,' he said, handing her a folded piece of paper.

Mary held it, embarrassed. She did not want to admit, in front of Ian Macgregor, that she would probably not be able to read it. Seeing what was happening, the countess leapt to the rescue.

'Mary, don't tell me that you've forgotten your glasses again? Really, you are too naughty; give me the note, and I'll read it for you.'

Mary handed her the note with a grateful smile.

'Oh,' said the countess, 'I'm afraid that you will have to go home.'

'The baby?' said Mary.

The countess nodded. 'I'll stay here with Jane, but I think that you had better go right away.'

'Shouldn't we all go?' asked Jane.

'Whatever for?' demanded the countess. 'What possible purpose could your presence serve? Besides, just look at Sir Ian's face.'

'I must say that I hope you don't have to leave, Miss Hardacre,' he said.

'Of course she must stay,' said Mary. 'I'm used to this sort of thing, and if owt went wrong thou'd only be in the way. Tell King I'm sorry I couldn't wait if he asks after me.' They all smiled as she left them.

'I'm terribly sorry that your mama had to go,' Ian said to Jane. 'My parents are in town, and I had hoped that we might have been able to get them together during the evening.'

'Well, don't worry about that, young man,' said the countess, 'why don't you bring them all round to tea tomorrow; I'll wager that you know where to find us.'

'But what about the baby?' asked Ian.

'Fiddlesticks,' said the countess, 'it's only just being born, or it might even be a false alarm, and in any case babies are very small and don't require a whole house; one room is ample.'

Mary found that getting out of the place was not as easy as she had thought and soon lost her way in the many corridors. At last she met a young naval officer, who seemed to know his way around.

'Young man,' she said, 'how dost a body get out of here?' she asked.

He proceeded to lead her, and as she explained her reason for leaving, he quickened his pace, but when they found a servant and the young man told him to get a carriage from the mews, Mary began to have suspicions.

'Might I ask who you are, sir?' enquired Mary.

'My name's George, I'm the Duke of York,' said the young man.

'Oh, please forgive me, Your Royal Highness,' said Mary.

'It was a pleasure,' said the Duke smiling. 'I think your carriage is here now, and good luck with your grandchild.'

Mary got to Grosvenor Square to find that Judith had gone into labour about an hour ago but it did not seem as if anything was imminent yet; the doctor had been summoned and would be there at any moment. Harry had been informed by telephone and would leave Hardacres for London first thing in the morning, as it was too late for him to get to York to catch the night train. Mary went straight in to see Judith and found her sitting up in bed quite bright and cheerful.

'When did it start?' asked Mary.

'I got the first pain about an hour ago,' replied Judith. 'I told them not to bother you; really, I am very well looked after, and nurse is so attentive – you could have enjoyed your evening.'

'I'd rather be here,' said Mary, and then as Judith stiffened in pain, 'Grab hold of summat and holler if thee wants to,' she said. 'There's nowt like a good yell to make it easier, especially when there aren't men about to think tha's dying.'

There was a tap at the door, and the doctor and nurse came in. They made a quick examination and asked one or two questions.

'Well, I don't think it will be here for an hour or so,' said the doctor, straightening up, 'so we will just have to sit it out.'

'That being the case, I'll go and arrange for a pot of tea,' said Mary.

Mary went below stairs and found cook. There was quite an air of excitement below stairs, and the servants plied her with questions about how it was going. She arranged for tea to be sent up, together with little sandwiches and cakes.

'I don't know about Judith, but I'm allus starving after I've had a baby,' she said.

Mary went back upstairs and then settled down to wait. Vanessa Judith Hardacre was born just before midnight. There were no complications, and the doctor pronounced a fine, healthy seven-pound baby girl.

At two o'clock in the morning Jane arrived home with the countess. They crept into the house and went into the sitting room, where they found Mary still up and about.

'It's a girl,' she said in answer to their unspoken question, 'and the tea in the pot should still be hot.'

'And Judith?' asked Jane.

'Grand,' said Mary, as the countess poured tea for the three of them. 'Now I want to hear all about the ball and that young man of yours.'

It was a somewhat garbled account of the evening but co-herent enough for Mary to gather that her daughter had had a wonderful evening and that Ian's parents were likely to call that afternoon and that Ian was the most handsome and gallant and dashing young officer in the whole of the United Kingdom.

Harry arrived in the early afternoon, just as they were finishing lunch. He found his wife sitting up in bed drinking a cup of tea with his sister while his mother sat in the arm-chair holding the baby.

When Harry came in Mary put the infant into the bed beside Judith.

'Come on, Jane,' she said.

'But, mummy, I ...'

'Come wi' me. If those two don't want to be alone together now, there's summat wrong with them. Come on.'

Judith smiled her thanks as Mary steered Jane out of the room. Harry, who had not yet said a word, came over to the bed and looked at his daughter. How that red, wrinkled piece of living humanity would ever grow into anything resembling a human being was for the moment beyond his comprehension.

'What do you think of her?' whispered Judith.

'She's beautiful, just like you,' Harry lied manfully, 'and her eyes are just as beautiful.'

'But Harry, she's asleep,' said Judith.

'I can tell, though,' said Harry, and they both laughed. Judith knew what Harry was thinking and also from past experience that within a week or two he would be boring everyone with his tales of how wonderful and beautiful his daughter was.

'How about you?' he asked. 'I must say you look well enough, and your colour's fine.'

'I feel great,' she replied. 'A little weak and a bit warm, but otherwise I'm fine. How is everybody at Hardacres?'

'Well, they all send you their love, that goes without saying. Noel is helping his grandfather to build a tree house in the garden.'

'I hope that he's not being a nuisance.'

'Oh, no. Dad's loving every minute of it. Joe arrived the day before yesterday; he apparently wants to talk business with the old man. It seems that he's got a fellow who designs flying machines and he wants to build one. He wants to do it in Yorkshire and at Hardacres because there's plenty of room and privacy.'

But Judith had gone to sleep. Harry let go of her hand and drew the blankets up over her. He kissed her lightly on the lips.

'Good night,' he murmured.

Harry tiptoed out of the room. The nurse was sitting on a chair by the door.

'Are you coming back, Mr Hardacre?' she asked.

'I'm going to see the others,' said Harry. 'My wife is asleep.'

'Then I'll just go and sit with her in case either of them needs anything,' she said.

'Thank you, nurse,' said Harry and went off in search of the others.

CHAPTER THREE

It was some time past midnight that there was a sharp knocking on Harry's door.

They had all retired early. It had been a most exhausting day for everyone, and none of them had had much sleep the night before. The Macgregors had called as arranged, armed with an invitation for the whole family to pay them a visit in the Highlands of Scotland the following month. After that they had tactfully left (it was quite obvious that the Hardacres were a very tired family), declining an invitation to stay on for dinner. Indeed, it was very shortly after dinner that they had started to drift off to bed.

'Mr Hardacre, Mr Hardacre, are you awake?' It was a strange woman's voice.

'Who's there?' called Harry.

'It's the night nurse' was the reply.

Harry was out of bed in a flash. He flung on a dressing gown and opened the door.

'What is it?' he demanded, 'is it Mrs Hardacre?'

'I think we should call the doctor, sir,' said the girl.

Harry pushed past the nurse and across the corridor into Judith's room. He turned up the gas light and went over to her bed.

'She's asleep,' he whispered.

'Yes, sir, but she's very restless, and just look at her face.'

Judith was flushed, and a fine perspiration was evident on her brow.

'Is it too warm in here?' asked Harry.

'No, sir, I don't think so, sir,' said the nurse. 'It might be a fever, sir, that's why I thought we'd better call a doctor.'

'Right,' said Harry, 'I'll telephone for him immediately.'

He ran downstairs to the telephone in the hall and asked for the doctor's number.

'There doesn't seem to be any reply,' said the operator.

'Keep ringing,' said Harry, 'they're probably asleep.'

At last the sleepy voice of a woman answered. 'Hello,' it said.

'Can I speak to Dr Johnson?' said Harry. 'I'm sorry, but this is an emergency.'

'There is no Doctor Johnson here,' said the voice, 'this is Mr Worthing's residence.'

Harry apologized and hung up. He was annoyed, and it did his temper no good when it took him about three or four minutes to get the operator again. He envisaged her sitting talking and giggling with the other operators, drinking tea while bells rang or lights flashed and emergencies all over London were ignored. When he finally got her again, he gave her Doctor Johnson's number and, through gritted teeth, demanded that she stay on the line until she was sure that a satisfactory connection had been made.

'Hello?' It was the calm, unemotional voice of the doctor, giving no hint that he had just been roused from a good night's sleep. 'This is Doctor Johnson speaking.'

'Hardacre here,' said Harry. 'Doctor, could you possibly come round to Grosvenor Square – I know it's late, but ...'

'One moment, young man,' said the doctor. 'You have a night nurse?'

'Yes,' he said, 'it was she who asked me to call you.'

'Oh,' said the doctor's voice, 'I was going to ask if I might have a word with her, but in that case I'll come over immediately.'

The doctor rang off, and Harry went back to Judith's room. 'Where's the baby?' he asked, noticing for the first time that the child was not in the bedroom.

'I took her into the dressing room, sir,' said the nurse. 'I thought that if Mrs Hardacre had an infection it might be as well for the baby to be kept in another room.'

The use of the word infection hit Harry hard. He had the usual useless layman's knowledge of things medical, but every parent dreaded the post-natal fever which could strike down an apparently healthy mother twenty-four hours after the birth of her child. 'Not that,' he prayed, 'dear God, not that.'

His morbid thoughts were interrupted by the arrival of Mary.

'What's going on?' she demanded. 'Telephones ringing and people shouting all over the place, a body can't get no sleep.'

'It's Judith, Mother,' said Harry. 'Nurse thinks she may have a fever.'

'Oh,' said Mary, suddenly serious. 'What is it, nurse?'

'She's sweating,' was the reply. 'I thought we had better call doctor.'

'I suppose that was all that telephoning I heard,' said Mary.

'Yes, Mother.'

'Well, you'd better let me have a look at her till the doctor gets here.'

Mary went over to the bed and looked at Judith; she put her hand on her brow.

'Well, she's certainly hot,' she said. 'Girl, thou go down to the kitchen and get me a bowl of water and some plain clean tea towels. Harry, you'd better get thy sen downstairs and wait for the doctor,' and as Harry hesitated, 'Now be off with you; I'll call you if she wakes.'

Harry spent the next fifteen minutes walking between the foot of the stairs and the front door, opening it frequently and looking out on the deserted streets.

At last Dr Johnson arrived. He went straight up to Judith's room, followed closely by Harry. He asked everyone to leave except for the nurse. Mary led Harry away and made tea for them all.

About ten minutes later the doctor came downstairs.

'You can go up now, Mr Hardacre,' he said. 'She is awake and wants to see you. She will not be awake long, for I have given her a sleeping draught which should see her through the night.'

Harry left the doctor with Mary.

'The lass is proper poorly, isn't she?' said Mary.

'I'm afraid she is,' said the doctor. 'I believe that her own parents are not in London?'

'That's right, they're in Yorkshire,' replied Mary.

'I think they had better be informed. Are they on the

telephone?'

'It's real serious, then,' said Mary.

'A fever after childbirth is never a light matter,' said the doctor, 'but the next few days will tell.'

Harry went into Judith's bedroom. She was lying back on the pillows and breathing quite heavily. He went over to her and sat down on the side of the bed. She had one hand outside the coverlet; Harry took this into his own and gently kissed the slender white fingers.

'Where's my baby?' she whispered.

'She's sleeping,' said Harry.

'I'd like to call her Vanessa,' said Judith, 'I don't know why – do you like the name?'

'I think it's a lovely name, darling; Vanessa it shall be.'

'You're a good husband, Harry,' she murmured.

'You're a good wife, sweetheart.'

There was no reply.

'She'll be asleep now,' said the nurse quietly. 'Why don't you go and get some rest? I'll call you if she asks for you.'

Harry went downstairs to the sitting room; Mary poured him out tea.

'Mr Hardacre,' said Dr Johnson, 'I should be doing less than my duty if I were not to warn you that your wife's condition gives cause for concern. I must return home now, but I shall be back tomorrow morning. I think that the sleeping draught will ensure a peaceful night, but if she should ... well, nurse will know whether to call me.'

'Thank you, doctor,' said Harry, leading him to the door. He was reacting like a man who was punch-drunk.

'Harry, get thee off to bed,' said Mary when he returned. 'You heard the doctor, there's nowt that can be done tonight.'

The next morning it seemed to Mary that Judith was weaker, so she telephoned the doctor at about eight o'clock. That was the time that the day nurse took over; she sat with Judith, applying cold compresses to her while Harry paced the room, waiting desperately for somebody to give him something to do, even when it was only to go and get another basin of cold water. Throughout, Mary was calm and in perfect control of the situation. The countess, on realizing what was happening, had tactfully retired to her room; this she accepted as a purely family matter where even she was better out of the way.

Poor Jane had been planning to go to lunch with the Macgregors but now felt it incumbent on her to stay at home until Mary turned on her and said, 'Go and have thy lunch, I'd a damned sight sooner not have thee under my feet.' They were hard words, but they worked, and Jane kept her luncheon appointment.

At eleven o'clock Sam arrived from Hardacres, followed fifteen minutes later by the doctor. Dr Johnson was more than half an hour with Judith; when he came down and let Harry go into her room, his face was grave. He took Sam over to a corner.

'Mr Hardacre, I fear that you are going to have to prepare your family for the worst.'

'You mean?'

'I mean that she is not responding to treatment, Mr Hardacre.'

'We're going to lose her?'

'I think so.'

'How long?' asked Sam.

'It could be hours, a couple of days at the most, unless there's a miracle.'

'Well, we can only pray for that,' said Sam. 'Meantime, will thee stay, doctor?'

'There's nothing that I can do.'

'Oh, aye, there is,' said Sam. 'When this is over, that lad's got to live with this. He's got to believe that everything possible is being done, and even if everything is nothing, it hasn't got to look like that.'

The doctor smiled. 'All right, Mr Hardacre, I understand; I'll stay.'

'Thank you, doctor,' said Sam. 'I'd better go up and tell Harry.'

He started upstairs as the telephone rang. Mary answered it. 'Mrs Hardacre here,' she said, and then, 'Lady Bainton, I wouldn't bother to have lunch first if I were thee, I think thou'd better get over here now; I don't know the full story,

267

but she's very, very ill.'

Sam went upstairs to Judith's room. He paused for quite a while before knocking.

'Come in.' It was Harry's voice.

He opened the door. Harry was sitting on the bed holding Judith's hand in both of his. She might have been asleep; anyway, she did not react to Sam's presence.

'Harry,' Sam spoke in a whisper, 'is Judith asleep?'

'I don't know, Dad; she hasn't spoken for some time,' replied Harry.

'Can thee come out for a minute?'

Tenderly Harry put Judith's hand down on the coverlet and came over to the door.

'I'm sorry, lad, but I've got to talk to thee. I think it would be better if tha came down to the study with me.'

Sam led his son down to the study, a leathery room set apart for Sam's exclusive use when he was in London. Harry followed his father, knowing that this was something important. Sam always reverted to his thees and thous when he was under stress.

In the study Sam motioned Harry to sit down and went to a drinks table which was stocked with three decanters and an array of glasses.

'Brandy?' asked Sam.

'No, thanks, Dad, it's much too early.'

Sam poured himself out a stiff one and then sat down facing Harry.

'Harry, boy, Judith's dying,' he said. It had to be said, and this was Sam Hardacre's way, straight out. He did not believe that breaking it gently was going to help his son at all.

Harry sat in silence for a long time; not a muscle of his face moved, and when he spoke it was very quietly. 'Are you quite sure?'

'Tha can talk to doctor if tha wants to, but he told me, not half an hour ago, that only a miracle would save her.'

'I think I'll have that brandy,' said Harry, going to the decanter and helping himself. 'Did he say how long?'

'A couple of days.' Sam looked up at his son's face. 'Don't

try and bottle it up, lad; go ahead and cry, Harry – I've cried in my time. There are few things in life that are worth a tear, but when you meet up with one don't be afraid of it. Come on now, boy, don't fight it; a good blub'll not make thee less of a man.'

Harry fell to his knees beside his father and wept. Sam put his arm around his son and sat silently gazing into the fire and trying to drive the bitterness from his heart.

'Lady Bainton is here, ma'am,' said the maid. 'I've put her in the parlour.'

'All right,' said Mary, 'I'll see to her.'

She went to the hall, where she found Lady Bainton waiting impatiently.

'Where is my daughter?' she demanded.

'I'll ask nurse if thee can see her,' said Mary. 'Thou'll have to wait here till I find out.'

'Very well, but please hurry, I'm already late for an appointment.'

Mary choked back an angry retort and went out. The nurse on duty in Judith's room told her that Judith had been asking for Harry.

'Where is he?' she asked.

'I don't know, madam,' said the nurse. 'He went downstairs with the master.'

Mary ran downstairs to the study and knocked on the door.

'Who is it?' asked Sam's voice.

'It's me, Mary; Judith's asking for Harry. Is he with you?'

The door opened, and Harry went out and up the stairs. He went straight past his mother without any sign or acknowledgement.

'Tha told him?' Mary asked.

'Aye,' said Sam.

'How was he?'

'He took it hard, lass, very hard indeed,' said Sam.

'Her mother's here,' said Mary.

'Oh?' said Sam. 'We could have done without yon.'

'It's a bloody shame,' said Mary, sniffing and wiping her

eyes, 'but I'd better go and see to the baby; we mu'nt forget that one.'

'What about Her Ladyship?' asked Sam.

'I suppose I'd better take her up for a minute first.'

Mary hurried away to the parlour to collect Lady Bainton, and to her surprise and annoyance found that she was no longer there. There was of course only one place that she could have gone, and so Mary hurried after her to Judith's room. She opened the door to find Harry, pale-faced with fists clenched so that the knuckles showed white, standing by the bed beside Judith, who was awake and facing an irate Lady Bainton.

'Please, Mama,' Judith was speaking in a thin little voice, 'we haven't got very long, don't you understand? I just want to be with Harry.'

'None of this would ever have happened if you had not got yourself mixed up with a family of fish-quay louts in the first place. I wonder if you realize the distress and annoyance this unfortunate marriage has caused both your father and myself ... and another thing ...'

She got no further. Mary had stepped up behind her and grabbed her by the arm, twisting it up behind her back.

'Say one more word and I'll break thy arm,' hissed Mary into her ear. 'Your mother's just going, Judith.' Then, again dropping her voice to a whisper, 'Now smile at thy daughter and wish her well.'

'Get well soon, Judith, dear,' gasped Lady Bainton, 'I, I ... really must go now.'

Mary steered her out of the room and closed the door. Lady Bainton opened her mouth to speak.

'Say one word here where that lass can hear thee and I'll knock tha teeth in,' hissed Mary, tightening her grip on the other's arm.

'You are hurting me.'

'Good,' said Mary, 'now get thee downstairs; I've a word or two to say to thee before thou goes.'

Mary guided her into the parlour, where she at last released her.

'Now just you listen to me, my good woman,' Lady Bainton started.

'Thou'd better shut up and listen to me, thou bitch.' There was genuine hatred in Mary's voice.

'I shall leave this house immediately.'

Mary drew back her hand as if she was about to strike the other woman across the face. 'Thou'll go nowhere till I've finished with thee.'

'I suppose you realize that I could take you to court over this behaviour.'

'At another time thou would make me laugh, but there is no place for laughter in this house today. Woman, don't thee know thy daughter's dying!' she almost shouted.

Lady Bainton stopped with her mouth open as if she had been hit. Her lip trembled. 'It's not true, for God's sake tell me it's not true.'

'I only wish I could.'

'Dear God in heaven, what have I done?'

'Thou's made a right bloody mess of everything as far as I can see,' said Mary, and suddenly her tone softened. 'Now, if thou wants to stay here, there's a room been prepared for thee so that thou can be near if she wants to see thee at all. But you've got to understand that it's what she wants that counts, nowt else; lass is dying, and the only other thing that anyone of us can do is to pray for a miracle.'

'But I can't stay here.'

'Whyever not?'

'After what I have said, how could I face her, I couldn't do it.'

'What else can thee do?' asked Mary, her tone hardening. 'Walk out and leave her?'

'I must. It's all I can do. Mrs Hardacre, I shall not ask for your forgiveness, nor that of my daughter, for I am well aware that I shall never forgive myself. Good-bye, Mrs Hardacre, I doubt that we shall ever see each other again.'

Lady Bainton left Mary, who looked after her with growing disgust.

Mary went off in search of her new granddaughter; the poor mite was being neglected, overshadowed as she was by the tragedy that stalked through the house.

Harry sat by his wife's bedside, changing the compresses against her brow, hoping against hope every time Dr Johnson came into the room, waiting and praying for the word or a sign that there was a chance, but no sign came.

It was late, halfway through the night, when Judith awoke and turned to him.

'Harry,' she said, 'is it you?'

'What is it, my darling?'

'Harry,' her voice was very quiet, barely a whisper. 'I feel better now, I have to go away for a while, look after my babies, and Harry . . .'

'Yes?' he dared not say more.

'Take me back to Hardacres.'

Her eyes closed, her face relaxed; Harry looked down at her, so peaceful, so beautiful, as silently she went to eternity.

CHAPTER FOUR

Judith had her wish; they took her back to Hardacres and laid her to rest in the family vault. Sam had had it constructed a couple of years back; he said it gave him a feeling of permanence. He had had a clearing made in the woods about half a mile from the house, and there fashioned a vault out of massive blocks of granite brought down from Scotland. It was to be a last resting place for his family for generations to come – but he had always believed that he would be its first occupant.

At the insistence of Sam, Mary, and Harry, Jane had stayed on in London for the remainder of the season. The countess stayed with her as chaperone on the party round. Harry had insisted that his sister should not go into mourning during the autumn in which she was entering society for the first time. To the delight of all concerned, Jane continued to see a great deal of Ian Macgregor, and the countess watched with approval as their friendship blossomed into romance. Sam and Mary, for their part, were highly flattered by the manner in which they were accepted by the Macgregors and the contrast to their experience with the Baintons.

It was late October, and Harry had been a widower for nearly a month. It was a dull, cold autumn. He remembered how he had first come to Hardacres. He had been a young boy in the grey, cold turning of the year. That season would always have a special meaning for him. Now it would have a new meaning.

For a while he had thought of leaving the place altogether, having decided in those first days of loneliness that he could not bear to live there without Judith. But it had been a hopeless desire – dramatic but useless. There was nowhere to go. Whatever his feelings, he had to live on without her. It was the land which kept reminding him. His farm workers, after the first week of polite murmured condolences and raised caps, began shuffling around uneasily when they saw him approach and awaited his instructions. Eventually his head ploughman announced bluntly that what did not get done in the autumn would have to be done in the spring. Winter would not wait for Harry Hardacre this or any other year.

Harry had been momentarily furious that neither his rank nor his grief were being respected. But the old ploughman stood impassive before him, sucking on his clay pipe and meeting Harry's angry gaze with quiet, kind eyes. Harry remembered that the old man had lost a son in the Boer War and an infant granddaughter to measles last winter. It had seemed little more than passing gossip at the time, but Harry was suddenly ashamed. He had neglected people in the past, and now he was neglecting the land.

He sent his ploughmen out the next day, and early in the morning they began turning the pasture that he and Judith had ridden across in the early spring.

He sat now, on his grey gelding, on a rise above the fields, watching the two teams of Clydesdales working slowly towards each other from opposite ends of the pasture. The morning sun was above the hill now, slanting across the lightly frosted ground, gleaming on the freshly turned furrows. Harry sat for a long time, watching the lines of dark earth closing in, wiping out the green. Before the two teams could meet, he turned his horse and rode off.

He rode down past the ruddy stubble of the oat field, where his Jersey cows were grazing on the remnants of the crop. Another time he would have stopped to enjoy the soft buff colours of the cows and straw, but now he could not. He cantered past the silver stubble of the barley field and under the brown, crusty, dead leaves of the birch wood. He wished there was something young and green and still growing, but he could find nothing. Even the lawns were greying in the melting frost. Mary's rose garden was scraggy with broken, spoiled blossoms, brown and decaying.

Harry trotted his horse briskly around the house and left it with a groom at the entrance to the mews. He hoped, ashamedly, that Noel would be with his grandmother and he would not have to face him. Mary seemed to be able to explain to him, to remind him gently, that the games he played in which Mummy always came back from London were not, after all, going to come true.

Then she would hold him and comfort him when he cried. Harry could do none of those things; he found himself even without the strength to be loving. Baby Vanessa – he reminded himself of her name – though to him she was a thing that was sexless, soulless, and joyless, was another matter. Deep down he knew that he would have to face her soon, before she was old enough to realize that he resented her and considered her no fair exchange for his wife. He tried to think of Judith and how she would have loved her baby, as they had both loved their first. He knew that Judith would have wanted him to love the infant twice as much, now that she was motherless. It was easy to say, and for other people to say. It was quite another thing to do it.

He determined to make an effort. He would go to the nursery today, now. He would hold the baby, talk to it, try to feel loving. He came in through the back door, by the kitchen, stood his riding crop into the umbrella stand, and struggled out of his riding boots. It was difficult, but to ask the help of a servant would mean talking to somebody. He stood the boots in a corner and limped, in his stockinged feet, across the flagstone floor to the back stairs. His leg was always stiffer after riding.

Hetty Cavandish was in the nursery, arranging the delicate silk organza canopy over the cradle. The cradle had just arrived from London that morning. Mrs Hardacre had specially requested that it be packed up in the house in Grosvenor Square and put on the train. She had insisted that her own daughter, Jane, personally do the packing. Hetty smiled, thinking of it. Jane Hardacre was such a lady, it was hard to imagine her nailing up a packing case. But Mrs Hardacre would trust no one with the cradle, and besides, she had assured Hetty that Jane, despite appearances, was surprisingly quite handy with masculine things such as tools and leather harness. Hard to imagine though, all the same.

Mrs Hardacre had personally unpacked the box and seen

that all was in order before Hetty was allowed to make up the bedding for Vanessa. Not that there was not a perfectly good, indeed very fine, cherrywood cradle at Hardacres already. But this new one had been the poor mother's delight in London, and now Mary Hardacre insisted that the baby should have it here.

It certainly was pretty, Hetty thought, lifting the woollen-shawl-wrapped bundle that was the sleeping Vanessa from her old cradle to her new one. She wrapped the shawl tighter, then piled coverlet after coverlet on top, so that the baby became a woolly mound. The room was not cold, with the roaring coal fire in the hearth, but one had to be so careful, particularly when the baby was not one's own. Hetty was conscious of the depth of her responsibility. She had known Harry Hardacre before, and liked him, and she knew him now. The difference was appalling and a measure of what he was suffering. Surely this baby was very, very important to him.

The baby was very dear to Hetty already, as was the older boy, Noel. It was natural for Hetty to love children; she was warm, giving, and with thoughts that did not stray from hearth and home. She made a good nanny, and it never occurred to her that she would have made an equally good mother. But children were not possible without marriage, and Hetty at thirty had passed the marrying age in her society. It had passed so quickly, that age; a few dances, a few house parties, but mostly a lot of hard work on her father's farm. She had older sisters; they had been their father's concern, and they had married. Then, suddenly, all the girls she had known at the village school were wives and mothers. Hetty knew the pattern her life would take already. Hopefully, she would have thirteen or fourteen years with the Hardacres. Then, when the children passed the age of needing her, she would move on and raise someone else's family. And in a series of half generations she would fill her life. In the end, no doubt she would finish on her parents' farm again – perhaps sooner, should they become ill or infirm. As the youngest daughter she would be expected to become their nursemaid.

Hetty tried not to think of that, or of much of the future, or of its possible uncertainties. Most of all, she tried not to think of the lurking potential of dismissal. She was a surrogate mother, she knew, who, at the whim or convenience of the master or some future mistress, could be dismissed in a day without notice. Another woman might one morning dress the children she had tucked into bed the night before. It was not a thing a woman like Hetty would choose to think about.

There was a rap on the nursery door, light but firm – not a servant's hand. Hetty said, come in, and the door opened. Harry Hardacre was standing there in his riding breeches and stockinged feet.

It was obvious that he had been out of doors, Hetty thought; you only had to look at his face. The frosty wind had given a ruddy colour to his cheeks, and his black hair was tangled and shaggy. Hetty had always thought him a handsome man; she thought, too, that in spite of his polished accent and manner, he looked, with his lean working-man's features and dark hair, like any Yorkshire farmer.

Hetty stepped back from the cradle, lifting the canopy above the sleeping baby.

'She's just down after her bath, Mr Hardacre,' she said, 'but I'll lift her for you if you like.'

Harry was still standing in the doorway, not speaking. Hetty suddenly realized that he was in a tearing fury. He seized her arm and turned her towards him, twisting her wrist so that she cried out with pain. That brought him up short; he dropped his hands and hesitated, obviously shocked at having hurt a woman but still furious. Trying hard to control his voice, he said, 'What right, what possible right have you to even touch that cradle?'

Hetty looked at him in amazement. She did not know what to say or do; she just stood there, holding her sore wrist, incredulous.

Harry said, 'Where did you get it? It was in London. How did it get here?'

'Mrs Hardacre sent for it, sir,' she said in a small voice.

'She told me ...' Hetty stopped, confused, not wanting to make it worse. She wanted to cry. No gentle person had ever treated her like that before.

Harry stood, his hands hanging at his sides, not looking at Hetty, trying not to look at the cradle either. He remembered it so well, standing beside Judith's bed in London and how they had taken it from the room when she was dying because she kept asking for the baby they could not give her to hold.

His anger – rare, and always fleeting – was gone. He looked around the nursery, at Noel's rocking horse, the toy train and the soldiers. At the small head of the sleeping baby. At the nanny, Hetty, with her round face and her trembling lips. A strand of hair had come loose from her bun and was hanging to her shoulder. Absurdly he noticed that it was a pretty colour, like the fur of a small field mouse.

He said, 'I'm sorry, Miss Cavandish. It wasn't your fault. I should have made my wishes better known. The cradle belonged to my wife, and I do not want it in the house. It will be removed tomorrow.' He was turning to go, expecting no answer, when Hetty spoke.

'No.'

He turned back, amazed. 'What did you say?'

'No, Mr Hardacre. The cradle wasn't your wife's. It is not hers now. It belongs to Vanessa. You cannot take it from her.'

Harry swallowed hard, fighting back his anger. 'Vanessa's? What possible difference can it make to her? She's just a baby. She can't care. Why should she have it?'

'Because it is hers,' Hetty said quietly. 'Your wife gave it to her. It's hers by right. Remember that she's a person too, Mr Hardacre.' Hetty was finding strength, the strength of hopelessness. She knew that her position here was lost already. She would be dismissed, but until Harry Hardacre threw her out of the door, she would fight for the children and what was theirs. 'And so is your son, not that you'd notice, for all the time you've given him. You haven't been here more than twice since you came from London. When you meet your son, you hardly give him a hello. You are the only parent he's got, God help him.'

278

Hetty was crying, and Harry, his fists clenching in frustration, stormed at her. 'Shut up, woman. I've lost my wife. I can't take this.'

'And they've just lost their mother. Have you thought of that, Mr Hardacre? You still have your mother, but Noel's not seven yet, and he's lost his. Now you want to take away your poor dead wife's gift to her daughter because it reminds you of your own loss. How do you think she'd take that? Have you thought? Have you ever thought about *her*, or do you only think of yourself, Mr Hardacre?' she shouted down the corridor, because Harry had turned and was running in his stockinged feet down the hallways of his own house.

Hetty did not leave, and the next morning a very subdued Harry came to the nursery to collect Noel. Hetty looked out of the nursery window and smiled at the sight of the pair of them as they walked around the house, hand in hand, in the direction of the mews.

Shortly after this, when Hardacres was managing to get back to a kind of normality, a formal invitation to visit the Macgregors arrived.

After expressing sympathy for their recent bereavement, Lord Macgregor went on to say that he hoped the family would find it possible to accept an invitation to spend a week or two at Castle Connon in the Scottish Highlands. He was aware that the request came at an unusual time, but he was thinking mainly of Ian and Jane. He concluded:

I trust that you will not regard this as an impertinence, but I do feel that in view of the obvious affection in which these two young people hold each other, we should put aside personal griefs and give them an opportunity to get to know each other away from the artificial environment of London.

It was Harry who finally persuaded them to accept. He insisted that his own loss should not be a bar to the possible future happiness of his sister. This argument, backed up by a letter from the countess, clinched the matter, and it was agreed that Sam and Mary would travel up from York and that Jane and the countess would go straight to Scotland in company with the Macgregors.

Leaving London, Jane was suitably impressed at the two private railway coaches, one for the family and one for the servants, which were attached, together with their private baggage van, to the Edinburgh train at Kings Cross Station. Lord Macgregor explained to Jane that these had been built by his father, who discovered that it was cheaper to move his eight children by private coach than to pay for individual tickets. The interior of the coach was beautifully furnished as a sitting room cum dining room. There was a series of separate, tiny bedrooms containing one or two beds each, and finally a kitchen where the Macgregors' own chef prepared their food.

They were going north for the stalking. The Macgregors owned a deer forest, and every year starting in late September they shot a limited number of stags, which provided venison for the table and trophies for the walls. Jane had to confess that, as far as she was aware, her father had never shot anything in his life, but she had no doubt that he would have a go.

It was for this reason that, a week later, one morning at about eight o'clock, Sam found himself, wet and miserable lying in soaking bracken and wearing a borrowed suit, looking down the sights of a borrowed rifle at somebody else's stag and listening to his gillie's orders.

'Now, sorr.'

Sam heaved at the trigger, there was the customary bang, the stag looked up, and then in company with his companions ran off.

'Ye missed, sorr,' said the gillie, who went by the name of Donnie.

'I suppose that we might as well go back now,' said Sam, who was quite determined to do the absolute minimum that honour would permit.

'Aye,' said Donnie, nodding his head and pitying his sassenach charge; they were not the same breed as the highlander. 'We might as weel go hame. I doubt if we'll find another beast within five miles.'

'Oh, what a pity,' lied Sam.

'We could try another hill,' said Donnie. 'This will be our fourth miss.'

'Perhaps tomorrow,' said Sam, not wishing to talk himself into any more.

'Do you wish to carry the gun, sorr?' asked Donnie.

'Eh?'

'Most of my gentlemen let me have it, so that I shall not forget to clean it.'

Gratefully Sam took the hint and handed the gun to Donnie.

'And then they are able to have a wee dram when their hands are free. It is necessary to keep out the cold for the journey home,' continued Donnie.

Obediently, Sam took out Ian Macgregor's hip flask. He took a generous swig himself, then passed the flask to Donnie and watched with unconcealed admiration as the gillie drained the entire contents in one swallow.

'That should see us home,' said Donnie, returning the empty flask to Sam.

It took a good hour of trudging through the fine drizzle and the knee-high bracken before they rounded the base of their hill and Castle Connon came into welcome view.

The castle was not a real castle; it was built more on the lines of a French chateau, with many little round turrets topped by spiky, slated roofs. It had been built at the beginning of the nineteenth century by the present Macgregor's great-grandfather to replace the ruin of old Castle Connon, which had been the ancestral home of the Macgregors centuries before.

Jane had been enchanted the first time she had seen the house.

'Why,' she had said, 'it looks just like the fairy castles in my old picture books.'

She delighted in her room, which had one of the little circular turrets in one corner. She could stand there and look

281

down the beautiful glen of Strathconnon and across to the mountains where the first snows had already fallen on their peaks.

One of the most unusual features of the house was the Caledonian pines. They had been planted in a perfect circle around the main building, and now, a hundred years later, they towered to heights of over a hundred feet, with their trunks having a girth of some eight feet. Mary had been so impressed on her first sight of them that she could not restrain herself from remarking to Sam that the way things were going they might all belong to Jane and Ian one day.

Sam dragged his dripping body through the circle of trees, across the lawn, and into the house. There he changed into dry things and wondered about the Scottish aristocracy who could find pleasure in such masochistic pursuits. He was due to meet The Macgregor in his study, so as soon as he was changed he went down.

Lord Macgregor was waiting for him and invited him to sit down by a blazing log fire. Sam accepted gratefully.

'Well, Hardacre, I thought it would be a good idea if you and I had a little chat before the party this evening.'

'Party?' said Sam.

'Yes, we're giving a little dinner in your honour.'

'That's right nice of you, Lord Macgregor.'

'Please call me Angus, and if I may, I'll call you Sam,' he said. 'The way things are going, it looks as if we'll be related very shortly.'

'Aye,' said Sam, tugging at his ear. 'How do you feel about that?' He was still very conscious of the opposition he had encountered from the Winstanleys.

The Macgregor laughed. He was a big man, in his way a sort of shaggy version of Sam himself, with greying, massive eyebrows overhanging deep-set blue eyes; a firm mouth; and a beard which always looked as if it would need trimming soon. He always wore the kilt when he was at home – by day a shepherd's plaid and in the evening the red-and-green Macgregor tartan. His face and legs were red and weather-beaten and hairy. 'Frankly, Sam,' he said, 'I'll be delighted if it comes off, but I would like to know how you feel.'

'That's easy. We all like Ian, and all I want is to see Jane happy. I don't mind admitting that I'd like to have a title in the family,' Sam grinned as he said this.

'You're an honest man, Sam Hardacre; what more could anyone ask except for a rich one, and you're both. I tell you straight, this estate needs a dollop of new capital, and I'm going to be old-fashioned enough to ask for a dowry.'

'By gum,' said Sam, full of admiration, 'thou don't beat about the bush.'

While the two men talked, the objects of their conversation were walking slowly, hand in hand, through the circling pines. Their talk was lovers' talk as they probed and questioned, searching for confirmation of what they both already knew.

'Hello, there!'

A loud hail interrupted them. It came from a tweedy lady. 'Hello there, Ian!' she called.

'Oh dear, it's Beryl,' said Ian. 'She's a neighbour of ours. I fear you'll find her a bit noisy, and I warn you, she's the local suffragette boss.'

Beryl joined them, and Jane was quite surprised to see that she was a comparatively young woman. Her dress was severe and practical, though there was nothing unusual in that – not in this climate.

'So this is the beautiful Miss Hardacre?' she said.

'How do you do?' said Jane.

'Must say you've picked a pretty one. How do you feel about women and the vote?'

'I can't say that I've given it much thought,' said Jane.

'I say, Beryl,' said Ian, 'I'm sure that Miss Hardacre doesn't want to talk politics.'

'Whyever not?' said Beryl.

'Well, you haven't even been introduced, have you?'

'Soon take care of that. I'm Beryl, you're Jane, how do you do? Care to come for a stroll? Just got Mrs Pankhurst's latest speech. I'd like to talk it over.'

'Not today, Beryl,' said Ian. 'Perhaps we'll get a chance to talk this evening.'

'Ah, yes, the party. Do please tell your mama that I'll be delighted to accept. Didn't get the invite till this morning, so

I hadn't time to write. Well, cheerio,' and she was off, striding away in the direction of the hills.

'I'd better warn you,' said Ian as she left, 'if ever you. go for a stroll with her, as she calls it, you'll not get back in under ten miles.'

The Macgregors were wonderful hosts, and dinner that evening was conducted in true Highland tradition. Their piper piped in the main course, a haunch of venison, and the assembled company made a glittering and colourful picture. The men, Sam excepted, were all in their kilts with velvet Montrose jackets, silver buckles and buttons, lace jabots, and furry sporrans. The ladies were dressed all in white and wearing sashes in their clan tartan, held at the shoulder with a large Cairngorm brooch.

It was Sam, uncomfortable as always in boiled shirt and tails, who started it.

He took a long drink of The Macgregor's excellent claret and asked, 'I suppose most of you saw *The Times* this morning? Did you notice that that damned fool Emily Pankhurst has been at it again?' He had little idea of the hornets' nest he was stirring up.

Sam was seated in the place of honour on Lady Macgregor's right, and on his left was Beryl Doig. She immediately sprang to the defence of her leader. 'I hardly think it is fair to refer to Mrs Pankhurst and her beliefs as "damned fool",' she said.

'Surely you don't think that women have any place in politics?' said Sam, turning to Lady Macgregor for support.

'I don't think I could give an opinion on that,' said Lady Macgregor, worried at the turn of the conversation.

'Do I understand that you feel that women are less responsible than men?' said Beryl.

'Of course not,' said Sam. 'In many things they're a lot more responsible, but I wouldn't include politics. You'll be saying next that we ought to have women members of Parliament.'

'Why not?' It was Jane, seated on the far side of the table.

'Well, it's laughable,' said Sam, but nobody laughed.

There was a rather uncomfortable pause, and The Macgregor signalled to his piper, who started to play a reel. The tension passed, and toes started to tap under the table as they continued their meal.

After the ladies had retired, The Macgregor spoke to Sam. 'Betcher don't know who that was sitting on your right?'

'Who was it? Miss Doig, I thought.'

'Aye, that's right, but she happens to be the secretary of the Highland Ladies Suffrage Movement.'

'Oh,' said Sam, 'happen I upset her?'

'A little, but don't let it worry you, she's used to it.'

When they joined the ladies, Sam sought Beryl out. 'Madam,' he said, 'I believe I owe you an apology. Not for what I said about woman's suffrage, because I meant every word. But if there was anything in the manner in which I said it that gave offence, then I'm sorry.'

No more was said on the subject that night, but something had happened.

After dinner Jane had sought out Beryl and questioned her at some length about her political convictions. She saw a lot of sense in what she had heard, though previously she had never given the matter much thought. After all, why should women not be in Parliament? And why should women be denied the vote? After all, the laws of the country applied as much to women as they did to men, yet women had no say in the making of those laws. It was all so reasonable and obvious.

During the remaining days of their stay, Jane and Beryl saw quite a lot of each other, and before she left, Beryl gave Jane a letter of introduction to the East Yorkshire Women's Suffrage Association.

At a conference between the two families on the night before the Hardacres left for England, it was decided that, as far as Jane and Ian were concerned, no definite announcement would be made yet. It was agreed that Jane was still very young, and so while no formal engagement would take place, all parties agreed that an 'understanding' existed between the young people.

As had become their custom, Ian and Jane walked in the

285

gardens together that night.

'Jane?'

'Yes, Ian?'

'There's been an awful lot of talk about you and me; have you realized that I have never asked you to marry me?'

'I know,' she said, then with a smile, 'Are you going to?'

'How would you feel about being a sailor's wife?'

'I think that being a sailor's wife must be very difficult.'

'How?'

'Well,' she said, 'there have to be long periods of separation.'

'Of course.'

'And the more she loves her husband, the lonelier those periods will become.'

'And?' he said.

'And each reunion will be another taste of paradise,' she smiled at him. 'Now are you going to ask me?'

'Dearest Jane, will you be my wife?'

'Of course, my darling, of course I will.'

Very gently, and for the first time, he kissed her on the lips. It would be two years before that happened again.

CHAPTER FIVE

The spring of 1908 had been warm and sunny, and by early July, all over the north of England, the first hay crop was being gathered in. The hot sun had dried yesterday's mown hay sufficiently for turning, and Harry Hardacre had been working since mid-morning. It was noon now, and Harry straightened his stiff back, rubbed his game leg, and leaned on the handle of his pitchfork, looking down the long lines of his workmen. They had begun stacking into small haycocks. The weather was holding well. He would have this field stacked by sunset.

It was not necessary that Harry should work with them, and it was certainly quite unusual. But he enjoyed the work. Leisure bored him and left him too much time to think. In the winter he could retreat to his books, but the summer light drew him out of doors, and, once there, he wanted to work. He justified himself on the grounds that another hand was always useful. Later, when the second crop was ready, and they also had the wheat, oats, and barley to bring in, they would hire casual labour, Irish boys who came to England every year for the harvest. But the first crop at Hardacres they did by themselves, and it was long, hard work.

Harry smiled as he looked towards the gate, where Noel was helping Kilner, his head ploughman, to bring in the first of the big hay wagons. The boy pleased him; he worked as hard as a man already, and would continue all day if allowed. He idolized Kilner, almost as much as he did his grandfather, and when he was not with the one he could almost certainly be found with the other. It was a good place to grow up, Harry thought, with the summers in the fields and the winters riding over the windy moors. He was always aware of it and of the contrast with his own childhood. Not that there had not been good times even then; he remembered the old cart and Adam and the games with Joe in the hedgerows. Thinking of Joe upset him; he had never reconciled the young boy he had once worshipped with the grown man whom he could not bring himself to like.

He turned back to his work and the cut, sweet-smelling hay, lifting and twisting the fork so that each forkful built neatly on to the growing stack; the rhythm came easy to him. When he next looked up and out over the golden field, he saw the cart had arrived with the kitchen maids, bringing the bread and cheese. They stopped near the tall elm, under whose shade the barrel of beer had been set up early in the morning, so that by lunch time the brew would have settled after its journey out to the fields. The girls began drawing the beer off into jugs and carrying them and wicker baskets of bread and cheese out to where the men waited in the field. Harry stopped to watch, finding them graceful and pretty as, with their skirts and aprons lifted slightly, they picked their way across the lying hay. The sun was strong now, and he would be glad of that beer. Overhead the sky was a cloudless rich blue, from the far reach of the pasture to the tall, dark-green elms that edged the near side. Beneath the elms the shadows were hard-cut, deep and summery.

Another cart drew up behind the first, and Harry recognized the small, brightly painted trap and the spotted pony he had given to Hetty to use for the children. She was such a tower of strength, he thought, with her farming background. She could harness a horse and drive as well as he could. She could cook and clean, not that she needed to – as nanny, all of that was done for her, but she could do it. No doubt she could pitch hay as well, given the chance. He smiled as she climbed down from the trap and lifted a large wicker basket down after her. She had brought Vanessa out to see him. He watched her as she walked out of the shadow of the trees and into the sunlight. She carried the basket in her arms, and Harry thought that she looked like something from the Bible, with her brown skirt drifting across the hay and her smooth hair covered with a kerchief. He went to meet her.

'Hello,' she said, quiet and shy as always, though Harry was not impressed by that; he had never considered her meek or shy since that day long ago when she had told him what

no one else had ever had the nerve to tell him. Her manner sometimes annoyed him – he was not yet used to being deferred to and was beginning to doubt if he ever would be.

'I came to see if Noel was getting tired, and I thought she might as well come with me,' Hetty said.

Harry had taken the baby from the basket and tossed her up and caught her in his calloused hands as she laughed. She had grown round and contented – a placid, happy creature. Her hair was turning soft brown like Judith's, but her face was like her grandfather's, solid and plain. Harry was secretly pleased, though Mary thought it a pity that the little girl should be plain, while Noel had his mother's fine delicate features. It was the way of things, he said, and was glad that she would not grow into a reflection of the woman he had lost.

Hetty was smiling at him still. 'I brought some lunch for Noel,' she said. 'Do you think he'll come and join me?' She was looking at the small, slim figure among the dark shapes of the men at the beer barrel.

'I doubt he'll thank us if we call him away,' said Harry. 'I am sure that Noel would much rather be with Kilner.'

'I'll just take his milk over to him, then,' said Hetty.

'No, I'll do it,' said Harry. He put the basket with Vanessa down on the grass and went off to find his son among the workmen.

Hetty watched him walk away; he was limping slightly, as he always did when he worked hard. It would be more sensible for him not to work, but she understood why he did. She liked looking at him, though it would not do for the nanny to be seen gawping after the master. But here there was no one to see, except Vanessa, and Vanessa was far too young to understand. Hetty was not quite sure that she understood herself. She knew she liked the way the sun touched his hair and the sharp strong line of his shoulders under his blue work shirt. She knew that watching him walk, watching him smile, listening to him talk made her feel good, and feel something else through her body, something different and exciting that did not bear explanation.

When Harry came back, he carried a pitcher of beer and

two tin mugs, as well as bread and cheese for both of them. Hetty said, 'Oh, you needn't have. I brought enough for all of us.'

Harry laughed, 'Then we'll have a feast. Come and sit down.'

She wondered for a moment, but she did as he asked. He came and sat quite near with the baby sitting up between them.

'She's had her lunch,' said Hetty, but she gave her a crust of hard bread, and she gnawed away contentedly, getting fingers and bread together in her mouth in a dribbly confusion. Harry watched, delighted. He knew that many of his friends found babies disgusting, to be seen only on those occasions when nanny had cleaned them carefully for presentation. It appalled him. And it wasn't only the men, but the women too, who visited their children only once a day at four o'clock for an obligatory hour before tea and saw them at no other time. It was one of the many facets of the upper-class life style that he found hard to accept. He smiled to himself, as he watched his daughter playing with her nanny's apron ribbons and felt suddenly that they were like a family. That would not do either, of course, he reminded himself, and he wondered if he might not be living in the wrong half of the world.

The sun dappled through the high branches of the elm, patchy on the grass, on Hetty and her blue kerchief. He looked carefully at her face, the freckles, the short nose, the round, blue-green eyes, and too-heavy eyebrows. He decided that she was pretty in a totally unconventional way and wondered again, because, until this moment, he had considered her downright homely.

He stretched himself out on the grass, leaning on one elbow, watching Vanessa crawl off to find a pile of sticks and turn them into playthings. His body ached with the good feeling of use and hard work. The air had become noon-day still, the workmen's voices were far distant. There was no one in sight. The beautiful scent of the hay was everywhere, on his clothes, in his hair. The sheer sensuality of it all became irresistible. He twisted over until he was close by Hetty,

almost touching, and called her name. She had been turned away, watching Vanessa, and when she turned back to him, she was surprised at his closeness. He put his arm across her body and pulled her down on to the grass and kissed her mouth, and when she did not protest, began to kiss her face and her throat, alive with sensations he had not known for a year.

She sat up suddenly as his hands started to move over her body and pulled away. 'Oh, Mr Hardacre.' Harry could have laughed; the response was so stereotyped, so damnably formal.

But he heard himself saying, out of the years of a gentleman's training, 'I'm terribly sorry, Hetty, I should never have done that. Please forgive me.'

She was gathering the food basket, Vanessa's wicker basinette, and Vanessa. Her face was down, turned away. She did not look at him or say anything. He realized that the rules decreed that she did not say anything. He knew also that he was supposed to say that it would not happen again, but he could not bring himself to do it.

He watched her walk, head down, arms full, back to the trap. He wanted to help her but did not dare. Instead he called once more, 'I'm sorry.'

Then he picked up his fork and walked back into the sunny field, jabbing it angrily into the first mound of hay, because he wasn't sorry at all.

CHAPTER SIX

In the early summer of 1909 Joe bought a field in Yorkshire. It lay just outside of Driffield on the right of the road which runs west from the town towards the ancient village of Kirkham. It was a very large, flat field, and when Joe built, in a corner near the road, a huge barn, the rumours and speculation started. The barn had large sliding doors facing the field, and these were always kept shut; it had no windows in its sides, though large skylights had been built into the roof and it was said that electric light had been installed.

Joe told no one, not even his family, what he was doing. He also bought a twelve-room house and a couple of cottages at Kirkham, and in September, much to Helen's annoyance, he moved north. He was accompanied by four men, who shared the two cottages. Apart from the fact that the four men and usually Joe went to the barn every day, no news leaked out as to what was going on, and the fact that large dogs were allowed to roam loose in the barn at night discouraged the curious from attempting to satisfy their curiosity.

Joe visited Hardacres quite frequently, mostly to see his mother, and it was she who persuaded him that they should have the whole family together for Christmas. Of Joe's brood, Emily and Maud were at Kirkham with a nanny, and Arnold was just starting at Eton. Noel and Vanessa, now a toddler of two, were of course at Hardacres. Poor Jane was unable to have her Ian with her, as he was serving aboard H.M.S. *Warrior* and would spend Christmas somewhere in the Indian Ocean. The countess was a very old lady but still as bright as a button and insisted on doing her share in preparing for the festivities.

'You'll have to do it without me soon enough now,' she would say.

Christmas morning was a bit of a pilgrimage for Sam and

Mary. Every year they drove to Bridlington and went to the old Priory Church. Mr Cox was no longer there, for he had died the previous year, but to Sam and Mary it was important. In a way they felt that it had all started here. There was an open invitation to any of the family to accompany them, and Sam always asked Wilson. This year Harry and Saunders went along. Joe had little time for religion.

'Not even an hour a year?' Sam had asked him.

'Time's too valuable to waste on things that don't matter,' Joe had replied.

Sam never mentioned the subject again.

In 1909 they went all the way by road for the first time. Sam had been finally persuaded that the horseless carriage was here to stay, and he had given himself one as a Christmas present, a Lagonda tourer which, much to Mary's relief, managed the two-way journey without blowing up or breaking down, both of which catastrophies she was convinced were imminent. Even Helen relaxed enough to enjoy the festivities. The traditional Christmas dinner was served at two o'clock in the afternoon, with the whole family present to eat goose, followed by plum pudding. Afterwards they all went down to the servants' hall, and Mary and Sam handed all the staff their Christmas presents. Excited but exhausted, the children were packed off to their rooms at about seven, and after a light dinner the men sat around in the dining room smoking and sipping brandy.

So relaxed indeed was the atmosphere that Sam was tempted to ask Joe about his barn.

'Joe,' he said, 'when are you going to tell us about yon barn? Or is it going to stay a secret?'

'You'll know soon,' was the reply.

'Come on, Joe,' said Sam, 'there's only me and Harry here, we can keep a secret.'

'I think I've got a fortune locked up in that barn.'

'And it's got summat to do with yon fellows you put into them cottages, I'll wager,' said Sam.

'Naturally.'

'What are they, Joe?' asked Harry.

'Engineers.'

'Come on, Joe,' said Harry, 'there's no point in us playing guessing games. Either you are going to tell us or you are not. Which is it to be?'

'If I tell you, it's to go no further.'

'That's reasonable,' said Sam.

'Agreed,' said Harry.

'I'm building a flying machine.'

'A what!' exclaimed Harry.

'Is that all?' said Sam, 'I can't see what's so damned secret about that. Plenty of folk do it, especially after yon froggy, what's his name?'

'Bleriot.'

'Aye, Bleriot. After he flew across the Channel.'

'It might be fun,' said Harry, 'but I can't see that there's a fortune in it.'

'Nor can I,' said Sam. 'There's got to be more to it than that.'

'War,' said Joe. 'I'm amazed that no one has yet seen the aeroplane as a weapon. It's early days yet, but I wouldn't mind betting that there'll be a dozen different ways that the army and possibly even the navy can use aeroplanes in wartime.'

Sam was suddenly serious. 'Why do you want to make money out of war, Joe?'

'I don't, Dad,' he replied, 'I just want to make money. Just now war seems to be a good investment. Just look at what Germany's doing; they're building ships almost as fast as we are.'

'Happen you wouldn't have taken a share in them as well?' Sam was heavily sarcastic.

'Naturally,' said Joe, unmoved by his father's tone.

Sam was amazed. 'Again?'

'I put another twenty-five thousand into Krupp of Essen last month. I can't see them failing.'

'I'll tell you one thing, Joe,' said Sam. 'It'll be a sad day for England if they don't,' and he left the room, unwilling, for Mary's sake, to start another row.

Joe watched him go, pitying him. 'Why won't Father ever understand that business is business and that there's nothing personal in it?' he said.

'You know,' said Harry, 'Dad's not such a bad businessman at that. You never had to gut herrings to make a living. As for there not being anything personal in it, I think there might be.'

'How do you mean?'

'Suppose, just suppose that we went to war with Germany. Not now, we're too strong at sea. But you said yourself that they're building up their fleet.'

'They'll never catch us up.'

'Don't be too sure.'

'Well, even if they did, I don't think it's the Germans we have to worry about, it's the French.'

'After what the King did in Paris? No.'

'Well, just supposing it did happen?' said Joe.

'Your Arnold's thirteen now; in five years he'll be of military age. You know he just could end up getting shot with a bullet that his father had paid for.'

'Oh, Harry, I sometimes think you're soft in the head; you're as daft as Dad.'

'That could well be so,' said Harry, 'but remember that I'm the only one of us who's seen war, me and Judith.' He paused for a moment; for two years now he could not mention her name without thinking about what might have been. 'That was a little war, and I only really saw one day of it, but it left me with this.' He tapped his game leg.

'I suppose that it's no use arguing with either of you,' said Joe.

'Not really,' said Harry, and he smiled. 'But in spite of Father, I am really interested in your machine. Will it fly?'

'I certainly hope so; I've got a couple of the best brains in the game working on it. Arnold knows about it; he says he wants to fly it himself.' They both laughed. 'But the important thing is that it is going to have a camera fitted to it.'

'How, what for?'

'Well, it will point straight down through the floor of the aeroplane. There will be two men in the machine, so it will have to be a big one, and one of them will work the camera and change the plates so that they can take pictures just like maps, but these maps will be right up to the minute, and you would be able to see what the enemy was doing and where his strength was and a whole host of other information.' Joe paused.

'You could also use it for map making,' said Harry, 'and we need accurate maps for all sorts of peaceful reasons.'

'Of course, but if I can sell it to the army, that's what counts.'

'And can you?'

'I think so.'

'When will it be ready? I'd like to see it when it flies.'

'And so you shall. It will be at Easter; I promised that to Arnold.'

Just before Easter Joe took the family to Driffield to see the machine. Even Sam was sufficiently curious to forget his prejudices and came along. Joe took them into the barn and had the doors opened. The two engineers were there in greasy white overalls, and there in the middle of the barn was It.

The body was shaped like an egg with two holes cut in the top where the crew would sit, with the engine and propeller behind them; four tubular strips of metal went from this to the tail, and its two wings were held apart by wooden struts and wire. The whole thing looked flimsy and fragile.

'I hope nobody kicks it,' said Sam. 'It looks as if it would fall to pieces.'

'It's tougher than it looks, Dad,' replied Joe.

'Doesn't it smell,' said Mary, and she was right – the whole atmosphere was pervaded with the mixed odours of dope, petrol, and castor oil.

Arnold was thrilled. He stroked it and patted it and finally turned to his father. 'Can I sit in it?'

'Of course you can,' said Joe.

A small stepladder was placed against the front of the machine, and Arnold climbed up; amidst warnings not to put his foot on to the canvas skin, he climbed into the front cockpit. Joe went up behind him.

'This is the pilot's cockpit. The photographer will sit behind,' he explained. He pointed out the various instruments

– altimeter, oil, temperature, and petrol gauges. Then he showed him the joystick, rudder bar, and throttle. Arnold moved the controls about and watched enchanted as the ailerons, elevators, and rudder moved.

'What's this?' he asked, pointing to what looked like an ordinary electric switch.

'Don't touch that,' said Joe. 'That's the magneto switch, if you turn that on, the engine might start.'

Sadly Arnold got out of the cockpit. 'I wish Aunt Jane was here,' he said. 'She'd love it.'

'So do I,' said Sam. He was worried about Jane. She had gone off to London a week ago, and they had not heard from her. 'When are you going to fly it? If it flies.'

'It'll fly all right,' said Joe. 'We won't have the camera ready for a couple of weeks yet, but we'll be test flying it on Saturday.'

'Can I go up in it?' asked Arnold.

'Not the first time, but if everything's all right, you'll have a go,' replied Joe.

'I bet I could fly it now,' said Arnold.

'And I'll bet you're not going to,' said Sam. 'Well, Joe, you know my feelings about your ideas, but in spite of them, I must say I'm very impressed with this. Is it going to have a name?'

'Not really,' said Joe. 'We're calling it the *J.H.1.*'

'That's a daft name,' said Mary. 'Can't thee think of owt pretty?'

They headed back to Hardacres with young Arnold, who had persuaded his father to let him spend the rest of the day with his grandfather. When they arrived, they were surprised to find Saunders waiting for them.

'Hallo, John,' said Sam, 'summat urgent?'

'I'm afraid so,' said Saunders. 'Could we talk privately?'

'Must we?'

'If you don't mind, Sam.'

'Excuse us,' Sam said to the others, and he took Saunders into the study. 'Well?'

'It's Jane.'

'She's not had an accident?'

'No, no, no, nothing like that; I'm afraid she's in prison.'

'What!' roared Sam. 'Who's done this? I'll ... I'll ...'

'No, you won't, Sam; it's the police. She's been arrested and is being held at Bow Street.'

'What for? What the hell has she been up to?'

'I don't know the details, but I suspect it is something to do with this women's suffrage business. I'm going down to London on the five o'clock from Hull. Her case comes up tomorrow morning, so I'll be able to see her first thing. What I want to know is what you intend to do?' Saunders said.

'I'm coming with you, naturally. What the hell are we going to tell Mary?'

'The truth?'

'If we do that, she'll want to come, and before we know where we are, we'll have the whole bloody lot of them. No, we'll have to think of something else.'

'Then we'd better just tell her that we have to go down to London to deal with some urgent business about the Grosvenor Square property,' said Saunders.

Having told their lies, and managed to persuade Mary that they did have to go to London right away, they left with the promise that they would be back in time to see the first flight on Saturday.

They took the train from Driffield to Hull and just managed to catch the evening express to London. They got to Grosvenor Square late that night and, having spent the night there, were on their way, in a hansom, to Bow Street at eight o'clock the next morning.

On arrival at Bow Street, Saunders presented his credentials and explained that he would be representing Miss Jane Hardacre. They were shown into the interview room, a cold grim-looking place with a plain table and four chairs. They had been waiting a minute or two when a policewoman came in with Jane.

Saunders had read the charge and had told Sam the gist of it.

'Lot of bloody nonsense,' said Sam.

'That's as may be,' replied Saunders, 'but I think you had better let me handle this, and if you possibly can bear it, 'please don't talk; let me do it all.'

When Jane arrived, Sam sat tight-lipped in a corner and, apart from a grunt of acknowledgement, managed by a supreme effort to hold his tongue.

'Well, Jane,' said Saunders, 'I've read the charge; you'd better tell me your side of the story.'

'Why?'

'Because you've been very foolish, and I'm going to represent you in court and try and persuade the magistrate not to send you to prison.'

'Prison?' Jane was suddenly frightened. 'They wouldn't do that to me.'

'Why not?' said Saunders. 'You're no different from anybody else. According to the charges, I would say that you have a very good chance of going to prison. So you had better tell me what happened.'

'I was chained to the railing of Kings Yard at Westminster outside the Houses of Parliament.'

'Why you?'

'It was my turn; we do it one day a week. Last week it was Sheila Baskerville, and this week it was me.'

'Go on.'

'I had "Votes for Women" written across my blouse, and quite a lot of people stood and stared at me. Some of them were sympathetic, and some, mostly women, were very rude.'

'How were they rude?'

'They called me awful names, and some of them swore at me.' She went on, 'After I'd been there about half an hour a policeman and a policewoman came along. The policeman had a big pair of shears, and he cut the chains. As soon as I was free, I tried to run away, and that was when I ... I ...' Jane was near to tears.

'That was when you what?'

'I hit the policewoman.'

'Oh, dear.'

'Is it bad?' she asked in a very small voice.

'It might be. Jane, I want you to do exactly as I tell you. When you go into court, they will read out the charge. It will sound awful, but don't worry about that. Then they will ask

299

you to plead guilty or not guilty. I want you to say guilty and not to utter another word unless the magistrate speaks to you directly.'

'Why should I say guilty? I don't feel guilty, just scared.'

'If you don't, you'll go to prison,' said Saunders, and then without waiting for a reply he turned to Sam, 'We'd better get into court.' He turned back to Jane. 'Guilty; and not another word.'

They left Jane with the policewoman and made their way towards the courtroom. Sam was pretty appalled at the sight of some of the people in the corridors. Among a few well-dressed individuals and court officials were scattered dirty, ragged, unkempt creatures, stinking of gin and stale sweat – the human garbage that had been swept from the streets of London during the night. Sam felt a twinge of conscience in his revulsion; it was not so many years since he used to rub shoulders daily with that kind of people – he was not all that far from the fish quay.

When they got into the court, a verminous old hag was receiving a three-month sentence for soliciting. As she was taken down, Saunders went to the well of the court and whispered to the clerk. He then took his seat on the front bench next to a police sergeant. Sam had to be content with a place at the back of the public gallery.

'Put up Jane Hardacre,' called the clerk.

The stipendiary magistrate must have been all of seventy. He was wearing a frock coat and black cravat. The yellowing skin of his face was drawn so tightly over the bones that his head looked like a skull with eyes and a tobacco-stained moustache. He leaned over his desk and addressed Saunders.

'You represent Miss Hardacre?'

'Yes, Your Worship, John Saunders solicitor.'

'I trust that you don't intend to drag this out,' snapped the magistrate, perching a pair of pince-nez on the end of his nose.

'I hope not, sir.'

The magistrate nodded to a corner of the court and Jane was brought into the dock by the policewoman. Sam, sitting at the back of the court, could barely see the top of her head over the pressmen in front of him.

The clerk of the court rose and read from a document in his hand, 'Jane Hardacre of Sixteen Grosvenor Square, London, West One. You are hereby charged that, on the fifteenth of April, in the year of our Lord nineteen hundred and ten, you did conduct yourself in a disorderly, unruly, noisome, and offensive manner, to the detriment of the public order and did thereby endanger the peace of His Sovereign Majesty the King; that you did utter in a public place abusive, insulting, and threatening language and did strike with your fist a Police Officer in the execution of her duty. How do you plead? Guilty or not guilty?'

There was a pause, and Jane glanced towards Saunders, who nodded.

'Guilty,' she said, in a voice barely above a whisper.

'Eh?' said the magistrate, cupping his hand to his ear.

Saunders stood up. 'My client has entered a plea of guilty, Your Worship.'

'Well, thank God for that,' said the magistrate. 'All right, get on with it.'

'Sergeant Owen,' said the clerk.

Sergeant Owen, who was sitting next to Saunders, got up and gave evidence as the arresting officer, reading from his notes in that soporific monotone common to all police witnesses. His story was pretty well the same as Jane had told to Saunders half an hour ago.

'I suppose you want to say something,' said the magistrate, glaring at Saunders.

'My client, a lady of gentle background, wishes to express her deep sorrow at having behaved in the manner for which she has been charged. She admits the truth of the sergeant's evidence and would only add that striking the policewoman was an accident caused by the fear and excitement of the moment. For this she would like to tender her sincere apologies to the lady concerned, together with the hope that she did not cause her any hurt.'

Saunders sat down. The magistrate adjusted his pince-nez and peered at Jane. 'Jane Hardacre, you have pleaded guilty to a series of serious offences which would ordinarily carry a substantial sentence. The argument on your behalf, while in no way constituting a defence, together with your extreme youth and sincerity and particularly the fact that you have pleaded guilty, thus saving a great deal of the court's time, has persuaded me to deal leniently with you. Ten pounds or thirty days.'

Sam, who had been suffering all sorts of torments while this was going on, suddenly blurted out, 'Bloody hell, has she got a choice?'

'Silence,' called the clerk, rapping his gavel.

They went to the office of the clerk of the court, where they found Jane, and Sam paid the fine.

'Well,' said Saunders as they left the office, 'I think we can count ourselves very fortunate.'

They were walking through the corridors on their way out, Sam tightlipped and silent.

'I shall be so glad to get away from all these terrible people,' said Jane, recovering her composure a little.

Sam stopped. 'What did you say?'

'Well, Daddy, you must admit they are awful; they're not even clean.'

Sam grabbed her by the arm and practically dragged her over to where a young woman was sitting on a plain bench suckling a baby. The woman could not have been any older than Jane; she was dirty, and her hair hung in long, greasy, matted lumps. She wore a skirt cut from an old hessian sack which still bore the imprint of the manufacturer whose goods it once contained. Her blouse was torn and dirty, and the child suckling at her breast was covered with sores. Her complexion was grey, and she looked up at them with brown, lacklustre eyes. Jane tried to pull herself away.

'Not so fast, young woman,' said Sam, pulling her back.

'Spare a copper, guvnor,' whispered the woman, looking quickly around to make sure that no one could hear her.

Sam shook Jane roughly. 'Do you see that? That would have been thy mother when I met her, and I wasn't much better me sen. You don't remember the fish quays, but I do and so does your mother; even Joe and Harry can remember. You're the lucky one, and do you know why you're lucky?

Because one day I cut my thumb. That's the only reason why you are where you are and not where she is. Today you cost me ten pounds and a heap of worry because you and a load of other bloody snobs have got crack-brained political ideas. Don't you think that ten pounds would have been a damned sight better spent if it had been spent on her?'

'I didn't mean ...' said Jane.

'Oh, aye, you did. I suppose it's my own fault, really. I've kept thee so much away from the real world that you've had to try and invent one. I can only hope that what you've learned today has taught you summat about folk as aren't as well off as you are.'

The woman watched them, understanding little. 'Are you going to gimme summat, mister?'

'Here you are, love,' said Sam, pressing several gold coins into her hand, 'get your bairn a decent meal and some clothes. I'm sorry I haven't got more, but it's better spent than the tenner my daughter just got out of me.'

Sam strode out of the door and on to the street; Jane ran after him.

CHAPTER SEVEN

They travelled to Hull that evening and got back to Hardacres the next morning, having spent the night in a hotel, just in time to leave for Driffield for the first flight of Joe's aeroplane. Mary was of course very curious to know what had happened in London, but Sam evaded her questions, and Jane dashed off to her room as soon as she got into the house and did not emerge until they were ready to leave for Driffield in the Lagonda.

There had been a small paragraph in *The Times* that morning about Jane's case, but luckily Mary seldom tried to read the papers, and Sam knew that Joe only read the financial news.

The weather was perfect when they arrived at Driffield. A morning sea mist had burned off and given way to a clear, blue sky with hardly a breath of wind. For the first time the machine was rolled out of the barn and exposed to the public view. A lot of interest had been aroused locally by the speculation about just what was going on in the Hardacres' barn. In any case it was not the sort of secret that could be kept indefinitely, and on Easter Sunday morning quite a small crowd had gathered along the roadside to watch.

The fabric covering of the machine was now painted with bright silver dope, stretching tight over the wings, tail, and cockpit shell. It looked fragile and flimsy as the two engineers fussed around it. Finally one of them put on a helmet and a pair of goggles and climbed into the front cockpit.

Joe and Arnold were standing apart from the others and very close to the machine.

'Dad,' said Arnold, 'if it works, can I go up in it?' It must have been the hundredth time he had asked.

'We'll see,' replied Joe. 'Watch now, there – they're going to start the motor.'

The engineer was now standing between the tubes where

the engine was mounted and was holding the propeller.

'Switch off, petrol on, suck in,' he called.

The pilot raised his hand, and the engineer swung the propeller several times.

'Contact,' called the engineer.

'Contact,' replied the pilot.

The engineer swung the propeller for the last time, stepping smartly back as he did so. There was a big puff of blue smoke from the engine as it coughed and spluttered into life.

The family watched, by now quite enthralled in the anticipation of seeing Joe's creation defy the laws of gravity.

'Looks as if it'll shake itself to bits,' said Sam, and indeed the contraption, which had looked flimsy before, now looked a hundred times more so as it trembled and shook to the vibration of the motor.

'I think they're ever so brave to go up in that thing,' said Mary.

'Or daft,' said Sam.

Hetty was holding little Vanessa, while Noel was standing wide-eyed in front of her. Harry went over to them and took Hetty's hand in his. She looked up at him but did not take her hand away.

The motor had now settled down to a smooth, steady note. The engineer came from behind the flying machine and pulled the wooden chocks away from in front of the wheels. The propeller started to accelerate, and finally became a whirling disc of transparent silver. Slowly the machine started to roll forward.

A cheer went up from the people watching, but this soon turned to disappointment and even a few jeers from the roadside as the aeroplane made no attempt to fly but simply taxied around the field. Joe explained to the family that the pilot was testing his controls on the ground before taking off. At length the machine rolled to a stop in front of the barn, and while the motor was ticking over, the engineer brought the steps to the front of the machine and climbed up. Here he spent a minute or so shouting at the pilot. He then got down, took the steps away, and quite quickly examined the wires and controls on the wings and tail. Finally he waved

305

to the pilot and gave the thumbs-up sign.

The pilot waggled his controls: ailerons, rudder, elevators; then he opened the throttle, and the machine started to roll forward again. This time, however, he headed straight across the field, accelerating all the time, and within seconds the aeroplane had lifted into the air.

'It works!' said Sam. 'Bloody hell, it works!' He could not conceal his amazement and delight.

'Well done, Joe,' shouted Harry, squeezing Hetty's hand.

Joe grinned back at him; then all eyes were on the aeroplane as it turned far beyond the end of the field and headed back towards them.

'It's not natural,' said Mary. 'I'm sure that the good God never meant folk to go gallivanting about in the sky.'

The machine flew across the field twice and then landed with such a series of bumps that it caused Sam to exclaim yet again, 'It'll shake itself to bits.'

However, Sam's prediction proved to be without foundation, and the machine taxied back across the field to the barn, where the pilot switched off the motor and climbed out of the cockpit. Then the two engineers and Arnold pushed it back into the barn and closed the doors. Joe explained to them that it would now have to be completely dismantled to find out if any parts showed signs of undue strain, so there would be no more flights for some time. It was a very cheerful party which headed back towards Hardacres to crack open a bottle or two of champagne and celebrate. The only one who did not go was Arnold. He stayed behind. He wanted to learn all he could about the machine before the Easter vacation was over, and above all he was determined to have a flight before returning to Eton if that were humanly possible.

As they reached the end of the drive at Hardacres, they were surprised to see a strange motorcar standing outside the house. When they went in, Wilson took Sam to one side and told him that Ian Macgregor had arrived and that he had asked to see him privately.

'Are you sure that it's not Jane he wants to see?'

'No, sir,' replied Wilson, 'he was quite specific. He said that he wanted to talk to you before he saw anybody else.'

'Where is he?' asked Sam.

'In the study, sir.'

'Hello, Ian,' said Sam, as he went into the study. 'This is a nice surprise; we thought that you were at sea.'

'I'm just back, sir,' said Ian.

'Well, what can I do for you?' asked Sam, and then as the thought struck him, 'Did you see *The Times* this morning?'

'Yes, sir, but that isn't the reason that I'm here.'

'Didn't it bother you at all?'

'Frankly, sir, I rather admired her spirit.'

'Surely you don't agree with her.'

'I don't know, I never really gave it much thought. I don't think that my Captain will approve,' he smiled.

'Happen he won't,' said Sam.

'You see, sir, I'm quite sure that women will get the vote sooner or later. It always struck me as incongruous that we could have a woman as a monarch while other women were not allowed to vote for the government.'

'Aye,' said Sam, 'I see your point. But if that isn't the reason you're here, what is?'

'I join H.M.S. *Monmouth* in three weeks' time.'

'That was the ship you were on when we met you.'

'That's right, sir, but the point is that shortly after that we sail for the China station. I shall be based at Hong Kong for at least three years.'

'I see,' said Sam. 'I think I'm beginning to get your drift; you'd better tell me the rest.'

'I want to marry Jane right away. I know we are not formally engaged, and I know that it's all rather sudden, but if we don't do it now ... well, three years is an awful long time.'

'What does Jane say?'

'I haven't asked her yet. I wanted to be sure that I had your permission before I did. I have already talked it over with my parents, and they are quite happy with the idea.'

'Well, Ian,' said Sam, 'as far as I'm concerned it's all up to Jane. Reckon you'd better go and see her and find out how she feels about it. If it's all right by her, it's all right by me.'

'Oh, thank you, sir; is she at home now?'

'Oh, aye, I brought her back last night. But don't rush; you can stay a couple of days, and she's not going anywhere.'

'Thank you, sir, I'd like to very much.'

'Good. Then you'd better have a drink before you go, and I'd better have a drink before I find her mother and tell her what's happening.'

'You think it will be all right with Mrs Hardacre?'

'Don't you worry about Mary, lad, you go out and worry about your lass. She's got spirit, and, handled right, she'll be a topper. Here, drink this.' He handed Ian a stiff whisky and took one himself. 'If she says yes, we'll have your folks down and have the wedding as soon as you like; good health.'

Helen watched disapprovingly as Sam helped Jane out of the landau. It really was too bad. Such a rush, and the King barely cold in his grave. That was the reason why half of the people who should have been there were not. She had very nearly refused to accept when Jane had asked her to be matron of honour, but that would have been difficult to explain to the children. Emily and Maud both wanted so much to be bridesmaids.

So far as Helen was concerned, the whole thing was suspicious. Whoever heard of anyone marrying only three weeks after announcing their engagement; it certainly made one think. Helen studied Jane's waistline carefully as she got out of the landau, but there was no sign – not yet anyway.

Mind you, it was not all bad – at least Ian Macgregor had a title and would inherit a Scottish chieftainship; better than that fool Harry, running around making sheep's eyes at a servant. They had just gone in – Harry and Henrietta Cavandish, together with Noel. Helen blamed Sam for the whole business; still, what could you expect from a guttie? It was a rotten time. The season would be ruined with the death of the King – not that any of the Hardacres would care – and Jane would be off to China quite soon.

Jane was out of the landau and standing, on her father's arm, waiting while Helen straightened out her train, which was to be carried by Emily and Maud, with Vanessa standing between them, wondering what this was all about and why she had not been allowed to play that morning.

They started to move towards the west front of the church. Maud put her tongue out at Emily, and Emily put her tongue out at Maud, and Vanessa giggled. For a moment they paused in the great, arched west door of Bridlington Priory, gazing down the nave, with its high, arched Gothic ceiling, towards the great square of the sanctuary just beyond the transepts. The organ struck up the wedding march. Sam had been asked if, in view of the nation's mourning for Edward VII, he would not rather have the ceremony without music, but he turned that idea down flat.

They started down the aisle towards where Ian and his best man, both in full-dress naval uniform, were waiting. Helen noted with disgust, as she passed them, that Harry and Hetty were holding hands and thought how nice it would be to get back to London and get away from the country bumpkins who now surrounded her. She would have to speak to Joe about that.

'Dearly beloved, we are gathered together here, in the sight of God and in the face of this congregation . . .'

The priest was beginning in that strange monotone which is neither speech nor song, and which is used exclusively by the clergy of the Established Church for conversation with God. Helen thought that the whole thing was so dull and so provincial, but at least it was short. Fifteen minutes later it was all over. Outside was a guard of honour from H.M.S. *Monmouth*, and Ian and Jane passed beneath an arch of the swords of Ian's brother officers. Then everybody threw confetti, and they all piled into motorcars and headed back to Hardacres for the reception.

Harry had been organizing the transport, and it was no accident that as the penultimate car drove off there was only himself and Hetty left. 'Come on,' he said, 'I'll drive you.'

He did not start the motor, but climbed into the car beside her. They had drawn closer over the last year or so, and he would occasionally take her hand when they were together. The incident at the haymaking was never repeated and never referred to, though they both thought of it often. Harry, for his part, could not get away from the feeling of family that he always found when he saw her with his children, and he was a frequent visitor to the nursery for tea. He was aware, too, that Hetty had an affection for him which went beyond that of a servant for a popular employer. Even so, it was not going to be easy. He knew that he did not love her, at least not in the way he had loved Judith; nothing could ever be like that again. He felt that, however, there was no reason why they, who already shared board and children, should not also share bed.

'Hetty,' he said, as she sat silently with her hands, palms down, on her knees, 'I don't know if it has ever occurred to you, as it has occurred to me, that you, Noel, Vanessa, and I, during these last two years, have grown very close and become a family in all save one thing.'

'And what would that be?' she asked quietly.

'Their mother and father are not married. I feel that we should put that right. No, please let me finish. I am not going to try to pretend anything which I do not know to be true. Don't ask me if I love you, for I could not answer that. I know only that your presence and your company give me great peace. Peace that I thought I would never know again when Judith died. We are neither of us children; I am sure we both know what we would be taking on. So if you accept this proposal, I shall remain true to you, and I shall love you and care for you as long as I live.'

Hetty was not surprised. This man, whom she had grown to love, was lonely; he needed a woman, her. She knew that she would never replace Judith; she knew that when he said love, he did not mean romantic love; and she knew that, one day, there might be someone else, but it was worth the risk. 'Yes, Harry, I'll marry you,' she replied. It was the first time she had called him Harry.

'Thank you, Hetty; I'll try and be worth it.' He kissed her very gently on the lips, and then, a little embarrassed, said, 'We'd better get to the reception.'

They waited until Jane and Ian had departed for destinations unknown before seeking out Sam and Mary and telling them the news. They were both delighted. They, too, had developed an affection for this quiet, unassuming girl and were more than happy to welcome her into the family.

'Happen he's only going to marry you to save your wages,' said Sam, but there was a twinkle in his eye.

'Sam Hardacre, you're not to say things like that, even in fun,' reprimanded Mary. 'Hetty, my dear, do you mind if we announce it tonight?'

'But I haven't bought her a ring yet,' said Harry.

'What difference does that make?' said Sam.

'Do just as you wish,' said Hetty. 'Personally I think it is silly to try and keep this sort of thing a secret, anyhow.'

There was a fairly large gathering at dinner that night. The Macgregors were staying on a few days before leaving for Scotland, and a few of the wedding guests were being put up overnight. When they sat down, there were a few raised eyebrows when it was seen that Hetty was seated on Sam's right.

'I do wish you'd speak to your father,' Helen hissed at Joe. 'He has no idea of how to treat servants.'

'They seem to stay with him, though,' replied Joe, 'which is more than you can say for ours.'

Helen found her place somewhere in the middle of the table; Lady Macgregor, who had already been let into the secret, was on Sam's left. Helen was in an extremely bad mood and managed to find something wrong with each course.

As the last course was being cleared from the table, and just before Mary rose, Sam tapped his glass with a fork.

'Ladies and gentlemen,' he said, 'before the ladies retire, I have an announcement to make. I'm going to give them summat to talk about, even though to do that to women is like taking coal to Newcastle. I am sure that it will be a great help to their conversation if they know that, today, Miss Henrietta Cavandish has done my boy Harry the great honour of consenting to become his wife.'

There were murmurs of surprise from around the table, and Helen dropped her fork.

'Now off you go, Mary,' continued Sam. 'You can congratulate Hetty; I'm sure Harry needs a glass of port to give him the strength to face you lot.'

Mary led the ladies into the sitting room, where they clustered around Hetty, congratulating her. The old countess, still wearing nothing but the most gorgeous of black gowns, but now walking with the aid of a silver-topped cane, tapped her way to be the first.

'Join the club, my dear,' said the countess, embracing Hetty and kissing her.

Helen and a friend of hers, Eileen Warburton, were sitting apart and not taking part in the general buzz of conversation. Helen waited for a lull in the talk and then said in a low, but very definitely audible, voice, 'Isn't it wonderful the way that servants can marry into the family these days? So democratic, you know.'

There was a complete silence in the room. Helen had made her challenge, and it was up to Mary now. Hetty blushed furiously, but it was to Mary that everyone looked, waiting for an explosion. It never came.

'I quite agree,' said Mary, smiling graciously in Helen's direction. 'You know Hetty, dear, my boys are really coming up in the world. They used to find their brides hiding under bits of tarpaulin in ships' lifeboats. More coffee, Helen dear?'

Helen got to her feet, hands clenched and eyes blazing. She pushed past Mary and flung open the door to the dining room.

'Joe,' she called, 'I'm leaving now; you can stay or come as you choose.'

With that she stormed out of the room.

Jane had a wonderful honeymoon. Sam had given them the use of the Grosvenor Square house, and they spent the first week there. Of course court mourning meant that a lot of the glitter was taken from the London scene, but there were still the famous restaurants, such as Rules and Romanos, and the theatres – which had closed only on the day of the funeral – and Ian took Jane to them all. But those things apart, all they really wanted was to be alone together and enjoy each other.

Apart from a handsome cash settlement, Sam had given them a factory in Lancashire.

'You need never go near it,' he had said. 'It's got my best manager running it, and he's promised that when he retires he'll find another as good. It should keep you for the rest of your lives if you don't go mad.'

With some of their cash they had bought a motorcar; it was an American model called a Ford 'T'. It seemed to be a frightful extravagance, as they had so little time before Ian sailed and Jane had had some doubts, but one go behind the wheel, and she was thoroughly converted.

They decided that it would be a great adventure to drive their new toy all the way to Scotland, where they had promised to spend a little time with Ian's parents before he sailed. After a week in London they set out up the Great North Road. They stopped the first night at the George in Stilton and sampled some of its famous cheese, and then continued on through familiar Yorkshire to Newcastle, where they spent the next night at the palatial Station Hotel. On the third day they continued their journey through Alnwick, Berwick-on-Tweed, and so into Scotland and to Edinburgh.

There they stayed one night with an aunt of Ian's and left their car with her, not wishing to risk it on the rough highland roads. They went on by train to Inverness, where Ian's father met them. He drove them out to a little lodge on the estate, which was to be their home. It was a lovely little house of six rooms, set right in the Glen of Strathconnon and looking out over the grouse moor, the pastures, the deer forest, and the mountains beyond. Jane called it her fairy castle; it seemed so far from the real world.

In view of Ian's leaving so soon, Jane insisted that they go up to the big house for at least one meal every day. They also spent a day in Inverness, where The Macgregor booked passage for Jane on the *Himalaya*, which sailed for the Orient six weeks after the *Monmouth*. While they were booking the passage and Ian was making sure that Jane had a portside cabin, Jane noticed that there was a P & O liner sailing on the day following the *Monmouth*'s departure.

'Why could I not go on the P & O boat?' she asked that evening at dinner.

There was a rather embarrassed silence.

'I am afraid that would not be very wise, my dear,' said Lady Macgregor, 'but we'll talk about it after dinner.'

When the two ladies had gone in for coffee, Lady Macgregor explained. 'You see, Jane, you may have conceived a child during your honeymoon. It would be an awful waste for you to go all the way out there only to have to turn round and come straight back.'

'But couldn't I have the baby out there?' asked Jane.

'Oh, my dear, that would be out of the question. Not in the Far East; much too dangerous. You would have to come home, where you could have the best attention.'

'What would Ian say?'

'I am quite sure that he would agree with me. It is just a fact. I know it would be terribly hard for you, a young bride, to have to stay behind, but it really is the only thing to do. Anyhow, we shall know in six weeks, and then, if you are not pregnant, you will be able to go straight out and join your husband.'

Soon, all too soon, the day came when they had to leave for Portsmouth. Ian's captain had been most generous and told Ian that he need not join the ship until the day of departure, but that day was drawing very near. They had planned that Ian would be accompanied by Jane to Portsmouth, where Sam and Mary would meet her. From there they would all go back to Hardacres to sit out the six weeks before she sailed to join him.

They went south as they had come north, in easy stages, but this time they did not take their little car. They spent the first night in Edinburgh and caught the 'Flying Scotsman' at ten o'clock in the morning to King's Cross in London. They spent the final two nights in London at Grosvenor Square. Jane would not allow the servants to touch Ian's sea chest, packing all of his uniforms and tropical kit herself.

Ian suggested that perhaps she would like to say good-bye there and not come to Portsmouth, but she would have none of it. She went to Portsmouth with him, and they were so completely immersed in each other that they did not even notice that Sam and Mary did not seem to have turned up. For the first time since their very first meeting, Jane went aboard H.M.S. *Monmouth* to say her last good-bye.

At last the moment of parting came, and she walked down the gangway to the quayside. Sam and Mary were waiting there for her. Tactfully, they had kept out of the way until this very last moment.

She saw them, but she did not speak; she went to Sam and took hold of his hand. Silently they watched as the armoured cruiser slowly edged away from the quay and headed out towards the Channel. She made a brave sight, all newly painted in light, tropical grey, her brasses gleaming in the evening sun, black smoke pouring from her funnels, and the ship's band playing 'Hearts of Oak' on the quarterdeck.

Jane searched the rapidly shrinking figures on the decks, hoping for a last glimpse of Ian, but she never saw him.

The following summer Arnold came to Hardacres to spend his vacation with his grandparents. His reasons were twofold. Now, approaching his sixteenth birthday, he was, if anything, keener than ever on flying. After his first success Joe had established a small factory at Driffield for the production and development of flying machines, based on his initial conceptions and certain that military contracts would come. Joe and Helen stayed in London – Joe to keep close to his financial interests in the City, and Helen because she was bored anywhere else. It suited them fine that their children should prefer to spend the long holidays with Sam and Mary, as Helen, at least, always regarded their presence as an encumbrance, and it was a blow to her vanity to have to admit that she had a child of sixteen. Arnold's other reason was that, along with his sisters Emily and Maud, he loved Hardacres and his grandparents – this love was fully reciprocated by Sam and Mary. At Hardacres there were ponies to ride, country rambles, the sea nearby, and a freedom which they would never find in the city.

Arnold was a good-looking youth, though still slim and with the awkwardness of adolescence; he had big bones which were already beginning to fill out as they began the process of turning the boy into a man. He was tall and fair, and his hair was the same colour as Sam's had been before it had gone grey. He was ruddy-complexioned and had a profusion of freckles, which lay across his rather snub nose. He had the Hardacre blue eyes and a huge, engaging grin which, combined with a great deal of charm, usually got him what he wanted. He possessed all of his father's intensity, but it was touched and softened with the humanity he had inherited from his grandfather. Eton, with its usual, public-school choice of monastic celibacy or homosexuality, had not spoiled him. He had, almost by accident, lived a rather sheltered life, due probably to the fact that his passions were usually diverted into less carnal pursuits, such as his current infatuation with flying machines.

He spent many days out at Driffield, where he struck up a real and genuine friendship with Roger Beresford, his father's manager and chief pilot, and finally, with Sam's consent, he persuaded Beresford to teach him to fly.

He was not disappointed. The joy of sitting in one of his father's two-seaters and watching the fields and hedgerows creeping slowly past beneath his wings was superseded only by the thrill of his first solo.

It happened one afternoon just after they had landed. Beresford got out of the front cockpit, leaving the engine running.

'All right, Arnold,' he shouted over the roar of the motor, 'take her round yourself.'

For a moment Arnold could hardly believe his ears.

'You mean I should?' he yelled.

'Go on,' shouted Beresford, 'take off; once round the circuit and land. You can do it.' With which he ducked out of the way, leaving Arnold alone.

Arnold's lips and mouth became brick-dry, and he sat there for quite a while as the reality came to him. Gingerly he pushed the throttle forward, his mind racing as he tried to remember all that he had been told. The flimsy machine started to roll forward and bump across the grass of the field. Faster and faster it went, until the tail came up. He overcorrected and felt a thump as the tail hit the turf, but in the same instant his wheels left the ground, and he was flying.

He climbed slowly away from the field and then put the aeroplane into a gentle turn and watched as the earth moved up beneath his port wings; he levelled out, eased back on the stick, and watched the horizon drop away until all that he could see in front of him was clear sky. It was the most thrilling moment of his life; sitting up there free of the bonds of earth, he felt almost godlike. But now it was time to make his approach and land. He turned a long way from the field and eased the throttle back, letting the nose drop and all the time watching the horizon come up. The ground beneath him swept past, faster and faster, as he approached touch-down and then hit the field. He hit it about four times before the machine finally stayed down and rolled to a stop.

He taxied back to the hangar and switched off the motor. Beresford was there waiting.

'Well, any landing you walk away from is a good one,' he said.

Arnold went back to Hardacres that evening, arriving just in time to change for dinner. He relived again and again in his mind the experience of the afternoon; he was almost drunk with the thrill of it all, and throughout dinner he talked about nothing else.

'Happen, if you're such a great aviator, I'll have to let you take me up,' said Sam.

'And me,' said Maud.

'And me,' said Emily.

'Sam, don't you go letting those girls get ideas like that,' said Mary. 'And you're not going up in any flying machines. It's not natural, I'm sure.'

'All right, lass,' said Sam, 'just for you I'll stay on the ground. But I would like to go up just once,' he mused.

'I'll take you, Granddad.' Arnold was full of enthusiasm.

'Later mebbe,' said Sam, 'when you get a bit more practised.'

It was a very exhausted and elated Arnold who went up to his room shortly after dinner and snuggled down between the sheets with a copy of Jules Verne's *From Earth to the Moon*. He was too excited to sleep or to concentrate on his book. It must have been about ten thirty when the door to his room slowly started to open.

'I just wondered if you wanted anything, Master Arnold?'

It was Betty, the upstairs maid. Betty was nineteen – a happy, buxom lass possessed of huge breasts and over-developed buttocks which were always encased in a tight skirt and swayed invitingly when she walked. Mary had wanted to speak to her on more than one occasion but had never managed to find the words.

Betty came over to his bed, shutting the door behind her.

'No, thank you, Betty, I don't think I need anything.'

318

She sat down on the side of the bed and leaned over him. Arnold's face was almost touching that magnificent cleavage. He swallowed hard, and his breathing became heavy as he smelled her cheap perfume.

'Are you quite sure that there is nothing you would like, Master Arnold?' said Betty, and she ran her hand down his body to where a little tepee had formed in the middle of the blanket. 'My word, aren't you big.'

'Am I?' said Arnold, whose mouth was brick-dry for the second time that day. He felt that he ought to say something else as well, but the words would not come, so he just lay there with his mouth open.

She kissed him. Arnold had heard talk of such kisses at school, and thinking about them had been one of his youthful sexual fantasies, but the reality! Her tongue darted in and out of his mouth, her teeth nibbled away at his lower lip, and then she pulled her blouse out of her skirt and put his hand on her breast. He was amazed at its softness; he squeezed it gently and stroked the nipple, which hardened under his touch. Suddenly Betty pulled away from him.

'Don't go,' he gasped, 'please don't go.'

'Bless your heart, dearie, I'm not going anywhere. I want to show you something.'

Quickly she darted to the door and slid the bolt. Then she slipped out of her skirt and blouse. She wore no underwear, only a pair of black stockings which came up to just below the knee. She rolled these off and stood there naked watching him.

'There now, what do you think?'

Arnold sat up in bed speechless. He had never seen a naked woman before, apart from an illicit picture smuggled into Eton. He licked his dry lips as she came towards him.

'Do you think we should?' he managed to say.

'Of course, it's going to be lovely.'

She was at the bed and fumbling with the cord of his pyjamas. She took his hand and placed it on her tummy.

'Smooth, isn't it? ... Oh, that's beautiful ... now, darling, I must have it now.'

She was on the bed, pulling him on top of her. Fiercely

she guided him inside her, her body writhed beneath him, and she started to moan; for a moment Arnold thought that he was hurting her, and he started to withdraw.

'No, no, right in, harder, slowly now, don't rush, slowly.'

When it was over, Arnold thought – for the second time that day – that it was the most wonderful experience he had ever known. Nothing, nothing could ever be more wonderful than this. Betty gently stroked his now relaxed body, and suddenly he tried to blurt out his love for her.

'That's silly, Master Arnold,' she said kindly. 'It's nice – I hope it's nice for both of us, and we'll do it again, never you fear. But I'm not the sort you fall in love with. Folk like you and me just have fun together.'

'But . . .'

'And you're not the sort that my sort fall in love with, and as long as we keep it like that we can enjoy each other whenever we want.' She was putting her clothes back on as she spoke. 'Now, just you have a good night's sleep, Master Arnold, and when you see me during the day try to remember that I'm Betty, the upstairs maid, and you're the master's grandson. That way I'll be able to come back; 'night.'

She went out into the corridor, leaving him exhausted and relaxed; within minutes he was fast asleep.

The next morning, not surprisingly, Arnold slept late. It was after ten when he eventually went downstairs. He wandered into the dining room to find it deserted. All of the breakfast things would have been cleared over an hour ago. He was very hungry, so he made his way below stairs to the kitchen, where Mrs Grey was holding her morning court and giving tea to the female servants. He saw Betty among them and was about to turn back, when Mrs Grey spotted him.

'Come in, Master Arnold,' she said, 'we've just finished.'

Betty got up and came towards him.

'Good morning, Betty,' he managed to gasp out.

'Good morning, sir,' said Betty matter-of-factly as she brushed past him and went away about her duties with no sign that anything had changed in the last twenty-four hours.

'Now, Master Arnold,' said Mrs Grey, 'what can we do

for you? Somebody slept in, I hear?'

'How did you know that?' he replied, surprised.

'There's not much going on in this house that I don't know about,' said Mrs Grey, quite unaware of the embarrassment that her statement caused. 'I suppose that you're looking for something to eat?'

'Yes, please, Mrs Grey,' he replied, 'just a bite, a piece of bread and butter or anything.'

Mrs Grey had fixed ideas about growing boys and their need to be thoroughly nourished. 'Sit down, and we'll do something about it. Betty, set a place for Master Arnold.'

'No, please, I didn't mean . . .'

'Of course you did,' said Mrs Grey. 'A slice of bread and butter indeed. None of my young gentlemen are going through till one o'clock with nothing inside them but a slice of bread and butter.'

Five minutes later he was sitting at the scrubbed whitewood kitchen table, facing three eggs, two thick slices of grilled York ham, bread and butter, and a steaming mug of tea. He ate every bit of it; when Mrs Grey fed you in her kitchen, you did not dare to leave scraps or you got the sharp edge of her tongue.

'Gosh, Mrs Grey,' he said as he finished, 'that was great, but I shan't be able to eat any lunch now.'

'Of course you will, Master Arnold,' she replied. 'Why don't you persuade your father to go riding with you? The exercise would do him good, I'm sure, living in that awful city the way he does; it might give him an appetite as well.'

'My father?' Arnold was surprised.

'Yes.'

'Is he here?'

'Bless my soul,' said Mrs Grey, 'didn't you know? I shall have to have a word with Mr Joseph. He came late last night. He's in the study with the master now.'

Arnold made his way back upstairs. He went across the hall to the door of his grandfather's study. He could hear raised voices inside; there was obviously a heated argument going on.

'I know he's only fifteen,' it was his father shouting, 'but

321

it's damned well time he started.'

'I said it once, and I'll say it again – it's up to the lad.' Arnold recognized Sam's growl.

Under normal circumstances he would not have dreamed of butting in, but as they were talking about him, he tapped on the door.

'Come in,' shouted Sam.

'Oh, it's you,' said Joe.

'Hello, Dad,' said Arnold, 'I only just heard that you were here; I slept in.'

'I got in at eleven.' Joe was making an effort to calm himself. 'I thought it was a bit late to come up and disturb you.'

Thank God he didn't, thought Arnold. 'I had a heavy day yesterday; I went solo.'

'Aye, so your grandfather tells me.' Joe did not sound very enthusiastic about his adventure. 'Arnold, I came up here because I wanted to have a word with you about the future. Now would seem to be as good a time as any, so shut the door and come in and sit down.'

Arnold did as he was bid and sat in one of the leather armchairs which flanked the fireplace.

'Are you staying?' Joe asked Sam; it was more a challenge than a question.

'You know bloody well I am,' snapped Sam.

Joe turned to his son, trying to ignore his father. 'How do you like Eton, Arnold?'

'It's all right, I suppose; I never gave it much thought.'

'That's just what I mean – the most expensive school in the country, and you never give it much thought. How would you feel about leaving?'

Sam was making a supreme effort to keep his mouth shut.

'I'd always assumed that I'd stay there until it was time to go on to university.'

'Book learning never got anyone anywhere,' said Joe.

'That's not fair,' said Sam.

'It bloody well didn't,' said Joe. 'Not in this family, any road. Look at Harry. For all of his fine learning, he's never made a penny for himself. Well, has he?'

'He runs the estate, and he runs it damned well,' growled Sam.

'Runs the estate,' said Joe scornfully. 'That's kids' stuff; it's your estate, you gutted bloody herring for it.'

'And what if I did, and where do you think you would be today, mister high-and-bloody-mighty, if I hadn't?' Sam was getting really angry.

'Please,' said Arnold, butting in, 'could somebody tell me what this is all about?'

'I'll tell you,' said Sam. 'Your father wants you to leave school and go into business with him. Go on, tell him,' he snapped at Joe.

'All right,' said Joe, 'but let's be calm about it. Arnold, I've got an opening for you in the City; you could start right away. Within eighteen months you would be earning a thousand a year, and your prospects, the way the world is at the moment, would be limitless.'

'What's the job?' asked Arnold.

'Armaments,' said his father. 'Every country in Europe is building up its military forces just now, and there's a fortune to be made by just sitting in the middle and arranging the deals. Remember that one and a half per cent of a million is fifteen thousand.'

'Aye, bloody Krupps,' Sam almost spat with contempt.

'One of the best arms firms in the world, if not the best,' retorted Joe.

'I don't want it, Dad,' said Arnold.

'What did you say?' Joe's voice was low and menacing.

Arnold paused and swallowed hard; he did not enjoy defying his father, but he had to say it. 'I don't want to live in the city, and I don't want to have anything to do with wars and killing.'

'Do you think that whether you take this job or not is going to make any difference? There's a hundred folk'll do it if you don't.'

'That's their business.'

'You ungrateful little sod, I suppose that you want to end up a farmer, a gentleman, and a parasite like Harry?'

'You'll take that back, Joe,' said Sam.

'Uncle Harry was wounded in the war,' said Arnold.

'I'm damned if I'll take anything back,' stormed Joe, 'and I'm damned if I'm going to keep on paying expensive school fees just to turn you into another bloody little snob. I offer you the chance to be a millionaire, and you turn it down. You're no son of mine if you do that.'

With that Joe stalked out of the room.

'Well, Arnold,' said Sam after he had gone, 'it must be quite plain to you that your father and I don't see eye to eye about this. I told him that it had to be up to you; I promise you that if you want to stay at school, you can. I'll see to that.'

'All right, then,' said Arnold.

'What does that mean, boy?'

'I'll stay with you, Granddad.'

CHAPTER NINE

H.M.S. *Monmouth* rode at anchor in the still waters of the bay of Hong Kong Island. From Victoria she stood back, lit by the setting sun, and her three thin funnels and fore and aft twin turrets were silhouetted against the evening sky. She was dressed with strings of bunting and twinkling electric lights passing from the stern, over the two tall masts, and down to the bow. All over the deck lights shone and were reflected in the polished brass and the gleaming tampions. A large awning stretched from the after six-inch turret to the stern, where the ship's band sat waiting.

Jane sat aboard the captain's pinnace, in company with the wives of other officers, as it crossed the bay towards the ship. There was to be a ball on board that evening. They were entertaining officers from the German armoured cruiser *Scharnhorst*, which was making a courtesy call on Hong Kong.

Scharnhorst had arrived a few days ago, and a party of officers from *Monmouth* had been invited aboard the previous day to take schnapps with their German opposite numbers in their wardroom. Four years younger than *Monmouth*, *Scharnhorst* was, apart from the Japanese and American navies, probably the most powerful ship in the Pacific Ocean. She carried a broadside of eight 8.2-inch and six 5.9-inch guns, all modern and giving her over twice the fire power of the British ship. Ian and his brother officers had been most impressed at the obvious efficiency and power of the German ship and had spent a very pleasant couple of hours aboard talking shop with the *Scharnhorst*'s officers.

The little pinnace pulled up alongside *Monmouth*, and the ladies were assisted aboard. Ian was waiting at the top of the gangway to greet Jane, and he took her down to the wardroom for a glass of sherry while they awaited their German guests. When the signal was given that the German pinnace was alongside, they all went up on to the quarterdeck to greet them. As the Germans came aboard, Ian sought out a tall, blond Lieutenant.

'Karl,' he greeted him, 'come and meet my wife. Jane, darling, this is Lieutenant Karl Muller. He is the chap who was my host on *Scharnhorst*. Karl, this is my wife, Jane.'

'Lady Jane,' said the German with just the trace of an accent, 'I am delighted to meet you.' He clicked his heels and made a little bow in the German manner.

'Lieutenant Muller,' said Jane, taking his hand, 'let me add my thanks to my husband's for the hospitality you showed him yesterday. I understand from him that you have a very fine ship.'

'She is a good boat, yes, but you know, Lady Jane, always we judge our ships by the standards of the Royal Navy.'

'Standards or not, I should not like to have to take you on in this old tub,' said Ian. 'I'll try and grab a steward and get us some drinks.'

As Ian went off, the band struck up the first waltz.

'May I claim a stranger's privilege and ask you for this dance, Lady Jane?' asked Muller.

As they danced, he told her a little about himself – that he was married and that they had a little house in Munich, where his wife Heidi lived with her mother when he was at sea. And he laughingly explained how Ian and he, the previous day, had told each other that they had each married the most beautiful woman in the world.

'I disputed his claim, of course,' said Muller, 'but now, having met you, I must concede a draw.'

They both laughed at this. When the dance finished, they found Ian waiting with a bottle of champagne.

'The Germans and the British may make magnificent ships,' said Muller, raising his glass, 'but it takes a Frenchman to make champagne. I understand that you will be sailing for home quite soon?'

'There's no secret about that,' said Ian. '*Monmouth* is due to go into reserve next year. And if you chaps are going to keep *Scharnhorst* in the Pacific, we'll need something a bit tougher than this to keep an eye on you.'

'You don't think?' said Jane.

'Of course not,' said Ian.

'Who knows what the Kaiser or the politicians will do,' said Muller. 'Then there are the Russians and the French and the Serbs and the Austrians. Sometimes I fear for the world. We have too many guns and too many ships; it would require such a tiny spark to blow it all up.'

'I can never see Britain and Germany fighting, though,' said Ian. 'Can you?'

'If they do,' replied Muller, 'nothing will ever be the same again.'

It proved a most delightful evening. Jane was very taken with the young German, and she and Ian asked him if he could possibly get shore leave for the next day. Muller's captain was a guest at the party, so they approached him together.

'In the interests of England, German, and Scottish relations, ja,' he said in extremely bad English.

While the *Monmouth* was at Hong Kong, Ian was able to live ashore, except when he was on duty or they were at sea. The following morning they got up early and went to the docks to meet the *Scharnhorst*'s cutter. When they arrived, it was already pulling back to the ship and Karl was standing on the quay waiting for them.

They had hired a phaeton with a pair of hackneys and a Chinese coachman, and they set off to give Karl a day of sightseeing around the island. They went up the steep hills away from the harbour, through the Chinese quarter, where the long, painted banners and signs and the profusion of shops, which sold almost every article one could think of, were of great interest to Karl.

Their coachman spoke some English and acted as interpreter when Karl wanted to buy some ivory trinkets to send to Heidi. They went on, climbing all the time, until from the heights above the city they could look across the bay to Kowloon and the Chinese mainland beyond. In the bay they could see both of their ships at anchor, looking grim and purposeful.

Here it was considerably cooler than in the stifling heat of the city. They were in an area of gracious dwellings occupied by wealthy Chinese merchants and the higher echelons of the British colonial officials. They went across the island and had lunch at Stanley. Jane had taken a picnic basket, and they sat eating cold duck and ham and gazing out across the South China Sea. Then they wandered slowly around the coast to Aberdeen, where they had afternoon tea and cucumber sandwiches; at last they went back to Victoria in time for a gourmet's Chinese dinner at one of the many fine restaurants in the city.

They dined early because Karl had to return to his ship on the ten-o'clock liberty boat, but it had been a lovely day. Nothing, not even parting, could take away the pleasure that they had had. They had talked and talked about their very different lives and homes. Ian and Jane, both country lovers with large houses and staffs to run them; Muller, the son of a doctor, living a middle-class urban existence whenever he was not at sea. It might have been considered strange that they took such delight in each other's company, so diverse were their origins, but they all felt that a real and lasting friendship had been formed that day, and it was amidst a welter of promises to keep in touch that they said good-bye, always leaving open the possibility that they might be able to meet the following day.

The next morning Ian had to report aboard at eight, so they were up at dawn.

'Ian, look,' said Jane, who was standing by the window overlooking the bay.

Ian looked out across the water. Belching black smoke from her funnels, *Scharnhorst* was getting under way, heading for the open sea.

'There goes Karl,' said Ian.

'He should have told us,' said Jane.

'He probably didn't know. I think they're like that in the German navy.'

'I wonder if we'll ever see him again,' said Jane.

'I'm sure we shall; he's got our address, and I think he'll write. By the way, did you get his?'

'I completely forgot,' she replied. 'It was such a lovely day, and I had so many things on my mind. Ian, darling, I'm going to have to leave you.'

'Leave me?' said Ian. 'You must be joking.'

'Not this time, my love; we are going to have a baby.'

Ian sat down with his mouth open. 'You mean a baby?'

'Yes.'

'Isn't that marvellous! Isn't that just too wonderful,' he said.

'Not really, darling; most people do it.'

'We'll call him Peter. Do you know, I think I need a drink.'

'Ian, at seven o'clock in the morning?'

'The time is immaterial, my dear. I am in a state of shock.' He went to the sideboard and poured out a brandy. 'How about you?'

'I'll try to preserve the decencies and have a cup of tea,' said Jane, smiling.

Ian raised his glass. 'Here's to Peter,' he said. 'I must say, you've timed it right; you'll be home for the summer. It will be January next year before I make it. You are quite sure, I suppose?'

'What about?' she asked.

'The baby, of course. How long have you known?'

'I suspected it a couple of weeks ago. Your ship's surgeon confirmed it the night of the dance.'

'The rotter. He never told me a thing.'

'I asked him not to.'

'I wonder if he'll want to go into the navy?' said Ian.

'Peter might be a girl.'

'That's ridiculous. Who ever heard of a girl called Peter?' said Ian. 'I must dash.'

'You haven't had your breakfast,' she called after him.

'I'll get something on board.'

'And you'll breathe alcohol all over the crew.'

'I'll suck a peppermint,' he shouted. 'Take it easy, now,' and he was gone.

When Jane arrived back at Hardacres at the beginning of June 1913, the old countess was very ill, and it did not seem that she would last much longer. Jane had always been her special favourite, and it was a great joy to her when she heard that she would be coming home. The day that Jane was due to arrive she insisted on getting out of bed and dressing. Mary and her maid helped her and then took her downstairs to the morning room, where they sat her in one of the chintz-covered armchairs. So well had she done her job of preparation that when Sam saw her sitting there it took him back over twenty-five years to their first meeting.

'By gum, Harriet, but you look gradely,' he said.

'It's an illusion, Sam dear,' she replied, 'but I wanted to look my best when I met Jane.'

'You were always a spunky one,' said Sam.

'And your language always left something to be desired,' she reproved. 'When will Jane be here?'

'Any minute now; the train was due in at Driffield half an hour ago.'

'You will bring her straight to me?'

'Aye, love, don't you worry.'

It was about fifteen minutes later when Jane arrived, and Mary took her straight to the morning room.

'Hello, Aunt Harriet,' she said with that awkwardness usually felt in the presence of the very ill.

'Come closer, child,' said the countess, 'I don't see as well as I used to.'

'But you look marvellous,' said Jane.

'It's an illusion, Jane, my dear. The sad thing about growing old is that you always want to do just one more thing, and one day there comes a point when you can't,' she said. 'So you're going to have a baby, Jane? How I should love to be able to see it, but I fear I shall not be able to wait. Now give me a kiss, and run along and get yourself settled in.'

Jane did as she was bid, and they left the countess alone.

When they returned to the morning room about half an hour later, she was still sitting in her armchair smiling slightly, but she did not reply when they spoke to her. Harriet, Countess of Lewiston, had left Hardacres at last.

There were other changes at Hardacres that year. Ian had been right; in November Jane gave birth to a baby boy, and they called him Peter. Early in the new year Ian returned from the Far East. *Monmouth*, now an ageing and out-of-

date ship by naval standards, was transferred to the reserve
fleet. As for Ian himself, he decided to leave the navy and
concentrate on their Scottish estate, so he, like his ship, transferred to the reserve, and they moved to their lodge on the
Connon estate with baby Peter.

Wilson, who was getting very old now, had gone into semi-
retirement. Sam had asked him to take a cottage on the estate
and a generous pension, but he would have none of it.

'What do you want to do, then?' Sam asked.

'With your permission, sir, I shall carry on with my duties.'

'Wilson,' said Sam, 'you're not bloody immortal, and you
may not have noticed it, but you're getting old.'

'Are you dissatisfied with my work, sir?'

'No, dammit, of course I'm not, it's just, well ... will you
at least engage an underbutler and teach him the ropes and
then start taking a bit of time off your sen?'

Wilson sulked a bit, but he engaged a man of about forty
by the name of Gunn. Gunn came with excellent references
and soon proved to be a valuable new addition to the household. Little by little Wilson delegated most of his duties to
Gunn, but he would not move out of his rooms in the house
and still kept an eye on everything.

His Majesty King George V was to review his navy, in the
Solent in the middle of July, and the Macgregors and Hardacres had taken a house in Southampton for the occasion. Ian
had been recalled to the colours, as the entire navy was being
mobilized for this occasion, and he had once again gone
aboard *Monmouth*, now crewed by reservists, for what he
imagined would be a couple of weeks at the most.

The Hardacre contingent joined the Macgregors in Southampton on the seventeenth while the fleet was completing
assembling. It was the greatest display of naval might in
history. The lines of grey ships stretched for thirty miles.
Fifty-eight of them were capital ships, battleships, and battle-
cruisers, headed by the flagship of the commander-in-chief,
H.M.S. *Iron Duke* flying the flag of Admiral Jellicoe; and
the royal yacht *Victoria and Albert*. It was certainly a most
magnificent sight; it was the power of empire. Surely any
nation which possessed such a mighty arm must be invulner-

able; that was how it looked to Sam.

For three days they watched the fleet, and in the evenings did the social round for the first time without the countess. They took little notice of the odd paragraph which appeared in the papers about how angry the central European powers were getting over the shooting of the heir to the throne of Austria, by some fanatic in Sarajevo. It had happened three weeks ago, and the only surprising thing was that it was still being mentioned.

'After all,' said Sam, 'these bloody foreigners are always shooting each other.'

'I've got a feeling that there's more to it this time,' said Harry, who was, without being unduly worried, a little perturbed by the events on the international scene.

'Anyhow, it's nowt to do with us,' said Sam.

At the end of the three-day review there was an air of almost intoxication in the national pride of those who had watched this once-in-a-lifetime sight, as the great ships finally steamed out of the Solent for a short exercise in the North Sea.

They stayed in Southampton a few more days but finally left for Yorkshire without Ian. They were not worried, least of all Jane; it was just one of those things that happened in the navy. They were quite sure that Ian would be back in time to go up to Scotland for the twelfth when the grouse shooting opened.

They would have been less complacent about Ian if they had known that *Monmouth* was at that moment ploughing her way to join Admiral Craddock at the Falkland Islands.

On the other side of the American continent, Admiral Von Spee raised his flag on *Scharnhorst*, aboard which was Karl Muller, and with his squadron slipped away to lose himself in the vastness of the Pacific Ocean.

CHAPTER TEN

On 4 August the whole family had gathered at Hardacres for lunch. With the exception of Ian, they were all there; the Macgregors had not yet left for Scotland. Joe and Helen were paying one of their rare visits north, and, as usual, Arnold, Emily, and Maud were spending their summer holiday with their grandparents. Harry and Hetty, with Noel and Vanessa, were there, and of course Jane, who would be leaving within the next day or two to accompany the Macgregors to Scotland while Sam and Mary would stay at Hardacres and come up with Ian.

Wilson had made an appearance at that lunch, supervising the meal as silently and efficiently as ever. It was during the last course; he had been out of the room for some time, then came over and murmured something to Sam. Sam nodded to him and tapped his spoon on the table.

'I've got an announcement to make, which is going to affect all of us here. You all heard yesterday that there was a chance that Britain would send an ultimatum to Germany? Well, Wilson has just been on the telephone to London, and I can tell you all that the ultimatum was sent and there was no reply. We are at war with Germany and have been for several hours.'

His announcement was greeted with silence. He turned to Wilson. 'Thou'd better get down to the servants' hall and tell them all. I'll come and talk to them later.'

He looked around the table, wondering what each of them was thinking. Jane was easy; she would be worried about where Ian was and sad in the realization that he would not be coming home for some considerable time. Joe? He looked at Joe; there was just the hint of a smile on Joe's face. Mercenary bastard, thought Sam. Joe would do well out of it. Arnold looked delighted. Both he and Noel were in the Officer Training Corps at Eton; if it lasted any time, Arnold would be able to go – he was nearly eighteen, and from the look on his face he wished he was already of military age. Harry was also looking at the boys; with his leg he was out of it, and he felt truly thankful that Noel was too young.

'Well,' said Sam, breaking the silence. 'Is there nobody going to say owt?'

'It can't last long,' said The Macgregor. 'You saw those ships the other day. And speaking of ships, I wonder where Ian is? I'll warrant you do too, my dear, eh?'

'I do hope he'll be all right,' Jane replied.

'Of course he will,' said The Macgregor. 'The navy's the safest place to be, I should think.'

'They must have expected this during the review,' said Harry. 'I mean with all the ships going to sea without warning and nobody knowing where they've gone.'

'I'll bet that was young Churchill's doing,' said Sam. 'He's a bright one, that.'

'Lucky for him there was a war,' said The Macgregor. 'He'd have had his head well and truly on the block if he'd done that and wasted all that money, and there hadn't been a war.' He turned to Jane. 'Well, my dear, the question now is what you are going to do; we shan't be offended if you decide that you'd rather stay with your own parents.'

'Thank you, I really would; I hope you understand.'

'How about you?' said Mary to the Macgregors. 'Why don't you stay here a bit longer?'

'Couldn't do that,' said The Macgregor. 'Half the estate workers are in the militia; there's going to be a hell of a mess up there.'

And so the conversation drifted on, discussing the war and what it would mean to them all. Joe decided that he and Helen had better get back to London immediately.

'What's the rush?' Sam asked.

'Well, the stock exchange is going to be going mad, and I've got a lot of investment to look after. And another thing – I've got the feeling that this is going to be a long war.'

'Great,' said Arnold.

'Don't talk like that,' said Mary.

'Sorry,' said Joe, 'but it's still true, and there's nothing that we can do about it.'

'Except make a profit,' said Sam with heavy sarcasm.

'Exactly,' said Joe. 'I see no reason why we can't make a killing.'

'I think that that is a rather unfortunate choice of words,' said Lady Macgregor.

'Again I'm sorry,' said Joe, 'but it stands to reason that everything in heavy industry is going to rocket sky high, and I'm going to be in on it. How about you, Dad?'

'No, thanks, Joe, I don't want that kind of money,' said Sam, compressing his lips

'Have it your way,' replied Joe casually.

'Listen, Joe, if you're going, you'd better get ready; if you want to be in London today, you'll have to catch the five o'clock from Hull.'

Sam could see that he was well on the way to another blazing row with Joe, and with the Macgregors around he wanted to avoid it if he could.

'What do you say, Helen?' asked Joe. 'Do you want to come?'

'Of course,' replied Helen, 'I wouldn't want you to go alone.'

Joe smiled cynically; he knew full well that Helen was always bored at Hardacres and longed for any excuse to get back to the city. Still, it suited him, so they agreed to leave the children with their grandparents and left early that afternoon.

Mary decided that they should take afternoon tea on the lawn, as it was such a beautiful day; Sam had sent into Driffield to get any newspapers that were still available. They were sitting around reading the reports and theorizing about the war when Gunn came to Jane with a silver salver.

'Lady Jane, there is a letter for you,' he said.

'Thank you, Gunn,' she replied, taking the envelope from the tray.

'It is from Germany, madam,' said Gunn. Jane looked at him sharply, but his face was impassive as he walked away.

'Who do you know in Germany?' asked Mary.

'It's from Karl Muller; he's the German officer I told you

about, the one we got to know in Hong Kong.' And then she added defensively, 'He's a friend of ours.'

'But he can't be your friend now,' said Mary. 'He's a German; he's an enemy.'

'Why don't you tell us what the letter says?' said Sam. 'Or would you rather take it into the house to read?'

'It was written two weeks ago, so I doubt if there is anything in it which you should not know,' replied Jane. 'Just give me a moment.'

They watched her in avid silence as she read the letter.

'Do you want to hear what it says?' asked Jane.

'It's up to you,' replied Sam, 'but I think it would be good for your mother to hear what it says. I can't see how this war business can turn a chap you like into a monster overnight.'

'I didn't mean that at all,' said Mary.

'Happen you didn't, love,' said Sam, 'but let Jane get on with the letter.'

'All right,' said Jane, 'this is what he says.'

Dear Lady Jane,

Please forgive me for not writing to you before. I had hoped that Heidi or I might have heard from you, until I realized that you might not have our address. I am sending this letter to Heidi and asking her to forward it to you. It is against our rules, but I feel that our friendship is worth a little risk, and I hope that she will be able to get it to you before events make it too difficult for us to communicate.

I cannot tell you how distressed we are at the thought that our two countries might become enemies. Having met you and your husband and all the charming people with whom I and my brother officers had the privilege of spending those happy days in Hong Kong, it seems wicked that events should have taken this dreadful turn. If war does come, I fear that it will be long and bitter. There are those Germans and, I have no doubt, many in your country, who say it will all be over in a few weeks, but I very much fear that this will not happen. Both of our nations are too strong. To me it is all very senseless; I do not hate England, and I hope and pray that you will not hate Germany.

For myself, if it happens I shall of course do my duty, and I know that Ian will do his. But it will always be my prayer that he and I will never meet in battle.

Always your friend,
Karl.

'Well that's it,' said Jane. 'It's just a letter from a friend who happens to be a very fine gentleman and a German.' She paused, and then, as her mother was about to speak, she said with a voice full of emotion, 'I'd rather no one said anything,' and ran into the house.

Sam watched her go and shook his head sadly. 'Happen that won't be the last tear to be shed over this lot,' he said.

CHAPTER ELEVEN

On 28 September 1914, H.M.S. *Monmouth* lay in the bay at Punta Arenas, sheltered temporarily from the fierce seas of the Horn which lay not many miles to the south.

She was under orders to sail for Port Stanley in the Falkland Islands on the other side of the tip of South America and to coal there. For Ian Macgregor and the rest of the crew the prospect was not a pleasant one. They had recently passed through the Straits of Magellan, and now they had to do it all over again in the opposite direction. The seas in those South American waters were among the most unfriendly in the whole world, made even worse in a ship which rolled up to thirty-five degrees – making everyone aboard cold, miserable, and if not actually seasick extremely uncomfortable. *Monmouth* had a main armament of fourteen 6-inch guns, but in any sort of sea the barbettes in her main deck were awash and could not be worked, thus reducing her fire power by half.

More alarming than the ship was the state of the crew. They were all brave and gallant men, who accepted the eternal diet of corned beef and nearly rotting potatoes and the myriads of cockroaches which shared their ship with them, but about 90 per cent of the ship's company of 675 officers and men were reservists. They had been, like Ian, called to the colours a couple of months ago and were completely without the basic training and 'working up' which a man-of-war requires in order to become an efficient fighting machine. Captain Brandt, commanding *Monmouth*, was as aware as Ian of the deficiencies of his ship and crew, and had confessed to Ian that he hoped that they would not be unfortunate enough to meet with Von Spee and his two modern armoured cruisers S.M.S. *Scharnhorst* and *Gneisenau*, either of which could sink *Monmouth* without ever having to take the risk of coming within range of her guns.

On 2 October they arrived at Port Stanley, and the filthy business of coaling began. The coal, which had been stored in huge dumps on the island, was loaded into sacks and then manhandled aboard a lighter, which took it out to the ship. There the sacks were hoisted aboard by means of the ship's derricks. The coal was transferred to wheelbarrows, which were taken across the deck and tipped down one of a number of holes which led to the bunkers below. In war conditions everyone, officers included, took part in coaling, and before the bunkers were filled, everything and everyone was covered with fine coal and dust. It was quite impossible to recognize even one's best friend.

When the beastly, backbreaking business was over and at last the bunkers were full, the ship was hosed down, and the crew washed – the hardier spirits, Ian among them, diving into the bay with a bar of coarse, naval-issue soap and spending a good half hour in the cold water removing the grime. As soon as he was clean and dressed, Ian was told that he was to accompany his captain and the first lieutenant and report to Admiral Craddock, aboard the flagship *Good Hope*. Craddock, a bearded veteran with twinkling eyes and the air of an Elizabethan privateer, commanded what must have been just about the most obsolete squadron in the Royal Navy.

The Admiral told them that he had information that the German China squadron, consisting of the two armoured cruisers and three light cruisers commanded by Admiral Von Spee, was at sea in the South Pacific. He had decided to detach *Monmouth* – accompanied by his only modern ship, the fast light cruiser *Glasgow* – to go into that area and conduct a search.

Their instructions were that they were on no account to attempt to engage the enemy, which would be tantamount to suicide, but in the event of finding any of the German force they were to use *Glasgow* to shadow them and wait.

'What do we wait for, sir?' asked Ian.

'You wait,' replied Craddock, 'until you are reinforced by the rest of the squadron before attempting an engagement.'

'Including *Canopus*?' asked Captain Brandt. *Canopus* was

an old pre-dreadnought battleship, mounting four 12-inch guns.

'Including *Canopus*,' said the Admiral. 'Without her, we would stand very little chance.'

They sailed again the following day, 3 October. Just before the ships weighed anchor, a launch came out from the shore to deliver and collect mail. Ian handed over letters to Jane and to his parents, and collected three letters in return, all from Jane. One of these related the text of Karl Muller's letter. Ian read it and realized that he too felt as Karl did. He wondered also if Karl were still aboard *Scharnhorst*. The ship had quite a reputation, having won the Kaiser's prize for gunnery two years running, and that meant a well-worked-up ship with a stable crew.

Once again they rounded the Horn and suffered. At times the ship behaved more like a submarine than a surface vessel; the decks were continually awash, as the bow pushed through one mountainous sea after another, and half the crew were so miserable that they did not care if the ship ever came up again. But at last it was over, and they entered the Pacific and started their sweep to the north, keeping a careful wireless watch in the hope of picking up enemy signals.

For twenty days they searched, and on 27 October, in Vallenar Roads – about halfway between the Horn and a small Chilean town called Coronel – they were joined by their admiral and *Good Hope*; then the filthy business of coaling began again. Hundreds of miles to the south the old battleship *Canopus*, the fortress around which they needed to fight any engagement with the armoured cruisers of the China squadron, lumbered its way as far as Punta Arenas.

As soon as the ships had coaled, Craddock, without waiting for the battleship, put to sea with his squadron in line abreast and spread out across a line of about twenty-five miles, and continued the sweep north. Ian realized that his admiral was not a complete fool and assumed, correctly, that there were in fact hopes of meeting with the German units singly. This would not be surprising, as the prime object of the China squadron would undoubtedly be to disrupt British and Allied shipping by commerce raiding in the Pacific. Even so, it could be argued that either *Scharnhorst* or *Gneisenau* alone could be regarded as a superior force to the whole of Craddock's squadron unless *Canopus* was with them.

On 30 October, *Glasgow* pulled out of the search on orders from the Admiral; she had been sent to Coronel to see if the British consul there had any signals from the Admiralty. For the others the seemingly endless search continued.

At midday on 1 November *Glasgow* rejoined the squadron, and the exciting news was flashed around the ships that she had intercepted wireless messages which appeared to come from the German light cruiser *Leipzig*. It seemed that *Leipzig* was alone, and if this was so, she would be a sitting duck for the British squadron.

Craddock formed his ships into line ahead and cleared for action, with *Good Hope* leading *Monmouth*. It was just after four in the afternoon that Ian, standing on the bridge of *Monmouth*, saw a smudge of smoke over the horizon to the east. The Admiral had seen it too, for he immediately altered course to converge on the ship that had been sighted.

It had to be one of the German ships. Had they found *Leipzig*? Their position was, at that time, ideal. The sun was getting low to the west, and the enemy to the east would be dazzled by it. In half an hour the picture changed completely.

It was not a lone *Leipzig* but the whole German China squadron. The British were now committed to battle, and their faster and more powerful enemy could dictate the terms on which it would be fought. Apart from wishing that *Canopus* were with them, Ian was surprised at his own feeling of almost complete detachment as the Germans kept just out of range. Ian realized what they were doing, and, as a professional, he respected them. They were waiting until the sun set. When that happened, the British would be silhouetted against the afterglow, while the Germans, now so brilliantly lit, would turn into mere smudges on the horizon. Ian thought of the letter he had been writing to Jane; it lay unfinished in his cabin. He thought of the son whom he might never see again, and then he thought of his friend who might, at this very moment, be standing on the deck of *Scharnhorst* looking at him.

The sun set, Von Spee started to close the range, and a little after seven o'clock there was a flicker of fire along the side of *Scharnhorst*. A few seconds later huge columns of water rose out of the sea around *Good Hope*, and then there was a flicker of light along the side of *Gneisenau*. The battle of Coronel was on.

Three days later rumours started to filter through to England that there had been a naval engagement in the southern seas. The first reaction of the British public was one of elation. After all, a naval engagement automatically meant a British victory to a nation which had been brought up on the belief that its fleet was invincible.

Back at Hardacres there was intense speculation about what had happened, not the least from the boys Arnold and Noel, who wanted to find out if Uncle Ian had been lucky enough to be in the fight. Both of them offered lurid accounts of what Uncle Ian's ship would have done to those wicked Germans. Only Jane had doubts; she had seen *Monmouth* and *Scharnhorst* lying together in friendship in Hong Kong, and she had listened while her husband jokingly told Karl Muller how he would not like to meet *Scharnhorst* in anger.

They were all gathered together in the morning room, discussing the rumour and the raid by four German battle cruisers off Yarmouth a couple of days ago, when Sam came into the room. He carried *The Times*, and his face was grim.

'Is there something wrong, Granddad?' asked Arnold.

Sam ignored him. 'Jane, your mother would like to see you. She's in her sitting room.'

With a heavy heart, for she feared what she might be about to hear, Jane climbed the stairs to her mother's sitting room. She found Mary sitting by the fire holding baby Peter.

'Come and sit down along of me, lass,' said Mary, indicating the chair opposite her.

'Mother, is it about Ian?'

'Aye, lass,' said Mary. 'Tha won't be seeing him again, he's gone. Yon battle we've been hearing about was no great victory. Your father just read the paper to me. We lost every one of our ships over on the other side of the world.'

'*Monmouth?*'

'She were one of them.'

'Were there any survivors?' Jane was clutching at straws. 'Surely they weren't all lost.'

'I only wish that I could give thee some hope, Jane, but I can't. The paper said the *Monmouth* and *Good Hope* were lost with all hands. I'm sorry, Jane, sorry for all of us, but for thee it mun be summat that none of us can comprehend.'

Jane sat silent. There was nothing to say, there was nothing she could say; she could only try to stem the pictures that flooded her mind, pictures of the cruel green waters, the shroud of the husband she loved so much.

'Dost tha want to be alone?' asked Mary quietly.

'It doesn't matter,' said Jane in a flat toneless voice. 'It doesn't matter.'

She got up and walked to the window and looked out over the green lawns and hedges; she thought of the mountains and the glens of the home that he had loved. 'It's hard to believe that he'll never see them again,' she said. 'It suddenly all seems so empty.'

'Jane,' said Mary, 'thou's got the bairn. Thou's still got thy baby to live for. Without Ian, thou's got to be father as well as mother to him.' She went over to her daughter at the window. 'Here, take him.' She put the child into Jane's arms. 'It might be better if I leave thee here with him. Send for me if tha wants owt.'

Mary went out, leaving Jane with the baby. She took Peter over to the fire and sat holding him close to her breast.

In the morning room, after Jane had left, there was a silence, and then Harry turned to his father. 'Is it bad, Dad?' he asked.

'Aye,' said Sam, 'it couldn't be worse.'

'Ian?' Harry asked.

'You'd better listen to this,' said Sam, opening the paper.

NAVAL BATTLE IN THE PACIFIC
A Valparaiso dispatch to the *New York Herald*
Just what happened before the battle is yet to be reported,

but this much is known.

The British ships, under Rear Admiral Sir Christopher Craddock, left port on Sunday to continue their search for the German raiders the *Gneisenau* and *Scharnhorst* and their companion cruisers. The Germans closed in and opened fire. The British ships apparently never came within good fighting range. The *Monmouth* continued the battle until her hull was riddled. She toppled over in the water and lay for a moment with her keel lapped by the waters and then plunged to the bottom with all hands.

After *Monmouth* disappeared, the Germans closed in on *Good Hope*, the big guns of the two armoured cruisers firing with marvellous accuracy. With flames bursting from her in a dozen places, her superstructure carried away, her guns out of commission, the *Good Hope* finally turned and ran ashore with water pouring into her hull. She could be seen settling in the water. The German report states that they, the Germans, followed her until darkness hid her from view.

The *Glasgow* was also seriously damaged.

'And that's the story,' said Sam.

'Is there nothing else?' asked Arnold. 'Didn't we get any of them at all?'

Sam shook his head.

'That's a German report,' said Harry. 'Is there no British comment? Surely the Admiralty has said something.'

'There's nowt,' said Sam, 'and I doubt if that would have been printed if they weren't damned sure it was true.'

For the next few days Hardacres was a quiet place. Even Arnold and his sisters were subdued. Everyone seemed to be waiting, though no one could have told you what they were waiting for. It came at last. The dreaded telegram arrived. It did not come to Hardacres but was sent to Castle Connon, and Lord Macgregor and his wife travelled overnight to Yorkshire rather than telephone the news. Sam was walking in the drive when their taxi pulled up beside him.

'Angus,' he said in surprise, 'what brings you here?'

'The telegram's come,' said The Macgregor. 'We just felt that we ought to be here.'

'That was kind,' said Sam.

The Macgregor took a buff envelope from his pocket, which was addressed to Jane, and handed it to Sam.

'The Admiralty regrets to announce the death in action of Lieutenant Sir Ian Macgregor R.N. Their Lordships wish to add their personal sympathy to that of His Majesty at this great loss to you and to the nation.'

'Shall I give it to her, or will you?' asked The Macgregor.

'I'd rather keep it for a while, if you don't mind,' said Sam. 'It doesn't tell her anything that she doesn't know. Tell her that you've had confirmation, but we'll not give her this, not yet, any road.'

They went back up to the house together and in silence.

Jane expressed a desire to stay on at Hardacres, for a while at least. As Lord Macgregor was to take up an appointment at the Admiralty, this suited everyone, especially as the Macgregors agreed to stay on at Hardacres until his appointment was due. Slowly normality began to filter back into the household.

The Macgregors had decided to stay until 12 November, when Lord Macgregor was to go to London to take up his post. So it was on the eleventh Sam decided to give them a farewell dinner party. That was the day that Jane got a letter with a Swiss postmark.

She said nothing about it, but shut herself up in her room with it and refused to come out until Mary persuaded her that she was being very rude to her in-laws. So, dressed in black, she came down to dinner.

To everyone's surprise Sam placed a copy of his newspaper beside his plate. It was unusual, but Sam made no remark about it while dinner was being served. He seemed to be in a brighter mood than he had been for the last month, since the news of Coronel had arrived. As they finished the last course and Gunn was clearing the table prior to the ladies' retirement, Sam rose to his feet.

'Gunn,' he said, 'we are all going to remain here for a little while. I have some important news, which I am sure everyone would like to hear. If any of the servants are around, you may bring them in.'

Sam would not answer any questions until Gunn returned with several of the servants, including Wilson, Mrs Grey, and several of the maids – including Betty.

When they were all assembled Sam began, 'We've got a bit of good news at last.' He picked up his newspaper. 'It's headed "NAVAL VICTORY".'

There was an interested murmur of appreciation, and Sam continued to read:

An important naval success is officially announced.

The German squadron under Admiral Graf von Spee, which on the first of November sank the *Good Hope* and *Monmouth* off the Chilean coast, was on Tuesday morning brought to action off the Falkland Islands by a British squadron under Vice-Admiral Sturdee.

The armoured cruisers *Scharnhorst* and *Gneisenau* and the light cruiser *Leipzig* were sunk. The light cruisers *Dresden* and *Nürnberg*, made off during the fight, but are being pursued.

The Admiralty statement, which was issued to the Press Bureau at 7:50 on Wednesday night, is as follows:

'At 7:30 A.M., December the eighth, the *Scharnhorst*, *Gneisenau*, *Nürnberg*, *Leipzig*, and *Dresden* were sighted near the Falkland Islands by a British squadron under Vice-Admiral Sir Doveton Sturdee.

'An action followed, in the course of which the *Scharnhorst*, flying the flag of Admiral Graf von Spee, the *Gneisenau*, and the *Leipzig* were sunk.

'The *Dresden* and the *Nürnberg* made off during the action and are being pursued. Two colliers were also captured.

'The Vice-Admiral reports that the British casualties were light.

'Some survivors have been picked up from the *Gneisenau* and the *Leipzig*.'

'Gunn,' said Sam, 'give everyone a glass of port, and we'll drink to the Royal Navy and damnation to the King's enemies.'

All of them cheered the news, and a loud hum of conversation broke out around the table as Gunn and Wilson filled glasses for everyone. Only Jane was silent. Suddenly she leapt to her feet and rushed out of the room.

There was an embarrassed silence until she returned a few moments later, clutching a letter. She took her place at the table, and Gunn placed a glass of port in front of her. Sam rose to his feet.

'I want to propose a toast,' he said. 'I want you all to stand and drink a health to the Royal Navy and to hell with the Germans.'

They all stood up.

'Stop it!' Jane was on her feet, shouting. 'Stop it, all of you, have you no shame?'

'Shame?' said Sam. 'What do you mean by that?'

'Jane!' said Mary.

'No, Mother,' she said, 'you're going to listen, all of you.' She waved the letter at them. 'Today I got this letter; do you know where it's from? It's from Germany.'

There was a hushed silence.

Jane continued. 'It was written three weeks ago, and it says:

Dear Lady Jane.

I have given this letter to a friend who will try to post it for me in Switzerland. I do hope that it manages to reach you.

We have just received news of the terrible battle in the Pacific Ocean. They have told us that the British ship *Monmouth* was sunk with all hands. I know how good you and your husband were to my dear Karl when he was in China, and he told me such a lot about you and how you all became such great friends. He was so fond of you and so admired your husband that, when our boy was born last June, we called him Ian.

I can only hope and pray that Sir Ian was no longer on the *Monmouth*, because if he was, then this would be a double tragedy, for Karl is still on the *Scharnhorst* and that would be too terrible for us all.

I thought that you would like to know that, after the battle, Karl tells me in a letter I received today, they put into a port where our consul proposed a toast, "Damnation to the British Navy". Our admiral, who is a very fine gentleman, got up and said, "I drink to the memory of a gallant and honourable foe." There can be little joy in the horrible necessity of war.

If this terrible thing has happened and your dear husband has been lost, I can only hope that the knowledge that his name lives on in our son will be of some small comfort to you.

Perhaps, when all this horrible business is over, we may be able to meet you at last.

Your friend,
Heidi Muller.'

Jane threw the letter on the table. 'That's from a woman I've never met, who considers herself my friend, who named her little boy after my Ian. Who probably doesn't even know yet that she too is a sailor's widow. Now, if you want to go ahead and drink "Damnation to the German Navy", please do.'

CHAPTER TWELVE

Arnold had disappeared. He had not returned to Eton after the Easter break for his final term, and no one at Hardacres had had any word from him. Even Joe had been worried and had taken a trip up north to try to see if there was anything that could be done to trace him. Arnold and Noel had left together to return to school, but Arnold had said nothing to Noel, whom he had accompanied as far as London, but who had not seen him since they left King's Cross Station. Noel had assumed that they had merely separated accidentally and would meet up again at Windsor.

In a country where hundreds of families were losing loved ones every day in the eternal static war of attrition which was being waged in Flanders, where every activity was subjugated to the war effort, the disappearance of one youth was of little importance to anyone except his immediate kith and kin.

In France, nothing moved. The lines of trenches stretched from the English Channel in the north to the Swiss frontier in the south, and men were living a semi-subterranean existence, pausing – as and when the opportunity arose – to kill one another. At home, after the first rush of recruits in 1914 and the appearance on the streets of the blinded and the maimed, people were beginning to ignore the poster of Kitchener pointing his finger at them and exhorting 'Your Country Needs You.' There were even rumours that conscription – that most un-British of concepts – was to be introduced soon.

At Hardacres in the spring of 1915 many things had changed. Jane had returned from Scotland and, though previously regarded with suspicion because of the letters she received from Germany, had now 'become accepted and popular as the first local war widow'. There were two villages within a mile or so of the house, Watton and Hutton Cranswick, and Mary, ever practical, had organized a ladies' committee for providing comforts for the troops, and in so doing had completely overturned the social order of the house, for Mrs Grey was the president. Sam had provided them with mountains of khaki wool, and together – servants, friends, and acquaintances – they gathered every Tuesday and Thursday in the drawing room, knitting, sewing, and packing bundles to be sent to the centre in Hull for shipment to France and distribution to the troops.

Harry, unaccepted for military services because of his game leg, had had as much of the estate as possible put to the plough, to provide food and animal feed for the nation's store. Sam visited every one of the businesses in which he held a controlling interest and made a speech to his employees. He told them that if they volunteered for the forces, he would guarantee that their jobs would be there waiting for them when they returned. He employed women to take the places of the men who answered the call and went to the front. Among them were Emily and Maud, and Sam was rather proud to think of them standing at a factory bench.

'I've spawned a race of little aristocrats,' he would say, 'but they've still got guts. There never was a Hardacre who was ashamed to gut a herring.'

The business of Arnold was a worry. There were rumours of cowardice – there were those who said that he had gone into hiding, fearing that he might be called up. Sam did not know and was not prepared to make a judgement. He blamed Joe for giving the boy the means to disappear in the shape of an allowance of two hundred pounds a year, and they had yet another of their rows over this. As for Joe, he was too busy to bother. His fortune was increasing at an incredible rate. Sam had made enough and wanted only to live in the comfort that his efforts had brought him, but Joe wanted money for its own sake and the power that it gave him. Helen lived with Joe in London, where she patronized every war charity which would secure her social advancement. Joe, who had little real affection for his wife, indulged her in this with cynical amusement.

On one occasion she was presented to the Prince of Wales. When she returned home, full of the event, Joe remarked, 'It's not bad to have come from a ship's lifeboat to the Royal

Family in twenty years.' But he did not mind; Helen's social contacts became Joe's business contacts.

Joe did not bother much about his children; he had practically handed them over to Sam and Mary. Not that the children minded, for they adored their grandparents, and their grandparents loved them and wanted them. As for Helen, she was delighted not to have the embarrassment of an eighteen-year-old son walk into a room where she was showing off her carefully and expensively preserved youth.

Arnold did return. He did not go to his parents but to Hardacres, which he always considered home.

It was eleven o'clock on 8 August 1915. Sam and Mary had just settled down to their glass of wine in the morning room when a young officer in service dress came in and stood just inside the door.

'Hello,' said Sam. He was not surprised, for strangers in uniform were common at Hardacres, where they kept open house for servicemen of all ranks. 'Come in and have a glass of wine.'

Mary had risen to her feet, an expression of horror on her face as she ran to the young man standing in the doorway. 'Arnold,' she cried, 'Arnold, what have you done?'

Sam stood up, and nobody spoke for a moment.

'I hope you weren't worried about me,' said Arnold.

'So that's where you've been,' said Sam. 'I might have guessed. Come on, lad, the offer of a glass of wine still stands; will you join us?'

Mary stood wiping the tears from her eyes.

'I'm sorry I did it this way,' said Arnold. 'Father was dead against it; he said he could get me a reserved job, but I didn't want that, and I didn't want any fuss. I'm in Uncle Harry's old regiment.'

'Does your father know yet?' asked Sam.

'Not yet,' replied Arnold.

'We'll have to tell him; I'll telephone him in a little while.'

'How long are you home for?' asked Mary.

'I've got two weeks' embarkation leave,' replied Arnold.

'Then?' said Sam.

'I don't know; France, I expect.'

351

'Arnold, why did you do it?' asked Mary.

'I felt that I had to, Grandma,' he replied. 'Ask Granddad; I think he understands.'

Sam heaved a big sigh. 'Aye, lad, I understand. Well, we must try and get Emily and Maud home for a few days; they're still working in Leeds. Harry and Hetty are still here, of course, and your aunt Jane; there's only your own folks still away.'

'I hope you don't mind if I spend most of my leave here,' said Arnold. 'I'd like to stay here for all of it, but of course I'll have to see Mother and Father before I go.'

'We'll see if we can't do summat about that,' said Sam. 'You hang on here with your grandma, and I'll see if I can get hold of your father on the telephone.'

Sam went to the study and finally located Joe in his office in the City.

'Arnold's here, he just walked in,' he said.

'Where's he been?' demanded Joe's voice.

'He's joined up, he's in the army,' said Sam.

'The bloody fool, the damned bloody fool.' Joe was angry. 'What the hell difference does he think he's going to make to the war?'

'Joe,' said Sam, and his voice was hard, 'that boy is doing his duty as he sees it. Any road, it's done now, and the lad's committed. We have got to stand by him. He said he wanted to spend his embarkation leave here at Hardacres, but he knows he must see you and Helen before he leaves for France.'

'Well, he knows where he can find us.'

'Listen to me, Joseph, you and Helen are coming up here for next week.'

'Father, I think you ought to realize that I am far too busy to take time off,' replied Joe.

'Joe,' growled Sam, 'can you hear me? Did you hear what I said?'

'I heard you.'

'I said that you were coming up here, and that's exactly what you're bloody well going to do.'

'And who's going to make us?'

352

'I am,' said Sam, 'because if you don't, I'll come to London and I'll knock the living daylights out of you, and don't you think that I couldn't or wouldn't. City life has made thee soft and flabby. So you're coming, and you can tell that to that woman of yours.'

'All right, all right,' said Joe, 'we'll come up for the weekend. I can't think what has got into the young idiot.'

'And there'll be none of that sort of talk while you're up here, leastways not in front of Arnold. Lad's going to war, and you're going to respect him. You're going to see that his leave is a happy one. I'll send a car to Driffield to pick you up off the London train,' and he rang off without waiting for a reply.

They did what they could to make Arnold's leave everything that they imagined it should be, but they weren't very good at it, and an air of forced gaiety pervaded the whole business. Of course the war was never mentioned, and Arnold was totally aware of why. He knew that Sam kept the newspapers, and their long casualty lists, hidden from the whole family, and he joined in the pretence that nothing was happening.

Joe and Helen came up for their weekend and left, and hardly anyone noticed that they had been there; Arnold exchanged barely a dozen sentences with his parents while they were there.

Arnold suffered much from the attempts to treat him the same as always, while knowing that he was the centre of all their attentions and that he had only to make a suggestion or express a wish for it to be granted immediately.

There were others, of course; it was impossible to hide the war. Mrs Grey's son was a corporal in the Duke of Wellington's regiment, and he was home convalescing from a wound received early in the year; he had been lucky. He had left Hardacres towards the end of 1914, a boy of nineteen, and had returned a few months later an old man of twenty who would talk little, and never about the war.

Harry was more philosophical. He had had his war and knew a little of what it was all about, and whenever the chance occurred he talked to Arnold. In a way Harry's conversations were a relief, because Harry was the only one who mentioned war. He tried to give Arnold what advice he could: 'Don't volunteer for anything, it's the easiest way to get yourself killed.' 'Keep your head down.' 'Don't try to be a hero. Just do your job and leave it at that.' Good advice as far as it went, but Harry had no conception of trench warfare – of the stagnation of life in that other world across the Channel so divorced from living, where the only realities were mud and rats and the systematic, scientific destruction of one's fellow men.

It was almost a relief to Arnold when his leave ended. On the morning of his departure from Hardacres, he got up at seven and dressed in his uniform and went down to breakfast at eight. They were all very brave, and none of the women cried. Arnold wished that they had; the stiff upper lip and forced bonhomie were more trying than any genuine breakdown. Sam gave him a pair of trench boots, the best he could find; he had had them made by a famous London bootmaker. Mary stuffed his case with warm underwear and woollen sweaters, and Harry and Hetty gave him a brandy flask filled with Napoleon brandy. Together they travelled down to London and had a farewell dinner at the Savoy, after which they spent the night at Grosvenor Square.

The next morning Sam and Mary accompanied him to Victoria and put him on the troop train leaving for Dover. They stood on the platform for a long time, watching the last coach disappear down the track and then, hand in hand, walked silently away.

Joe had a business appointment and could not make it.

Arnold settled down in his first-class compartment with what amounted to a sense of relief. It had had to be done, and he loved his grandparents and Hardacres, which he always looked upon as home, but he was glad that it was all over and that he was at last on his way to whatever destiny held for him.

There were five other officers in the compartment – three more second lieutenants, as fresh and as green as Arnold, a lieutenant, and a captain, who wore the ribbon of the Military

Cross. They got to talking, and one of them produced a bottle of whisky and another a box of Dutch Agio cigars. They smoked and chatted and drank their way to Dover. For the first time Arnold talked about the war, which everyone now seemed convinced would last for ever. The four second lieutenants hung on every word that the captain, a regular with the Cameron Highlanders, said. He told them a little of what to expect and surprised them with the information that the front line was probably the safest place in the war, unless of course the brass hats decided to launch another futile attack. Apparently it was the support and reserve trenches which received most of the attention from Jerry artillery and mortars, but if you were in the front line, as long as you kept your head down and didn't try to do any unnecessary fighting, you were comparatively safe.

Their conversation grew more lively and raucous as the level of the whisky fell, and they flung the empty bottle out of the carriage window just before the train pulled into Dover.

At Dover they were herded aboard a grey, rust-streaked steamer, packed together on deck for the hour-and-a-half crossing. They sailed out of the harbour, watching the fast little ships of the Dover Patrol fussing around, into a heavy sea. That was when Arnold discovered that he was no sailor. He leaned in abject misery over the lee rail and wished heartily that they had decided to fight the war in Kent and Sussex instead of Flanders. Anyhow, he thought, as the boat pulled into Calais, it could have been worse. He could have joined the navy.

They landed in Calais and were given a hot meal of soup and bread and sweet tea. Then, to their surprise, they were loaded aboard London buses which still bore the trade mark of the General Omnibus Company; the one that Arnold got on to still had a destination board 'Piccadilly'. They drove on the solid tyres over fifty miles of bumpy, uncomfortable roads. They travelled south until they arrived at Bethune. There they were handed over to the divisional transport and billeting officer. That worthy found them billets for the night, straw palliasses on the floor of an old school hall, and then informed them that they would be joining their regiment, which was bivouacked just outside of town, the following morning.

Arnold found that they were only a few miles from the front, and that evening, after dark, he stood a while outside his billet listening to the distant guns and watching the flashes of light in the sky to the east. That was where the war was, he thought; that was where there was a man he was going to kill, a man he had never met, or perhaps the man was going to kill him.

However, all of that was tomorrow; tonight life still went on.

'Hello,' said a voice beside him.

Arnold looked at the man who had spoken to him; it was another second lieutenant. 'Hello,' he replied.

'Just arrived?' asked the other.

'Yes,' said Arnold, 'I'm Hardacre.'

'I've just arrived too, James is the name. You with the Twenty-Third?'

'Yes.'

'We bivouac tomorrow, and I hear we'll be moving up soon. There's going to be a big show. I'm glad I got here in time.'

'Aren't you scared?' asked Arnold.

'I suppose I am, but what's the use? Here, have a fag.'

'No, thanks, you have one of these.' Arnold produced the last two of his share of the Agios, and the two young men stood silently smoking, looking towards the distant firing.

CHAPTER THIRTEEN

At six thirty on the afternoon of 23 September, Arnold's battalion marched from their bivouacs. They were to reinforce a battalion of the Loyal Regiment in the line facing a small village called Loos. When they arrived, the Loyals were to retire to the support trenches, and Arnold's battalion would take over the front line.

As they marched, the sounds of desultory firing drew closer; it was possible to distinguish the crack of a rifle and the occasional rat-tat-tat of a machine gun, now and then punctuated by the dull crump of mortar or shell. Arnold had been given command of Number Three Platoon of B Company, and his friend James of the previous night had been given Number Two Platoon. Arnold's platoon sergeant was a regular, a Boer War veteran called Sergeant Holtby. Arnold knew that he was fortunate in this, in having a regular soldier to rely upon as his Uncle Harry had had fifteen years ago.

They were about a quarter of a mile from the support trenches when there was a whining, whistling noise in the air. 'Take cover!' The shout went up, and they all dived for the mud at the sides of the road.

Crunch, crunch, crunch. They got up after the shells had landed and continued forward in a more open formation. Arnold was surprised with what little regard his men treated this incident. Around him, as they started to move forward again, Arnold could see the litter and debris of war. A skeleton of broken masonry that had once been someone's home; a dead horse, bloated and rotting, covered with enormous blue flies; and suddenly a red slimy mass of what looked like offal on a butcher's slab, running blood. It was only the bits of khaki clinging to it that told him that it was one of his battalion, whom the shells had not missed; nobody else seemed to give the mess a second glance.

'Poor bastard never knew what hit him,' said Sergeant Holtby, seeing Arnold looking at it.

Near it a couple of medical orderlies wearing Red Cross armbands were trying to patch up a couple of men who had been badly wounded, probably by the same shell.

'Well, there won't be any more for a half hour,' said Holtby. 'You can count on Jerry, very methodical he is. Three H.E. every half hour on the road and that's all, unless there's a show on. Then it can get bloody dangerous.'

Arnold felt a bit sick. His immaculate new uniform was now covered with its first coating of Flanders mud. As they walked, a small group of walking wounded passed them, going towards the rear. One of them was on crutches with a bandaged foot.

'He's for it,' said Holtby, indicating the man on crutches. 'S.I.W.'

'S.I.W.?' asked Arnold.

'Self-inflicted wound, sir,' said the Sergeant.

'You mean that men really do shoot themselves?'

'Look, sir,' said Holtby, 'the best thing that can happen to you out here is to get blighty.'

'Blighty?'

'That's a wound that's just bad enough to get you home and out of it. They do it, all right, the poor buggers, only some of them haven't got very much imagination and get themselves caught. I can't blame them; most of them's kids and shit-scared. I reckon that the bloody brass ought to come down a bit more and find out what it's like for themselves; there's not many of them that spend a night in the trenches.'

Arnold was getting his first lesson in the contempt which the front-line soldier felt for the staff at the rear.

'I beg your pardon, sir, I shouldn't have said that.'

'That's all right, Sergeant,' replied Arnold.

They marched a little farther in silence, and then they came to a small crossroad.

'Well, sir,' said Holtby, 'here we go.'

'Go where?' asked Arnold.

'Other side of the road and we're in the reserve trenches.'

Arnold noticed for the first time the beginnings of the lines of ditches which were to be his home.

'We'll send the platoon across three at a time, sir, if you don't mind,' said Holtby. 'Just in case there's a sniper around watching us.'

They got into the support trench without incident and made their way through the slits in the earth past groups of tired and weary men until they found themselves in a wider, deeper trench with a sand-bagged parapet over which men were peering at intervals standing on the fire step, that raised earth ridge which allowed you to look out towards the enemy.

The Loyals moved out as soon as they arrived and started to thread their way back. Sergeant Holtby detailed off a lance corporal and two men to take positions on the fire step in the section that the company commander, Captain Beamish, had allocated to Arnold. Arnold saw to the placing of the platoon's Lewis gun at the head of their sap, a small piece of trench jutting out in the direction of the German lines.

'Well, sir,' said Holtby, 'welcome to the war.'

'How far away are the Germans?' asked Arnold.

'Hundred, hundred and fifty yards, but you don't want to have anything to do with them; just keep your head down, and you'll be all right.'

Captain Beamish was going around his company's section of the line and stopped to have a word with Arnold, when a lieutenant and two soldiers whom Arnold had not seen came into his section and started to set up a trench mortar.

'Just a minute,' said Beamish to Arnold and went to the Lieutenant. 'Now, just what the hell do you think you are doing?'

'Just two bombs, and then we'll be off,' said the Lieutenant cheerfully.

'Not in my bloody sector,' said Beamish. 'Get on your way and take your little toy with you.'

'But I have a job to do,' protested the Lieutenant.

'And you can bloody well do it somewhere else,' said Beamish.

The Lieutenant left with very bad grace, muttering something about the Colonel hearing about this.

Beamish turned back to Arnold. 'You've got to watch them. They lob a couple of mortar bombs into Jerry's front line, then they get to hell out of it. A minute later Jerry throws every bit of scrap iron he can lay his hands on right where the bombs came from, and that'll be you if you let them get away with it.'

'I see, sir,' said Arnold, wondering if anybody wanted to fight the war.

'Well, lad,' said Beamish, 'just try and stay alive. We've got the Camerons on our right; you can't beat the jocks if there's any trouble. I've got to report to the Colonel now; your sergeant will show you your dugout. I'll let you know what's happening later.'

Arnold found himself sharing a dugout with James and an older man, Lieutenant Spittle, an ex-ranker and second-in-command of the company. Spittle, who had been a regular Regimental Sergeant-Major, had been commissioned in the field and wore the ribbon of the Military Medal. They settled down to a meal of bully beef and biscuits with plum and apple jam, which was the staple diet of the British front-line soldier. The company cook brought them in some mugs of tea.

'Ugh,' said Arnold as a rat the size of a large cat scuttled across the earth floor of the dugout.

Spittle picked up the handle of an entrenching tool and hit the beast over the head, then threw the corpse outside.

'Don't know why I bother,' he said, 'they never try to pinch the grub.'

'Never?' Arnold was surprised.

'Too much fresh meat for them over there,' replied Spittle, nodding in the direction of no-man's-land.

Arnold felt sick and pushed the tin plate containing his food aside.

'Eat your grub, mate,' said Spittle. 'You'll get used to lots worse than that around here.'

At that moment the Company Sergeant-Major pushed his head around the corner of the dugout. 'Captain wants to see all officers in his dugout right away.' The head disappeared.

'Well, when father calls we all must obey,' said Spittle. 'Come on, you two, I'll show you where to find him.'

They went out and along the trench, and Spittle led them into a much larger dugout, where several of the company officers were gathered. Beamish looked up as they entered.

'Good, we're all here,' he said.

'Come on, George, tell us the worst,' said Spittle. 'Is it a show?'

'Tomorrow morning,' said Beamish, 'if the wind is right.'

'Pray for an easterly,' said Spittle.

'I don't understand,' said James; neither did Arnold.

'It means we're going to make an attack,' said Spittle. 'But only if the wind is in the right direction, from the west, and we can use gas. So, if it's easterly, we live another day, and if it keeps up long enough some other poor bastards have to do it.'

'All right, Ken,' said Beamish, 'you've had your little joke; now let's get down to details.'

The attack was timed to start early the next morning. Arnold could not sleep. He lay on his palliasse through the long dark hours, staring at the earth ceiling. He listened to the sounds of the night – Spittle snoring, the clank of the gas cylinders being moved into position, and the restless movements of James in the third bunk. Arnold wondered if he, too, were awake, but he did not speak.

Occasionally a shot would ring out, as some nervous look-out imagined he had seen someone moving outside the wire. Then there would be a rustle as a rat scurried across the floor of the dugout. Arnold tried to imagine the other side, only a hundred yards away from where he lay; there were men and boys like himself, listening to sounds as he was. Men without hatred but men who would, in a few hours, turn into animals, killing and being killed as the attack got under way.

Arnold had few illusions about his chances. He knew that they were small, but they were better than James'. James' platoon was to be first over the top; Arnold was to follow a minute later. If James' platoon did their job well and were lucky, then Arnold's chances would be better than even, if not … but you did not think about that.

Their orders were to stand to in the trench at a quarter to six and wait for the artillery. This, according to Spittle, was our way of letting Jerry know that we were coming so that he could be ready for us. After the artillery, the chlorine gas would be released and, hopefully, be blown over the enemy lines. Then, under cover of smoke – an idea borrowed from the navy and to be tried out for the first time – the battalion would attack in open order with bayonets fixed. They would advance through the gaps which the sappers were even now cutting in the enemy wire. At least, that was what was supposed to happen.

At last the night drew towards its close and the order to stand to was given. Arnold was not a religious man, but he said a prayer to Somebody and hoped it would be heard. He saw that James was saying the Rosary.

They crept out of their dugout and got their five grenades each, checked their ammunition, and moved around their men with words of encouragement and hope which did not really ring true. Now they were in the cold, dark, damp air, standing below the fire step, occupied by James' platoon, waiting for the artillery which would tell them that the attack was on.

'It's bloody southwest,' Spittle had said, pouring maledictions on the wind. 'That means that we're for it.'

At exactly ten minutes to six the bombardment started. There were less than one hundred and fifty heavy field pieces, but to Arnold it sounded as if the whole earth had erupted in one gigantic explosion.

They waited, so deafened by the bombardment that they could think of nothing but the noise.

'Gas!'

The order was given to put on their crude respirators and open the gas cylinders. The whole trench took on an unreal aspect as the men stood like creatures from another world, hideous in their gasmasks. The billowing clouds of chlorine started to roll hesitantly towards the German lines. The wind had dropped; it did not seem to know whose side it was supposed to be on.

Still the bombardment continued, throwing up huge columns of earth around the German front line. Then there was a moment's pause, an incredible silence as the shelling stopped and the gunners raised their sights to concentrate on the German support trenches.

In the silence the whistles blew.

The men on the fire step scrambled over the parapet; Arnold watched in horror as several of them fell straight back into the trench, dead or wounded. Now the sound of small-arms fire added to the confusion, as the rifles and machine guns opened up.

The whistles blew again.

'That's us, sir!' yelled Sergeant Holtby.

They were up and over the parapet, Arnold clutching his Webley and peering through the smoke and gas. He saw shadowy figures around him, but so dense was the smoke that he could not tell whether they were friend or foe. Suddenly they were in clear air, and the whole landscape stood bright and sunlit before him. The wind had changed, and now a good stiff breeze was blowing from the east. The smoke and gas were blowing back across the British lines; they were all sitting targets for the German riflemen and machine gunners. Men were falling all around him as the Germans opened up their systematic massacre of the exposed British forces. Everyone was diving for cover. The great attack had never even got started.

Arnold dived into a shell hole. There was a British officer already there, unrecognizable under his gas mask. Arnold tore off his own gas mask and started to creep through the mud towards him. As he was doing this, a German soldier dived into the hole, bayonet at the ready. Instinctively Arnold fired his revolver. A neat hole appeared in the German's head, and he fell backwards into the mud.

Arnold crouched motionless, staring at his victim; a moment ago that had been a man, like himself, and Arnold Hardacre had killed him. Why, he wondered, did he feel nothing at all – neither remorse, pity, nor jubilation.

He pulled himself together and holstered his revolver. The British officer was moving slightly and moaning. Arnold crawled to him and pulled off his gas mask. It was James.

James' eyes flickered in recognition, and then he coughed and a great gob of blood and something white oozed from his mouth. Arnold was searching for a clean piece of cloth

363

or a handkerchief; he knew that it was idiotic, but he felt that he had to wipe the boy's face – he couldn't let him die all covered in that filth.

As he was doing this, another figure crawled into the shell hole, a soldier in field grey. This was it, thought Arnold; like a fool he had put his revolver away to attend to James, but the German took no notice of him. Instead he took out a strip of purple cloth and put it around his neck; then he went over to the man that Arnold had killed and leaned over him.

My God, thought Arnold, it's a padre; he was interrupted by James, who was trying to say something – at last he made out the word.

'Priest.'

Of course, James was a Catholic. 'Padre!' Arnold shouted.

The German looked around and smiled at him. Arnold pointed to James. 'Catholic,' he yelled, 'Catholic, dying.'

The German nodded and crept over to them. 'Ja ja,' he said to Arnold and leaned over James. '*Ego te absolvo ...*' He murmured the words of absolution over the dying boy, then he turned to Arnold and made the sign of the cross over him, 'Gott bless you, mein son,' he said in crude English and then scrambled out of the shell hole.

James was dead, and Arnold had a long day ahead of him. He knew the rules. He had to stay there till dark, eleven or twelve hours away, and then try to creep back to his own lines. So this was war, and of all the people he had met the only man who seemed to know what he was doing was the German padre.

Arnold pulled a bar of chocolate out of his pocket and started to eat.

CHAPTER FOURTEEN

The Arnold who returned to Hardacres in the spring of 1916 was a stranger. Sam, now in his late sixties, in the presence of Arnold felt that he was younger than the boy. No one in the family could get near to him mentally. His letters from France had been short and getting shorter; they never mentioned the war or the life he was leading in the trenches. As for Arnold himself, he was the only member of his original platoon who was still alive; how or why was beyond his comprehension. Even the apparently indestructible Sergeant Holtby had gone. A mortar bomb had got him a month ago and he had become just another unrecognizable mess.

Arnold was not on leave. Sickened with all that he had seen and lived through, he had applied and been accepted for transfer to the Royal Flying Corps. When he went before the selection board and told them that he was already able to fly and that one of his father's factories was producing the D.H. 2 scout plane, his acceptance had been automatic.

For a couple of weeks he hung around divisional headquarters, doing a variety of odd jobs, until his transfer was completed and he was ordered to Driffield for flying training. But he hated the divisional H.Q. more than he hated the trenches, populated as it was with young, fit men in immaculate uniforms, most of whom were there as a result of wealth or nepotism. They would never see anything of the war, apart from brief trips around quiet sectors of the line in the company of high-ranking officers and visiting notables.

It was neither the risks nor his companions which had caused Arnold to apply for transfer; it was the mud. The risks he accepted with a sort of weary fatalism; he was sure that he would not get through, but he wanted to die with dignity. The men around him were his comrades; he admired them more than he admired himself, though he was proud to number himself one of them. But the mud, the dirt, the rats and the lice, the sweet cloying stench of rotting flesh that had once been men, the moaning of some poor creature, wounded and impaled on barbed wire – these things drove him nearly to the point of madness. He had seen others lose their reason; he did not want it to happen to him.

As for the Royal Flying Corps, it was out of the frying pan. If anything, his chances would be less, but it would be clean. There would be a bed to sleep in with sheets and a pillow. A table to eat at, maybe even a tablecloth and places to go to when you were not fighting. It might even be possible to become a human being again.

His posting to Driffield was no accident; he had asked at the selection board for this on the grounds that it had been his father's property until taken over by the army in the middle of the preceding year. His request had been granted. So, with two days to go before he reported for training, he was back at Hardacres.

Hardacres itself had lost something. A lot of the polish had gone. Almost all of the young men had left to join the army or work in the mines and factories, and the women too were busy on one or another kind of war work. Some of them of course, under Harry's management, were working the farm at full pressure. But the lawns were not quite so well kept; the flowerbeds, except for Mary's roses, not so well tended; the brasses a little duller; and the ornaments a little dustier. But it was still home to Arnold, even though his sisters were away, working in the factory in Leeds, and his parents had not bothered to come up to see him. Harry and Hetty now occupied the farmhouse, so as to be nearer the job, but they were only half a mile away from the main house in which Sam and Mary still lived with Jane and little Peter. Gunn had gone to war, and Wilson – now seventy – butled spasmodically. Mrs Grey was still busy in the kitchen, where she now supplied meals for farm workers and any passing soldiers who might call; her husband and son, now no longer fit for military service, did what they could around the grounds and in the stables.

As for the rest, Betty had left to live in the far north of Scotland, where she would be nearer to her sailor husband,

and there were a couple of maids whom Arnold had never seen before. Mary was always busy around the house or tending her flowers, and Jane was fully involved in war charities, dragging little Peter with her everywhere as she organized, badgered, and cajoled people into giving and helping.

For Arnold none of this was real; the reality was over there in the mud and filth of Flanders, and he was not sorry to get to Driffield and start training. This proved a simple business for him, and within a matter of three weeks he was off to France again to join an operational squadron which was located to the rear of the sector opposite Lens and just south of the trenches he had occupied during that cold and miserable winter past.

There was no doubt about Arnold's skill as a pilot, and on his second trip over the lines he made his first kill. It was a Halberstadt two-seater observation aeroplane, and he had managed to get his D.H. 2, a type that bore the unflattering nickname of the 'flying incinerator', back to base – avoiding the attentions of two Albatross scouts which were supposed to be guarding his victim.

At stand-down that evening, it was pointed out to him that he had a duty to perform. Having made his first kill, he was required to take the other members of his flight to the estaminet in the nearby village and supply them with wine.

They went. Six of them, and Arnold ordered the wine. They were served by the daughter of the house, who was introduced to Arnold as Madelene, a tiny girl of perhaps twenty, with black hair and huge bright-brown eyes that always seemed to be smiling. Arnold had been warned about Madelene. She was beautiful, she was friendly, she loved the British, she had lost two brothers at the front, and she was a good girl. You did not touch, you only looked and admired and envied and wished.

The party was soon in full swing, and the wine flowed freely. Arnold was no drinker, and he sat sipping a single glass while the others were downing it by the bottle. They sang 'Tipperary', 'Little Dolly Daydream', and a host of other popular songs as the wine loosened their tongues and raised their spirits. It was then that Madelene came in with a large basket of eggs.

'Omelettes!' shouted one of the pilots.

He solemnly took an egg from the basket and, with great deliberation and ceremony, cracked it over the head of his neighbour. The now be-egged one did likewise, and the basket passed around the table until there was not a single egg left. The group of young pilots presented a sorry sight, each of them dripping with raw egg and trying to scrape the mess off with the back of a knife.

Arnold took no part in the egg ceremony. He stood to one side, feeling awkward and embarrassed, as one does when one is the only sober member of a party. Madelene came into the room again; this time she was carrying a bottle of champagne. She ignored the others and took it straight to Arnold.

'This is for the victory,' she said in good but heavily accented English.

'Will you drink it with me?' asked Arnold. 'I'm sure that they don't want any more.'

Madelene paused. 'A little only would give me the great pleasure,' she said.

She got a couple of glasses, and they went outside. The night was warm and clear, the raucous sounds of the party were now muted, and only the occasional faint rumble to the east told them that the war was still going on. Arnold opened the bottle; it was a little warm, and the cork shot a great distance, followed by a spurt of spume. They both laughed as he managed to get some of it into the glasses. He handed one of the glasses to Madelene and raised his own.

'To France,' he said.

'To England,' she replied, looking straight into his eyes over her glass as she drank.

They sipped the wine, their free hands resting on the little wooden table less than an inch apart. Arnold spread his hand, and the tips of their little fingers touched. She made no move to withdraw her hand, and gently he covered it with his own.

Day followed interminable day. The Germans were now equipped with new Albatross scouts and were taking an increasing toll of the antique D.H. 2s which Arnold's squadron was still flying. Somehow he managed to survive; he was promoted to Captain and given command of B flight. He had five kills to his credit, and he lived only by his superb flying ability. They kept hearing rumours of a new British fighter which was going into production at Sopwiths, but they saw nothing of it and cursed the powers that be for letting them die while they waited for a reasonable aeroplane.

In the evenings at sunset, after the last plane had landed, Arnold would, whenever possible, borrow one of the squadron's motorcycles and ride down to the village. There he would walk hand in hand with Madelene, smelling the smells and listening to the sounds of summer; sometimes hardly a word would pass between them – they were content with the gentle peace that they found in one another's company. Arnold was afraid of his feelings. He knew that he loved her, and what frightened him even more, he knew that she loved him. He was living on borrowed time; what was there that he could offer to her? It was different, so different to anything that he had ever known. He never, in his mind, belittled the relationship he had had with Betty, but he could not help drawing comparisons. That had been fierce and animal and gay; this was gentle and warm and filled with a complete peace.

All that he wanted was to be with her, to spend all the time that he had left in her company. Every time he returned from a mission at the end of the day, he thanked God that he would see her again, that once more he would know a few hours of peace and contentment in their solitude, but always with the knowledge that the following morning he would probably watch another youth in his squadron burn, or maybe he would kill another man.

One night she said to him, 'The war is not important. What is important is life, and we must live it together. Perhaps there will not be another night after tonight, perhaps there will be a hundred or even thousands and thousands.'

That was the night that they made love for the first time, and two days later he gave her an engagement ring and started to take instruction in the Catholic faith from the local Roman Catholic chaplain.

Over a month passed, and there was still no sign of the new fighters. It was dawn on 14 September 1916, and as the grey streaks in the east grew brighter, the squadron commander briefed B flight for the dawn patrol.

The alarms, empty shell cases banged with a metal rod, started to clang out a warning, and they could hear the sound of approaching aircraft. They rushed out of the flight hut to find their opposite numbers, of the German air force, flying their bright new Albatrosses and attacking the airfield with incendiary bullets.

The Albatrosses made their first pass over the field, and three of the parked D.H. 2s burst into flames. All was confusion as fires began to break out all over the place. The ground crews were heaving and tugging at the undamaged planes to get them away from the flames.

Arnold led the rush to the aircraft. His own was still undamaged, and as he scrambled into the cockpit, a mechanic, seeing what was happening, ran to swing the propeller for him.

'Contact,' yelled Arnold.

The cold motor fired the first time, and, without trying to warm his engine – all the time keeping his eyes on the Albatrosses, which were turning and lining up for another attack – he thrust forward on the throttle and started to bump across the field. The Albatrosses came in again, and miraculously they did not hit him, but his was the only D.H. 2 to get airborne that day.

Accounts of what happened in the next fifteen minutes varied, but many watched in awe, and one thing was certain. Handling his aeroplane like a man possessed and flying as even he had never flown before, Arnold broke up the attack. How many planes he shot down was never quite certain; it was at least three, and maybe five. One German who survived and was taken prisoner was sure that they had been attacked by a whole flight of D.H. 2s. But the inevitable happened, and flames started to appear behind Arnold's cockpit; like a falling torch the D.H. 2 plunged into the earth at the edge of the field.

They would not let Madelene see the body.

CHAPTER FIFTEEN

It was 14 December 1916, three months to the day since Arnold had died. Sam and Mary were staying at Grosvenor Square, for they had a very important appointment the following day. They were commanded to attend Buckingham Palace for the presentation, by the King, of the Victoria Cross, which had been awarded to Arnold for the terrific single-handed fight he had put up the day he had died.

Joe and Helen, to whom the original invitation had been offered, would not be at the palace. After Arnold's death, Joe had decided to return to the United States and had booked a passage for himself and Helen aboard an American ship from still-neutral Spain. Helen would not risk sailing out of an English port because of the risk of submarines, so after a great deal of string pulling they crossed the Channel and went by train across western France to Spain and thence to New York. Neither of their daughters wanted to accompany them. Both Emily and Maud wanted to stay at Hardacres and carry on with their war jobs, and Sam and Mary – who had come to regard them as their own children – were delighted. So Joe and Helen sailed alone in October.

But they were dark days at Hardacres. The glowing accounts of Arnold's gallant action in the national press did little to assuage the grief which they all felt at his loss.

'I don't want no bloody hero,' Mary had said. 'I want t'lad.'

Not that they regarded their grief or loss as anything unusual or spectacular. So many were dying. There were so many acts of unbelievable courage; there was barely a street in Britain that did not mourn the loss of one or more of its sons.

The royal command to attend the investiture had seemed, to Sam, strangely worded, for it gave no indication of who was to receive the actual award. However, that did not really matter and would undoubtedly be sorted out when they arrived at the palace.

On the morning of the fifteenth they dressed carefully. Sam wore the obligatory morning suit and Mary a long black gown. They took a taxi to the palace and were there ushered into the same room, where, in happier times, Jane had been presented to Edward VII several years ago.

As Arnold's was the only Victoria Cross to be presented that day, his would be the first award, the V.C. taking precedence over all other awards and orders; so they waited, along with a small group of dignitaries and officials.

The King arrived wearing the service dress uniform of a field marshal. The ladies curtsied, the men bowed, and His Majesty took his place on the dais.

The King nodded to an officer standing near him, and the officer began to read.

'The Victoria Cross. Awarded to Captain Arnold Hardacre of the Royal Flying Corps, for extreme gallantry and devotion above and beyond the call of duty . . .' The citation rambled on, describing the fight Arnold had put up against impossible odds, and finally came the words, 'This award is posthumous.'

A tiny, attractive, and quite obviously pregnant girl was ushered to the dais, where she had a few moments of murmured conversation with the King, none of which Sam or Mary could understand, as they were speaking French.

'What the hell's going on?' Sam whispered to Mary.

The girl, holding Arnold's medal, was being brought towards them.

'I think I can guess,' said Mary. 'Come on, Sam, I'll introduce you to your new granddaughter-in-law.'

'That one?' He suddenly grinned. 'She's a right good-looker, Mary; we Hardacres could allus pick 'em. But he should have told us he got wed.'

Book Three

The Pensioners

CHAPTER ONE

'If you will all be seated, I shall commence.'

They were in the morning room at Hardacres, gathered for the reading of Sam's will. A table had been arranged in front of the French windows, and on this Saunders had laid his briefcase, from which he had taken a sealed envelope. It was September 1919.

Mary, now in her mid-sixties, was seated in an armchair in the middle of the room, dressed in pale violet. She did not believe in mourning. Sam had been a good man, and Mary, strong in her faith, was convinced that there was nothing to mourn in his passing. Even at the funeral, three months earlier, she had refused to wear black.

'If tha believes in heaven, it's only selfish to begrudge him getting there,' she had said.

Sam had died in June. He had not been ill, but he had been suffering a little from nagging chest pains, most of which he had been putting down to attacks of indigestion. That evening they had been particularly irritating, and he had decided to go to bed early. He had not, however, been able to get to sleep, and around half past eleven he got out of bed, put on his dressing gown, and wandered along the corridors to Wilson's room. Wilson had already retired, but he came to the door when Sam knocked.

'Wilson,' said Sam, 'can I ask thee a favour? I'd like thee to come down to t'study with me.'

'Of course, sir,' said Wilson, 'there's nothing wrong, is there?'

'No, not as I think of,' said Sam. 'I can't sleep, and I felt that I wanted a bit of company.'

Sam went down to the study and waited by the dying embers of the fire until Wilson arrived. The old butler was fully dressed when he came in.

'Nay, Wilson, thou needn't have gone to all that bother,' said Sam. 'I just wanted thee t' come down and have a drink and a chat with me.'

'Sit down, sir?' Wilson was surprised at the impropriety.

'Aye, Wilson,' replied Sam, 'I know what tha's going to say, but don't say it. I mind well the first day us came here. Tha wouldn't shake my hand because it weren't proper. I'll tell thee summat else that tha doesn't know.'

'What's that, sir?'

'I don't believe I've ever seen thee sitting down. It were on that first day that tha told me about special occasions. This is one.'

'Why, sir?'

'I don't know, I just feel it is. I'm asking thee, not as the master of the house but as a friend, for that's what thou art, to sit down and let me pour thee a drink in return for the hundreds, nay thousands, that thee must have poured for me.'

'Under the circumstances I can hardly refuse, sir,' said Wilson, and he sat down very uncomfortably on the edge of one of the big leather armchairs.

'What's thy pleasure?' asked Sam.

'A very small glass of whisky, sir, if I may.'

Sam poured out two glasses of whisky. 'Owt in it?'

'A dash of soda, sir.'

Sam handed Wilson his glass. 'I hope I didn't ruin tha night,' said Sam, 'it's only that I suddenly got the feeling that I'd never really said thank you to thee for all that tha's done over the years for me and mine.'

'It has been my pleasure sir,' replied Wilson.

'That's as maybe, but thou's been a good friend, at least that's how I've allus thought of thee; I've never known better. Us has been through a lot together, and I know how it must have been for thee at the beginning. I've allus been an awkward bugger, and I shouldn't think I've changed much.'

'Oh, no, sir, if I may say so, it is I who have been fortunate,' said Wilson, 'it has been a great privilege to serve you.'

Sam had lapsed completely into the strong Yorkshire dialect of his youth, and they sipped their whisky and talked for about half an hour. Then Sam suddenly felt very tired, so they said good night, and both of them went off to bed.

Sam got between the sheets, and within a few minutes he was asleep, and within an hour he was dead. They found him there the following morning, silent and peaceful.

The reading of the will had been delayed. Helen had insisted on Joe bringing her back from the United States, where they had made their home. They were sitting with Harry, Hetty, and Jane beside Mary. Behind them sat Sam's grandchildren – Emily, Maud, and Noel, and with them was Arnold's widow Madelene. Vanessa, who was only twelve; Peter, now Lord Macregor, his other grandfather having died a year ago; and Madelene's twin babies, Sam and Terry, had been expelled to the schoolroom. Behind the children were the principal servants, including Wilson and Mrs Grey, both of whom were now well into their seventies.

The murmur of conversation stopped as Saunders broke open the seal on the envelope and commenced to read from it.

This is the last will and testament of me, Samuel Hardacre, of Hardacres, by Driffield, East Yorkshire, made by me being of sound mind and of my own volition.

I appoint my dear friend and solicitor, John Saunders, and my beloved son Harold as my executors and trustees, and I do convey the whole means of my estate, real and personal, wheresoever situated, to John Saunders and Harold Hardacre, upon these trusts only.

'Here we have a lengthy clause regarding the settlement of his debts and other expenses, which I shall with your permission omit,' said Saunders.

There was a murmur of assent from the family. 'Aye, let's get on with the meat,' said Joe.

Saunders looked at Joe over the top of his spectacles and then continued, 'To each and every person who is in my employ at the time of my death or who has gone into honourable retirement, I leave the sum of ten pounds for each year they have been in my service, the total sum in no case to be less than fifty pounds. And in the case of any dependants of my servants who were left bereaved by the war that sum is to be doubled.'

There was a murmur of appreciation from the rear of the room.

'To Mrs Margaret Grey, who cooked for us so well and looked after us so magnificently, I leave the cottage which she at present occupies, together with five acres of arable land around it and a pension of two hundred pounds a year.'

Mrs Grey sniffed and said, 'Thanks, but I'd rather have the master.'

Saunders looked up and said, 'I must apologize for the language in the next phrase, but Mr Hardacre insisted on it being put in this form.

'To my friend Wilson: why the bloody hell did you never tell me your other name? I leave any house of his choosing, on or off the estate, to the value of five hundred pounds, ten acres of land to be picked mutually by him and Harry, and one thousand pounds per year for the rest of his life on one condition – that he reveals his Christian name to the assembled company here and now, and remember, I'll be listening.

'Well, Wilson?' said Saunders.

'Clarence,' said Wilson, in a scarcely audible voice.

'I beg your pardon?' said Saunders.

'Clarence.' He almost shouted it and then blushed.

'Thank you, Mr Wilson,' said Saunders, and, as the others started to titter, 'Hush.'

Saunders continued the reading.

'The residue of the means of my estate I leave to my beloved son Harold.'

'What?' shouted Helen.

'Please, Mrs Hardacre,' said Saunders, 'there are some exceptions.' He read on. 'Except for two provisions: First, that my beloved wife, Mary, shall have whatever income she

376

wants within the means of my estate and the absolute right of tenure of Hardacres for the remainder of her life. Secondly ...'

'This is it,' said Helen.

'Secondly,' repeated Saunders, frowning, 'I have something for my eldest son Joseph, but first I want to say something to him. Joe, you're probably a lot richer than I am, so there's nothing I can give you except perhaps to remind you and that woman of yours where you came from. In the middle drawer of my desk you'll find an envelope. It is addressed to you; take it, Joe, keep it, and remember.'

Saunders sat down.

'Well,' said Helen, 'is that all?'

'I fear that it is,' said Saunders.

Helen snorted, 'I suppose that we'd better go and see what the damned thing is.'

'There's no hurry,' said Joe. 'I've got a feeling that I can guess.' He grinned. 'By the way, Mr Saunders, I noticed that there was no mention of Jane.'

'I knew that there would not be,' said Jane. 'When Father made my marriage settlement, he was extremely generous and he told Ian and me that would be our lot and you all know Father, he meant it.'

'But what about the children?' asked Joe.

'All of that was left to Harry,' said Saunders. 'Your father's attitude was that, when he died, he would have no idea of the needs of various members of the family or of their circumstances. He decided that it would be better and fairer if Harry were to deal with these matters as events dictated.'

'And how do we know that we can trust him?' demanded Helen.

'You don't,' said Harry, 'but Father thought he could, so you're stuck with me.'

'You're no businessman,' said Joe without malice; he was simply stating a fact.

'I'm certainly not in your class, Joe,' replied Harry, 'but I'll manage. Our father wanted to keep the home in one piece. I think he had the idea of a sort of Hardacre dynasty becoming one of the great families of the land. In order to do that he needed to pass on the authority as an entity and, rightly or wrongly, he decided that I should have the job. For myself and Henrietta, I can only say that Hardacres is your home, and that is not charity – it is yours of right. I know that that is what Father wanted. Madelene and the twins and both of your daughters, Joe, have already made their home here, and there's plenty of room for more, isn't there, Mother?'

'Aye,' said Mary, 'that's the way Sam wanted it, so that's the way it's got to be. Wilson,' she said, changing the subject, 'thou remember yon cottage the master offered thee a few years back?'

'Yes, madam, I remember it well,' said Wilson. 'A charming little place.'

'Would tha be wanting it?'

'I'd really much rather keep my old rooms in the house, where I can enjoy the companionship of the servants' hall. That is, if Mr Harry has no objection.'

'Help yourself, Wilson,' said Harry. 'Mother, what is this all to do with?'

'I'm going to have yon cottage,' said Mary. 'I've allus fancied it, and I'm going to have it. I'm going to move in right away.'

'But there's only three rooms,' said Jane.

'And that's one too many,' said Mary. 'I want to tell you lot summat, summat that I could never tell you while Sam was alive. The happiest time of my life was when we was going around the racecourses. It were exciting, and I had a little place where there was allus summat to do, where I could care for my own and do it all me sen. I never said owt to Sam, of course, but I never really liked living in a big house. Now that he's gone, yon cottage is just what I want. There'll be a sitting room and a spare bedroom, where I can put up a friend whenever I want to.'

'If that's what you really want, Mother.' Harry sounded a little doubtful.

'Aye, Harry, it's what I want. Tha knows I was never cut out to be a great lady, in spite of what thy father said. So me mind's made up, and that's the way it's going to be for me, any road.'

'But it's only a farm-labourer's cottage,' said Helen. 'Whatever would people say?'

'I don't give a bugger what they say,' snapped Mary. 'And what's wrong with farm labourers, miss high-and-mighty?'

'I think,' said Joe, intervening quickly, 'we had better go and collect our legacy.'

'You'll be going back to the States soon, I suppose,' said Harry as Joe started to move.

'Yes,' replied Joe, 'we'll take the evening train to London, and we sail on the *Aquitania* on Thursday.' He turned to his daughters. 'Are you two quite sure that you don't want to come to New York?'

'If you don't mind, Papa, I think that we really would rather stay here,' said Emily.

'We will come and visit you, though,' said Maud.

'All right,' said Joe. 'Coming, Helen?' They started to move towards the door.

'Perhaps I had better accompany you,' said Saunders. 'I am aware of the package in question, though I have no idea of its contents.'

'We're not going to steal anything,' said Joe.

'Oh, please,' said Saunders. 'I also have the keys, I have not handed them over to Harry yet.'

As they went across the hall towards the study, Joe said to Saunders, 'I notice that you weren't mentioned either,' he said.

'Sam made more than ample provision for me when I retired from the business. I suppose that this will be my last professional act,' said Saunders.

They went into the study, and Saunders opened the desk drawer. There was, as Sam had indicated, a long manilla envelope addressed to Joe.

'This would appear to be it,' said Saunders. 'Would you rather be alone while you open it?'

'If I'm right, I think we'd better,' said Joe.

Saunders left the room, and Joe stood weighing the package in his hand.

'Well, get on with it,' said Helen.

Joe was still smiling as he ripped the top off the envelope and drew out a leather case.

379

'How lovely,' said Helen.

It was indeed a beautiful case. Covered in fine leather with a profusion of gold tooling and solid gold clasps.

'It must be jewellery,' she said.

'You think so?' said Joe.

There was a small envelope attached to the case. Joe opened this and read;

Joe, inside this case is the foundation of everything that you and I possess. I shouldn't think it will be of much use to you, but then I doubt it would be of much use to anybody else. You will look after it, though, Joe, won't you?

'Well, Helen,' said Joe, 'shall we look?'

'Oh, Joe, stop being so childish.' She tried to grab the case from him. 'Give it to me.'

'All right,' he said, putting it down on the desk. 'Open it and see for yourself.'

Joe went and sat in one of the leather armchairs and watched cynically as Helen approached the case as if it was the Crown Jewels. First she stroked the soft leather, then she lifted one of the side catches, and then the other, and finally she released the centre clasp.

'Now,' she said, and slowly raised the lid of the case. 'The bastard, the dirty, rotten bastard.'

Joe grinned. He had been right; he did not need to look.

Inside the case and lying on the velvet lining was a razor-sharp piece of steel with a plain wooden handle bound with string. It was Sam's gutting knife.

CHAPTER TWO

'But, Mother, you can't take that,' said Harry.

'And why not, I should like to know?' replied Mary.

'Your parlour's so small, and this is enormous.'

'Harry,' said Mary, 'this aspidistra came to Hardacres with me. Before that it went round the fish quays and then round the racecourses. I'm not deserting it now, whatever thee or anybody else says.'

It went. She had one of the servants carry it out for her, along with the Tin Box and the Victoria and Albert mug. Mary had borrowed Hetty's pony and trap for the journey to the cottage. Her clothing and the few small items of furniture she was bringing from the big house had been sent down with the servants, in one of the farm carts. But these few precious items were not to be trusted to anyone but herself. Harry had asked a groom to come with the pony, but Mary sent him away. The black-and-white pony was gentle, and Mary was quite happy to handle him herself. Harry settled the aspidistra firmly in the centre of the cart, and Mary placed the Tin Box and the cloth-wrapped mug beside it. Then she went familiarly to the pony's head and took hold of the bridle to lead him off.

'You could ride, Mother,' Harry said uncertainly; 'I'll drive if you like.'

'Thanks, but I'd rather walk.' She started off down the curving gravel drive, and Harry, not sure he was welcome, stood at the doorway. She seemed so secretive, so privately happy. He watched the tail of the cart and his mother's small, grey figure, seeming smaller against the vast lawns all around. She did not look back, and he felt odd, worried.

Suddenly he called, 'Wait, I'll come with you,' and half ran, lurching awkwardly, after her. Mary turned, stopped the pony, and waited for Harry to catch up. The house behind him looked immense and unfamiliar.

Then mother and son walked with the cart and the spotted pony down the long drive, past the rose gardens, and the yew maze to the edge of the beechwood. A small earth drive turned off the main gravel one, ran a while beside the beechwood, and ended in a small patch of vegetable garden; behind that was Mary's cottage.

Harry knew the cottage well. He remembered when he had first come to Hardacres; a family called Scobie had lived there. The man was one of the farmworkers, and his wife had kept hens and the garden; there were several children, and Harry played with them during his first holidays from Barlow's. After that they had all emigrated to Australia, and he had missed them. They had been easier, less demanding companions than Joe.

The cottage had stood empty ever afterwards. It was awkwardly placed; there were others, more convenient to the home farm. Sam had left it unoccupied, always keeping it in mind for Wilson's future retirement.

It was built of the same red brick as the main house and all the farm buildings, but the roof was thatch, steep and sloping, heavily overhanging the eaves. It was a simple rectangular shape, with a lean-to scullery at the back. The windows were narrow, with many diamond-shaped, leaded panes; there were four at the front, balanced two and two on either side of the painted plank door. Above were three garret windows, each with its hat of thatch. The thatch was new as was the cream-coloured paint. Inside, every room had been freshly painted and papered, and the household staff had been down half the week cleaning. They were, none of them, very happy to see Mary go off to live here, but if she was determined, they were equally determined to make the place as comfortable and as pleasant as possible. They were still not sure that her leaving the big house was not in some way a judgement on their abilities.

Harry left the pony outside the garden gate, walked up the brick path, lifted the heavy iron latch, and pushed open the door. The wood was rough and uneven, and scraped the flagstone floor. He himself had not been in the house since childhood. It didn't really look any different. Fires had been

382

lit in each of the fireplaces to warm up the long-cold chimneys, and their light flickered on the plain wood furnishings, the paint work, and the brasses around the fireplaces. The copper kettle that he remembered still sat by the hearth. The oven doors on either side of the fire were freshly black-leaded, but the old pothooks were permanently encrusted with soot.

'It's right homey, in't it, Harry?' said Mary. She was standing in the doorway watching him explore the room. He remembered the chintz curtains (these seemed identical to the old ones) pulled tight against the dark of a rainy evening; the fire; chestnuts roasting on the brick hearth; and himself, a boy awkward in his good suit, side by side with the ragged farm children, their dogs, and their cats. There had even been a pet duck in a box by the fire. When it was time to go, the dark outside had been long and ominous between him and the big house. Mr Scobie would always get up from his seat by the fire, saying nothing, and walk Harry as far as the rose garden and the lights of Hardacres.

'I like it, Mother,' Harry said slowly. 'It's just what I remember it to be.'

Mary led him through the house, showing him the broad pine sideboard in the parlour, where he was to place her aspidistra; then she took him up the stairs to show off the brass bedstead she had salvaged from the old furnishings and had cleaned herself. Thick carpets had been laid on the old rough board floors, and their richness looked slightly out of place. He had insisted on them; the cottage must be warm, if not fancy, and there were only the very best carpets in the big house.

Mary had rooted around Hardacres for all the oldest and plainest tables, chairs, and chests of drawers to make up what was missing from the existing furnishings. She said that any better would look wrong, and he saw that she had been right. He bent his head under the exposed oak beams of the bedroom ceiling and leaned to look out of the low window. The view was of beech trees and meadow. It could be any small farmhouse in Yorkshire.

Mary led him back down the stairs, so steep and narrow that he found them difficult to negotiate with his game leg.

When he reached the bottom and the small entrance hall, she was already away into the kitchen-living room.

'Wilt tha have some tea, Harry?' she called, and he was immediately aware that she was a more certain hostess here than he had ever seen her. He realized that she had taken possession here in a way she never really had at Hardacres.

He sat on a plain wooden chair by the fire, and Mary put the copper kettle on the hob and swung it over the fire. She went into the scullery and found an earthenware teapot and two white mugs in the old cupboard. Mrs Grey had sent two kitchen maids to stock the larder with everything Mary could conceivably need, but Mary saw many things that she knew she would never touch. Now she could cook and eat what she liked. She found tea for the pot and brought it back into the living room. Harry was sitting quietly, looking into the fire. Mary thought suddenly that he was beginning to look like Sam. Not his face – which was like her own – but his manner, his shape by the fire. She told him something she would never have dared to tell Sam.

'Harry, lad, dost tha know summat? When your dad first said he'd buy me a house in t'country, tha know what I thought it ud be like?' She paused to pour boiling water from the kettle. 'I thought it ud be like this. How I wanted a place when thee lads were still little, and finding road so hard. I used to think on it, cold nights, sleeping by cart. I used to think on it a lot.' She stirred the tea in the pot and poured a cup for each of them. 'And tha knows, lad, even after we came to big house, I still used to think on it, just every now and then.'

Harry didn't know what to say. They had forgotten to bring fresh milk, so he drank his tea the way it was, too hot and bitter.

When he left, he did not turn and look back. He walked on in the fading light until the great hulk of Hardacres almost filled his vision; that was home. He thought of the four of them who had come here all those years ago. Sam who needed it, Mary who was afraid of it, Joe who ignored it, and Harry Hardacre, who loved it.

*   *   *

384

Madelene Hardacre stood by her dressing table in her bed-room at Hardacres. She wore black – a narrow dress which fell from a simple square neck in a straight line to its hem at mid-calf. She was adjusting a black lace mantilla over her dark, shining curls. Madelene wore her hair short now, which, like the dress, was very much in fashion. She was no longer in mourning for Arnold, but she wore black because it was Sunday and she was going to Mass. At home, black was always worn in church. Madelene was not at home now, she re-minded herself, wondering if perhaps she should not try to become more English – to give up Sunday black perhaps, to give up thinking in French and expressing certain free opinions that were for ever shocking someone, such as Hetty or even Maud. She smiled; young girls today in England thought themselves so modern, and they were so innocent. Even Emily, who was trying so hard to be shocking herself that she did not have time to be shocked by anyone else.

Madelene looked beyond the gilt-framed mirror, in which her reflection seemed altogether too dark against the flowered beige wallpaper and the pale-peach chintz furnishings.

Outside the spring was brightening the Hardacres lawns with hundreds of daffodils. It was a beautiful place – Arnold's home, she thought, because he had always thought of it as home. That was why she had stayed. Because Arnold had not been able to come home. At least his children could. There were other reasons. France was gone, destroyed – the France she had known. Her village was a ruin, her parents dead, her friends and family lost and scattered. She was deeply French, deeply loyal, and felt great guilt at her lack of courage; but she could not go back there, alone with her two babies. How could she take them from this to the heap of rubble which was what remained of her home?

She would stay now, stay at Hardacres and try as best she could to become English, to be a good mother, a loyal widow. She was young, and the face in the mirror was beautiful. She would not find widowhood easy.

Madelene shook her head abruptly with characteristic impatience, took her black gloves, Missal, and Rosary from the dresser and left the room.

She went down the hall and rapped lightly on Hetty's door. Hetty's voice called, 'Come in,' but Madelene opened the door hesitantly. She knew that, though it was early, Harry would already be out. Farm work started at first light, even on Sunday. Still, she was conscious that the bedroom was his, and entering it made her uneasy.

Hetty was still dressing, sitting on a brocade stool in a dark pink slip, pulling on heavy lisle stockings. She looked awkward and heavy, with her grey-brown hair still braided from bed. Madelene did not understand English women; they seemed not to care how they looked, or how their men saw them. But she realized, as a fact and not unkindly, that Hetty had never been beautiful. She had a peasant's face and a peasant's figure, and that pale English complexion that was exquisite on young girls but aged badly. Her face was broadening now, her jaw growing heavy, and the tendency to dark shadows beneath her eyes was accentuated. But such features were common, and all women aged, though not all women grew old. In France she had known farmers' wives and working women with broad faces and greying hair who still kept their men fluttering around them like lost moths. Their charms had more to do with a sparkle in the eyes and a swaying of the hips that, Madelene knew instinctively, had more to do with the soul than the body. English women did not seem to understand that.

'Are you going now?' Hetty asked; her voice was a soft, tired monotone.

'The babies are sleeping,' Madelene replied.

'Never mind, dear,' said Hetty, 'I'll see that they have their breakfast when they wake. Are you away, then?'

'If it's all right,' said Madelene, apologetic. Hetty was so good to her, always willing to help with the children.

'Is Harry waiting for you?'

'I think so.' Madelene was suddenly flustered. 'He said he would drive me to Beverley; it is very kind ...'

Hetty returned to the brocade stool, kicking suddenly at an overturned shoe. Then she jerked the second stocking on angrily and hooked it roughly to her garters. She stood up and walked to the window. Harry was standing by the motorcar on the gravel terrace. His back was to the house, and he was looking over the lawns towards the beeches. The morning sun was still thin, spring-misty. His hair was greyer now, but his body was still tough and strong. Why was it that age treated men so well and women so unkindly?

Hetty slipped on her skirt, brown tweed reaching to her ankles, and a pale-yellow lambswool twin-set. The colours did not clash, but they did not go together either. Emily was always making polite suggestions about Hetty's clothes. Hetty ignored them. She knew that Emily was right, but she was too old to change. She was forty-three. Too old for many things; too old now to give Harry the child which she had always hoped and prayed for.

She did not approve of Madelene. She had no reason and felt guilty as a result. The guilt made her treat Madelene more kindly than she needed to and at the same time resent her even more.

To begin with, Madelene was foreign. Not bad foreign like the Germans – indeed the French were recent allies and supposedly good friends. But they were different. One could not understand them; they did not look or think or talk like ordinary people. Added to that, Madelene was a Catholic. Hetty resented that – an unfair, added strangeness. Hetty knew nothing about the Catholic religion, for her family had been very Low Church and had found even the Anglican High Church unacceptable. Madelene's sons would be brought up Catholic, and Hetty resented that too. Hetty thought of Catholicism in the same way she thought of Madelene – too much passion and earthly beauty, even in sombre black. Hetty did not approve.

It disturbed her, perhaps annoyed her, that Emily and Maud admired Madelene and thought her charming. And even Noel, whom she regarded as her own son, she suspected felt the same. Not that Noel would say or do anything about it, she knew. He was barely three years younger than Madelene, but the gap between the young French war widow and a nineteen-year-old undergraduate at Kings, Cambridge, was not measurable in years. Madelene considered Noel a child.

He was not that, Hetty knew, though he was not precisely

a normal young man either. Hetty could not imagine him having girl friends. But it was neither shyness nor disinterest. He admired Madelene, he admired other women. She was a woman herself and could see that. But there was a wall between Noel and other people, particularly people of his own class, and particularly women. He did not give freely of himself – not his time, not his company, and most of all not his own, very private, self. He was closer to Hetty than to anyone; he considered her his mother, but for all that he told her little of what he thought, hoped, or planned. Sometimes she thought he had never really hoped for anything after, as a little boy, he gave up hoping that Judith would come back to him from London.

Noel loved the farm, and because of that he loved his father. As farmers they understood each other. But only as farmers. When Harry entertained, which he did occasionally and with grace, Noel sat silent and remote, avoiding conversation and leaving as soon as acceptably possible. For his own pleasure he retired to the village pub, where, Harry told Hetty, he sat drinking and playing darts with the farmhands. In that company he was at ease and content. But he would not find a wife there; Hetty knew that, and it worried her.

He was a surprisingly handsome man, with fine, delicate features, but he was small and slightly built, which he resented. He had missed the war, partly because of his age and partly, as only his parents and Mary knew, because Sam had pulled every possible string to keep him out. He had had no bad conscience about doing so: he had given two of his family, Ian and Arnold, and he felt that was more than enough. Hetty had always feared what Noel might do, should he ever find out. As it was, he was called up, but it was only days before the armistice, and he never saw action.

His slim, almost frail-looking body and thin, pale face led people to assume ill health kept him from active service. The suggestion infuriated him; he had grown up to hard work and was fit and tough. Once, in the pub, a farm boy, back from the war, came closer to the truth, suggesting that his rich grandfather had kept him out. Noel had turned on him with sudden anger and beaten him viciously. There had been trouble about

388

it; rich young men who threw their weight, even slight weight, around were unpopular. Noel did not care, and Harry guiltily sympathized, but for the first time he realized that his quiet, studious son had a dangerous potential for violence. It shook him, and he regarded Noel in a new and cautious light. Hetty, somewhat reasonably, defended Noel almost without question. She felt that life had dealt unfairly with him, and she was intent on evening the balance in his favour.

Hetty waited to hear the noise of the motor starting. Perversely, she had to know that Harry and Madelene were away before she could start the day.

Madelene paused in the hallway to readjust her mantilla at the huge gilt-framed mirror above the heavy-footed hall stand. The sound of her feet echoed on the mosaic tiles; it made the house sound empty. The house was too quiet; it needed more people. She had not been really happy here since Sam had died. She had really loved him – the big, warm, kindly old man who had made her so welcome from the first. He had loved Arnold, and he had understood. Now Sam was gone, and Mary too, who loved the babies and spoke so honestly, no longer lived in the house. But it was all right as long as Jane was at home. Jane was her friend. She was different – English, but open and understanding. She could talk freely to Jane without fear of offending or shocking her. Jane was strong, and most important, she also was a young widow. She understood things that no one else could.

As for Harry's children, Noel was always away at Cambridge or out on the farm, and that odd child Vanessa was always going on about breeding horses and dogs. She seemed to think of nothing but breeding and used the most appallingly graphic language. The English were so odd; love between people was never mentioned, but love between beasts was a fit topic for twelve-year-old girls. Even at the dinner table.

Madelene shrugged. Sometimes she was very glad she was French. She went out, shutting the heavy door firmly behind her.

Harry watched Madelene walk from the door to where he waited by the side of the brown Humber. She looked so beautiful with her rich, warm complexion and the shining hair beneath the lacy veil. And so young.

Emily came out that winter and begged to be allowed to stay in London. In some ways she was Helen's daughter, though she lacked Helen's avaricious streak. Hardacres bored her. In the excitement of the immediate post-war years she wanted to be where the action was, among the bright urban lights where young people fought hard to capture the gaiety which had been for so long missing from their lives. Maud was much quieter and much more intense. She had definite artistic talent, and – though Mary thought it an indulgence – Harry sent her to art school, where she was able to express herself in sculpture. She was one of the moderns; her work was mainly abstract and not to the taste of the older generation and the traditionalists – Mary, least of all.

'What is it?' Mary would ask when Maud showed her her latest piece of work.

'It's a thought, a shape,' Maud explained, trying to make Mary understand.

'Well, owt that tha can see's got shape; tha can pick things like that up on the beach, but tha can't see a thought.'

And Maud would give up. It was no good; old people would never understand the intensity of the feeling that she was trying to express. Mind you, Harry was not too bad; at least he tried, though she suspected that his praise was somewhat forced and contained a suggestion of indulgence that she did not want.

'What I really need, Uncle,' she said to him one day, 'is a studio in Chelsea.'

'What's wrong with Driffield or Bridlington, or Hardacres for that matter?'

'You don't really understand, do you?'

'No,' he said, smiling.

'If you want to work in the arts, atmosphere is all-important. You need people around you who think and feel as you do.' (She said 'feel' with a very long 'ee'.) 'Honestly, it's terribly important to me.'

'A bit later perhaps, when you're a little older.'

And there the matter would rest until the next time.

Jane spent most of her time at Hardacres, but she had to live for part of the year at Castle Connon, where the dowager Lady Macgregor still carried on the estate. She owed this to Peter, who had now inherited the title and would, everyone assumed, take over the Scottish estate as soon as he was old enough to do so. One thing that gave Jane great joy was that she found herself in a position to be able to help Heidi Muller, with whom she was now in frequent correspondence. When inflation hit and the German economy was paralysed, Jane was able to let Heidi have some small amounts of British money to help tide her over those difficult days. With memories of her suffragette days still strong, she admired the independent spirit that both Maud and Emily were showing, and encouraged them in their desire to go it alone.

When Philip Barton called one day late in 1923, she began to wonder if perhaps she had encouraged them a little too much.

Number 43 Gerrard Street in London's Soho was the 'in' night club. It was patronized by everybody – which was that set of 'gay young things', the flappers, who lived in the environment of a never-ending round of parties. These parties were such that it was possible, if one knew the right people, to go to a series of fancy-dress affairs which would carry one through a week or more without ever being recognized and without ever seeing the light of day. It was, in the language of the time, all too devastating. Of course, all the best parties ended up at Gerrard Street. It was even whispered that royalty went there. All of the women smoked black Russian cigarettes with gold tips, from long holders, and everybody drank cocktails. There were, however, sinister overtones to the activities in Gerrard Street. It was rumoured that it was possible to obtain more exotic stimulants than mere alcohol and tobacco if one could afford to pay for them and knew whom to ask. That was the reason why Philip Barton was sitting near the bar in Number 43, glancing at his watch on the night of 1 September at about two o'clock in the morning.

'Columbine' came and sat down at the bar next to him. Philip looked at her, casually at first and then with greater interest. She was in her early twenties and attractive, with wisps of auburn hair escaping from the black skullcap which encased her head. She had either lost or discarded her mask, her lipstick was smudged, and she was struggling to put a cigarette into a long ivory holder.

'Why don't you go home, young lady?' he said.

She looked at him and said nothing.

'I said, why don't you go home? I'll call a taxi for you if you would like.'

'I don't think that I know you,' she said, with an attempt at dignity which was ruined by the slurred speech, and then turned away from him.

Why he should suddenly pick on this girl out of all the others who were there was something that Philip Barton was never able to explain. She was, like most of the others, drunk, with the kind of ingrained drunkenness which comes from long periods of alcohol with very little food.

'Listen,' he said, 'I'm only trying to help. Tell me where you live, and I'll take you there.'

'Oh, no, you wouldn't.'

'I would, I swear it.'

'Listen, mister, whoever you are, I may look like a tart, but I'm not one.'

Philip smiled; in his job he knew practically every tart in Soho, and he was pretty certain she was not one of them. He really did want to help.

'Look,' he said, 'I can't tell you why, but you'll be doing yourself a big favour if you go home now. I meant it when I said that I'd take you home, and that was all that I meant. Just tell me where you live, and I'll leave you there with your people.'

She made no reply, but Philip persisted. 'Don't be a damned little fool.'

Emily looked at him. He was a good-enough-looking man – tall, about six feet, and fair, with honest brown eyes; also, he seemed to be sober, which was quite unusual for the time and place.

392

'You don't mean it,' she said.

'I promise you I do. Where is your home?'

'Yorkshire.'

'Oh.'

She laughed at him.

'Well,' he said, 'I made the offer, so it stands.' He looked at his watch. 'I think you have approximately five minutes in which to make up your mind.'

'What's so important about five minutes?'

'You'll see,' he said. 'My car's outside; I'll drive you straight up there. How about it?'

'How do I know I can trust you?' she said, swaying slightly.

'You don't. You only have my word.' He paused. 'Well, what do you say?'

'All right.'

She collapsed into his arms just as the first police whistle blew, and the raid on 43 Gerrard Street was on.

A couple of hours later Philip stopped his car in the parking lot of Jack's Hill Café. He turned to the sleeping figure in the back seat and shook her.

'Wake up,' he said.

Emily groaned and sat up in the back of the car. 'Who are you?' she demanded, then giggled.

'Chief Detective Inspector Philip Barton, Special Branch,' he replied.

Emily was impressed; she tried to pull herself together. 'Am I ... did I ... ?'

'You're not under arrest, if that's what you want to know,' he said. 'You ought to be, but you're not.'

'Then will you please tell me where I am?'

'Just outside Baldock on the Great North Road,' he replied. 'Do you know where that is?'

'Are you abducting me?' she asked. 'How simply divine.'

'Don't be a fool,' he replied. 'I am taking you home, but first I am going to get some food inside of you. Come on.'

He half carried Emily into the café, which was a regular stop for the long-distance lorry drivers. There were a few of them in, having breakfast – stolid types who scarcely raised an eyebrow at the sight of Emily in her rather bedraggled

393

Columbine costume. He sat her down in front of a large plate of ham, eggs, bread and butter, and tea. She started to eat, tentatively at first to see if it would stay down, and then ravenously.

'What time is it?' she asked.

'About five o'clock.'

'Morning or afternoon?'

'Morning. What's your name?'

'Emily Hardacre,' she replied. 'Are you really a detective?'

'And where do you live, Miss Hardacre?'

'You don't know? I thought you were taking me home.'

'I only know that you live in Yorkshire.'

'I don't think I'll go home,' she said. 'I'm over twenty-one.'

'Listen, young lady,' said Philip firmly, 'I am taking you home. In order for me to be able to do that, you are going to tell me exactly where you live, because if you don't, I shall put you across my knee and spank you until you do.'

'You wouldn't dare.'

'Wouldn't I?'

She looked straight at him. 'Yes, you would. I live at Hardacres. If you take me as far as Beverley or Hull, I'll get a train from there. Can I?'

'No.'

'You won't be able to find it.'

'I'm a policeman, remember. I shall take you as far as Beverley, lock you in a cell, and while you are there I shall have enquiries made and find out how to get to Hardacres.'

Emily gave up. 'All right; go to Beverley, then take the Driffield road, and I'll direct you from there.'

'Thank you,' said Philip, smiling.

'I hate you,' said Emily.

'In that case we had better get going and get this over with.'

Philip ordered a package of sandwiches and took her out to the car.

It was about 180 miles to Hardacres, and the drive took them five and a half hours. Emily protested at intervals. First she was cold; Philip gave her a rug. Then she was hungry; Philip tossed her a sandwich. When she said that she was thirsty, they stopped at Doncaster and had a cup of tea. Apart from these occasional protests, there was little or no conversation, except when Philip started to sing and Emily told him to shut up.

After they left Beverley, she made one last attempt to get him to allow her to go home alone, but he would have none of it and threatened her again with a cell. It was just after eleven thirty when they turned into the drive at Hardacres. Gunn answered the door, and the moment he opened it, Emily shot past him and disappeared upstairs.

'Miss Emily!' Gunn was startled more by her appearance than anything else.

'Let her go,' said Philip; he handed Gunn a card. 'I should like to see the master of the house.'

Gunn looked at the card, impressed. 'If you would care to wait in the study, Chief Inspector,' he said.

Philip followed him across the hall and into the study. It intrigued him to see the way the grand formality of the hall gave way to the warm intimacy of the study, with its leather furnishings and dark oak panels. Three people came into the study. They were a middle-aged man and woman, the man greying and the woman rather plain, dressed in a brown tweed skirt and twin-set. The other woman was more the sort of person he had expected to see in such a house – tall and fine-featured. Philip reckoned she would be in her early thirties; her black hair was immaculately groomed, and she was wearing a pale-lemon-coloured silk day dress. He was not surprised to see that they all looked somewhat worried.

'Chief Inspector Barton?' said the man. 'I'm Harry Hardacre; this is my wife and my sister, Lady Jane Macgregor. Emily's parents are in America; I am her uncle.'

'I see,' said Philip.

'What's wrong?' asked Jane.

'Is she in some sort of trouble?' said Hetty.

'No, she's not, though she ought to be,' said Philip. 'Don't you think that I ought to explain to Mr Hardacre privately?'

'No,' said Harry, 'these ladies are Emily's aunts. If there is anything to know, then I feel that it is better for us all to know the worst.'

'As you wish, sir,' said Philip. 'Do you mind if I sit down?

I have been up all night.'

'Forgive me,' said Harry. 'Perhaps I could get you something? A drink or some food?'

'No, thank you, Mr Hardacre; some strong black coffee might not be a bad idea, though.'

'Of course; I'll get it right away,' said Hetty and arranged for the coffee.

'Ought we to get Emily down?' asked Jane when they had all settled.

'I doubt if that would do any good,' said Philip, and he started to recount the events of the previous twelve hours.

'And that's it,' he finished. 'It's not my place to say so, but in your position I should try very hard to keep that young lady away from London for some considerable time.'

There was a long silence after Philip stopped speaking.

'I had no idea,' said Jane. 'I feel in part responsible, for I actually encouraged her to be independent.'

'You need not blame yourself, Lady Macgregor,' said Philip. 'She just got in with a bad lot – it happens all the time; I see a lot of it in my job.'

'Well,' said Harry, 'I can't tell you how grateful we all are to you for what you have done. You'll stay the night, of course. You cannot possibly drive all the way back to London today.'

'That's very kind of you, Mr Hardacre,' said Philip. 'If I might just use your telephone first to contact the Yard and let them know where I am. Though how I am going to explain this to them, I just don't know.'

'Why did you do it?' asked Hetty.

'I can't answer that one either. When she came in and sat beside me, she just looked as if she needed help. Honestly, I don't know.'

Philip telephoned through to Scotland Yard and then went upstairs to the room that had been prepared for him and got himself a couple of hours' sleep. When he woke, he had a quick bath and dressed and then went down.

The family were having afternoon tea. Emily, now cleaned up and looking very pretty in a printed cotton dress, glared at him when he came in.

'You,' she said, 'I don't know how you have the nerve to stay here. I just want you to know that you are the most loathsome, beastly, ungentlemanly, horrible man I have ever met in my life, and I have no intention of speaking to you ever again even if you come and live here.' With this she stormed out of the room.

They were married within twelve months.

CHAPTER THREE

It wasn't only Emily. Her sudden and dramatic return to Hardacres had set them all worrying about Maud. Jane had interceded with Harry, and they had finally given Maud permission to go to London, where she had rented a studio in the artists' colony in Chelsea. When she saw that she was going to get her way, she had tried for Paris, but no one – not even Madelene – would agree that that was a good idea, so she settled for the compromise and went down to London with Jane. They found her two rooms on the top floor of a large old building just off the King's Road. It was a pleasant little apartment, and the larger of the two rooms made an excellent studio, having a very large north-facing window.

For the first few months she worked away, living on a small allowance. She continued to sculpt her abstracts from stone and marble, and even had the thrill of making a couple of sales. They were not earth-shattering, but they were sales, and they told her that there were at least some people who wanted her work. She received two pounds for one and two pounds, ten shillings for the other. She began to realize, though, that even if sculpture provided for her an interesting hobby, she was not destined to become one of the great or fashionable artists.

The house in which she lived was occupied by two other artists and a musician. Her immediate neighbour was the musician – a jazz trumpeter by the name of Albert Chandler. He was working fairly regularly, managing to get a fair number of engagements with various dance bands playing around the West End. Maud had been in the apartment for about three months before she met him for the first time, though they had nodded to one another on the stairs.

It was an egg that they met over. There was a tap on the door of her apartment, and when she opened it Albert was standing there.

'I'm your neighbour,' he said. 'Albert Chandler.'

'Yes, I know,' she replied. 'Was there something you wanted?'

'An egg,' he said.

'An egg?' She was surprised.

'I suppose it sounds silly, but I always have bacon and an egg for breakfast. I fry the bacon and then the egg in the bacon fat – well, I've cooked the bacon and find that I haven't got an egg.'

'I'll get you one,' she said. 'Do you usually have breakfast at two o'clock in the afternoon?'

'I was working until five,' he said, taking the egg. 'Thank you. Would you like a cup of tea? I've got a fresh pot.'

'Thank you.'

'I'll bring one round.'

'I'll come with you if you like.'

'Oh,' he said without enthusiasm, 'it's not very tidy.'

When she saw the state of his room, she realized why he had been so reluctant to invite her in. It was chaotic.

'You're not very house-trained, are you?' she said as they sipped their teas.

'Not very,' he replied, and they both laughed.

'I'll tell you what,' she said. 'Are you working tonight?'

'Yes.'

'Then, if you leave your room open, I'll come in after you have gone and tidy up.'

'Oh, but I couldn't possibly let you do that; it wouldn't be right,' he said.

But she did.

Over the next few weeks a warm friendship developed between them. It was a friendship without any complications of sex or emotion. Maud kept his room reasonably tidy for him and performed other little tasks like sewing on the odd button or ironing a shirt. Albert, when he had a night off, would take her out to one of the little restaurants with which Chelsea abounded and buy her a modest meal.

They were both alone in London, and in their different ways they were both rather shy people. They did take a genuine interest in each other's work. In a manner they were both moderns: Albert was principally interested in jazz, though most of his paid work was ragtime and dance music, while Maud was of course still working on her abstract sculpture. He would come into her studio and sometimes admire and other times criticize her work, and she in return, though she did not really like it, would listen to him improvising on the trumpet. Their relationship developed in a pleasant, easy-going, uncomplicated way until one day when Albert told her that he was going away for a week to play with a new band at Brighton.

It was almost casual, the way it happened. She went down to hear him play on the Friday night – not because she really wanted to but because she knew that he wanted her to. The concert was at the Pavilion Theatre in Brighton, and afterwards they all went along to the small hotel where the band was staying. They had a meal and then sat around as various groups of the musicians played and improvised in an impromptu concert. It was all very pleasant and Maud enjoyed herself a lot, but she missed the last train back to London.

Albert tried to get her a room, but the hotel was full, so he offered Maud his. At first she would not hear of it, but when she was assured that he would be able to share with George, the alto saxophonist, she consented. He took her up to show her the room and tidy up a bit; then he started to leave.

'Don't go yet,' said Maud.

'I must,' he replied. 'You're tired, and I'm sure you must want to get some sleep.'

'Not just yet.'

She felt strangely excited. She really did want him to stay; he finally agreed, and they sat down, she on the bed and he on the only chair, and talked. They chatted on for over an hour – they talked about every subject under the sun – and then, for the very first time, he kissed her.

There was no logical explanation for what followed other than the most logical of all. Two healthy, normal people, a man and a woman, alone together with the world locked out behind their door. They became lovers.

A few weeks later Maud began to suspect that she was

pregnant. She was surprised at her own feelings about this; she did not mind. It was, to her, a simple issue. They loved each other, and it would merely be a matter of marrying earlier rather than later. However, she decided to wait to tell him another week or two, until she was quite certain.

There was a loud knocking at her door. It was Albert. He came in obviously excited and very elated.

'Darling,' he said, 'I've had the most wonderful news.'

'What is it?' she asked, feeling his joy and taking his mood.

'An offer, the chance of a lifetime. I'm going on a tour of the United States as lead trumpet in one of the big American bands.'

'The United States?' She tried not to show her apprehension.

'Yes. I don't want to leave you, but I won't be away long, a year at the most. And, Maud ...'

'Yes?' She tried hard to smile.

'We'll be able to marry as soon as I get back.'

'But a whole year?'

'At the very most, and if it was any longer, I could send for you and we could get married over there.'

'Can't I come with you now?' She was pleading with him.

'I thought of that,' he replied. 'I even suggested it, but they wouldn't hear of it. If I'd insisted, I'd have lost the job.'

'But, Albert, there's something else.'

'No, my darling, not until the first tour is over. You see, it's going to be coast-to-coast. You know the sort of thing – one-night stands and long train journeys every day or two.'

'I wouldn't mind, honestly.'

'But I would; even if it were possible, it would be no life for you – you must see that.'

'Is it that you don't want me to come?' She had to say it. It was as if she had hit him across the face. If only she could be certain of his feelings – were they guilt or remorse?

'That's a beastly thing to say,' he replied.

She wanted to tell him about the child, but she didn't. She wanted to throw herself into his arms, but she didn't. She wanted to cry, to stay with him and be with him always, but she didn't. She did none of those things. Instead, she had a flaming row with him and caught the next train to Hardacres.

When she got home, she did not go to the big house but straight to her grandmother's cottage. There she found Mary alone, polishing the leaves of her aspidistra with olive oil.

'Hello, Grandma,' she said.

'Maud?' Mary was surprised. 'Is it really thee? I didn't know tha was back.'

'I've only just arrived,' said Maud. 'I haven't been to the big house; I came straight here.'

'That was right nice of thee,' said Mary. 'Now, just thee sit thee sen down, and I'll make a pot of tea before tha goes over.'

'Grandma, I don't want to go over. Please, can I stay here with you?'

'Well, of course tha can, love. I've got yon spare bedroom, but it's a mite small, and there's a lot more room in the big house. Come on, then; I'll make tea – kettle's on – and then tha can tell me what has happened.'

Mary busied herself in the kitchen and came out with a tray on which was a cup of tea for Maud, the Victoria and Albert mug for herself, and a plate of hot muffins dripping with butter. At the sight of the muffins Maud felt a feeling of nausea and put her hand over her mouth.

'I take it that tha doesn't want owt to eat,' said Mary, and she took the muffins away.

Maud nodded.

'All right, love, just drink tha tea and tell me what's wrong,' said Mary.

'Everything,' said Maud. She was near to tears.

'It's a man, isn't it?'

'How did you know?' Maud was startled.

'It weren't so hard to guess,' said Mary. 'I'm a woman, Maud, and I've been young me sen. I know how a young lass feels, and I also know that there's nowt so bad as it cannot be put right.'

'But you don't understand, Grandma, there is, there is.'

Mary sipped her tea for a moment and then spoke very gently. 'Maud, when's baby due?'

Maud gasped. 'It doesn't show, does it?'

'Not in tha body, though it will – there's nowt that can stop that. It's in thee sen that it shows. Dost tha love him?'

'Yes.'

'And him, does he love thee?'

'He's gone to America.'

'And tha never told him?'

'No.'

'Well, that's that; are tha going to write to him?'

'I wouldn't know how to get in touch with him.'

'Well, then,' said Mary, smiling, 'isn't this a lovely surprise?'

Maud looked up, wondering if her grandmother had gone mad. 'Lovely surprise?'

'Aye. Imagine, another baby about the house. Reckon it's just what we needed. And don't thee fret; thou can stay here with me for a day or two or as long as tha wants to. Just leave it all to me, I'll tell the others ...'

'Must you tell them?'

'They'll know soon enough if I don't. I'll tell them, pet, and don't thee worry, everything'll be fine.'

'Oh, Grandma!' She burst into tears. 'You're so wonderful.'

'There, there, my baby,' said Mary, 'thou's nobbut a kid.' She took Maud into her arms.

That evening Mary got Maud off to bed early and then went over to Hardacres. She found them – Harry, Hetty, Jane, Madelene, and Emily – in the drawing room having after-dinner coffee.

'Mother, this is a nice surprise,' said Harry, rising and offering Mary a chair.

'No thanks, Harry,' said Mary, 'I've summat important to tell thee, and I'll feel better standing up.'

'What is it?' asked Jane.

'Maud's back.'

'Maud – when, where?' said Emily with a murmur of surprise.

'This afternoon. She's over at my place now. She's in bed, and I hope asleep. She's going to have a baby.'

'A baby? But ... But ... She didn't tell us that she was married,' said Hetty.

'She's not.'

403

There was a silence before Emily spoke. 'The stupid little fool,' she said.

'That's enough of that,' snapped Mary. 'It could have happened to any woman here.'

'Oh, come now, Mother,' said Harry.

'And tha can stop that, Harry,' said Mary. 'I want no pious claptrap from anybody. She's frightened, and she's lonely, and if anybody's got owt to say, they'd better say it now and get it off their chests, because if I catch anybody upsetting her, they'll have me to deal with.' She paused. 'Well, if that's all, I'll be getting back.'

'What are people going to say?' said Emily.

'I suppose that we shall have to keep it quiet,' said Hetty.

'Why is there the fuss?' asked Madelene. 'If my Arnold had died a week earlier, it would have been the same for me.'

'Madelene!' Emily was shocked.

'But, of course – in this modern world, who is there who does not do it?' said Madelene. 'You?'

'Are you suggesting . . .' Emily was angry.

'Only if you think so,' replied Madelene. 'Perhaps you were one of the lucky ones.'

'All right,' said Harry, intervening before they got to blows. 'You all heard what Mother said. That's the way it's got to be. I, for one, don't feel like arguing with her. You know, she seems to be getting more and more like Father.'

'I've seen that in her too,' said Jane, 'and as far as Maud is concerned, we've all got to rally round; there's nothing else that we can do. Of course, there are going to be nasty things said in the village, and you can't keep this sort of thing secret even if you want to. I am sure that Mother and Madelene are right, and for you, Emily, if your husband was here, he'd agree with them. He's probably seen more of life than all of us put together. If any of you are shocked, you'd better not show it. It won't only be Mother you'll have to deal with if you do; for God's sake, don't go patronizing Maud.'

And there the matter rested. Maud continued to live with her grandmother. Mary gave her the front bedroom of her cottage – a sweet little room with a dormer window overlooking the little flower garden in the front. It had flowered wallpaper, showing a profusion of pink rosebuds, and a fire-place with a rocking chair, where Maud would spend many hours reading or knitting or thinking.

For Mary the whole business was like a new lease of life. She loved having someone really to look after once more. She was, now in her late sixties, quite grey and a little heavier than she had been, but she still had masses of energy, which had been so repressed and frustrated when she had been surrounded by servants in the big house. She cooked all their meals except Sunday lunch. The family always lunched to-gether at Hardacres after church on Sundays. At first Maud had not wanted to go to church – she did not want to be on public view – but again Mary's will proved the stronger.

'Tha's not going to hide,' she had said. 'If there are tongues that want to wag, they'll wag any road, and it's better that they do it in front of tha face rather than behind tha back.'

So Maud went to church. She also went into Driffield once a week alone, always on Fridays. When there she went to the public library and searched the pages of *Variety* to see if she could find some mention of Albert. His name began to appear – occasionally at first, and then with greater fre-quency. It seemed that he was being quite a success in America, and he had formed his own band, which was be-coming more and more noticed.

When the baby was born – a girl, Janet – Maud missed four Fridays, but as soon as she was allowed out and about, she was off to Driffield again and looking through the back numbers of the magazine.

When Janet was about three months old, *Variety* con-tained a large announcement to the effect that Albert Chandler and his band would be appearing at the Pavilion Theatre in London's Piccadilly Circus, in about two weeks' time. She resolved that she would go to London while he was there and possibly see him.

She made the trip with Jane on the pretext that she was going on a shopping expedition. Mary made no objection; she was only too pleased to have the baby to herself for a few days. They stayed at Grosvenor Square, and Maud per-suaded Jane to come with her to the Pavilion on the second of their two-night stay.

'But I thought that you did not like modern music,' Jane said when Maud suggested it.

'I'm beginning to see something in it,' Maud lied.

Jane, quite a jazz fan, was only too delighted to go. They sat for two and a half hours in the theatre, and Maud was thankful for the darkness of the auditorium, which hid her emotions. She sat there watching Albert, so near to her on the apron of the stage, terrified that at any moment he would look into the audience and recognize her and at the same time praying that he would.

She could not bring herself to go around and see him. It had all been too much. She decided that the whole expedition had been a mistake and that it would have been better if she had never come.

With all the old heartache renewed within her, Maud returned to Hardacres. Mary noticed the change in her and tackled Jane about it.

'What happened to yon lass in London?' she said.

'Nothing that I know of,' replied Jane. 'We were together the whole time.'

'She didn't go off anywhere on her own?'

'No.'

'Summat happened,' said Mary. 'Are tha sure there was nowt that you can remember?'

'All we did was buy a few clothes and go to the theatre,' replied Jane.

'What did tha see?'

'It was one of the big jazz bands, Albert Chandler's,' said Jane.

'I wonder,' said Mary, but she would say no more.

Albert Chandler stood in the post office in Driffield; he had discovered that Maud came from somewhere in that area. As soon as his engagement was over, he had gone up to Bridlington, where he had discovered that some people called Hardacre lived near Driffield.

'I wonder if you could tell me where the Hardacres live?' he asked the woman behind the counter.

'They live near Watton; it's about five miles down the Beverley road,' she replied.

'Is it hard to find?' he asked.

'Nay,' was the reply. 'Just ask anyone for Hardacres; it's the biggest house around these parts.'

'But it is a family called Hardacre that I'm looking for.'

'That's right,' she said, 'same name as the house.'

He drove to Watton and was then directed to the entrance to Hardacres. He was most impressed when he saw the magnificent old mansion; he had no idea that Maud came from so grand a background. He got out of his car and rang the bell. Gunn answered the door.

'I am trying to find a Miss Maud Hardacre,' said Albert. 'I was given to understand that she may live here.'

'Not exactly, sir,' replied Gunn. 'She lives in a cottage with her grandmother. It's about half a mile from here, across the fields.'

'Could you show me how to get there? I'm an old friend of Miss Hardacre,' he added by way of explanation.

'Certainly, sir,' said Gunn, and he directed him to Mary's cottage.

Albert left his car and walked across the garden towards the little cottage.

'Excuse me,' he said, when Mary answered the door, 'I'm looking for a lady. Her name is Maud Hardacre, and they told me at the big house that I might find her here.'

Mary looked her visitor over – a personable young man, she thought. Nicely spoken. By Mary's standards, he looked as if a few weeks in the country might take the city pallor from his cheeks. Still, he had charming manners and looked her straight in the eye when he spoke. His fair hair was plastered down in the fashionable manner, and his clothes were smart and a little, but not too, flamboyant – and was there just a trace of an American accent? Mary smiled a greeting. 'She lives here, but she's not in at the moment,' she said. 'And who might thee be?'

'I'm Albert Chandler,' he replied, a little surprised at Mary's broad Yorkshire accent. 'I'm a sort of – well, you might say that I'm an old friend of hers.'

'Well, that makes two of us,' said Mary. 'I'm her grandmother. I suppose that tha'd better come into t'house and wait for her, Mr Chandler; she won't be long.'

'Thank you very much,' said Albert as Mary took him into her tiny sitting room.

'Might I ask why tha wanted to see her?' asked Mary. 'If it's not too personal a question.'

'We were very good friends; I lived in the same apartment house as she did. I've been in America for about a year.'

'But there's more than that,' said Mary.

'Oh, yes,' he replied. 'We had a stupid row just before I left, and I haven't been in touch since.'

'Tha could have written.'

'Oh, I did, but I only had her London address, and I gather that she left rather suddenly, and the house we were staying in changed hands, so I just couldn't contact her. I've been working in London for a few weeks, and I've spent every spare moment trying to trace her.' He paused.

'Tha must have wanted to see her very much,' said Mary.

'I did, I still do, that's why I'm here,' said Albert. 'You see ... I've got something to offer her now.'

'Happen she's got summat to offer thee an' all,' said Mary.

'I don't understand,' said Albert.

'Oh, but tha will,' said Mary, smiling because she knew now that it was going to be all right. 'I think, Mr Chandler, that while tha's waiting for her I'd better bring tha daughter down so that thee two can get acquainted.'

CHAPTER FOUR

Joe was seated at his desk, in his office on the top floor of a building on Wall Street; he was gazing at the gutting knife. Much to Helen's disgust he had had it silver-mounted on a black marble base. It was sitting in the centre of his desk, and it seemed to be staring back at him. It was almost as if he could hear his father speaking to him as he sat there.

'That's all I needed, Joe – that and guts. Money's nowt. It's got no meaning unless it works for thee and gives work to them as depends on thee . . . it's in the land that tha'll find real wealth, the land gives life. A million pounds is no bloody use to a hungry man if there isn't a baker to sell him a loaf of bread for tuppence . . . if thou makes money thy god, it will destroy thee, but as long as tha has a trade, as long as tha can handle a tool and do summat wi' thy hands, tha can allus start again.'

Joe grinned. At fifty-five he was beyond starting again. Back home at Hardacres – somehow he always thought of Hardacres as home – he had a grandchild he had never seen and two grandsons who would be nearly twelve; he had not seen them either, not since they were babies. Both of his daughters had been in some sort of trouble, but that was all over; with his mother's help they had both managed to come through. None of this worried him; none of it, that was, except for his mother.

Mary still wrote to him every month; he wondered why, for he hardly ever wrote to her, though there was never a word of recrimination in any of her letters. The whole thing was cumulative; sometimes he prayed for Christmas to come around so that he would have a reason to write the letter which he had written daily in his mind for months but had always left until tomorrow. If Joe regretted anything, it was not his marriage – he believed that he and Helen deserved each other; it was not his lack of friends, for he had never laid much store by friendship; it was every letter that he had not written to his mother.

Apart from Mary, it was doubtful if Joe had any real affection for anyone. The hard, brittle circle of acquaintances in which he moved was a source of social satisfaction to Helen and of contemptuous amusement for Joe. It was now, in October 1929, that he was beginning to realize that there was nothing real in his world. He dealt in pieces of paper with cardboard characters; now, somehow the whole lot had caught fire, and Joe watched with cynical pleasure as their world turned to ashes around them.

He looked back over the preceding few months. Not long ago, only a couple of weeks or so, he could have counted his fortune in millions – and now? Tomorrow was settling day, and Joe could not settle. He could not settle even if he sold his house on Long Island, his apartment in midtown Manhattan, his cars, and all of his possessions. Joe was broke. He had joined the hundreds, the thousands of others who had been swept up in the hysteria of buying on the stock markets. They bought more and more and watched prices soar as they mortgaged themselves up to the hilt. And then one day, quite recently, some unknown individual decided to sell his pieces of paper. That one had been joined by another, then another, and another, until all the pieces of paper became just that and nothing more, and the margins that they had bought – because they were an even quicker way of acquiring more pieces of paper – became due.

Down and down the market had plunged. It was almost inconceivable, but it was true; there was nothing left.

Sam would have shrugged his shoulders, picked up his gutting knife, and started again. Joe could not do that; he was tired, and he lacked his father's resilience. Besides, Sam would have had something to work for, a family. Joe had sired a family, but they were not his – they never had been. They belonged, three thousand miles away, to a country estate in Yorkshire.

Then there was Helen. Joe almost laughed when he thought about Helen. It was funny how she had stuck with him, ever since the day he had found her in the lifeboat. There had never been much warmth and affection between them; Helen had invested her body in him, and always she wanted a higher return on her capital. She had believed that wealth would buy her happiness, but she had been wrong; it had only served to make their discontent more comfortable. She had borne him three children and had resented every one. Even Arnold's death and heroism had failed to move her as a mother should have been moved, and she had, like Joe, never met her daughters' husbands.

Most of all, she resented being a grandmother, and whenever Joe taunted her with the fact, she would fly off to the most expensive beauty salon she could find and hand over large sums of cash in return for reassurance about her youthfulness. In spite of all this Joe pitied her, but she suspected it, and it made her more bitter than ever. He was sorry for her because he felt that, beneath the glossy façade, there was still a frightened little girl trying to get out. A little girl who had been ill-used by such as himself, to such an extent that she had run away and hidden herself aboard a big ship. She had been running ever since.

When Helen came into the office wearing a silver-fox fur, a mauve cloche hat, and matching costume in fine wool, Joe looked up admiringly; she had style, you had to give her that. He lifted the telephone receiver off the hook and laid it down beside the instrument. There would be no important calls – only creditors who themselves were afraid of their creditors, and so on *ad infinitum*.

'Well?' she demanded.

'Well, what?' he asked, raising an eyebrow and smiling slightly.

'What are we going to do about this mess?'

'My dear, there is nothing we can do; the bubble has burst, and we are quite broke.'

'That is ridiculous.'

'Yes, dear, quite ridiculous. It is also very funny, and it is also true.'

'Joe, I need a thousand dollars, and I need it now.'

Joe fished about in his pockets and produced two dollar bills and thirty-three cents in small change; he laid them on the desk in front of her. 'Here you are, my dear – the family fortune; you can have it all, every last cent of it.'

'Joe, I shall leave you.'

'Will you, my dear?' his tone was bored.

'I shall go back to England. I can raise the fare; I shall go back to England and ... and ...'

'Live off Harry?'

'That fool,' she snapped. 'But anyway, why not? Half of what he has is yours by rights.'

'No, it's not,' said Joe. 'Hardacres belongs to Harry. I got this, remember?' he tapped the gutting knife.

'I'm through with you, Joe,' she said. 'Do you understand? I'm through.'

'It doesn't matter,' said Joe.

She flung her silver fox around her neck and flounced out of the office.

Joe went over to the window and opened it. Down there below was Wall Street, and all of the people hurrying along were in various stages of Depression fever. Funny, her mentioning Harry. He smiled again as he thought of his brother, of Adam and the cart, and of the darkness when they played under the tarpaulin. He leaned farther out.

Officer O'Mally heard the screams and ran down the street in their direction. It was another one. O'Mally wished that they wouldn't do it on his beat. He elbowed his way into the crowd, calling to them to stand back. The body was lying on the sidewalk. There was an elegantly dressed woman standing looking at it; she wore a silver fox fur and a mauve cloche hat.

'You fool,' she said, 'you cowardly fool.'

And in the silence that followed, O'Mally could hear her heels tip-tapping on the sidewalk as she walked away.

They tried very hard to keep the news from Mary, but it did not work out. The Hardacres were too well known in the whole of the county, and the papers got hold of it. The local paper ran the whole tale, in all of its lurid detail, as the lead story of the day, and there was mention of the tragedy on the wireless. Mary never said a word, but she suddenly appeared wearing black. Harry had never seen his mother in black before, and the implication did not escape him. He decided that he would tax her with it.

'Mother,' he said, 'I thought that you didn't believe in it – mourning, I mean. It's for Joe, isn't it?'

'Aye,' replied Mary.

'But you never even wore black for Father.'

'No, Harry, I didn't,' she said. 'Thy father were a good man, and he got his reward – he went easy and without bitterness. Joe needs our prayers; what he done were wrong, and there's many around these parts as would condemn him for it. That's why I'm wearing black. I want to tell folk that I know how he died, and I want them to know that, no matter what, he were my son and I loved him.'

They left it at that. Harry never brought up the subject again and warned the others not to discuss Joe in Mary's presence.

It was late November 1929, and, in spite of his brother's recent death, Harry was uncommonly happy. The day was cold but dry, and the mid-day sun still surprisingly strong in the sheltered square of the kitchen garden. Winter was near; it showed in the frost contained by the shadowed side of the brick walls. It would not last, but there was still an hour or two of sun and work and companionship. Harry was lifting the garden potatoes from the long rows of dead, blackened stalks, and Madelene was helping him. It was a rare moment, but Harry had learned to savour such moments fully when they came; life did not give happiness for long.

He was not working the kitchen garden by choice. Harry was a farmer, and gardening was another profession, small in scope and somewhat beneath him. But Mary had abandoned her garden, along with everything else, when Joe died. She maintained she was feeling arthritis. Perhaps it was so, Harry thought, but the onslaught had been swifter and more sudden than winter. He wondered uneasily if Mary would ever come back here.

Even if she eventually did, the potatoes were needed today. They were depending more heavily on the kitchen garden every year. And now there was just the one gardener – he was a young man, a neighbour who had come, odd and confused, back from France in 1918. He had once been to Cambridge and shown promise, but that was all gone, lost somewhere in the trenches. Harry hired him for the garden out of kindness. He did not do badly, considering, but he was busy now with winter pruning and lifting the dahlia corms and gladioli bulbs. Harry wondered about the flower gardens. He saw them more and more as an extravagance, to which he was perhaps not entitled in this new, changed world. But stripping the house of her gardens would be like stripping a lady of her jewels or a bride of her veil. He could not bear to do it, though one day, he imagined, he might have to.

It was nearly four years since the General Strike. Harry's family had spent the nine days gleefully playing at running the Driffield railway station. Harry had been alone on the farm, working hard and counting in his heart the cost of Hardacres in terms of the poverty of others. They had come out of it financially bruised but in no way permanently scarred. But it doubly shook Harry. He had always distrusted security in the financial world, and now it had become even less certain. The justification for his elegant life style became even more uncertain. Harry's response was to work and make the land he so loved work.

Still, he had a guilty awareness that the work he did with his hands remained something of a fraud. He did not have to do it; he could hire someone else or redirect the existing labour. But what else was there for him? Noel handled the business management of the home farm and the estate – and handled it better than Harry had ever done. So Harry found himself making his repayment for the good life by working as a farm labourer. He was good at it, better than he was at any other trade; but he knew that, for him, hard work would always be balanced by luxury. At the end of the day he would come in, shed his muddy clothes for others to wash, his boots for someone else to clean, and find waiting for him a hot bath drawn by his footman. Afterwards he would put on a dinner suit and dine with ladies in long gowns at his own splendid table, on fine food and wine extravagantly prepared by his kitchen staff. The farm labourer spent his evenings surrounded by fine china and glass, silver and wines, good music and good company. Deep down he knew that he was playing at farming just as much as his family had played at railways during those nine days in 1926.

But it was all he could do, other than watch his country still trying to restructure itself in some new, workable way after the shaking its foundations had taken in the war. It intrigued and worried Harry how much they still felt that war, and how much their lives still turned on its effects. Here was his gardener, a man who had been destined to be a university don. Here was his new cook, Mrs Porter, who should have been raising a family but now would cook for him until she died a childless widow. Madelene and Jane were more fortunate; the war had given them enough time for children, but both, he knew, would never marry again. And there was Noel, his own son, fortunate to have missed the fighting but marked nonetheless by what he did not do, as much as others were marked by what they had done. Jane had probably come out of it best. She still kept in touch with Heidi Muller, and though they had never met, their friendship seemed to take a lot of the bitterness out of the past.

It was hard being the head of the family, responsible for the house and all its people. It was hard and tiring, and he sometimes wished that there was someone to whom he could turn and hand the whole thing over. But there was not anyone. Noel was a good farmer and administrator, but he was not a gentleman interested in a decaying life style. So Harry kept on, wondering what Sam would have done, had he ever felt the same?

He looked up from his fork, shaking the earth and the hard golden roots loose beside the ridge. Madelene was at the far end of the row, working towards him. Her head was down, bent over her work, and her red head-scarf had slipped off, letting the dark curls fall over her forehead. She wore old jodhpurs, a loose green sweater, and Wellington boots. She was thirty-two and as slim as a girl. He watched contentedly, until she saw him looking and smiled – that quick, expressive smile – then he went back to his work. Hetty knew that they were together here and could have joined them, but she did not, preferring to remain in the house with Maud and little Janet. He was glad that they had come; the child was sweet, and Hetty loved her. Harry knew how much she looked forward to their visits when Albert was away touring and Maud left their little house near Sloane Square for the family companionship of Hardacres. Now Maud was here for two weeks, and that was why Hetty, in spite of being asked, would not join them. Harry felt guilty and glad.

How many years, he wondered – thrusting his fork viciously into the black earth – could this go on? Hetty was not a complainer. She never said anything – that was the trouble. Only once did resentment give rise to words, and that was oblique and unexpected.

Jane's son, Peter, was at Eton. The twin boys, Sam and Terry, were bright, high-spirited, and thoroughly presentable; Eton would certainly have accepted them, too, but Madelene would not accept Eton. Madelene had requested that, after their Catholic prep school in Sussex, they go to Beaumont. It was a stone's throw from Eton, but it was run by Jesuits. Its very nearness to Eton and to Peter infuriated Hetty. She considered it an insult to her, to her family, to her country, and to her religion. If Eton was sufficient for the young Lord Macgregor, it should be doubly so for the sons of Madelene Bisset Hardacre. Madelene was hurt and quiet and unrelenting. Harry, miserable between them, defended Madelene. It was his money, he said. But that was just what Hetty resented most. Nevertheless, that September, Sam and Terry had gone off with Peter, on the same train, but to very different schools. Then the odd, tense, quiet life resumed among the three of them. Harry remained uneasy about the decision but stood by it. He hated hurting anyone, Hetty most of all; she was so kind and gentle in most all other things, and her narrowness was the inheritance of her childhood. But religion was important and serious to Madelene – not simply social, as it was to himself and probably to Hetty as well. Strangely, he felt that it was also serious to Madelene's two odd, wild sons, with their dark French eyes and irrepressible laughter. They scandalized country house parties with their practical jokes but would never dream of missing Mass and even served as altar boys. It was a picture Harry found so incongruously amusing that one Sunday he went to Mass with them, just to see. There they were, two little angels, who the week before had put live toads in poor Mrs Porter's bed.

Harry and Madelene found themselves together in the centre of the garden; their turned potato ridges had met. Harry threw a last handful of potatoes into the wicker basket and straightened up, feeling the stiffness in his back and the old ache in his leg. Madelene smiled and suggested they rest; he nodded, putting his muddied hand lightly on her shoulder as they walked to the sheltered sunlight of the grape arbour. They stood side by side under the scattering shadow of the bare vines, leaning against the sun-warmed brick wall. The path beneath their boots was thick with yellowing dead leaves. Harry held Madelene's hand and closed his eyes, listening to the breeze and feeling the sun. He remembered Judith; it seemed so long ago. He was getting old – he knew that now, and he was finding both work and life increasingly tiring. He opened his eyes again and looked out across the black earth, the neat rows of winter greens, and then back to Madelene beside him. He would probably be dead before she was old. He leaned over and kissed her familiarly, on the mouth. She returned his kiss, and for a moment they held each other in the November sunlight. Then they separated, except for their hands, and leaned back against the wall.

Harry had closed his eyes again and did not see Vanessa

coming, but felt the sudden, familiar jerk as Madelene pulled her hand away. He looked up, alert, thinking of the times unnumbered he had felt her do that.

'Hello, Daddy,' Vanessa shouted, striding down the brick wall towards them. 'Jolly super finding you. I'm just off for a quick gallop. How about coming along?'

She was obviously just back, for the weekend, from Bridlington, where she taught at a school, and Harry wondered perversely if she had changed into jodhpurs on the bus. She had hardly had time to have gone into the big house. Maybe she wore them in the class room? His tired mind insisted on searching for the last time he had seen Vanessa not wearing jodhpurs in daylight.

'No, thank you, Vanessa,' he said, 'we still have to finish here.'

Vanessa stood slapping her boot with her crop. Harry realized that she never seemed to think that there was any work to be done around the place, unless it applied specifically to horses. 'Nice to see you back,' he added.

'Oh, yes, rather,' she replied. 'Cheers, Daddy. I'm off. Cheers, Madelene.' She strode away – her ponytail of straight sandy hair bouncing – swiping at the odd potato stalk with her crop.

Harry watched silently. Vanessa always exhausted him. Madelene, who had been very quiet, now said in a small voice, 'Do you think she saw anything?'

'Saw what?' said Harry, then remembering, 'Oh, that? Not Vanessa. It wouldn't register. She never notices anything that hasn't got four legs and whinnies.'

Madelene giggled. 'She is young yet.'

'My God, Madelene, she's twenty-three. I wish she would notice something. She might get some ideas.'

'Harry!' Madelene was shocked. 'Your own daughter? Surely you would not want her to ... ?'

'Anything,' said Harry, 'just as long as it's not horses.'

Madelene straightened up. 'You better take the basket into the kitchen; I'll tidy up here. The sun will be down soon, and there will be a frost.'

Harry nodded. He lifted his fork, laid it against the wall,

and, limping, carried the basket through the dead stalks. The day was too short at this time of the year.

Gunn met him at the kitchen door as he came in, muddy and getting cold, in his heavy boots and worn tweeds.

'Excuse me, sir, someone has called,' said Gunn. 'Mrs Joseph.'

'Helen?' Harry was amazed. 'Where is she?'

'I left her in the morning room, sir.'

Helen gave the lie to the popular conception of the impoverished widow.

She had had her hair dyed platinum blonde in the current Jean Harlow vogue. She wore a dark green afternoon coat of fine velvet trimmed with silver fox and a hat of the same material. The ministrations of various beauticians had managed to make her, except on close inspection, look considerably younger than her over-fifty years.

After Joe's suicide she had sold, with reluctance, some of her considerable store of jewels in order to pay for a first-class passage to Southampton aboard the *Mauretania* and for sufficient funds to arrive at Hardacres in style. She announced her coming to no one, and when her taxi arrived at the door, Gunn failed to recognize her.

'Whom did you wish to see, madam?' asked Gunn.

'I want to see Mr Harry Hardacre,' she replied.

'If you will wait for a moment, I will see if the master is in,' said Gunn, 'and who shall I tell him is calling?'

'You can tell him that it is his sister-in-law,' she said. 'I am Mr Joseph's widow, Gunn.'

Gunn was quite taken aback. 'Forgive me, Mrs Hardacre, I should have recognized you,' he said. 'If you would care to go into the morning room, I'll find the master and tell him that you are here.'

She went in and looked around the familiar room. They had not changed it at all. The same chintz covers – a little threadbare here and there, the same pictures on the walls, and the same windows overlooking the same gardens. As far as she could see, not a stick had been altered since she had last been in the room ten years ago; it might just as well have been yesterday.

'Hello, Helen,' Harry said quietly as he entered the room.

'Hello, Harry.' She looked hard at his muddied appearance. 'Welcome back.'

She made no move, not even to offer her hand. 'I shan't be staying so please don't bother to prepare a room for me.'

'A night or two at least,' he said. 'How long is it? Ten years or more.'

'No, Harry.' She was quite firm. 'I have come here on a matter of business, and when that has been dealt with I shall leave.'

She meant it. She had never liked Hardacres; they were all too damned nice, and she found the atmosphere repressive.

'I'm not quite sure what you can mean by business, Helen,' said Harry, 'apart from the fact that you will always be a member of the family. We were all very sorry about Joe, and if there is anything at all that we can do, you only have to ask.'

'No, thank you, Harry. I'm not in the market for charity, and I have no intention of becoming one of the Hardacres' pensioners. There are, however, things which I do wish to discuss, things which I regard as my rights.'

Harry was wary of the turn the conversation was taking. He was aware that Mary would, in all probability, be over shortly, and he did not want her to meet Helen until he had got this business, whatever it might be, sorted out. He did not really want her to meet Helen at all. He knew how Mary felt towards her, and, if Helen meant what she said and was going to leave almost immediately, it might be possible to get her away without them meeting.

'Why don't you come over to the study, where we can talk this matter over in privacy?' he said.

'As you wish,' said Helen, and they went across the hall into the study.

'Right,' said Harry, 'what is it?'

'I want my share of the estate.'

'You want what share of what estate?'

'Your father died a wealthy man. He had three children. He made a massive settlement on his daughter when she

420

married; he left all of his estate to you; and he left your brother, my husband, a sixpenny gutting knife.'

'I see,' said Harry.

'I doubt if you do,' she replied. 'Sam Hardacre died a senile old man . . .'

'Sam Hardacre was never senile.' Mary had come into the study unnoticed by both of them. 'His mind was as sharp on the day he died as it was the day he bought his first cran of herring on Bridlington fish quay.'

'Mother!' said Harry, 'I didn't see you come in.'

'Happen tha didn't, Harry,' replied Mary. 'Well, madam,' she said, turning on Helen, 'Gunn told me that tha was here. I would like to know what this is all about.'

'I don't think that this is anything to do with you,' said Helen. 'This is a matter between Harry and myself.'

'Happen tha would much rather deal wi'him,' snapped Mary, seating herself in one of the leather armchairs. 'Happen tha think he's a softer touch than I am.'

'Mother, please,' said Harry.

'I'll please me sen, Harry, lad,' said Mary. 'Thee two just get on wi'tha talk. I'll sit here and listen, I'll have my say when tha's all finished.'

'I think that Helen is right,' said Harry. 'It might be better if we discussed this alone.'

Mary did not move. 'When I came in, tha was saying that my husband was a senile old man. Why don't thee just go on from there?'

Helen's lips hardened into a tight line. 'Have it your way,' she said. 'Well, Harry, if you want to know, I think that your father's will was manifestly unfair.'

'Why?' asked Harry.

'Because he left nothing to Joe and everything to you.'

'You know, Helen, I never believed that,' replied Harry. 'I always believed that Father left me in a position of trust. It was obvious to me, at least, that he did not want the estate split. He felt that Hardacres should always be here, that it belonged to all of us, and that it should always be ready to provide a home for any of the family who either wanted it or needed it.'

'How very charming,' replied Helen with heavy sarcasm. 'For myself I can only regard that as a pretty way of saving your conscience. You cannot expect me to believe that claptrap. You know that Joe was entitled to every bit as much as you were. For a start, I'll take Grosvenor Square.'

'I hardly think that entitlement entered into the matter. Besides, we're selling Grosvenor Square. And Joe was very much more wealthy than Father was when he died.'

'And Joe died a pauper.' Helen almost spat the words out.

'I don't deny that,' said Harry. 'As far as you yourself are concerned, I feel that I have a duty which I owe to you – that is, to offer you, as Joe's widow, a home here at Hardacres.'

'But you wouldn't like it if I accepted,' declared Helen.

'No,' said Harry quietly, 'I would not like it if you accepted.'

There was a pause. All of this time Mary had sat in her chair, breathing heavily but saying nothing.

'Are you two done?' asked Mary.

'Not yet,' retorted Helen, and she turned back to Harry. 'Well, at least you're honest about not wanting me here. As for myself, I couldn't bear to live in the place. I have no desire to become one of your pensioners, leading a life of seedy grandeur. I think that Hardacres would drive me insane. I suppose that you have some alternative in mind.'

'Yes,' said Harry.

'Then I'd better hear it.'

'We are not nearly as well off as we were ten years ago,' said Harry, 'but that apart, as I have said, I do feel that I owe you a duty. I propose that I settle upon you an allowance. I am sorry that it cannot be a large one, but I would make certain that it would be sufficient to keep you in modest comfort for the rest of your life and enable you to choose where you wanted to live.'

'And how much do you estimate that would be?' Helen did not like the term 'modest allowance'.

'If I did that,' said Harry, ignoring her interruption, 'it would be of advantage to both of us. You would not become a "pensioner", as you put it, and we would be free of our obligation towards you.'

'How much?'

'I thought that something in the region of three to four hundred pounds a year would be about the right figure.'

Helen snorted, 'Three to four hundred a year? That would just about pay my hairdresser.'

'Then tha can bloody well brush thy own hair,' said Mary, stung to speech at last. 'Listen to me, missus, Harry's offered thee a damned sight more than I would have done. I'd have given thee nowt. But now he's made the offer, he'll stand by it, and I'll not stop him. I've nowt but contempt for the likes of thee. Tha took my Joe and tha drove him, allus wanting more and more, until tha killed him.'

'How dare you!' Helen almost screamed the words and started towards the door.

'Wait!' shouted Mary. Helen stopped. 'If thou walks out of yon door afore I've said my piece, I'll make it my personal business to see that thou doesn't get a penny, whatever Harry says.'

Helen turned, her face white with anger.

'That's better,' said Mary. 'Thou's a right bitch. Hast tha ever asked tha sen what thou's ever done for anybody? Three kids thou's had and wanted rid of them almost as soon as they were born. They was lucky that tha did, and they was lucky that, when they was in trouble, they had Hardacres to fall back on. Thou's a parasite. I suppose Harry's right, it is worth summat to be rid of thee. Tha can go now, tha'll get thy allowance, never fear, but there's one last thing. Before tha gets it, thou's got summat that I want from thee.'

'And what is that?' hissed Helen.

'Sam's guttie knife. I want it back, and until it's back in my hands not one single penny dost tha get. Good-bye, Mrs Hardacre.'

Helen looked at Harry, embarrassed by his mother's outburst. She looked at Mary, hard and uncompromising. For a moment she wanted to tell them all to go to hell, but she wanted the money more. Thank God, she had kept the knife.

She turned on her heel and walked out of the room and out of their lives.

CHAPTER SIX

The sign on the railway station read 'München'. As their train rolled gently to a halt, Jane and Peter looked out on to the large, clean concourse, dotted here and there by young men in paramilitary uniforms with swastika armbands. The whole area had an almost clinical cleanliness and was liberally adorned with the swastika motif. The young men in the brown-and-black uniforms seemed to be some kind of an elite, and people moved out of their way as they strutted around the station. Jane and Peter got out of their carriage and stood on the platform, admiring.

Jane had not heard from Heidi Muller for about two years. Reading between the lines of her last two letters, she had sensed that there was something wrong. For one thing, there had been no mention of her son Ian, and this was unusual, as Heidi's letters typically contained a large proportion of details about Ian. Jane had written several times during the past year but had received no reply; when she had made enquiries at the German consulate, though she had been treated with formal politeness and a superficial air of help, she had ended up with no information whatsoever.

Over the past few months Jane had several times discussed the question of Heidi with Mary. Mary, still spry and lively, though she was approaching eighty, had urged her to go to Germany and find out for herself.

'Tha's been going to go ever since t'war ended,' she had said; 'I don't rightly understand thee, Jane. Tha's never been a one for shilly-shallying, and yet tha's never seemed to be able to make tha mind up about this.'

When Peter had come down from Oxford for the summer vacation of 1935, she had decided that it was indeed about time that she acted or just forgot about Heidi altogether. Peter had readily agreed; Germany in 1935 was a fascinating prospect to an educated young man of the day. Germany's new ruler, Adolf Hitler, was apparently pulling the nation up by its boot straps and recreating that sense of national pride which had been dormant since the dark days of 1918. There had been rumours of oppression, of course, but the general feeling was that most of this could be put down to the jealousy of frustrated political opponents of the new regime.

They had travelled by sea to Bremerhaven and, after spending a night there, had taken the train for Munich. The train took them south through Hanover and Nuremberg, through large industrial towns and rolling farmland. Everywhere they were impressed by the amount of activity and well-ordered discipline which seemed to pervade the whole country. There were many attractive villages and small towns, especially after they had left Nuremberg and were heading through the hills of Bavaria. In the glorious summer weather it was really a feast for the eye. They were particularly taken by the beautiful countryside just north of Munich between two sleepy, peaceful towns called Ingolstadt and Dachau; whenever the train slowed and they managed a more detailed look, they expressed their admiration.

At last, and exactly on time, the train rolled to a halt in Munich.

They took a taxi to their hotel in Stachus Square and were shown to their rooms – neatly furnished and, like everything else that they had seen, spotlessly clean. It was well into evening by the time they had settled, and they went down to dinner, having decided to leave their search until the following day.

They had an excellent meal and went to bed early. The following morning, after breakfast, they summoned a taxi and showed the driver a card on which they had printed Heidi Muller's address. He drove them out to a pleasant middle-class suburb and stopped outside a house. It stood in about a quarter of an acre of flower garden, which was neatly arranged around a flagpole; from it hung the by-now familiar red banner with a swastika in a white circle in the centre.

'Are you sure that this is the right place?' asked Jane, pointing at the card and then at the house.

'Ja, ja,' replied the driver, pointing firmly at the house.

Peter paid the cab and turned to his mother, who was staring at the house.

'Somehow that,' she said, indicating the house, 'doesn't look like Heidi to me.'

'You mean the flag?' said Peter. 'But nearly everyone seems to do it.'

'Anyhow, I suppose there's no harm in asking,' said Jane.

They went to the door, and a tall young man with close-cropped blond hair answered. He was wearing a black shirt, black breeches, and boots.

'Excuse me,' said Jane, 'do you speak English?'

The young man paused before replying. 'What does you want?' he said, speaking with a very thick accent.

'I am looking for a Frau Muller,' Jane spoke very slowly. 'Frau Heidi Muller. She used to live here,' said Jane, pointing at the house

'Nein.'

'Two years ago,' said Jane. 'Before.'

The man gazed at her uncomprehendingly. 'Not Muller here.'

'Perhaps you know where she is now.'

'Mein English, she is bad.' And with that he shut the door in their faces.

'Charming,' said Peter, and he and his mother looked at each other. 'I can't say that I think much of that one; the point is, what do we do now?'

'We could try the neighbours,' said Jane. 'We might find one who speaks English. Somebody must remember Heidi; after all, it's only two years since she was living here.'

They started to work outwards from the address they had tried. At the house on the right there was no reply, and the woman who answered the door of the house on the left stared at them blankly when they spoke, said something in German, and slammed the door in their faces.

'We really ought to get ourselves an interpreter,' said Peter as they approached the third house.

This time the door was answered by a youth. He was about fifteen years old and wearing short brown leather trousers, a light-coloured shirt, and a swastika armband. His hair was closely cropped, and he seemed very correct and almost military in his manner.

When Jane asked him if he spoke English, he replied, 'Mein mutter, she speak English very well. I get her.'

A few moments later a woman of about Jane's age came to the door. 'You were looking for someone who spoke English?' she asked, with only the trace of an accent.

'Thank goodness,' replied Peter, but he noticed that the youth was hanging around within earshot.

'I used to teach English, and I have spent many years in England,' the woman went on.

'That's wonderful,' said Jane. 'Perhaps you will be able to help us.'

'If I can, I shall be delighted,' replied the woman, smiling.

'Would you mind telling us how long you have lived here?' asked Jane.

'Seven or eight years,' she replied, 'but why do you ask?'

'You must remember the lady who lived next door but one,' said Jane 'Frau Muller.'

At the mention of Heidi's name the woman looked quickly back into the house, then stepped outside, pulling the door closed behind her.

'I am sorry,' she said, 'that is a name I do not know.'

'But you must,' said Peter. 'Heidi Muller.'

'No, I do not know this woman.'

'She was here in 1933,' Peter continued. 'We know that for a fact; my mother was writing to her at this address.'

'No,' said the woman.

'She had a son about the same age as me. He had a Scottish name, Ian.'

'I remember no Frau Muller, and I remember no Ian,' said the woman. 'Please to go.'

'Has something happened to her?' asked Jane. 'Is that why you don't want to talk about her?'

'I am sorry, but I am not able to help you,' said the woman, and she went back into the house and shut the door.

Peter was about to follow her. 'Don't bother,' said Jane. 'She's frightened of something, she won't tell us anything.'

'I wonder what on earth's going on,' said Peter. 'Shall we

try somewhere else?'

'I don't think it would be any use,' said Jane. 'I think we ought to go and have a word with the British consul.'

In 1935 there were still certain advantages in having a title. When they arrived at the consulate, Peter asked for an interview with the consul.

'I am sorry, but you will need to make an appointment,' replied the rather glossy young man who was attending to them.

'It is rather urgent,' said Jane. 'Would it be possible to arrange it for today?'

'I have no idea, madam,' said the young man. 'Everyone who comes here thinks that their own business is urgent. However, if you care to leave your name and a telephone number where you can be contacted, I will see what can be done.'

Jane glanced at Peter and nodded.

'Lord Macgregor of Connon,' said Peter.

'Oh,' said the young man, 'of course, sir. If you could wait just one moment ...' He hurried through a door and into an inner office.

Five minutes later they were closeted with the consul and having morning coffee.

'I feel, Lady Jane,' said the consul when Jane had finished telling her story, 'I feel that you would be well advised to forget the whole matter and return home.'

'Why?' demanded Peter.

'There are strange things happening in this country, Lord Macgregor,' replied the consul. 'People do disappear, and often it is wise not to enquire too deeply into the reason for their disappearance. It could be so in the case of your friend. In view of the attitude of her neighbours, I should not be surprised if it is.'

'But that sounds medieval,' said Peter.

'Probably because it is medieval,' replied the consul.

'And there is nothing that you can do?' asked Jane.

'I am sorry,' was the reply. 'You see, it's none of our business. Your friend is a German national. It would be an unwarranted intrusion for us to attempt to interfere.'

They wandered back to their hotel feeling rather let down.

'I suppose you can't blame the consul,' said Peter. 'Even if he could help, I don't suppose it would be right for him to do so, not in his position. I don't understand this place; everything seems so fine and right, and yet there is something – it's an atmosphere more than anything.'

'I know what you mean, Peter,' said his mother. 'I know that foreigners tend to behave rather badly towards their political opponents, but I can't imagine Heidi being political. The point is, what do we do now?'

This question was answered about an hour later. Their suite was on the third floor of their hotel, and they had been back some little time when they got a telephone call from reception. It was one of the undermanagers, and he told them that he had a young man downstairs who was asking for an English couple. Apparently the enquirer could describe, but not name, the people he was looking for.

'Did he give any name?' asked Peter.

'No, sir,' replied the manager. 'And he says you do not know him, but he would like to see you, if only to find out if you are the people he is looking for.'

'This all sounds odd,' said Peter. 'Could he give us some indication of why?'

There was a muttered conversation in German at the other end of the line; then the manager came back on. 'He says that if you are the people he is looking for, he spoke to you this morning.'

'Just hold the line,' said Peter, and he explained the other half of the conversation to Jane, who nodded. 'All right,' he said into the telephone, 'send him up.' He rang off and turned again to Jane. 'I wonder who the devil it can be?'

'We'll soon know,' replied Jane as there was a tap on the door. 'He got here quickly enough.'

Peter opened the door to reveal the youth in the short leather trousers to whom they had spoken earlier in the day.

'Come in,' said Peter.

The youth stepped into the room, raised his right hand, clicked his heels, and said 'Heil, Hitler.'

'Oh yes, of course,' said Peter.

'Me Hitler youth,' said the young man in his very bad English, 'but Frau Muller my friend. She good to me.'

'You know where she is?' asked Jane, trying to conceal her excitement.

'Ja . . . yes; you take her to England?'

'If she wants to come, she will be most welcome,' said Jane.

'Good. Go to there, you find her perhaps.' He handed a piece of paper to Peter. 'Do not take der frau,' he said, indicating Jane, and before either of them could speak, he was out of the door and away.

'What on earth do you make of that?' said Peter after the youth had gone.

'Strange,' replied Jane. 'Did you get the impression this morning that his mother, if it was his mother, was afraid of him?'

'I don't know. She was certainly afraid of something.'

'What's on the paper he gave you?' asked Jane.

'It's an address.'

'Then we'd better go,' she said.

'He said not to take you.'

'I heard,' replied Jane.

They went down and called a taxi. Peter showed the driver the address he had been given. At the sight of this the man shook his head and drove off. When this happened a second and then a third time, they went to the reception desk inside the hotel.

'I am trying to get a taxi to take me to this place,' said Peter, showing the girl the paper. 'Can you tell me why I cannot get one?'

The receptionist looked at the paper. 'It is difficult,' she said. 'This is not a good part of the city; the drivers do not like to be seen going there.'

'What's wrong with it?' asked Peter.

'It is not good to go there.'

'How far is it?' asked Peter.

'About two kilometres is all,' replied the receptionist.

Peter went back to his mother and told her what the receptionist had said. Jane would not hear of Peter going alone, so they decided to walk. They found a street plan of Munich from which they gathered that the address they wanted was about a mile from the hotel.

As they walked, the buildings began to take on a shabbier aspect; the change was really quite dramatic as they approached their destination. There was garbage left in the unswept streets, and, as if to emphasize the gloomy atmosphere, clouds began to darken the sky. The shops were dirty, and here and there whitewashed slogans and the inevitable swastikas appeared daubed on the walls. Some of the shops had broken windows, and others had their fronts boarded up. Groups of brown-shirted youths, neat in their uniforms, paraded around the streets. They all seemed grim and purposeful, and looked enquiringly at Jane and Peter when they passed.

'What do you think?' asked Peter. 'Don't you think you ought to go back to the hotel and let me go on?'

'No.' Jane was quite firm. 'But I don't like it.'

It was as if they had lifted a stone to reveal dark and sinister creatures crawling about underneath.

'It's the other side of the coin,' said Jane.

'Yes,' replied Peter. 'What does "Jude" mean?' He was referring to a word which appeared over and over again, daubed on walls and doors and shop fronts.

'I don't know; Judas perhaps?' said Jane.

They passed yet another group of brown-shirts. These had with them a bearded old man who wore a long black coat. They were pummelling him and pushing him and laughing at their sport. Peter made a move as if to go to the old man's aid.

'No, Peter,' said Jane, grabbing his arm. 'There's a dozen of them; you might only make it worse for the old boy.'

Reluctantly they left the old man to his fate and at last arrived at the address they had been given. The street comprised four-storey, terraced houses – relics of an affluence long past. The pavements were cracked, and paintwork peeled from rotting doors and window frames. Here and there a dejected-looking figure sat morosely on steps leading to a dirty front porch. No one gave them more than an expressionless stare and then looked quickly away. Jane was sickened by the

431

piles of uncollected rubbish in the street and the mangy cats scrabbling away in the garbage. Though they did not see any rats, they had to be there. The smell and the squalor, the greyness of everything – including the people, who moved around in purposeless silence – gave the impression of frightened ghosts drifting through a colourless limbo.

They reached the house. There was no door, only a pair of rotting hinges. The opening led into a musty, damp, unlit corridor. They paused and glanced at each other, knowing that neither wanted to go on and aware that they must. At last Peter stepped inside. He had gone only a couple of paces when he stumbled over something; it was soft, and it moved. He bent forward and grabbed a small boy. The child was frightened and emaciated and did not even struggle as Peter held him by the shoulder.

Jane, becoming accustomed to the gloom, watched horrified as the child held his free arm across his face, cringing in Peter's grasp.

'We're not going to hurt you,' said Peter. 'Muller, Muller, here?'

There was no reply.

'Muller,' repeated Peter, pulling a twenty-mark note from his pocket and holding it for the boy to see.

The child stopped struggling and looked, amazed, at the money. He ran his tongue over his lips and nodded, trying to grab at the note.

'No, no,' said Peter, holding the money out of the boy's reach. 'First Frau Muller.'

The boy nodded, and Peter released him. He led them up a disintegrating, bare wooden staircase to the second floor, where he pointed at a door.

'Frau Muller,' he said, snatching at the note and running off.

Jane and Peter exchanged glances, and then Peter knocked at the door.

'Kommen,' said a woman's voice from inside the room.

Jane opened the door, and they went in. Many years ago, it had been an imposing bedroom; there was a fireplace, with no fire. A small paraffin stove stood on a wooden table beside half a loaf of stale-looking black bread. The walls had once been covered in a flower-patterned wallpaper, patches of which still remained. There was a rickety bed in one corner, neatly made with grey, patched blankets, and before the fireplace lay the remains of a rag rug. Over the mantelpiece hung a single picture in a gilt frame. It looked surprisingly out of place in its dingy surrounds; it was of an officer in the uniform of the Imperial German Navy.

A thin, greying, pinch-faced woman was backing away against the far wall as they entered. She had on a thin, shapeless black dress. Her dark eyes were wide with fear, and her hand flew to cover the six-pointed yellow star which was sewn on to the dress over her left breast. She looked up at them like a frightened animal as Jane spoke.

'Frau Muller?' said Jane.

'Ja?' was the whispered reply.

'I'm Jane Macgregor. This is my son; we've come to visit you.'

There was a long, awkward silence, and Heidi went slowly across the room towards them.

'Jane?' she whispered. 'I am not dreaming? It is really you? From England?'

'Yes, Heidi, of course, it's really me,' said Jane. 'We were worried about you; we had not heard from you for so long, so we came to look for you.'

The two women embraced. Jane was conscious of the thin, wasted little body that she was holding and conscious of the tears that streamed down Heidi's cheeks.

'You must sit down, and we must talk, but you must not stay long,' said Heidi. 'This is not a good part of the city, and after dark it is dangerous.'

'Heidi, what has happened? Why this? Where is your son?' The questions came flooding out as Jane tried hard to rationalize this macabre situation in which she found herself.

'My Ian has gone,' said Heidi, and there was something horribly final in the words she spoke.

'Gone? Gone where?' said Jane.

'They took him away. In Germany today it is not permitted to oppose our new masters. They took my Ian away, and I shall never see him again.'

'But that doesn't make sense,' said Peter.

'You are Peter, yes?' said Heidi. 'In this country it is one sin to oppose the government. It is an even greater sin to have a Jewish mother.' She struck the yellow star on her breast.

Jane was horrified. She would never have believed it without the evidence of her own eyes and ears. Heidi told them how, one night at three in the morning, she had been woken up in her little house by men in grey trench coats, men who spoke harshly through thin lips and wore hats pulled down over their eyes. How, with no further warning, she had been thrown out of her home there and then, with only what she could carry. They had left one of their number in the house, and she had stood on the pavement and watched as they bundled Ian into a motorcar and drove off. That was the last she had seen or heard of her son. She had found this room, after sleeping rough for several nights, in a Jewish house. 'We help each other now,' she said. After she had told him her story, the owner had given her this room, but she was living on charity.

'All Jews are living on charity in Germany today,' she concluded.

When Heidi finished, Jane and Peter sat for a while in silence. Then Jane said, 'You must come back to England with us, Heidi.'

'Of course,' said Peter, 'we'll arrange that right away. And when we get you safely back, I'll see what I can do about tracing your son.'

She looked up at them with a tired smile. 'And how will I come to England?' she asked. 'I have no passport; I think that they will not give me one. I am a Jew, and my son is an enemy of the state.'

'We'll work it out somehow,' said Jane. 'For the moment, you can come back to the hotel with us, and we can all go and have a word with the consul tomorrow.'

'I go to your hotel!' Heidi laughed and tapped the yellow star. 'You forget who I am. I am sorry, Jane, but this is not possible.'

'Have you any clothes?' asked Jane, ignoring her protestations.

'This is my wardrobe,' said Heidi, indicating her dress.

'Peter,' said Jane, 'stay here with Heidi while I run into town and get some clothes for her to wear. I'll come back and collect you both. We needn't book her into the hotel; she can share my bedroom for tonight, and with any luck we'll be on our way tomorrow morning.'

'What you suggest is impossible,' said Heidi.

'In that case we might not get away till the afternoon,' said Jane.

'And, Jane, you must not go out alone,' pleaded Heidi.

'Stuff and nonsense,' said Jane.

'It's a waste of time trying to argue with Mother,' said Peter as Jane went out.

'And where is Frau Muller now?' asked the consul.

It was nine thirty the next morning, and Jane and Peter were once more sipping coffee with the British consul. They had explained to him about their adventures the previous evening and how they had brought Heidi back to the hotel, completely kitted out with new clothes. The consul had listened patiently to their story, sitting behind his desk with his fingertips joined.

'She's still at the hotel,' said Peter.

'Lord Macgregor,' said the consul, 'it is not possible for us to interfere in the internal affairs of a sovereign state. Our duty is to provide assistance to those British subjects who might have need of our services. Now, if your friend had a passport, then I could, and would have, given her a visa to enter Britain, but in my position, without that, it is impossible for me to help you.'

'You mean that there is nothing you can do?' said Jane.

'Less than nothing, I fear, for not only can I not assist you, but I am afraid that it is also my duty to reprimand you for breaking the laws of this country.'

'But those laws are ridiculous,' said Jane. 'They are wicked laws, and I'm quite sure that you believe that every bit as much as I do.'

'My personal opinion,' replied the consul, 'is neither here nor there. I think that it would be as well for all of us if we were to assume that this conversation had never taken place.'

'You refuse to help us, then?' said Peter. 'And that is all you have to say?'

'Officially, yes,' replied the consul, and then as Peter rose to leave, 'I think we should all sit down and finish our coffee. There's a story I'd like to tell you.'

'I am afraid we must be leaving,' said Peter.

'Sit down, Peter,' said Jane.

'What for?'

'Sit down,' she repeated, 'I want to hear the consul's story.' She turned to the consul. 'You were about to say?'

'Thank you, Lady Jane,' said the consul, 'it is a simple tale, and the telling will be brief. It concerns two foreigners who were accompanied by a German national when they left Munich. They left by train for Ulm, where they changed trains for Friedrichshaven, which lies on the shore of Lake Constance in the middle of the most beautiful tourist country. At Friedrichshaven they booked into a hotel for a week. On the second day they took a bus ride along the shore of the lake to the eastern end; here they left the bus and went walking. Unfortunately, they had no knowledge of German and were unable to read the notices which abound in that area. Quite by accident they wandered across the Swiss frontier. They were lucky not to have been noticed by one of the frequent patrols – there is one every ninety minutes – for, had they been seen, they would certainly have been fired on. Anyhow, they got into Switzerland, where they found a road and managed to get a lift into Zurich. They went straight to the consul there; he suggested that it would be better if they returned direct to the United Kingdom, as, had they gone back into Germany, they may have had to answer some awkward questions. He issued the German member of the party with temporary documents, and they left for home. Interesting, don't you think?'

'Very,' said Peter, smiling, 'and thank you.'

'Before you go, there is one other point,' said the consul.

'It was necessary for them to pay in advance for the hotel at Friedrichshaven; by doing that, it cut down the paper work at this end when they were missed.' The consul rose and offered his hand. 'Good day to you, Lady Jane; good day, Lord Macgregor.'

Forty-eight hours later the three of them were standing on the Swiss shore of Lake Constance looking back into Germany. Two German policemen, accompanied by German shepherds and carrying rifles, passed across their range of vision. Peter glanced at his watch.

'You've got to give them marks for punctuality,' he said. 'Exactly ninety minutes.'

'You know,' said Jane, 'it smells different.'

'What does?' asked Heidi.

'The air. The tension's gone; there was something unreal and oppressive over there. Even before we found you, I always felt that we were looking over our shoulders. I didn't realize until now, but do you know, you really can smell freedom.'

The remainder of their journey passed without incident. The consul at Zurich proved to be most helpful. They felt that this was not the first time he had had to deal with such a situation.

Within a couple of days they were on their way by train, through France and across the Channel to England. For the first time Jane felt quite sentimental at the sight of the white cliffs of Dover, and when they disembarked, the slight griminess of the harbour station seemed so much more welcoming and comfortable than the antiseptic cleanliness they had found in Germany.

In London they left the train at Victoria and called a taxi to take them to Grosvenor Square, where they were to spend the night. Jane telephoned Harry and told him that they would be arriving the next day. The following morning they took Heidi shopping for clothes and other necessities.

While they were on their shopping expedition they saw a squad of Oswald Mosley's black-shirted Fascists marching towards Hyde Park. Heidi cringed at the sight of them.

'Don't worry,' said Jane, 'it will never happen here, not once they understand.'

'Providing that they understand before it happens,' Heidi said. 'In Germany we did not.'

'You are among friends now,' said Peter. 'You don't have to worry any more.'

'You are a strange people,' said Heidi. 'My husband was on the ship which sank your father, so that you cannot now remember him, and yet you welcome me into your home and show me all this kindness.'

'We are not quite home yet,' said Jane, 'but we'll be at Hardacres tomorrow.'

CHAPTER SEVEN

'Oh, Peter, how positively too, too quaint,' said Bunty.

Peter winced slightly. They were in Peter's brand-new 1938 MG Magnette; he slammed on the brakes and stopped in front of his grandmother's cottage. He was beginning to have doubts about bringing Bunty down to meet Mary. In fact, he was beginning to have doubts about Bunty. It had started as soon as they had arrived on Friday evening, when Bunty had bounced all over Uncle Harry like a cairn terrier and Harry had produced that slightly pained expression which he always wore around his daughter Vanessa. Not that Harry's opinion mattered that much; he liked his women old-fashioned and very feminine. Still, Peter would have liked to impress the family. Bunty was, after all, singularly attractive – in a fluffy, blonde way – and she had fabulous legs, which she was for ever showing off with short, shimmery dresses. He recalled that those legs and one of those satiny little cocktail outfits had really started the whole thing, some months back, in a London club. Odd, how that shrieking little giggle of hers seemed so, so right in London and so, so wrong in the drawing room at Hardacres. God, thought Peter, I hope she behaves herself with Grandmother.

Mary pulled aside the chintz curtain of her kitchen–sitting room when she heard the rare sound of a motor outside her gate. The car was small and red and unfamiliar, but there was Peter climbing out. He looked well – with his wavy, almost ginger, hair slicked smooth down and his country, casual tweeds, open-necked shirt, and dark-red cravat. He reminded her of Ian, his father, for he was near the age at which they had known him. It was odd to think of Ian, all those years ago, frozen in their minds, in eternal youth. They had all grown up and grown old. Even, Jane, her daughter, was a middle-aged woman.

Peter was elaborately helping a young woman out of the little motorcar. Mary studied her with old age's unashamed curiosity. She saw a thin, tall girl with wide eyes that never left Peter. She wore a short, skimpy dress and looked cold. Mary wondered why young ladies chose to wear such summery dresses in this part of the world, where summer was such an uncertain season. It was July, but with grey and drizzling rain. Peter said something to the girl that Mary could not hear, but she could see by the sudden hurt expression that it was something harsh. She dropped the curtain and went to the door, feeling disapproval. She had seen her handsome grandson with young ladies before, and she knew that he was not always kind. Perhaps it was a misfortune to be rich and attractive and still so young.

Bunty stood slightly behind Peter as the painted plank door swung inward. She was scared of meeting his grandmother. So far the weekend had been unnerving, with Peter's country farmer uncle stomping about the place in his Wellington boots and with his two peculiar cousins, Noel and Vanessa. Noel she could not have distinguished from any other of the Yorkshire farmworkers about the place; in fact, he did not act like family. He did not even come in to dinner the evening before. Apparently he preferred ham and eggs in the village pub. Vanessa was worse; she came to dinner wearing jodhpurs. Still, Bunty took comfort from the realization that Harry had been as appalled as she was. Harry's wife, Hetty, seemed nice enough, but very middle-class; then there was the Frenchwoman and her two sons who, this morning, had been flying a kite from the top of the balustraded roof of the big house. Peter had told her that they were both reading law at Cambridge, but Bunty flatly disbelieved him. She had already heard of Peter's cousin, Maud, who was married to the band leader Albert Chandler. That rather thrilled her, and she was hoping that the Chandlers would be here this weekend, but they were not. But then there was his other cousin, Emily, whom Peter had insisted had married her policeman husband after he had tried to arrest her. She sensed dimly that Peter was deliberately making his unorthodox family sound more peculiar than they really were; they made her very uneasy. She would frankly have had doubts about Peter being Lord Macgregor of Strathconnon, but she had met his mother in

London and had been very impressed. Lady Macgregor had invited them both to Castle Connon for the Twelfth, but Peter had not mentioned it lately. She hoped he would.

'Hello, luv,' said Mary, 'thou's looking gradley.'

'Grandma,' Peter said, pulling Bunty forward, 'this is Bunty, Bunty Marjoribanks.'

Bunty extended her hand and said, 'How do you do, Mrs Hardacre?'

'Fine, how's thee sen?'

Bunty looked blankly at Peter, got no help, and nodded awkwardly, shaking hands with Mary and hoping she would not ask any more questions she could not understand. Peter had told her that his grandmother spoke broad Yorkshire, but she thought he had been joking. She had also heard that his grandfather had started life gutting herrings on a fish quay, but she had not really believed that either. Everybody nowadays was claiming some sort of perfectly ghastly family origin. It was the fashion.

Bunty followed Mary into her sitting room. The old woman walked with a stick and was grey and wrinkled. Old people upset Bunty; she did not like to look at them and did not know what to say to them.

'Sit thee sen down, lass,' Mary said.

Bunty glanced at Peter, but he was expressionless. She guessed she was to sit and found a straight chair in the corner of the room on which she sat, nervously, on the edge. Peter then flopped into the rocking chair by the fire, not really looking at her. She noticed Mary getting a decanter of wine from the sideboard. It looked out of place, and she guessed, rightly, that it had come from the big house. Mary went into the scullery and returned with a plate of cut cake. Bunty had wondered why the old lady lived alone here and not in the big house, but now she knew. If she had a grandmother like Mary Hardacre, she too would keep her well out of sight.

She wondered why Peter had been so insistent on her meeting the old lady. Surely he did not need to turn to this uneducated woman for approval. Bunty was well aware of Peter's potential as a husband. This weekend could be the start of a very bright future for her. She determined to be charming

441

and ladylike, even if the old grandmother could not be expected to notice.

Mary laid plates and silver cake forks on the white cotton lace tablecloth. They all sat around the table while Peter poured the wine. Cautiously Bunty nibbled at the cherry cake and found it good; she sipped the Madeira and found it very good. She accepted another piece of cake from Mary's twisted arthritic hand. She had never eaten at such a table in her life, with an open door leading directly into a lean-to kitchen at the back. Still, the place was spotlessly clean, even if there was just the faintest smell of smoked fish and steamy soup. She sipped again at her wine, listening to Peter and his grandmother talking, silent and wishing the visit would end.

Mary watched as Bunty and Peter walked down her brick garden path and Bunty clambered awkwardly, in her short skirt, into the car. The girl had enthused about the visit; it had been 'too, too super'. Mary smiled sadly; she knew when a young lass was having a miserable time because of a man. Mary had seen women in love before, and men. She could see clearly that Bunty was, and Peter was not. She sighed as she returned the decanter to the sideboard and cleared away the plates. She had so hoped for another wedding, another Hardacre baby, before she went, and now she doubted that there would be one.

Peter had been her last hope, particularly when she heard he was bringing a young lady to Hardacres for the weekend. But Peter would not marry yet, not Bunty Marjoribanks, no matter how much the poor lass wished it.

On Noel Mary had long ago given up. That one was not the marrying kind. Perhaps that was just as well; she would not wish that dark nature and sullen temper on anyone. Better he should spend his evenings with men, playing darts and drinking too much and getting into fights. At least there was not some poor woman waiting alone by the fireside. It was a pity, because he was a good worker and would have made a good provider. And Harry needed someone, a grandson, to keep his father's big house. It meant so much to Harry, and all the rest around here just took it for granted.

For a while she had counted on Vanessa. After all, all women wanted to marry and have children; and though Vanessa was plain, and a bit clumsy and loud, Mary had seen plainer women marry and make good wives. But Vanessa was thirty-one and had never had a man to pay her court. Mary was not sure which was more unseemly – Vanessa stalking about in breeches or Vanessa in a blue dress with a white collar, hands folded on her lap like a schoolgirl. The lass did not know how to be a woman.

Maud's daughter, Janet, was a future possibility, though she was already showing interest in a theatrical career, and heaven knew what would happen to her then. She was not likely to become mistress of Hardacres in that direction. Anyhow, she was far too young – not yet sixteen – even to think of marriage. Mary stopped, her hands in the dishwater, thinking. She had been about that age when she herself married. Not that you could compare herself to Janet Chandler. Life was different now, very different, thank God. Mary often thought about these sleekly groomed young men and bright, frilly girls. What would they do if they were suddenly handed the life which she and Sam had known? But that did not happen. You grew up with it, and it made you for ever, irrevocably different, tough and strong and hard. Or you did not survive. She was happy that her grandchildren did not need that kind of strength, though she sometimes wondered if any of the boys would ever be half the man that Sam had been.

Oddly, it was the twins, Sam and Terry, who she believed would come closest. And it *was* odd, too, because they were the most different. Hetty, she knew, did not even consider them as part of the family, with their dark French looks and their alien religion. Mary considered them family, and more too – they had Sam's humour, more of it than he had had, but they had more time for humour. They were warm and forgiving, and they played boyish jokes on her – the way Sam had once done, years ago, in the yew maze. They had a way of not caring what people thought, and Mary liked that. Peter was not like that; Peter had to be approved of. That was why he had come to her today with his lass.

And Noel, too, cared what people thought, even though he covered up by ignoring the social graces and the way people were supposed to act. But he cared – so much that he was afraid to try his hand at the thing, afraid of parties where he might look awkward. And he cared enough to fight with people who, he thought, looked down on him. She could not fathom why; was it because of the war or because his grandfather had been a guttie?

But Sam and Terry, they were something unique. Mary felt they had a special future, like Sam had had. They would be something unusual, unpredicted. She wondered about their studying law; it did not suit them – too dry, too cold. Harry had encouraged it because the boys were bright at school, excelling in the arts and Latin. Still, Mary could see them better in something human and extraordinary – perhaps the theatre? Or perhaps they would be politicians, something in the centre of everything, but also something deep. Because they were thinkers. Mary saw that, when even their own mother despaired of their ever being serious. Mary knew how they thought and read books and talked privately and intensely between themselves. It was Terry and Sam – and not Harry or Noel, or even Peter, who had been to Germany, and who said that this man Hitler would not be finished until there was no peace left in the world. That frightened Mary, because she felt too old to face her country going to war again. You needed strength and youth for that.

Though she loved them, she doubted they would satisfy her longing for an heir to Sam's Hardacres. It would be years before those two settled down enough for wives and bairns. And they seemed so self-sufficient, the two of them. That was being twins, she guessed, no need to go searching for someone to be close to. They were two people and one person at the same time.

Mary shrugged, hung her dishcloth on its hook, and wiped her hands on her apron. She was past the years when these things were for her to worry over and to try and sort out. Whatever her brood decided to do with their world, it was their problem now. Mary went through to the kitchen fire, nudged the coals into a better shape with the brass poker, and sat down in the rocking chair. As she drifted off to sleep, her eyes moved instinctively and comfortably along the wooden mantelpiece, with its Tin Box, the guttie's knife, and the Victoria and Albert mug.

'Oh, God,' said Harry, wincing, 'here it comes again.'

He was standing at the heavily curtained library window, watching Peter's MG as it swung around the house to the balustraded terrace. He had had a fire laid in the library this morning, because he intended having a quiet Saturday reading – and July or not, it was chilly. At least, he felt it was; he could never be sure now – he felt the cold in all damp weather, and his leg ached abominably. It was beginning to make him bad-tempered and snappy with people, and he hated himself for it. He had had enough years of living and working with Noel to know what a moody nature did to other people.

Hetty looked up from her knitting – a vast grey heap of cardigan, half finished. She had come in earlier and had joined him – without speaking, and he had been pleased. She was such an easy, quiet person to have around. When he felt full of strength he could cope with anyone – Noel; or Madelene, with her high, exciting spirit and her unpredictable fiery temper; or even Bunty, bouncing around like a fluffy yellow budgerigar, but a loud one. Today, however, he was tired and cold, and he wanted to sit and read and listen to the quiet, slurred clicking of Hetty's knitting. She was really a blessing when he needed comfort.

'We must go and see them,' Hetty said softly. 'Or would you rather I went and you could stay here?'

Harry smiled. 'I would rather, but it wouldn't be right. Thanks, all the same.' She was always kind, always thinking of him first. At times he felt desperately guilty at having, over the years, caused her what must have been a considerable amount of pain. Right now he was too tired for guilt. He would forget about it for now; it was something he had done many times before.

He crossed the room and followed Hetty to the door. She was wearing a plain tweed skirt, her perennial lisle stockings, and old but sturdy laced shoes. More comfortable, she had said. Also the layers of mismatched sweaters to keep warm. Hetty liked old things; he used to buy her newer, more

445

fashionable things, until he realized that she only wore them to please him, and so he gave up. He looked down at her head; it was iron-grey now – the hair that had once been mouse-dark and soft, that day long ago in the hayfield. Hetty was sixty-two and looked every day of it. Once he had resented her lack of effort in such things, but it didn't seem to matter any more. He saw himself in the gilt-edged mirror over the fire, as he turned to close the library door. He was as grey as she.

Peter pulled up in front of the house.

'Peter,' said Bunty, 'can't we go for a drive? The weather's clearing; it might turn out to be a super day.'

'All right,' said Peter, shrugging, 'anything you say; we'll take a run up the coast.'

'How super,' said Bunty.

They drove off just as Harry got to the door.

They went north to Bridlington and then on to the coast road towards Scarborough. Three miles out of Bridlington and just as they were passing the little private airfield that lay there, a notice caught their eyes.

LEARN TO FLY AT THE EAST RIDING FLYING CLUB
TRIAL LESSON 10/-

Peter looked at the board bearing the notice and then at Bunty. Bunty had been a great disappointment.

'I feel like having a go,' he said.

'Oh, super,' said Bunty, who seldom said anything else.

They drove on the extra few hundred yards to the airfield entrance and turned in. There they found a wooden hut which served as office-cum-bar-cum-clubroom. As, apart from a small hangar, it was the only building that the airfield boasted, they went in.

The room was occupied by a dozen or so youngish men and women who were drinking beer or sipping cups of coffee and talking loudly about aeroplanes. Upon seeing Bunty and Peter, a tall, lean individual who had been lounging in one of the worn armchairs which furnished the clubhouse in great profusion unfolded himself and came over to them.

'Can I help you?' he asked.

'I saw your poster and thought I might take a stab at this

446

flying business,' said Peter. 'Can you tell me the form?'

'Nothing to it, old boy,' replied the tall one. 'By the way, I'm Charles Hill, club secretary, call me Charles, not Charlie.'

'Oh,' replied Peter and then, realizing that introductions were the order of the day, 'I'm Peter Macgregor, and this is Miss Bunty Marjoribanks.'

Charles Hill shook hands with them both, and Bunty gushed.

'Well, the form's really quite simple. You take a trial lesson – that costs ten bob – then, if you fancy the idea, you join the club, and we teach you to fly. We have two qualified instructors, and we can take you as far as "A" licence. Want to have a go?'

'Yes, rather,' said Peter.

'How simply super,' said Bunty.

Peter flinched. He went over to an old rolltop desk with Charles Hill and was handed a form.

'Read that and sign it. It's just to say that we're not responsible if we happen to kill you; we call it a blood chit.'

Peter signed the document without bothering to read it. He then handed over a ten-shilling note, saying, 'Just in case I don't come back.'

'We don't charge if that happens,' said Charles, but he took the money.

Charles rummaged in a drawer and produced a pair of goggles and a leather helmet which had tubes coming out of the ear flaps, rather like a stethoscope. He handed these to Peter.

'Let's go, then,' said Charles.

'Who's the instructor?' asked Peter.

'You're talking to him, old man,' replied Charles. 'Miss Marjoribanks, if you care to sit on the bench in front of the shop, you'll be able to watch.'

'How perfectly super,' said Bunty.

The two men walked across the grass to the hangar. Standing outside were two Tiger Moths, an Avro 504N and a very grand-looking cabin monoplane which Charles said was a Percival Mew Gull.

'We'll take one of the Tigers,' said Charles. 'Have you ever flown before?'

'No, never,' said Peter.

447

'Absolutely nothing to it,' said Charles. 'Piece of cake, really, and a damned sight easier than driving a car.'

As they approached the little biplane, Peter felt the same sort of thrill as he had when they sneaked across the German border into Switzerland.

'George!' Charles shouted.

A man wearing white overalls which had been liberally smeared with grease emerged from the hangar.

'George, is BAV O.K.?'

'Aye, she's ready, and the tank's full. Want a swing?'

'We'll take her now,' said Charles.

George wiped his hands on a piece of cotton waste, slipped a pair of chocks under the aeroplane's wheels, and stood waiting.

Charles turned to Peter. 'You get in front. Put your helmet on and keep your goggles down all the time.'

Peter did as requested and clambered into the front cockpit. Charles leaned over him and connected the end of his ear tubes to another tube inside the cockpit, fastened a safety harness around him, slapped him on the back, and climbed into the rear cockpit.

A voice came through the tubes into Peter's ears. 'You should be able to hear me, but I will not be able to hear you. Nod your head if it's O.K.'

Peter nodded his head. The mystery of the tubes was solved – it was a primitive intercommunication system.

'Comfortable?' said Charles' voice.

Peter nodded.

'Good. Don't touch anything unless I tell you to and don't worry – I'll give you a go at handling her when we are airborne.'

George was now standing by the airscrew.

'Switches off, petrol on, suck in,' shouted Charles.

George seized the propeller and gave it three or four swings.

'Contact,' called Charles.

George swung the propeller again, this time stepping back as he did so. The engine fired.

After warming up the motor Charles taxied out, turned the plane into the wind and stopped.

'We're going to take off now,' he said to Peter. 'Just relax and enjoy yourself.'

The aircraft started to roll forward. Peter sat in the cockpit, watching the controls as they moved gently. He felt the plane bumping and shuddering as it gathered speed across the field, and suddenly everything went smooth and they were flying.

They flew out over the coast, climbing slowly until the altimeter registered two thousand feet. Charles' voice again came through the ear tubes.

'If I ask you anything, raise your right hand for yes, your left for no. Got that?'

Peter raised his right hand.

'Would you like to fly her?'

Peter raised his right hand.

'O.K. You see that stick between your legs?'

Peter raised his right hand.

'Hold it gently with your right hand. Good. Now, if you move it forward, we go down; back, we go up. At your feet there is a metal bar. Put one foot on each end of that. Right foot forward ... no, no, not yet. Right foot forward, and we turn to the right. Left foot forward, and we go left. Ready to take over?'

Peter raised his right hand.

Charles repeated the instructions and then said, 'O.K., she's all yours. If I yell, drop it, take your feet off and leave go of the stick. Try her now.'

Peter was thrilled. For a moment he did nothing but just sit there holding the stick.

'Go on, move her about a bit,' came Charles' voice.

Gently Peter pushed the stick forward, and he watched the horizon rise in front of him; then he eased it back and found himself gazing at nothing but sky. He tried to bring the aircraft back level but succeeded in flying it like a roller coaster.

'Try to keep the horizon level with your engine cowling,' called Charles.

He soon got the hang of it. He kicked the left rudder bar, and the world swung away to the right. He kicked the right rudder bar and swung it back again. For ten glorious minutes he had control. His decision was made long before his time was up. He was going to learn to fly.

They landed, and the aircraft rolled to a stop outside the hangar. They got out and went over to the clubroom, where Bunty was dutifully waiting for them on the bench, surrounded by three of the young men – one of whom was the owner of the Percival Mew Gull and all of whom were trying to date her. She got up and came over to them as they approached.

'Was it super?' she asked.

'Great,' replied Peter, and he turned to Charles. 'Can you tell me what happens now?'

'Well, if you want to carry on and you live locally, the best thing to do is to join the club. It's five pounds a year, and we charge one pound an hour for flying instruction.'

'And that's all there is to it?' asked Peter.

'That's all.'

'I'll do it,' said Peter, and he went with Charles into the clubroom, where he filled in the necessary forms and handed over a cheque for five pounds. He had completely forgotten Bunty, who, somewhat slighted, went back to the bench and dated the owner of the Percival Mew Gull.

'If you keep at it,' said Charles, 'you could solo after ten hours and take your "A" licence after forty.'

'What is an "A" licence?' asked Peter.

'It allows you to fly to other airfields and to carry passengers as long as you are not doing it for money.'

Peter decided that he would give Scotland a miss that summer and concentrate on his new-found love. When he told his mother, Jane, seeing his obvious enthusiasm, brought up no objections and decided that she would stay at Hardacres as well. He saw very little of Bunty after that; she moved out of Hardacres the following day but not out of the district. She had left him for the more glamorous Percival Mew Gull and its very wealthy owner.

Peter took his flying with a dedication that surprised all of them. Every day he would leave for the club shortly after nine and return in the late afternoon. During the evenings he would spend his time poring over manuals of air navigation and the theory of flight; he had certainly become a devotee.

He had been going up for less than two weeks. They landed a little earlier than usual, and Charles who was now his instructor, instead of switching off the motor jumped out of the rear cockpit, leaving the engine running. He leaned into Peter's cockpit.

'O.K.,' he shouted over the roar of the engine, 'take her round by yourself.'

If Peter's first flight had been a happy experience, then his first solo was sheer ecstasy. When Charles told him to go, at first he did not think much of it, and he climbed to a thousand feet before he fully realized that he was alone. He kept looking round into the rear cockpit to make sure that it was really true, that he was in fact alone in the empty sky. As he circled the field in wide sweeps, he got a feeling akin to grandeur, looking down upon the world beneath his feet. He went into his approach, determined to make his first landing a perfect three-pointer, but he overconcentrated. Thump ... thump ... thump – the Tiger Moth bounced over the grass shaking up every bone in his body, but it was all right, he managed to steady the machine and bring it to a stop outside the hangar. He switched off the engine and sat for a full minute in a state of perfect happiness until Charles came up and tore him off a strip for that foul landing.

By September he was ready to take the test for his 'A' licence. It was comparatively simple, and he passed it with little bother. The day after his licence was confirmed, he took his mother up for her first flight. Jane loved the experience; it made her almost as great an enthusiast as her son. When they landed, they went laughing, arm in arm, into the clubroom for a celebratory drink. They were surprised to find the bar deserted and all the members clustered around the antique wireless set.

Peter sought out Charles. 'What is going on?' he asked.

'It's Chamberlain,' replied Charles. 'Good news, he's back from Munich; he has signed some sort of treaty with Hitler. He says it means "peace in our time".'

Peter and Jane looked at each other. Their gaiety was gone; they knew more than these young people around the wireless, for they had seen Hitler's Germany.

'I really do not know what young people are coming to today,' said Harry. 'God help us if there is another war.'

Sam and Terry grinned sheepishly at their uncle. They were in the study at Hardacres on the morning after the 'farmer's ball' which had been held in the house the previous night.

It had all started with a stuffed fox. The twins had brought the creature into the house and mounted it on a pedestal just outside the door of the morning room, which was doing service as a bar for the evening. They had wired up its tail and, taking turns, had concealed themselves. As the farmers, in varying stages of intoxication, had passed, the concealed one had tweaked at the wire, causing the tail to wag. The results had been quite spectacular.

'Yon fox is alive,' said one.

'Don't be daft, it's stuffed,' said his companion.

'I tell you it's alive, it wagged its tail,' said the first.

'It bloody didn't,' said the second, pausing and looking at the fox.

'It bloody did!'

These and like comments had soon produced a small crowd, which rapidly divided itself into rival factions of believers and disbelievers. That would have still been all right if a fight had not broken out, with resultant, not inconsiderable, damage.

But that was not all. The band took its break at about midnight, and when they returned, the drummer complained that someone had stolen his drums. They were not recovered until dawn, when they were found at the end of the south pier at Bridlington by a somewhat irate harbour master. Someone had been playing them during the night, and when a harbour official had gone to investigate he had seen two shadowy figures dancing what appeared to be Indian war dances on the end of the pier. Unfortunately he had not been able to apprehend the miscreants; they had driven off in a blue Austin Ten tourer before he could get to the end of the pier. The official did not get the licence number of the car, but after he had reported the incident to the harbour master, and the harbour master had reported it to the chairman of the Harbour Commissioners, the chairman had telephoned Harry.

It did not require a Sherlock Holmes to solve the mystery. The twins possessed a blue Austin tourer; they had not been seen at Hardacres after midnight, when the drummer had made his complaint; and Madelene had admitted that they had not slept in their beds that night. Madelene had asked Harry, as head of the family, to deal with the matter, and upon their return to Hardacres, they had been summoned to the study.

They were still wearing their dinner suits, dishevelled and grimy, and both were looking like miniatures of their great-grandfather. Harry glared at them.

'Now, Sam,' said Harry.

'I'm Terry,' said the one he was addressing.

The statement may or may not have been true; even now, when the twins were twenty-one, only Madelene could be sure which of them was which.

'All right, then, both of you,' snapped Harry, 'have you any explanation for this childish behaviour?'

'Yes,' said Sam.

'No,' said Terry.

'One at a time, please,' said Harry.

'Well,' said Sam.

'It's like this,' said Terry. 'It's all true, and we had a lot of fun, but we spent the night catching rabbits.'

They had, in fact, driven around the country lanes with their headlights on and one of them sitting on the bonnet. When the lights mesmerized a rabbit, the idea was that the one on the bonnet should dive off and grab it. They had nothing to show for this except the grime with which they were now covered.

'Really,' said Harry coldly.

'Well,' said Sam, 'we're sorry if we upset anyone ... I think,' he added lamely.

'But only if they were really upset,' said Terry, 'not if they were just fussing.'

'You are supposed to be going to London to stay with your Aunt Maud and Uncle Albert in a couple of days.'

'Well,' said Sam defiantly, 'we're over twenty-one; we can do what we like.'

'Oh, I can't stop you, not legally at any rate,' said Harry, 'but I do still control the purse strings; I could cut off funds.'

'Oh,' said Terry and glanced at his brother. They both knew that Uncle Harry did not make idle threats.

'When do you leave?' asked Harry. 'If you leave.'

'August the thirtieth,' said Sam.

'Very well, I'll tell you what I want,' said Harry. 'I want a letter of apology to the chairman of the Harbour Commissioners and another similar letter to the drummer. If that is done, then I am prepared to overlook this incident, but I warn you, it will be the last time.'

The twins looked at each other. London and their now-famous Uncle Albert represented the high spot of the year. Albert and Maud were indulgent and gay. There were dances and concerts, parties and girls. They had no desire to miss all of the fun that their trip meant. Of course there was a lot of talk about war, but they had no intention of allowing that to interfere with their pleasure. Hitler was again making his 'last' territorial claim in Europe. This time it was Poland, but of course it would not happen; it would all blow over, just as it had done before, when it was the Saar, Austria, Czechoslovakia, and the rest. No, they did not want either Hitler or Harry to spoil their trip, and as Harry appeared to be the major threat, they capitulated to him. They agreed to write the letters.

As events turned out, they did not go to London. Things began to happen with gathering speed. On 29 August, Peter, who was in Scotland at the time, was called to the colours. He had joined the Royal Air Force Volunteer Reserve, and he was ordered to report to the new R.A.F. station at Lossiemouth for advanced flying and operational training. Later on the same day that Peter was called up, Albert rang Harry and asked if he could bring Maud and Janet up to Hardacres;

naturally Harry agreed, and Albert said they would arrive on 1 September.

By the Thursday of that momentous week things were beginning to look very serious, and Harry, realizing that London would not be a good place to be if hostilities broke out, telephoned to Philip Barton and suggested he might like to send Emily to Hardacres if the balloon went up. Emily would have none of it. She knew that her husband's job would keep him in the metropolis and had no intention of being separated from him.

When the news of the German–Soviet non-aggression pact came through, Harry began to realize that now things were quite serious, though he, like so many others, could still not bring himself to believe that it could happen.

The Chandlers duly arrived on the first as arranged, and Harry gave a dinner party at Hardacres on the same day. They were unaware of the fact, but as they rose to join the ladies, the British ambassador in Berlin was handing His Majesty's government's ultimatum to Herr von Ribbentrop. That morning the German armies and air forces had invaded Poland.

Saturday, 2 September, was an unreal day. Everyone was extremely subdued. There was none of the hysteria which had greeted the run-up to the war of 1914. The nation knew what modern war could be like. Mary telephoned to Jane, who was alone at Castle Connon. Mary wanted to have her daughter with her, and Jane agreed that she would come down if it really did come to war. On the Sunday morning they all went to church in Driffield, except for Madelene and the twins.

The service was due to begin at eleven, but at that hour the vicar came out and announced to his packed congregation that he had heard that the Prime Minister was to broadcast to the nation at eleven fifteen.

'My friends,' he continued, 'I am sure that we all fear what it is he will tell us, but nevertheless I am equally sure that you will all wish to hear his words. I have therefore had a wireless set placed in the church and will turn it on just before a quarter past. Might I suggest that we all spend the next fifteen minutes or so in private prayer and ask our Lord to grant peace to the world.'

For the next quarter of an hour there was a hushed stillness in the church. The congregation was silent, kneeling. The vicar knelt before the altar with his hands laid upon it, motionless until the moment arrived.

Just before eleven fifteen the vicar went to the radio and switched it on; they all listened as Neville Chamberlain informed the nation that a state of war had existed between Britain and Germany for over an hour.

When it was all over, they prayed for victory and sang 'Fight the Good Fight' and 'Onward, Christian Soldiers' and the National Anthem. Then, silent and subdued, they all filed out of the church.

Lunch was a quiet business. Harry looked around the table, and it took him back twenty-five years. Then, Sam had been occupying the chair he was sitting in. The whole family had been there; many of them were still there now, but there were new faces. Sam and Terry, Madelene, Heidi, Janet and Albert Chandler. And there were the faces that they would never see again – Joe, Ian, the Macgregors, Arnold, and of course Sam himself. Harry remembered vividly how his father had announced the outbreak of hostilities and the letter that Jane had received from Heidi – and how suspicion had rested on Jane as a German sympathizer. Harry looked sadly around the table; it was happening all over again.

Harry was not, and knew that he never could be, a Sam. He was too easy-going, for one thing, and he lacked his father's authority and drive. As he sat there, barely eating, he wondered what Sam would have said.

'It is evil things that we shall be fighting . . .' That was what the Prime Minister had said in his broadcast.

We would fight all right, but at what cost? How many of them here now would be able to gather around that table when it was all over? There would be no talk of 'over by Christmas', not this time. This time they knew the enemy, and they knew that the struggle would be long and hard and bitter.

'Will there be anything further, sir?' Gunn was speaking.

'No, thank you, Gunn,' said Harry, 'you can just leave the

coffee and come back and clear away later.'

Why did no one say anything, thought Harry. It was different this time. There had been no cheering in the streets of Driffield, nor, so far as anyone could tell from the radio, had there been anywhere else. This was a country which was not seeking glory in battle but one entering solemnly upon a loathsome task because they knew that their cause was just. But right would not be enough. How ready were they? One was uncomfortably aware of the wave of pacifism and the desire for disarmament which had swept the country over the preceding years. Winston Churchill and Lord Beaverbrook had been condemned and berated as warmongers for preaching self-defence, and people had laughed at them when they talked of the inevitability of the conflict which was now upon them. And it would not be like the last time. The whole country would feel the pestilence; there would be air raids, cities and towns would be destroyed, women and little children would be slaughtered in the holocaust.

And what of the foe? No one knew just how strong Germany was, how long it would take, or how many lives it would cost.

It was Vanessa who broke the silence.

'Daddy,' she said, 'I think I should join the Women's Land Army, don't you?'

'What's that?' asked Mary.

'Women,' replied Harry. 'They're being recruited for agricultural work so that men can be released for service with the armed forces.'

'There doesn't seem to be much point in your doing that, Vanessa,' said Noel. 'We're all fully employed on the land right here, or if we're not, we jolly soon can be. I cannot see that the wearing of a uniform will make any difference.'

'Your brother's right,' said Harry to Vanessa. 'We're going to need every hand we can get right here at Hardacres. As I see it, we should use every square yard of land for food or grazing. The lawns – everything – will have to go under the plough.'

'Not my roses,' said Mary. 'Tha can take everything else if tha must, but not my roses.'

457

Harry smiled. 'All right, Mother,' he said, 'you shall keep your roses, I'll see to that.'

'Tha'd better,' said Mary.

'I suppose we had better enlist,' said Terry.

'Join up, eh?' said Sam. 'Good idea.'

'There is no need for that, not yet,' Madelene spoke quickly. 'I think it would be wise to wait and see what the government wants you to do.'

Madelene was all too conscious of her own brief marriage, of memories of living close to the lines in the last lot and watching the ambulance trains with their cargo of maimed and broken bodies. She looked at her sons, fine wholesome men; she couldn't bear to see them broken, torn apart by the dogs of war. 'Besides,' she continued urgently, 'there will be plenty to do on the farm; you heard Harry – someone must do the work, someone must feed the country.'

'Not me,' said Sam.

'Nor me,' said Terry.

'All right,' Harry interrupted, 'there is no need to make decisions yet, not here and now, anyway.'

'We could join your old regiment,' said Sam.

'Good idea,' said Terry.

'Perhaps,' said Harry, 'but we can discuss all of that sort of thing later.'

'I wonder if they would take me?' said Noel. 'Or do you think that thirty-nine is too old?'

'I have a feeling that they're a lot better organized than last time,' said Harry. 'I think that if they want you for anything they'll let you know, and you might only gum up the works if you start volunteering all over the place. In any case, Noel, you're not going anywhere; you must stay on the farm.'

Two or three of them started speaking at once; the ice had been broken, and the conversation was beginning to become alive when it was partially interrupted by the reappearance of Gunn.

'Excuse me, sir,' he said quietly to Harry, 'there are two gentlemen here asking for Mrs Muller.'

'Mrs Muller?' Harry was surprised.

'I think it's the police, sir,' Gunn whispered.

'I'll come and take care of it myself,' said Harry. 'Excuse me, will you?' he announced. 'There is someone I have to see.'

Harry accompanied Gunn out. He had a nasty feeling that he knew what all of this was about. Silly of him not to have thought of it before. Heidi was a German.

'Where are they, Gunn?'

'I took them into your study, sir,' replied the butler.

'All right,' said Harry. 'You carry on with whatever you are doing; I'll see to them.'

'Thank you, sir,' said Gunn.

Harry went into the study, and two men rose to meet him. He recognized the elder of the two.

'Inspector Barry, isn't it?' he said.

'That's right, Mr Hardacre, and this is Sergeant Young.'

'How do you do, Sergeant,' said Harry.

'I'm sorry about this,' continued the Inspector, 'but I'm afraid that we have to take Mrs Muller in.'

'Whatever for?' asked Harry.

'Enemy alien, sir.'

'But you surely don't think that Mrs Muller ... why, it's preposterous – she's probably a much greater enemy of Hitler than we are.'

'I realize that, sir,' said the Inspector. 'I know the lady, but there's nothing I can do. She's got to be screened, and then she will probably be released if everything's all right. Of course, she'll have to report more frequently, but that's no great inconvenience.'

'You know,' said Harry, 'she must be nearly sixty, and as far as we know, she's already lost a son fighting Hitler, and she's a Jew.'

'I'm sorry, sir,' said the Inspector, 'perhaps if you get on to the Home Office?'

'All right, I know it's not your doing. Where will she be held?'

'Initially at Beverley, sir,' said the Inspector. 'I could keep her there for about a week; you could come down and see her and take her out for walks. But if you don't manage to get me fresh instructions inside a week, she'll have to go to the Isle of Man.'

459

'All right,' said Harry, 'I'll go and talk to her; it's a bloody shame, isn't it?'

'Yes, sir, I'm afraid that enemy aliens are guilty until they are proved innocent.'

'Wait here, and I'll get her,' said Harry.

At first Heidi was terrified. She knew only of German prisons, but Harry managed to persuade her that it would not be too bad and that she was being taken away by her old friend Inspector Barry of the Immigration Department. Harry promised that he would get on to the Home Office immediately and pull whatever strings he could.

'All right, Harry,' said Heidi. 'I understand – we are at war with Germany, I am German, and you must be careful with all Germans in this country. There are some, I am sure, who will be loyal to the Nazis.'

With that they went back into the study. The two police officers rose as they entered.

'Mrs Muller,' said the Inspector, greeting her; then he turned to Harry. 'Mr Hardacre, you said that you intended to contact the Home Office in the matter.'

'That's right,' said Harry.

'Might I ask who it is that you intend to get in touch with?'

'One of the permanent undersecretaries. He was at school with my brother and me. His name is Tarrant.'

'I have heard of Mr Tarrant, sir,' said the Inspector. 'I should say that he is certainly in a position to help you. Mrs Muller?'

'Yes, Inspector?' said Heidi.

'I hope you realize that I am sorry about all of this, but I want you to understand that at this stage we are not able to make exceptions.'

'Of course, Inspector, I understand,' said Heidi.

The Inspector turned back to Harry. 'Mr Hardacre, when do you intend to contact Mr Tarrant?'

'Today, if possible; certainly no later than tomorrow,' replied Harry.

'Well, sir,' said the Inspector, 'I don't know that I should do this, but I think that we can afford to bend the rules a little in your case.'

'How do you mean, Inspector?'

'We will allow Mrs Muller to remain here in your custody until Thursday. That might give you time to get something in writing from your friend. She will have to report daily to the constable at Watton, and I shall return on Thursday. I hope you will have something by then.'

'Thank you, thank you very much,' said Heidi.

'Not at all, ma'am,' said the Inspector. 'Come along, Sergeant.'

Harry and Heidi watched them go. Heidi turned to Harry.

'You are right, Harry,' she said, 'it could not happen here.'

CHAPTER NINE

It was, in the parlance of the Royal Air Force, 09.45 hours on the morning of 9 August 1940, somewhere in Kent. The sky was clear and empty, save for half a dozen wispy white clouds which hung around at about five thousand feet in an atmosphere so soporific that they could be persuaded neither to disperse nor to move.

'A' flight of Number 683 Squadron, Royal Air Force, had been at readiness for about two hours. Their Supermarine Spitfires sat in organized disarray around the dispersal hut, their engines warm, tanks topped up, and ammunition belts full. The NAAFI wagon was just about due, bringing with it a welcome supply of hot, sweet tea made with condensed milk and a peculiar confection, much beloved by all ranks, consisting of hard pink icing in a cracker sandwich and known euphemistically as a cream slice.

The ground crews drowsed beside their aircraft, with either fitter or rigger in the cockpit ready to start the Rolls-Royce Merlin engine and hand over to the pilot in the event of a 'scramble'. The Flight Sergeant Engineer strode majestically from aircraft to aircraft, pausing every now and then to issue a word of admonition to one of the crews; but there was a certain lethargy, even in this.

The phoney war had come to an abrupt halt; France had fallen, and ever since 683 Squadron had been waiting for the onslaught. Farther south on the Channel coast, there had been plenty of activity as Goering's Luftwaffe carried out a series of attacks on convoys of shipping. Squadrons stationed near the coast had seen a fair amount of action. For 683, however, there had been no combat. They were one of the units which Air Marshal 'Stuffy' Dowding had held back against the threatened invasion. So it was that, day after day, while the three flights of 683 alternated among readiness, standby, and training, nothing had happened.

At 09.46 hours two things happened, the NAAFI wagon was sighted and the Tannoy, the public-address system, crackled into life.

'Scramble! "A" Flight, scramble! This is not an exercise. "A" Flight, scramble,' it blared.

The expected had been expected for so long and had not happened that it took a second or two for the nine pilots, some of whom were kicking a ball about and the rest merely loafing, to realize what was happening.

'SCRAMBLE!' shouted the Tannoy.

The message got home, and all nine were sprinting towards their aircraft. The engines, not yet cold from their last warm-up, fired and instantly came to life. Pilots grabbed helmets and goggles from the rigger and then changed places with the man in the cockpit, who then stood over them and strapped them into their parachutes and then their Sutton harnesses.

Riggers flung themselves across the tail of their aircraft as the pilots ran their engines up to full revs and then throttled back. A wave from the pilot, chocks whipped away from the landing wheels, throttles eased open, and the aircraft were slowly rolling towards takeoff.

The Flight Commander clipped his oxygen mask-cum-microphone across his nose and mouth.

'This is Badger, Red Leader, calling Tango control; clear for takeoff?'

'Tango control calling Badger, Red Leader. Roger, orbit base, angels one five.'

The Flight Commander acknowledged this, then fixed his eyes on the watch office, as his aircraft formed up in sections behind him. He pulled down his goggles and drew the cockpit canopy shut. A green Very light arched away from the watch office.

'O.K., Red Section, go. Blue and Green follow.'

As he finished speaking, the first three Spitfires – in 'V' formation, throttles wide open, airscrews screaming in fine pitch as they reached takeoff revs – started to bump over the grassy surface of the airfield.

Eight and a half minutes later the flight was in formation

and still climbing in a gentle turn, as they circled base.

'I wish we hadn't had that bloody party last night,' said an aggrieved voice over the ether.

'Cut the chatter,' snapped the Flight Commander – then more formally, 'This is Badger Leader calling Tango control. Present position base; angels eleven and climbing. Acknowledge.'

'Tango control to Badger Leader. Vector one seven zero; angels one eight. Acknowledge.'

The Flight Commander acknowledged and passed the instructions on to his flight. The nine Spitfires turned on to course, still climbing and now heading just east of south. Their radios were silent; each man was alone with his thoughts and apprehensions, listening for the next set of instructions from the operations room fifteen thousand feet below. A couple of minutes later control spoke again.

'Tango to Badger Leader. Vector one five five.'

'Roger, Tango. Badger aircraft, vector one five five ... now.'

The flight swung fifteen degrees to port.

'Tango control to Badger Leader. Thirty plus bandits, angels one five. Maintain course and intercept two minutes from ... now.'

'Roger, Tango. All Badger aircraft, clear guns and check.'

Each Spitfire shuddered as its pilot fired a short burst from its eight wing-mounted Browning machine guns.

'Blue leader, check, skipper.'

'Green leader, check.'

'Red two, check.'

'Red three, check,' said Peter Macgregor.

'Green three, to Red Leader. Aircraft at two o'clock low.'

The Flight Commander saw them, below and slightly to his right. It was a formation of Heinkel 111s.

'All Badger aircraft,' called the Flight Commander. 'Bandits at two o'clock low. Green section, right leg; Blue, left; Red two, follow me, we take Bandit leader. Red three, top cover. Buster! Tallyho!'

Red three eased his throttle forward and pulled gently back on the stick. As he climbed, Peter Macgregor could see the

464

formation of Heinkels below him. There were about twenty of them, black and menacing and apparently oblivious of the presence of 'A' Flight, who were peeling off and diving to the attack. It looked like a piece of cake.

Peter rocked his wings to give himself a better view of the action. He did not hear the voices of his comrades as they crackled across the ether. His VHF radio was on transmit. It was his job to watch and wait, to avoid combat and to report any other aircraft that might be around.

The sun was proving a bit of a nuisance. It kept flashing in his rear view mirror and he kicked the rudder stirrups back and forth to give himself a better view behind.

Well, he thought, he wasn't likely to get a Jerry today, but he was going to have a magnificent grandstand view of the action. He levelled off when he had climbed to 18,500 feet. He was finding himself distracted from his main purpose by the impending action below and his own private thoughts. It was that sort of a day. Too pleasant, too soporific – he found that he could not even sum up any hatred for the Huns below. It was not a day for killing; it was a day to live and let live, a day to enjoy the good things of life.

Pilot Officer Lord Macgregor had joined 683 Squadron at Usworth in County Durham. He was posted there from Lossiemouth after finishing training. Peter saw his first Spitfire on the last day of May 1940, and he fell in love with it at first sight.

The squadron was re-equipping and standing guard over a sector of the northeast coast, a relatively quiet sector. Peter was interviewed by the squadron commander, Squadron Leader Tirrell, who assigned him to 'A' Flight led by Flight Lieutenant Nigel Austin.

'Good afternoon; Macgregor, isn't it?' Austin greeted him when he reported to the flight office.

'Yes, sir,' replied Peter.

'Flown Spits before?'

'No, sir, Gladiators and Gauntlets.'

'Join the club. You'd better do the same as the rest of us. Draw a manual from the orderly room and read it up. You can have a go tomorrow morning. Sorry about your billet.'

'Why, sir?'

''Fraid you've got to share. We've put you in with Pilot Officer Mackenzie. He's a Canadian, nice chap. By the way, off duty, my name is Nigel.'

'I'm Peter, sir ... er ... Nigel.'

Peter wandered over to the officers' mess and was directed to his quarters by the mess steward. These comprised a room in a Nissen hut. As he entered, a long, red-headed figure unwound itself from one of the beds.

'Hi, I'm Donald; you must be Macgregor; they call me Mac.'

'Hello,' said Peter. 'I'm Peter – better call me that, I suppose, can't have another Mac.'

'Glad to know you,' said Mackenzie, shaking hands. 'Got any Scotch?'

'Sorry.'

'It's a helluva war. Scotch is harder to get than ice cubes in the Sahara. Have a beer.'

Mac produced a screw-top bottle of Newcastle brown ale and two rather grimy glasses.

'Cheers,' said Peter, taking his beer.

They chatted for half an hour or so, and Mac established that Peter really was a lord; they got on very well, and Mac suggested that it was about time to adjourn to the Three Horseshoes. This was a pub on the main road which bisected the camp. The bar was the main meeting place for the pilots of 683, and the barmaid could usually supply them with classified information about twenty-four hours before it was released through official channels.

When they arrived, the only other occupant of the bar was an attractive-looking girl in WAAF uniform. She was sitting, with her back towards them, at a table near the fire. For a moment Peter could hardly believe his eyes. There could only be one woman who looked like that.

'Bunty!' he said.

She turned to look at them, and it wasn't. They went over to her.

466

'Hello, Mac,' she said, 'who's your friend?'

'I say, I'm terribly sorry,' said Peter, 'I thought for a moment that you were someone else.'

'I almost wish I was,' she said and smiled.

'I'm glad you're not,' said Peter.

'This is Mavis. Mavis, meet Peter, new boy,' said Mac. 'Geordie not been over yet?'

'He's orderly officer, but he said he would try and slip away for a short time.'

'Who's Geordie?' asked Peter.

'Flying Officer Emmerson, regular, ex-ranker, red-hot socialist, flies number two to the skipper. Watch him, bud, he doesn't go for the establishment. He hates you already because he knows you're a lord.'

'Are you really?' said Mavis.

'I'm afraid I am,' said Peter. 'Sorry.'

'Don't let it worry you,' said Mavis, laughing. 'By the way, Doris says you're moving south next week. Hope you get near us. I'm on leave, go back tomorrow night,' she added by way of explanation.

'Doris is the bartender here; you get all the gen from her,' said Mac. 'Hi, Doris, three large Scotches.'

The lady in question emerged from an adjoining bar. 'You must be joking. One small one each, and that's your lot until tomorrow.'

Mac walked over to the bar. 'Whisky for you, Mavis?'

'And a gin and tonic,' she replied.

'I say . . .' Peter was astonished.

Mavis laughed, it was an attractive laugh. Then she whispered, 'You need training. If I have a gin and tonic, then Mac gets my whisky.'

'Is Mr Emmerson your husband?' asked Peter.

'I wouldn't marry him if he was the last man on earth,' she said good-naturedly. 'Don't look shocked; he's my brother.'

Peter felt relieved. 'Where do you live?'

'Newcastle.'

'And you're leaving tomorrow?'

'Well, sort of, it's really the day after. My train goes at one

467

o'clock in the morning.'

'Have dinner with me tomorrow night,' Peter said on impulse.

'You don't waste much time.'

'There isn't much of it.' He knew that she was going to say yes. 'You'll have to tell me where to meet you – I don't know Newcastle.'

'Cocktail bar, Station Hotel, seven o'clock.'

She spoke quickly, as Mac was already bearing down on them armed with three whiskys and a gin.

During the evening he met several other pilots from the squadron, including Geordie, who dropped in for a quarter of an hour to say good-bye to his sister. As predicted, Geordie showed his disapproval of Peter, but that apart, he felt among friends.

The next morning he spent an hour going over the cockpit drill of a Spitfire, then spent another hour taxiing and taking off and landing. His first impression was confirmed – the Spit was a beautiful bird, even if she was a bit temperamental in landing.

He managed to get away from the camp at about six in the evening. He caught the Newcastle bus and found his way to the Station Hotel by a quarter to seven. Mavis did not show up until a quarter past, by which time he found himself worrying.

She apologized for her lateness, which she said had been caused by a protracted farewell to her parents, whom she had, with great difficulty, dissuaded from coming to the station to see her off.

It was a quiet dinner; they started to get to know each other silently. Over coffee in the comfortable lounge Mavis asked him, 'Who was Bunty?'

'Someone a long time ago.'

'Did you love her?'

'Her body? Yes. The rest? No.'

There was a long silence.

'Do you want me?'

'Yes.' It was true he did; then, after a pause, he added, 'But it seems terribly important.'

'You can if you want to, but I'd rather wait.'

'There'll be other times?'

'Yes, please, lots of other times.'

They sat and held hands until it was time for her to go. Then he took her on to the platform, and, as the train came in, he took her, ever so gently, into his arms. Suddenly she was holding him fiercely, her mouth open as she pressed her body into his.

'I meant that,' she said.

'I know,' he replied solemnly. 'So did I.'

And then she was gone. He had missed the last bus, but it didn't matter. He set out to walk the ten miles back to camp.

Doris had been right. Two weeks later they were moved, fully operational, to southern England, and Mavis had her wish – they were only eight miles from her station.

Peter was enjoying himself. He loved flying, and today, he thought, he would not have to fight. He put his hand against his breast pocket – it was still there; he would give Mavis her engagement ring tonight. That was when he saw them.

A dozen or more black specks, like flies crawling across the cockpit canopy, floating down towards the attacking 'A' Flight.

'Watchdog to Badger leader,' he called excitedly. 'Bogies, six o'clock high, twelve plus.'

'Roger, Watchdog,' came Nigel Austin's calm voice. 'Keep watching. Leader to all Badger aircraft. Press home attack, then evade. Bogies high and behind. I see them.'

Peter watched as the first shots were fired in the Battle of Britain; he saw a couple of Heinkels going down, trailing smoke, and then saw one of the Messerschmidt 109s on the tail of a Spitfire. Suddenly an agonized voice broke through the ether; Peter thought he recognized it as young Michael Wykham.

'Save me ... is there no one? Can't you help ... Mother! Sweet Jesus, I want my mummy ...'

Peter watched as the ME opened fire and Michael Wykham died.

Peter saw the ME break away and start heading south. There was nothing else around, so Peter put his Spitfire into a long dive and gave chase. He tore through the sky after the ME. They were over the coast, and Peter was closing in for the kill. The German saw him and put his machine into a tight turn. Peter followed with grim satisfaction; he had him now. He knew that the ME's fuel must be getting low and that he would not be able to wait long. Long before Peter would have to break the circle, the 109 would have to head for France, and when he broke the circle, Peter would kill him.

The two fighters were chasing each other around and around. The ME had throttled back in order to give him the advantage of his superior acceleration when he broke. Peter did not mind. As soon as the other man broke the circle, he would open fire, and by now the circle was so small that he knew that he could not miss.

The German pushed his canopy back as if preparing to bail out, should it become necessary. He waved at Peter, and that made Peter feel guilty. The anger was gone; he did not want to kill this young man he had never known, but he was sure that he would. Then the German pointed down and waved again.

Peter had been so intent on keeping his quarry in view that he had not looked down to where he knew the Channel must be. He took a quick glance. Where there should have been sea was a rolling fog bank less than a hundred feet below.

So that was it; the Hun knew what he was doing, after all. Peter slid his own canopy back and waved to his enemy; the German cut his throttle and disappeared into the fog.

Peter knew that he shouldn't, but he was feeling glad – it had all suddenly become too personal. He opened his throttle and started to climb away to the north and into the empty sky.

CHAPTER TEN

The London contingent of the family had a party. It was 7 September, and Peter had been given a forty-eight-hour stand-down, so, with Mavis, now proudly wearing his engagement ring, he had come up to London to spend the night with Emily and Philip Barton. The twins were on embarkation leave. They had managed to get into Harry's old regiment and had made such a fuss that the powers that be had agreed that they would be posted together wherever the exigencies of the service permitted. They had completed their training and had been given leave together, prior to departure for places unknown. They were staying with Maud and Albert Chandler out at their pleasant home in Shepperton, some fifteen miles from the West End.

Peter had got in touch with Emily and had asked her if it would be all right to spend the night there in company with Mavis. Emily had been delighted and had phoned Maud, and between them they had arranged to spend the evening in the West End. They were to have an early dinner, do a show, and spend the rest of the evening wining and dining and supping at the Café de Paris to the music of Snake-Hips Johnson, which activity should take them well into the small hours of the morning. Albert was appearing at the Hippodrome with his band, as one of the stars of one of the revues which had become popular among sophisticated Londoners just before the war. As only Maud had seen the show, they decided that they would go there and that, after the show, Albert would join them for the remainder of the evening.

Peter and Mavis arrived from Kent at about five o'clock in the evening to find that everyone was almost ready to go. The twins had been behaving with predictable irresponsibility during their leave, but they had promised that they would behave themselves in a gentlemanly fashion in the presence of Peter's new fiancée. This promise had been received by

Emily and Maud with some doubt and a fair amount of concern.

Mavis was a little bemused at the company in which she found herself. Her fiancé was a Scottish peer, holder of one of the oldest and noblest titles in that country, and his relations included a band leader, a policeman, and a late grandfather who had gutted on fish quays. She had found out about Sam when Peter had given her the ring and she had told him that she was only a miner's daughter. Peter had been quick to point out that his mother was a guttie's daughter, so if anyone was social-climbing, it was him and not her. Nevertheless meeting, for the first time, other members of his family had been a bit scary. The twins helped a lot. When Mavis and Peter arrived at Emily's little house in Charlotte Street, just around the corner from Sloane Square, the twins subjected Mavis to a searching but good-humoured inspection and interrogation.

'I say,' said Terry, smiling as he shook hands, 'not bad.'

'Not at all bad, brother,' said Sam, shaking hands himself. 'Congrats, Peter, I must say you seem to have an eye for them.'

'Cut it out,' said Peter, 'Mavis doesn't know you yet, and if she has any sense at all . . .'

'She can't have, she's too beautiful,' said Sam.

'And she wouldn't have said yes to you,' said Terry. 'She'd have saved herself for us.'

'If she has any sense at all,' Peter repeated, grinning, 'she'll avoid getting to know you, like the plague.'

'Never,' said Sam. 'We're nice.'

'Any sisters?' asked Terry.

'Only a brother,' said Mavis.

'What a waste,' said Sam. 'Miss Emmerson, anyone who was fortunate enough to produce a girl as lovely as you should certainly have produced more and not wasted their time having boys.'

'There should have been at least two more,' said Terry. 'May we call you Mavis?'

'Of course,' said Mavis, and she smiled at their flattery.

Emily came into the room with Maud. 'Come on, you lot,' she said, 'I've just done the blackout for when we get back.'

'You needn't have bothered,' said Sam.

'We won't be home till the morning,' said Terry.

'Never mind about that,' said Emily. 'Philip's meeting us at the restaurant, and if we don't go now we'll be keeping him waiting and won't have time to eat before the show. We have a table at Gennaro's for six thirty. Sam, be a brick and run into Sloane Square and see if you can grab a taxi.'

'I'm Terry,' was the reply, 'but don't worry, we'll both go.'

The twins went out, and Emily turned to Mavis and Peter. 'You know,' she said, 'I'm quite sure they lie about who they are, but how is one supposed to tell?'

'Emily,' said Peter, changing the subject, 'have you been on to Hardacres today?'

'Yes,' said Emily.

'How's Grandmother?'

'Pretty much the same.'

'I wonder if I should have gone up. It would have been such a rush. Up today and back down tomorrow.'

'I don't think that would have done any good at all,' said Maud. 'I was up there last week, and she hardly recognized me.'

Emily turned to Mavis. 'Well, Mavis,' she said, 'welcome to the clan. I suppose that you'll find us all a bit nutty, but don't let it worry you; we're comparatively harmless.'

'Except the twins,' said Peter, grinning. 'They're lethal.'

They were interrupted by the triumphant return of Sam and Terry.

'Did you get one?' asked Emily.

'Of course,' said Terry. 'Sam had to lie down in the middle of the road, but we got one. You are talking about a taxi, I hope.'

They all piled into the taxi and headed for Soho. Gennaro's Rendezvous in Dean Street still maintained a superb service; the ladies received a rose from white-haired old Gennaro himself when they entered, and the chef managed to produce some gastronomic miracles with the restricted and sometimes unusual war-time rations.

Peter, of course, was the hero of the day. Since the start of the Battle of Britain, a fighter pilot found it quite difficult to pay for anything in London. His brevet and the undone top button of his tunic, which had become the unofficial mark of the fighter pilot, opened all doors – and even more remarkable, when they approached the cocktail bar, they were offered whisky.

They had an excellent, if somewhat hurried, meal, in which they were joined by Philip Barton, who had come directly there from Scotland Yard. When the meal was over, they made their way on foot down Dean Street and then along Old Compton Street and into Cambridge Circus to the Hippodrome. It was only a matter of a couple of hundred yards, but in the complete blackout it took some little time. As they passed doorways, torches would flash on for a moment to reveal a shapely leg.

'What are they doing?' asked Mavis.

'Working,' replied Philip Barton, but in the dark she could not see him smile.

They got through the light trap and started blinking in the brightly lit foyer. Maud collected the tickets, and they had just settled into their seats in the third row of the stalls when the curtain went up on the first number.

They were about halfway through the show. Albert and his band were the next item due to appear. Vic Oliver, the funny man with the violin, was in the middle of his act and the packed audience were enjoying themselves immensely, when, from somewhere outside the building, came a long, high-pitched, intermittent wailing sound. It rose and fell for some time, and it produced a buzz of conversation around the auditorium. The artist looked off into the wings and then left the stage; the curtain fell. After a moment's pause a man dressed in a black dinner suit appeared in front of the curtain.

'Ladies and gentlemen,' he called, raising his hands for silence, 'ladies and gentlemen, I am the theatre manager, and I am sorry to have to tell you that the air-raid warning has just sounded.'

Everybody started talking at once.

'Please, ladies and gentlemen, may I have your attention?'

said the manager. 'There will be some of you, I know, who will want to get home and some of you who have essential duties to perform. We will have a short interval. If, during that time, those of you who wish to leave will do so, the show will then continue.'

There was an answering cheer from the audience. Philip Barton, who was sitting between Emily and Maud, turned to them.

'I suppose I had better get back to the Yard right away,' he said. 'This is my department.'

Philip started to move down the row of seats.

'What do you think we should do?' asked Maud as Philip left.

'Stay here,' said Sam.

'We've paid for the show, let's see it,' said Terry.

'No, you didn't,' said Emily. 'Albert got the tickets; they were free.'

'But we might as well stay,' said Peter.

About half of the audience started quietly for the doors. The remainder, at the request of the manager, made their way from the circle and gallery into the stalls, and then the show continued.

London was living through a new experience. There had, until now, been no night raids on the capital, but now for the first time the enemy was occupying the darkened skies over the metropolis.

When the performance came to an end, the whole audience rose to their feet and sang 'God Save the King'. The curtain stayed up, and the manager again came to the footlights and addressed them.

'Ladies and gentlemen. The raid is still in progress,' he announced. 'If you wish to remain here, Mr Chandler and the rest of the company have agreed to entertain you until the all-clear sounds. I ought to tell you that there may be some difficulty in getting transport home, and if you have not got your own cars or do not live within walking distance of the theatre, it would probably be wise to remain in the theatre.'

Outside there was a 'crump, crump, crump'.

'You see what I mean?' said the manager.

'Bugger the Kaiser,' cried a voice from the back of the stalls.

'Wrong war,' retorted Vic Oliver.

'Can't remember the new fellow's name,' shouted the gentleman in the stalls.

Everybody laughed.

'What shall we do now?' asked Peter.

'I'm staying if Albert is going to continue playing,' said Maud. 'In any case, we can't walk all the way to Sloane Square.'

'We'll all stay,' said Emily firmly.

The twins, who had been having a whispered conversation, got up. 'We won't be long,' said Terry.

'Where are you off to?' demanded Peter.

'Don't worry, we're not going,' said Sam; 'we'll be back soon.'

They edged their way out of their seats and went down into the stalls bar. There they failed to find what they were looking for, so they went out to the foyer. After a word with the commissionaire to make sure they would be able to get back, they went out into the streets.

Cambridge Circus was strangely quiet, even for war-time London at ten o'clock at night. In the sky long, white pencils of light from the searchlights surrounding the city probed and stabbed through the darkness, and they could hear the pulsating drone of aircraft engines – punctuated occasionally by an explosion.

'Doesn't seem too bad,' said Terry.

'I think it's the East End,' said Sam. 'Probably the docks.'

'Where shall we go?' said Terry.

'Anywhere,' said Sam. 'Why don't we try the nearest one?'

They went into a pub. The contrast with the cool September night was enormous. The place was packed; everybody was singing, and the atmosphere was hot and steamy. A barmaid was dancing on the bar counter to the music of an accordion being played by a street musician, who had obviously been dragged in and plied with large quantities of alcohol. Sam and Terry looked at each other.

'We'll never get served here,' said Terry.

'Let's try a hotel,' said Sam.

'O.K.' said Terry.

They walked down a deserted Shaftesbury Avenue and into the Regent Palace at Piccadilly Circus. The restaurant was just closing, but there was evidence of several parties starting up in the lounges and foyer. Sam and Terry went into the restaurant, where they managed to get hold of the head waiter. After a *sotto voce* conversation and the transfer of several bank notes, the waiter went out.

'Looks like being a night,' said Sam.

'Bit of a lark,' said Terry.

The waiter returned and handed them a large carton.

'Thanks,' said Sam and Terry together.

Carrying their burden carefully, they returned to the theatre, tipped the commissionaire five shillings, and pushed their way back to their seats in the stalls.

'Where have you two been?' hissed Peter.

'Blowing up the Houses of Parliament,' replied Terry.

Albert and his band were playing a selection of popular numbers. As they finished 'Run, Rabbit, Run', Sam rose to his feet.

'Can we have some light out here?' he shouted.

There was a chorus of approval from the audience, and in a moment the house lights came on.

Sam and Terry opened their box and revealed their purchases. They had brought half a dozen bottles of champagne and a selection of glasses.

'We've going to have a party,' shouted Sam, waving a bottle of champagne above his head.

There was an answering cheer from the audience.

'And if there is anybody here who can do a turn,' called Albert from the stage, 'come up and do it.'

The manager came back on to the stage. 'The bars have been opened,' he called. 'Is there any lady or ladies who would care to make sandwiches?'

'I will,' replied Mavis.

She was joined by Maud and Emily and one or two others, and the whole theatre began to have a giant midnight picnic.

A man got on to the stage and recited 'Gunga Din' very badly, but nobody cared and everyone cheered, and, once the ice had been broken, there was a rush of volunteers to sing or dance.

'Better than the Café de Paris,' said Sam, sipping his third glass of champagne.

'I'll say,' said Terry.

And soon the party was in full swing.

There was another side to the raid. Philip Barton had gone straight back to the Yard. The bombs were dropping out in the East End of London, as Sam had guessed. Late into the night Philip had taken a squad car and gone out to inspect the damage. There he saw the devastated homes where firemen and rescue workers sweated, trying to get people out from beneath piles of rubble. He watched in the light of the fires as the dead and the maimed were taken away. He saw a woman's hand sticking out of the rubble of one bombed building. He went to it and started to move it. There was blood on the arm but no body: the arm had been severed at the elbow. He turned away in disgust.

As the grey dawn started to streak the sky, at long last the sirens wailed the all-clear, and everybody went home except the rescue workers, who carried on until their task was done.

It would be two months before they were to know a night without bombs.

CHAPTER ELEVEN

Even the momentous happenings in the sky over southern England had no effect; while the Battle of Britain raged and the country struggled for its life, at Hardacres it all had little impact. Not even the involvement of Peter could detract from the drama which was being played out within the family. Mary Hardacre was dying. She was in her eighty-third year. She had finally been moved into the big house a couple of months ago, where she and her treasures occupied the master bedroom and sitting room. By the beginning of August the issue had passed beyond all possible doubt. She had become bedridden, and her sitting room had been converted into a bedroom for the nurse, who was in constant attendance. There was nothing wrong with Mary – nothing that could be given a name; she was just worn out, her body was tired, and she was willing and ready to give up the struggle.

The family came and went, as and when their war work would allow. Harry and Jane were there all the time, all through August and into September. It was on the fifteenth, around eleven in the morning, that the nurse called for Harry and Jane.

'She's asking for you, Mr Hardacre,' she said, and the expression on her face caused Harry to ask, 'Is she . . . ?'

'I can't say, sir; I've sent for doctor,' replied the nurse.

Together, Jane and Harry went up to Mary's room. She was propped up by a veritable mountain of cushions. For the first time in her life Mary looked frail. Her skin, drawn tight across the bones of her face, had taken on an almost transparent hue. Her eyes had taken on an incredible brightness, and her mouth opened and closed in little gasps as she drew breath.

'Come and sit along o' me, Sam,' she said.

Jane and Harry looked at each other.

'Do what she says,' said Jane. 'She thinks you are Father.'

Harry went and sat on the end of the bed. He took one of her hands into his and wondered at how thin and cold it was.

'Eeh, Sam, we'll need to be off soon,' she said.

'Aye, lass,' said Harry in a passable imitation of his father's voice.

'Is cart ready?' she asked.

'It's all ready,' said Harry.

'Joe's gone for Adam, 'as he?'

'He'll be back soon,' said Harry.

'Then tha'd better give me Tin Box and us'll be on our way. Sam ...'

Mary paused.

'What is it, luv?'

'Usn's got a long way to go, but we'll get there by dark.'

'Happen us will,' said Harry.

Jane thrust the Tin Box into Harry's hands, and he put it under his mother's.

'Tha's never let it get empty, Sam; tha's a good man. Shall us be off now?'

'Aye, we'll be off.'

Harry got up from the side of the bed and went over to Jane. 'What do we do now?' he whispered.

Mary's eyes had closed for a moment; then they flickered open.

'Sam,' she said.

'What is it, luv?' asked Harry.

'Hang on a minute; Peter want to come along of us.'

Her eyes closed again. Harry looked at Jane. There was terror in her face; her hand flew to her mouth, and she ran from the room. There was not any reason to stay, for Mary Hardacre was dead.

That same evening the radio announced that the RAF had shot down a total of 183 German aircraft for the loss of less than forty of their own.

Peter Macgregor was one of those.

CHAPTER TWELVE

Harry stood on the terrace of Hardacres in late November
1940, his shoulders hunched against the cold wind whipping
around the corner of the house and his hands cold and stiff
on the sandstone balustrade. The smoke was heavy and rich
from the fires beyond the lawn. It filled the air, thickened it,
darkened the afternoon, and half hid the distant beechwood.
They were burning the yew maze.

The ring and thud of the axes carried clear and plain, above
the sound of the wind. Noel was down there, and the gardener, and half a dozen of the farmhands. Harry fancied
grimly that Noel was enjoying it; he could see him clearly –
his thin, small body hunched over his swinging axe, the
rhythm easy and mindless, accomplishing a simple, satisfying
destruction.

The wood smoke and the distant axes were doubly dis-
tracting, tossing Harry's mind back and forth between an old,
old memory and a new, harsh reality. Smoke and new fire,
a damp evening and the sound of axes – it was a doorway to
his childhood and the racecourses and his parents, both gone
now. But it was a new door as well, opening forward on to a
long, lonely corridor. The war was real; it would be long and
hard, and it was going to be lonely. Harry felt that his family
was like a severed tree, the roots gone and the branches gone.
He was left, isolated, without past or future, like deadwood.

Now they were chopping down the dark yew hedges where
he had played with his brother in a long-gone childhood. The
boughs were going to the fire, the roots would be torn out by
tractors and ropes, and then the earth would go under the
plough. It had taken four hundred years to plant it and grow
it. What kind of a man, Harry thought, can put his wit and
will into a thing that won't be right until his very gravestone
is rotting to dust? He tried to think of four hundred years
hence but gave up. There would be no more yew mazes.

He had won, from Noel, the rose gardens – a last, grim victory. The yew must go, and the lawns. But not his mother's roses. Foursquare in the centre of the lawn they sat, and there they would remain, even when, next spring, the lawn was an oatfield. Noel had been incredulous, then angry, and then, foolishly, mocking. For the first time in their long, uneasy half friendship, father and son had nearly come to blows. Now Noel was working out his anger on the gnarled roots of the yew, and Harry was exploring in his mind the odd discovery that, son or not, there were times when he hated him.

But if the lawns had to be destroyed, Harry would do it himself. He was a good ploughman with a team of Clydesdales, or, as it was done now, with a tractor. He prided himself in straight, clean furrows and scarce any waste at the field's edge. He would be the executioner and do the job right.

Harry slapped his hands together, blew on them for warmth, and turned his back on the pall of smoke.

Madelene heard the clash and rumble of the tractor and the roar of the diesel engine and dashed to the kitchen door in time to see Harry clattering by at speed, along the cobbled drive, the ploughshares raised clear of the stones and Harry's grey hair blowing wildly in the wind. She ran through the house calling to Hetty, and the two of them came out the front door, ran down the terrace, and saw the tractor roar around the corner of the house and on to the lawn.

Harry stopped the tractor and sat quietly, listening to the sudden silence. Through it the sound of the axes grew gradually. He looked up at the house and saw Hetty and Madelene, side by side, an old woman and a middle-aged woman, both in country work clothes. They were watching him, waiting.

He sighted along the front of the terrace to a small Japanese cherry tree at the edge of the drive. That would be his line. He looked once more over the soft green sweep of it. Then he thrust the lever forward and felt the ploughshares thud solidly down behind him. He kept his eyes on his marker, then slammed the tractor into gear. The turf resisted for a fraction of a moment – it was tough and firm – but the ploughshares were steel; then he was moving, drawing a thin, dark triple line to the cherry tree. He did not look back until he had reached the tree. He was far from the house; Hetty and Madelene were dark shadows on the terrace. The smoky afternoon sun was drawing through the clouds and lighting a dull, black shine on his three furrows. They were straight and true, and Harry suddenly saw how beautiful they were, new and clean. Elated, he jerked the lever back, raised the plough, wheeled the lumbering machine about, and eager now, set plough to earth again.

He crossed and crisscrossed all afternoon, and by dusk there was nothing left of that rolling sweep of green – only black earth, crisp and lined like corduroy. Exhausted and cold, Harry stopped the tractor and switched off the diesel engine. The silence was complete; Noel and the axeman had left the yew maze, now a dark outline of roots and smouldering branches. Harry looked across the blackness which was soaking up what remained of the daylight. The windows of Hardacres were stately and sad, with soft, yellow light. Harry could already see the thin spring lines of seedling corn and the ripe, rippling flow of summer and the autumn stubble in a smoky peace. The land had come alive, out of its grave of turf; now the seasons and the year would circle again, and the land could grow and give. Harry stepped down from the tractor and left it at the foot of the lawn, by the smouldering yew. He limped slowly and patiently across his fresh-cut furrows. When he reached the terrace, he climbed the steps, whose feet were now in black earth. He turned at the top, holding the balustrade for support and said softly, his voice shaky with weariness, 'Now, damn thee, thou'll work.'

CHAPTER THIRTEEN

Jane told the taxi driver to stop halfway up the drive and got out. They joked about saving petrol, but it was not the reason. The morning, in late spring of 1941, was soft and warm, and she wanted to see the place again, for a few minutes, alone. She had gone north a week after the day that Mary and Peter died, and this was her first return.

The elms and the beechwood were the same as always, the peacocks drifting among the brown leaves on the ground – and an odd touch of glory in their hard, new world. She walked quietly, thinking, on to the end of the beechwood, glancing instinctively down the gravel drive to what had been Mary's cottage. It all looked very much the same. What had once been parkland was now grazed by cattle, but that change had come years ago, during the Depression. Then she reached the cattle fence where gardens had begun and the yew maze should have been. It was gone. She had expected that, but what she had not expected was to see still the rolling haze of green, climbing up the long rise to the red brick of Hardacres. Harry had told her the lawns were gone. She stopped, shading her eyes, and seeing gradually that the green was too blue-rich for the time of the year; it rippled like silk moiré in the soft wind. Hardacres stood in a sea of young oats. She smiled, seeing the dark, neat geometric shapes in the centre of the oatfield. Harry had saved the roses, as he had sworn he would.

Jane shifted her small handcase to her other hand and continued walking. In the distance she saw an old man, grey-haired, bent over a fence post at the side of the gravel drive.

Harry straightened his back, shifting his leg painfully, and stood the mell up beside the new fence post. Damn the beast – two posts down for the sake of the greener grass on the other side of the fence. The thought was comfortable; mending fences was part of life, and not really resented. But it was heavy work, and he could have done with less of that just now. So could they all.

He let his eyes rove contentedly over the green oatfield and back, down the backs of his grazing cattle, and away towards the beechwood. He saw the woman; she was walking up the drive. He could not make out a face, at that distance, any longer, but he saw the figure as slim, aristocratic, and dignified, even in the short, utilitarian skirt and mannish jacket.

Harry watched, curious, for several moments. Then he saw it was Jane and started to run, as best he could, and called her name. Jane stopped short, recognizing him with sudden shock, and then she too ran. Brother and sister met and embraced in the middle of the long drive.

Then Harry drew back and held Jane at arm's length, surveying her with pleasure and pride. She was past fifty, though he found it hard to believe; her face had grown more beautiful with age. The strength and the good, honest bone structure held true, when more pretty faces had sagged away to puffy wrinkles. She wore her hair, as she had done for years, in a heavy, simple bun at the back, and it was still more dark than grey. But there was more than that – there was the easy, sure carriage, the confident direct blue eyes; Jane alone looked as if she really belonged to Hardacres and had the breeding of generations to prove it. It amused him and pleased him, and he said, quietly teasing, 'Lady Jane.'

She shook her head, smiling but serious, and pulled away. 'No. Not any more. Just Jane, Jane Hardacre.'

'Do you mean that?' he said, because he could see that she did.

'Yes. It's all over now. It's all gone. I'm Jane Hardacre again.' She paused and looked out over the fields. 'It's odd. It's almost as if I was never anything else. As if it all never happened.'

'But it did happen, Jane,' said Harry, suddenly earnest. 'You had Ian, you were his wife.'

'For four years.'

'But Peter?'

'Peter's gone now. It's done, Harry. I just want to come home.' She sounded weary, and he knew he shouldn't pursue it, but he couldn't let it rest.

'Jane, Ian made you Lady Macgregor, willingly and happily. It pleased Father more than anything in his life, I sometimes think. Please, for Father, keep the title.'

'Father's dead many years,' Jane said flatly. 'He can neither know nor care. Anyhow, it isn't just me, Harry. It's all over for them, too, up there. They've nothing left. The earldom has gone to a cousin in Canada. Lady Macgregor is eighty-five. Do you know, she begged Heidi, pleaded with her to stay. She's the only thing she has left of Ian now. Poor Heidi; I hope she'll be happy there.'

Harry nodded, slowly. 'She's always welcome here, of course, if she'd rather.'

'She knows. She's staying out of kindness. I was glad. I felt cruel leaving, but I had to come home.'

'How are they doing up there – I mean, the estate?'

Jane smiled, her eyes still on the rippling green of the oats. 'The same as us. They're working. They're working with their hands, just as we are. It's odd, though, because they're so surprisingly good at it. I mean, for us it's all so recent. But how long since the Macgregors of Strathconnon have had to work with their hands? But they're very good at it.' She paused and then said, very slowly, 'Do you see what I mean, Harry? It really is all over. For all of us. It will never be like that again.'

Harry smiled and put his arm across her shoulders, taking her case in his other hand, as they began walking towards the house. She was probably right. But somehow it didn't matter any more.

Nothing mattered except the green, growing corn, and the grazing beasts, and the warm spring sun. The year was young, and he felt elated and young inside, like a man at the start of a new love affair.

Jane asked, 'How is Noel? Is he here?'

'He's seeding turnips in the bottom field. He works all day here, and half the night he's at Watton, training in the Home Guard. I don't know how he does it. I couldn't.'

'He's a lot younger than you.'

'He's a lot tougher than I ever was. He's like Dad, in spite

486

of the way he looks. You would think that by now he'd have lost the need to be proving it all the time.'

'Still the same?'

'There was a bit of trouble at the pub last week. Somebody spoke out of turn. The usual thing.'

'Doesn't it help, being in uniform at last?'

'It should, but it doesn't. You know Noel. He doesn't regard it as a proper uniform. He doesn't consider himself a proper soldier. God knows he'd be soldier enough if the Germans got here.'

Jane shuddered. 'Let's hope it doesn't come to that.'

'Aye,' said Harry. 'I don't imagine it will any more. Peter and his lot took care of that.'

Jane smiled, 'If that's so, that's something, anyhow. What do you hear of Sam and Terry?'

'Quite a bit,' Harry said. 'They write every week; of course, it's often months before their letters get here. But they're very good about that. They're still in North Africa, of course.'

'How are they taking it?'

'As you'd expect. They're treating it like a lark. On the surface, anyhow.'

'And underneath?'

'It's shaking them. Madelene and I – well, we read between the lines. They don't much care for killing, war or not. I don't blame them. I didn't like it much either.'

'Peter never spoke of it that way.'

'It was different for Peter. He was isolated, apart. It was one machine against another. It wasn't personal. Sam and Terry are fighting a ground war. It's face to face. Individuals. And they're killing people. It's hard. They're pretty deep, you know.'

'Yes,' Jane said slowly. 'It took me a long time to see it. But I think you're right. I wonder, though, about Peter. If he'd have seen it that way, or not?'

Harry shook his head. There were so many people and questions that would never be fully understood now.

Jane stopped him as they reached the end of the oatfield, at the foot of the balustraded terrace. She turned to face him, her hand on his arm.

'And how are things with you now? You and Hetty and Madelene?'

Harry turned away, looking back the way they had come, away from the house. She watched the slow, gentle smile that she loved and the wind tousling his grey hair. Harry said, very softly, still looking away:

> *Though Margery is stricken dumb*
> *If thrown in Madge's way*
> *We three make up a solitude;*
> *For none alive today*
> *Can know the stories that we know*
> *Or say the things we say …*

Jane smiled understanding. 'That's Yeats, surely?' she said. 'One of your favourites.'

'Why, Jane,' Harry retorted quickly with mock surprise, 'you've learned to read.'

She shoved him girlishly and laughed – her sharp, upper-class laugh.

'That's enough from you, Harry Hardacre. I'm not such a philistine as all that, even if I don't have my nose in a book as often as some people. Besides, what else is there to do now that we've all grown old?'

'You're not old,' Harry said, suddenly serious, 'not you.'

'We're all getting there,' Jane said, smiling easily. 'Anyway, I've always liked Yeats.' She shut her eyes, thinking carefully, and said a little triumphantly:

> *How such a pair loved many years*
> *And such a pair but one,*
> *Stories of the bed of straw*
> *Or the bed of down.*

Harry nodded eager approval, still surprised, but said quite automatically, 'You missed out a line.'

Saying it made him stop suddenly, as far down a memory was touched and stirred lightly. He thought for a moment but could not recall what it had been. Jane shoved him again and said, 'My God, but you're a hard teacher. Go on, let's go in.'

He put his arm around her shoulder again, and they walked to the front door.

'Do you know, Jane,' he said, pausing on the threshold and looking back over the green field, 'half the world is at war, and I've never in my life felt so much at peace.'

CHAPTER FOURTEEN

Jane rode the tractor down the long drive from the upper pastures to the mews. It was a frozen January morning in 1943, and she was wishing ironically that they still used a horse and cart for this kind of work. A horse was warm, at least, and you could climb up on to its back and bury your hands in its thick, rough mane or rub its soft nose until it warmed you with its heavy, steamy breath. Cold comfort from a hard metal tractor seat. She grinned, though, pleased with herself that she could handle the big machine, and drive it at speed down the rough gravel – the barrow, empty now, bouncing and clattering behind. She always rather fancied herself as a racing driver, or then again, an engineer. She loved machinery and wartime meant that she could at last indulge her pleasure in it. It was just past eight and she had already taken two barrowloads of turnips up to the Jersey heifers. She had saved Harry a cold job on a very cold morning and she was pleased.

At the entrance to the mews she parked the tractor neatly in its accustomed place, climbed down, and started for the house. Then she remembered they would need greens for lunch and collected a wicker basket from the toolshed; then she walked out to the kitchen garden, a tall, almost rangy figure in dungarees, a man's work jacket, and Wellington boots.

The Brussels-sprouts plants were bushy and almost hip high – and solidly frozen in the morning shadow of the brick wall. Jane, knowing from habit that only bare hands would do the job, slipped her wool gloves off and into her pockets, and began picking. The sprouts were knobs of dull, green ice down the smooth stems, and they snapped stiffly free in her fingers. Within minutes her hands were white with cold and bitterly painful. She clenched her teeth against the pain, stamping her boots to ease the frozen tingle of her feet. She reminded herself harshly that the gypsy harvesters in their fields did this work day-long, for weeks at a time, and small children among them. It set her mind better, but it did not ease the pain. She worked her way down the row, slowly filling the basket, thinking of warm things – the house, the fire, the steamy kitchen where Madelene and Hetty worked to feed them all. She smiled, suddenly, and winced because it hurt her chapped lips. Sam and Terry – *they* were warm, anyhow, if no one else was. She felt at the moment she could willingly change places with Sam, in the desert, or even Terry in his Italian prisoner-of-war camp.

They had heard just last Thursday, from the Red Cross, that he was safe and well in Catania; this ended the long weeks of worry since he had been reported missing. Sam had written at the time that Terry had gone off, on a one-man, totally unsanctioned attempt to capture General Rommel. They were not sure that Sam wasn't joking, though it sounded like Terry, and Sam, worried about his brother, was unlikely to be in a humorous mood. But now, anyhow, he was safe, and for the time being, his war was over. Jane wondered how the twins would take this, their first separation.

Jane was pleased that it was Italy and not Germany. Harry assured her that everybody played the thing according to the Geneva Convention, but having glimpsed, through Heidi, the underside of Germany, she had private doubts, which she expressed to no one.

Jane shifted the full basket of sprouts on to her forearm, pulling her jacket collar tighter around her throat, and walked, shivering, towards the house.

As she approached the kitchen door, she saw a young man step out, letting the door bang behind him. He saw her, but did not speak, and stalked away around the corner of the house. He was well-dressed in civilian clothes – too well-dressed, Jane thought, for the meagre extent of the ration book, and looked healthy and strong, as if he ought to be in the forces.

When Jane came through the long, cold flagstone hallway and into the kitchen, having left her boots at the door, she found a sharp, awkward silence. Harry was working studiously

491

at the heaps of government papers that took more of his time than they should have done. He worked in the kitchen because, to save coal, they lit no fires in the daytime, and the kitchen alone was warm. Hetty was stirring soup with too much deliberation, and Madelene was making bread on the broad kitchen table. No one spoke, even when Jane entered, and the only sound was the heavy thumping of the dough as Madelene twisted, tossed, and kneaded it mercilessly.

'What was that all about?' Jane asked.

'What was what all about?' Harry said mildly, not looking up.

'The man I saw leaving just now. What did he want?'

'Oh,' said Harry, elaborately casual, 'him? He wanted to do business. I didn't, so he left.'

'What kind of business?' Jane asked, genuinely curious.

Madelene lifted the dough up clear of the table and threw it solidly down with a great thud. 'Business!' she shouted not at Jane, but at Harry. 'Just a little bit of business; that would have made everything just a little bit easier, but apparently, making things easier is such a terrible thing these days ...'

'I will not do business with profiteers,' Harry shouted, suddenly angry, slamming his books shut.

'Profiteers,' Madelene echoed, mocking. 'You give them a name, and suddenly they are criminals ...'

'They *are* criminals,' Harry retorted, getting to his feet.

'Then everybody is a criminal. Everybody does it, just a little, one way or another.'

'No. Not everybody does it. And anyhow, I don't do it.'

'Oh, no,' Madelene said angrily, thumping the dough again, 'not you. You wouldn't do it.'

'Do what?' shouted Jane.

'The man wanted to buy some pigs,' Hetty said mildly, still stirring the soup. 'He said he would collect them at night, and we could say they had been stolen. No one would ever know, of course,' Hetty related in a flat tone and seemed to make no judgement. Harry's judgement had always sufficed for her; she would never oppose him.

'Well,' said Jane, smoothly practical, having finally got the facts, 'Harry is quite right, of course. We don't deal on the black market.' She considered the argument finished and started towards the door. She thought briefly of Joe; he would have done it, and Hardacres would have grown rich again out of the war. Many around them were doing it. Not Harry, though, and she realized with an odd twinge that he was throwing everything they owned into the effort. If the war continued very much longer they would come out of it paupers, for all their grand house.

Madelene was not finished, however; she looked across at Harry, stuffing her hair under its kerchief with floury hand. 'I do not see why we cannot kill a pig. For ourselves. We could cure it and make our own bacon and have our own hams, and then there would be all the other meat, and I could make soup that would not taste like dishwater ...'

'Your soup is very good, Madelene; it's beautiful,' Harry said honestly.

'Don't flatter me, Harry Hardacre,' Madelene shouted back. 'Why can't we kill a pig?'

Harry sat down at the kitchen table, facing her. 'Listen, Madelene, it would be very nice, I know, but all the pigs we grow have to go to the ministry. We are not allowed to keep one for our own use.'

'Barry Gray does,' said Madelene. 'He keeps one in the garden behind his shop in Driffield.'

'Ah,' said Harry, 'that's different. That's all right, you see. You're allowed to have a single pig and keep it for your own use, but if you are a producer, like us, you cannot.'

'That is a stupid rule,' said Madelene, thumping the bread dough with her fist.

'No, it's not,' said Harry. 'If you were allowed to make exceptions for yourself, you might start making them for somebody else, and soon the whole rationing system would fall apart. Besides, Barry Gray will never kill that pig; it's a pet.'

'Everybody does it; every farmer around except you.'

'It's against the rules,' Harry said patiently, looking up at her gently.

'The rules. Always the rules. Damn you and your rules, Harry. Everyone breaks the rules sometimes in this life. Except Harry Hardacre, God's saint on earth. Damn you, Harry, and damn your rules! All of them!' She shook her head, angrily, and the kerchief slipped down over her still-dark curls which fell over her face. She pushed them back with the back of her hand, smearing flour over her forehead.

Hetty slipped her arm through Jane's and walked quietly to the door. As they stepped through into the hall, she said mildly, to no one in particular, 'The best bread is made in anger.'

Jane fought a smile. Hetty had that unique English country talent of using a platitude like a bayonet.

Harry started to rise, reaching across the table. 'I'm sorry, Madelene, really I am.'

'Harry Hardacre, you are a stupid man, and you make me sick.' She lifted the dough with a sudden jerk, raised it shoulder high, and pressed it firmly down on Harry's head.

'And now you've ruined my bread,' she shouted, whirled around, and stormed out of the kitchen door.

Harry sat amazed and bemused for a full half minute. Then the door banged open again, and he looked up, expecting Madelene, repentant. But it wasn't Madelene; it was Vanessa.

She was wearing dungarees, having been working in the mews or in the fields, and she was munching a large, red apple. Between bites she said casually, 'Daddy, I'm going to get married.' She took another bite, waiting for an answer. When she did not get one immediately, she looked more fully at her father, took another bite of apple, and said, 'Daddy, there's something on your head.'

'Yes, dear, I had noticed,' said Harry, removing the dough in a sodden lump and brushing flour from behind his ears. 'Shall we start again? You came in just now, and I think you said ...'

'Yes, Daddy, I said I was going to get married.' She munched again, with an equine munch, and Harry suddenly leapt to his feet and shouted, 'Put that bloody apple down!'

Vanessa's eyes opened wide, harmless and blue. She was impossible to offend. 'Yes, Daddy,' she said.

Harry sat down again, brushed his hand through his floury

hair, closed his eyes, and said, 'Who or what are you going to marry?'

Vanessa squawked a sharp, loud laugh. 'I say, Daddy, that's good, who or what! Jolly good you can take the whole thing so calmly, what? I rather thought you might get upset – I mean, after all these years.'

'No dear, I'm not upset,' Harry said a little more gently. He wasn't. Just astounded, but he didn't say that. 'Well, I suppose you had better tell me all about it.'

Vanessa pulled out a chair and sat astride it. 'I had dinner in Driffield last night, with Rodney.'

'Vanessa,' Harry said patiently, 'who is Rodney?'

'That's right, Daddy. He asked me to marry him.'

'And what did you say?' asked Harry.

'I said yes, rather.'

'At the risk of seeming to repeat myself,' said Harry, 'who is this Rodney?'

'He's got an Arab stallion.'

'Indeed?' said Harry, raising an eyebrow. 'How very nice, but what is he like?'

'Beautiful,' said Vanessa, and Harry raised the other eyebrow. 'He's beautifully balanced and responds awfully well.'

'Really?' said Harry.

'And he's got such a gentle mouth.' Vanessa was waxing enthusiastic. 'You really ought to see him.'

'I'm sure I should.'

'Deep-chested, high withers – oh, Daddy, he's all but perfect.'

'I see,' said Harry who did not see at all. 'And how old is he?'

'Five,' replied Vanessa.

'Ah,' said Harry, understanding at last. 'You're talking about the horse.'

'Of course I am; what did you think I was talking about?'

'Never mind,' said Harry. 'But what about Rodney? Is he well balanced? And has he a gentle mouth?'

'Oh, Daddy,' said Vanessa, 'you're laughing at me, and this is terribly serious.'

'No darling,' said Harry, 'I'm not laughing at you. Sit down

495

properly and tell me all about your Rodney.'

Rodney, it transpired, had an honours degree in the sciences and was engaged on essential war work at a large chemical plant near Leeds. It was their mutual love of horses that had brought him and Vanessa together. In spite of war-time difficulties, he had managed to preserve his Arab stallion – thus, naturally, becoming an object of admiration to Vanessa. They had been seeing quite a lot of each other in recent months, and Vanessa had just not bothered to tell anybody about him until this particular evening. They had had dinner at the Bell in Driffield, where Rodney was staying for the weekend, and during the main course, halfway through a discussion of the difficulties of getting winter feed, he had asked her to marry him. Vanessa had decided that, as their interests were so compatible, it would be a 'jolly good idea', and she had accepted him there and then. She had arranged for him to come over to Hardacres the following morning – Sunday, after church – to meet her parents. As Hetty had retired almost immediately after dinner, it was left to Harry to hear the saga of Rodney.

Rodney turned out to be a likeable enough fellow, even if he was not exactly Harry's type. He was an intellectual, with a high-domed forehead, and he was some fifteen years older than Vanessa, but there could be no doubt of the regard in which he and Vanessa held each other. They seemed to be very well suited, and neither Harry nor Hetty raised any objection to the match. The wedding was arranged for early 1944, and Harry was amazed when Rodney – who, it appeared, had no family, having been brought up in one of Dr Barnardo's homes for orphans – came to him shortly before the wedding with a detailed list of the costs involved and suggested that they split the bill.

Of course, Harry would not hear of this, and he gave his daughter the best wedding that he could manage in those restricted days, dipping deep into the remains of his cellar for wines, and as a gesture to the thing that they both loved more than self, he provided a horse-drawn landau to take them to and from church. When they got to the church, Vanessa cantered up to the altar on her father's arm, whinnied her consent, and the deed was done.

It was a happy interlude for Hardacres, a bright spot in the grim days of war. Harry gave them Mary's old cottage and, almost with tongue in cheek, he gave them the mews. It turned out to be a good marriage; the couple did not mix much and kept very much to themselves, but Vanessa, even when she became pregnant, never neglected her work on the farm. Rodney, too, proved a tower of strength. His interest in horses had given him a fairly substantial empirical knowledge of livestock, and he worked alongside the rest of them for every spare moment he had away from his factory.

In February 1945 Vanessa produced a baby girl. Harry said that she threw a filly and ought to have it registered in the stud book, but it was a bonny child – not unlike Mary, after whom it was named.

In March the peace of Hardacres was again disrupted by the return of Sam and Terry, now liberated, on a month's leave. They had seen action for the last time, and soon it was only a question of days before the final victory would be celebrated; at midnight on 8/9 May the war in Europe came to an end.

CHAPTER FIFTEEN

Corporal Molly Smith, steward of the officers' mess at Melton Mowbray camp, set two pints of bitter down on the table between the two young officers. They stretched luxuriously in two leather armchairs before the fire, in the anteroom. Molly glanced, with a quick blush, from one to the other of the two, dark, handsome faces. They both smiled simultaneously, as they seemed to do everything else, and then one of them – God knew which, thought Molly – took the bill from her and signed it. They were really quite extraordinary, and even had there been only one of them, Molly would undoubtedly have known about that one. As it was, with two, they were unmistakable. They were the Hardacre twins, both captains, and identical in every way – tall, lean, and dark, with a darkness accentuated by a recent Italian suntan. They both had unnerving, near-black eyes and odd-quirked eyebrows, permanently quizzical or mocking. Molly wasn't sure which. They both had that long, slow smile, with a look of assessment behind it. It was said that, in spite of their uncompromising Yorkshire names, Sam and Terry Hardacre were half French. That was supposed to explain it all, though Molly rather primly considered that even being French did not justify the shocking trick they had played on the occasional young lady, who, confident to have been entertaining one gentleman, unwittingly entertained two.

Molly accepted the bill from the twin on the left and turned smartly. She, for one, was not getting mixed up with anything as unpredictable as those two.

Sam stretched one arm just far enough to reach the nearest pint, lifted it, and drank with great satisfaction.

'Well,' he said slowly, 'it's over.'

Terry smiled. 'In Europe, anyhow. I don't suppose it's over for us yet.'

'It will be soon enough. Japan can't possibly hold out long.

Then it will really be all over. For all of us.' Sam set his glass down and lifted the poker by the fire, casually poking at the coals. 'The question is, what now?'

'Now?' Terry looked surprised. 'We have a party, of course, what else?'

Sam laughed, jabbing at the fire. It was Terry's immediate reaction to every situation, just as it had always been his own. Still, their minds were twin minds, unnaturally close, unnaturally perceptive. Terry knew what he meant and was deliberately avoiding the question.

'Have you changed your mind, then?' Sam asked.

Terry looked into the fire, vaguely annoyed as always when forced into his inner self. 'Of course not,' he said quietly. 'But it's not yet time; there's the Far East, still, and anyhow, even this bit isn't over till the eighth, and that's not until tomorrow. Today, we'll have a party.' He sounded grimly determined now, rather than enthusiastic.

Sam conceded. 'All right, we'll have a party. Shall I round up the birds while you round up the booze, or vice versa?'

'No,' said Terry, still rather darkly, 'no birds.'

'No birds?' said Sam, with mock shock.

'No.' Terry was serious. 'I don't want any. I want a family party. Just the family. God knows, it will probably be the last. The next time everybody is all together in England, we probably won't be a family any more.'

'That's an odd way to put it,' Sam said sharply. 'I don't see it like that ...'

'But that's the way it is, Sam; it's like getting married, only more so. We'll have a new family then, but we'll have lost this one for ever.'

'I don't like that,' Sam said quickly.

'Neither do I, but you think about it. That's what it is. That's what it has to be. Everything has a price, and this one's rather high. Still, it's worth it.'

'Yes,' said Sam slowly, 'of course.' He felt a bit down now and disturbed, the muddy waters of his complicated mind thoroughly stirred. 'C'mon, let's have that party before I change my mind.'

'Where?' said Terry, suddenly thinking of it. 'Hardacres?'

'No. London. London's the place to be for this. You ring Harry, and I'll liberate a jeep. Go on, you've got ten minutes, then we're off.' Sam stood up, leaving his pint half finished, and strode out, retreating into quick action, his first line of defence against the dark recesses of his mind.

Harry replaced the phone on its hook in the hall and walked slowly into the drawing room, where he stood in front of the fire, ruffling his hair thoughtfully.

Hetty looked up from her knitting expectantly.

'That was Terry,' he said. 'He's invited us to a party.'

'Where?' asked Jane, laying down her open book.

'Surely they are not expecting us to come down to Melton Mowbray just for a party?' Hetty demanded, annoyed at the very idea.

'Well, actually no,' Harry said, smiling to himself.

'I should think not,' Madelene replied defensively. 'They wouldn't dream of such a thing.'

'No,' Harry answered, still smiling, 'the party's in London.'

Hetty turned a satisfied look of cool disdain upon Madelene, which Madelene was too astonished to notice.

Jane stood up from her seat by the fire, smoothed her trim tweed skirt easily, and said, 'Well, we'd best be off, then; it will take a bit of time to get there. I'm going to change.' She smiled brightly at Hetty and Madelene and walked out of the room.

Harry laughed, delighted, and then said quickly, 'It is a very special day, tomorrow. Perhaps VE Day does deserve a special celebration. The twins are contacting Maud and Emily. The party starts with breakfast at the Savoy.'

Madelene looked once, guiltily, at Hetty and walked quietly to the door. She turned in the doorway and said uncertainly to Hetty, 'Does one dress for breakfast at the Savoy?'

Harry, watching Hetty, said, 'I doubt it; not tomorrow, anyhow.'

She left them, and he stood, still watching Hetty who was hunched over the fire, comfortable and secure. Very gently he said, 'They can go, but I won't, not without you.'

She looked up and smiled suddenly – a warm grateful smile.

'I was only thinking, can we find someone to look after The Filly, for Vanessa and Rodney?'

'You'll come?' Harry was amazed and suddenly refreshed.

'I think that nice girl from the farm cottage, Peggy, she'd come up. I'll go and see her now.'

Harry went out to the kitchen door and then stopped still in the cobbled courtyard. The night was moonlit and cold for early May. He stuffed his hands into his pockets and stood watching the lacy pattern of the moonlight through clumps of young ash leaves on the cobbles. He had just invited everyone to London, and realized now he could not possibly get them all there. There was the car, of course, but there would be seven of them, if Noel agreed to come. They'd not all fit, and besides he hadn't anything like enough petrol coupons for the trip, even with the small car. If he took them in the old Bentley, which was the only thing which would hold them all, his month's petrol ration would probably get them as far as Beverley.

Disheartened, he wandered across the cobbles and into the converted half of the mews, where cars and tractors had replaced horses. The Bentley was far back in the cobwebby darkness. It had been out on only a handful of occasions since the outbreak of war. Far too extravagant for these times. He found his way to it and stood stroking the once-fine finish in the dim light of the single bare bulb. The last time he had used it was when the tractor had broken down. He'd hauled hay in the back, and turnips. He winced mentally, remembering the scratching of the bales across the elegant leather seats. Wisps of hay were still caught in the doors and tucked under the seats. Then, of course, he had used his generous allowance of agricultural petrol to fuel the Bentley. Harry's hand stopped suddenly on the cold, smooth surface.

When Jane came into the mews, looking for Harry, she found him standing beside the Bentley, carefully replacing the petrol cap with one hand and holding an empty petrol can in the other. He jerked erect as she came in and whirled around. He looked remarkably boyish and guilty.

'I thought, perhaps,' he started, 'I mean, it is a very special

501

occasion, and, well, the war is over ... I'll replace it later, with coupons, of course.'

Jane leaned against the dusty mews door and laughed until she felt weak. Harry watched, confused and still guilty. Eventually Jane managed to say, between gasps, 'Well, thank God. After all these years. Thank God.' She went out into the courtyard, still laughing.

When the twins had phoned, Emily and Philip Barton were in bed in their little house in Charlotte Street. Maud, Albert, and Janet Chandler were in the Grand Hotel at Bristol, where Albert had just given a concert in aid of the refugees in Europe. Nonetheless, at half past eight the next morning, with the sole exception of baby Mary, they were all together in the grill room of the Savoy Hotel, just off London's Strand. Even Noel had been keen to come and, to Harry's amazement, had remarked. 'Today the bloody farm can look after itself.' They were having breakfast of kippers and champagne. None of them had slept, but none of them was tired. It was going to be a wonderful day. There would be no more air raids, no more flying bombs, no more V2s bringing death, unheard and unseen at any time, no more seamen dying in the Atlantic as their ships were torpedoed under them. The nation had made it, and now they paused for a moment to celebrate.

It was Albert who managed the minor miracle of securing them a table in the grill room, and it was the twins who, by a mixture of bribery and charm, had 'organized' the champagne; by eight fifteen they were all together in the lobby of the hotel waiting for breakfast and making plans for the day ahead.

And what a day it was. After breakfast, with the champagne just beginning to make itself felt, they held a conference. As far as the making of decisions went, this was a complete failure; everyone talked at once, and nobody heard anything that anyone else was saying. Nobody really knew what they should do, but nobody in the country knew what they should do, and it did not matter. By ten o'clock the streets were full of people on foot, and motor traffic had been brought to a virtual standstill. Everywhere there were people – singing, laughing, and dancing. Total strangers embraced, and all the girls kissed all the men in uniform. Albert had brought his trumpet, and they all marched down the Strand towards Trafalgar Square. Albert started to play, and he was soon joined by a man with a clarinet and another with a violin, and soon they had quite a respectable orchestra. Albert and his fellow musicians commandeered one of the lions which guarded Nelson's Column and played while everyone danced.

'Let's go and see the King,' shouted a voice from the crowd.

A great cheer went up. Albert struck up 'Roll Out the Barrel,' and they all started marching and dancing their way through Admiralty Arch and into the Mall.

There must have been fifty thousand or more by the time they got to Buckingham Palace, and when they got there the chant, which was to be kept up all day, started.

'We want the King. We want the King ... we want the King ...'

The demands of thousands of people, from every corner of the empire, was not to be denied, and after they had been standing there singing and chanting for about half an hour, the doors behind the balcony in the centre of the façade of the palace opened.

George VI, who had shared so much of the sufferings of his people, even to the extent of having his own home bombed, appeared on the balcony dressed in naval uniform and accompanied by that most beloved lady, the Queen, his consort. Happy and smiling, he waved to the multitude below. They cheered him, and then they all sang the National Anthem.

'Where's Winnie?' someone roared.

'We want Winston!' the chant began.

The King spread out his hands; Winston was not there. Then the King turned to go, and a storm of protest arose.

'Let him go, he wants his lunch,' shouted someone as the King turned back to the balcony.

Then they all sang 'For He's a Jolly Good Fellow', and after that the King really did go.

'Let's see if we can find Winston,' shouted Sam. By some miracle they had managed to keep together.

There was a chorus of approval. Albert raised his trumpet, and they set off through St James' Park in the direction of Westminster.

By the time they found him, it was late afternoon. They were in Whitehall, and a Salvation Army band was playing outside the Ministry of Health building. Quite a crowd had gathered around the band and were busy singing 'Land of Hope and Glory' when on the balcony above appeared the great man himself, in company with Clem Attlee and Herbert Morrison.

More cheering as soon as he had been spotted.

'Where's your cigar, Winnie?' shouted someone.

Churchill produced one, and everybody cheered. He produced a box of matches, and everybody cheered again. He lit the cigar, and they cheered even louder. Then a man brought a microphone out of the building and placed it before him. The crowd was silent.

'My friends,' he said, and they cheered.

'There is something in life I still want to do.'

'Do it, Winnie,' they all shouted.

'I want to conduct an orchestra, and I see you have one there.' He waved his cigar in the direction of the Salvation Army band. 'Do you, ladies and gentlemen, happen to know "Onward, Christian Soldiers"?'

They all cheered again and then were quiet as Churchill raised his cigar like a baton. The crowd sang, the band played, and Winston Churchill conducted the Salvation Army band with a cigar.

It was a wonderful day. They went and saw the King again, and after darkness fell, they danced in Piccadilly Circus; Pat Kirkwood appeared at a window above the Criterion and sang, 'I'm Going to Get Lit Up When the Lights Go on in London'.

Deep in the night – unable to get back to their cars, unable to find accommodation, tired and happy – they found themselves in Hyde Park. The crowds were still around, but here and there you could make out groups of people who had given up and were sleeping out in the park. They managed to find a coffee stall that had not run out of coffee, and the day that had started with champagne and kippers ended with coffee and dry rolls.

They sat in a circle on the grass and talked about the day and how wonderful it had been for all of them to get together.

'Why don't we do it every year?' said Emily.

'What? On VE Day?' asked Harry.

'Of course,' said Jane. 'I think that is a superb idea. We could all meet at Hardacres, just for a day. It would keep the family together. I think that Mother and Father would like that.'

They were tired, desperately tired. There was nowhere to go; they could not even face the walk to Charlotte Street, so, like many hundreds of others, they slept where they were. They managed an improvised shelter of furcoats, greatcoats, and whatever anyone was willing to discard for the good of all. They slept lying over one another, in a heap under the improvised shelter. Harry lay awake for a long time, stroking Hetty's hair as she slept with her head on his lap. It was so like it had been, all those years ago. He had done it all before, or had he? Was he the same person as that seven-year-old boy who had snuggled up against his brother under the tarpaulin? Or was he someone quite, quite different? But he was too exhausted to follow even his own thought; his eyes were heavy, and soon he was asleep.

He awoke at dawn and started to crawl from under their shelter.

'Harry?' It was Jane. 'Where are you going?'

'I'm going to catch the first train home. There's work to be done.'

'Shall I come?' she whispered.

'No, get them breakfast and come up this afternoon.'

He crept out from under the coats. Jane stuck her head out and watched him go – a tall, lean figure, limping slightly as he made his way across Hyde Park and into the morning mist.

CHAPTER SIXTEEN

It was nearly midnight on 8 May, 1950, when Harry came into the morning room. He had gone to bed an hour earlier but had been unable to sleep, so he slipped on a dressing gown and slippers, came down, and stoked the dying fire. The house was dark and quiet, though there was a warmth and fullness from the family who slept under its roof. That evening, for the fifth time, they had all – almost all – gathered around the table at Hardacres for dinner.

When Harry had looked around the dining table that night, he had seen not the great dynasty which Sam had hoped to found, but a really quite ordinary group of people; he smiled as he thought about it. The Hardacres were not aristocrats; they had never quite made it, except for Jane. It was not the husband or the son she had lost, or the title she had now abandoned which had made his sister a lady – she just was. Somehow it had all come out in her. Jane would always be a lady. Harry grinned; Sam would have been proud of her, but it would have been pride mixed with sadness, for Jane was the end of the line.

He had had great hopes for the twins, but they were no longer here. They were happy, though – probably happier than any of them. Funny how none of them had realized what they had in mind, or how desperately serious they were beneath their façade of gay irresponsibility. He remembered the day well; it had been in 1946, or was it '47? They had come into the study looking sheepish, with the same manner that they had had years ago when he had had them on the carpet for some practical joke.

'We're going away,' they said together.

'Not very far,' said Sam.

'But we won't be able to see you very often,' said Terry.

'Will you tell me what you are talking about?' he had asked. He was busy with the farm returns and had wanted to get on.

'We're going to be monks,' said Sam.

'At Ampleforth,' said Terry.

They had stood there, gazing at their shoes, while Harry had tried to take it all in. 'You mean ... ?'

They both nodded. 'How long ... I mean, when did you decide?'

'In the desert, during the war,' said Sam.

'About four years ago,' said Terry.

And that was how they had become Brother Erkenwald and Brother Jude, O.S.B. It had been a surprise to them all, and yet, in retrospect, Harry was aware that it should not have been. The lighthearted irresponsibility had had to be a cover for something – something very deep and very private.

Last year they had all gone to their religious profession – all, that is, except Hetty. Poor Hetty, Harry thought; it was the only prejudice she was never able to get over. Though she loved the twins dearly, Roman Catholics would always be foreigners to Hetty. Madelene had cried as she watched her sons lying prostrate before the Abbot. It was the only time Harry had ever seen her in tears; she was still as beautiful as ever, but the fire was no longer there.

Harry looked at the decanter of Madeira on the sideboard. He always kept it there, just as he had kept the Tin Box and the Victoria and Albert mug and the aspidistra. They all still lived in the morning room; Mary would have liked it that way.

'Why not?' he murmured and poured out a generous glass, then settled down in front of the fire, where the coals were beginning to catch and the flames were flickering up the chimney.

The Chandlers had not been there tonight, either. They had emigrated to California two years ago. Albert had been given a lucrative contract to compose and direct music for motion pictures. It had been nice to get their phone call, though. It had come during dinner; they had all had a word, and the soup had gone cold. But they had not forgotten.

They all seemed to be getting so old. Noel was fifty, and though he now got on well with his father, there was no longer any chance of him marrying. The name Hardacre

507

had barely a generation to run.

Harry stretched comfortably. The wine was soporific, and he let his thoughts wander where they would.

The last five years had not been easy, but they had managed. It was true, though – the days of the great estates were numbered. On paper he was still a wealthy man, but their industrial interests were all gone. It was love for Hardacres which had made him sacrifice everything else to keep the place going and try to maintain a life style that was fast becoming an anachronism in the new welfare state in which they now lived.

Harry wondered what Sam would have done. He knew that he did not possess his father's flair. Sam would have probably pulled off something; Joe certainly would. Joe would have come out of the war a very wealthy man. Harry smiled. His way was not Joe's way; he would rather be able to live with himself than be able to live with riches. Besides, he was a farmer and his son was a farmer – a damned good one – and the farm was doing all right. Not, of course, well enough to cover the taxes on the house and the threatening death duties, but he had taken care of that. It had been his one master stroke, his one business triumph – only it was not in the world of business, it was in the world of art and of beauty that had been the salvation of Hardacres.

He almost laughed aloud when he remembered their faces when he stood up after dinner and started speaking with the words, 'I think you will all be interested to hear that I have given Hardacres away ...'

It had been so simple, really. Eighteen months ago, it had started. The tax bills were piling up, and in a fit of temper he had said to his solicitor that he was thinking of demolishing the house. He had not meant it, of course, nor could he possibly have been aware of the consequences of that remark, but it had set the ball rolling.

The only red-brick Tudor mansion in East Yorkshire could not be allowed to fall to the bulldozers. His solicitor had told someone, in confidence, who had told someone else, in confidence, until the Press had got hold of the story. Harry had been amazed at the reaction. Conservationists, the National

Trust, minor preservation societies, and even the Ministry of Works had all beaten a path to his door.

Harry saw his opportunity. He did not lie, but he managed never to deny that he was considering knocking Hardacres down. He finally settled for the National Trust. He let them persuade him to hand over the title to the house on condition that the west wing would be maintained, in perpetuity, for any descendant of Sam Hardacre. With that, and with Noel running the farm, they were all right for the foreseeable future.

Harry tried hard to analyse his feelings. He had no resentment. There was a price to be paid for the fact that they now lived in a country where people, ordinary people, no longer needed to fear hunger, and Harry was glad to pay that price and live as a pensioner in his own home.

True, the drive to get out of the gutter, the drive which had taken his father from the fish quays to this house was no longer there, but it was better this way.

Harry thought back over the years to their beginnings. Mutton pie and sweet tea. The smell of fish, the cart, Adam, the racecourses, camping out, collecting wood, putting up the stall, and suddenly all of this.

It had been a long time. Three wars – Ian, Arnold, and Peter, and all the others they had known who had not come back. It would be better tomorrow, it had to be.

He was nearly asleep; he managed to get himself out of the chair and stood for a moment looking at the mantelpiece. He picked up the Tin Box; it still held two gold half sovereigns. He put it down and looked around the room. He was really the only one left, the only one who had seen it all.

He was just about to go through the door when something caught his eye. He grinned, it wasn't true – he was not the only one.

'No,' he murmured. 'Not just me, me and the biggest aspidistra in the world.'

OUTSTANDING WOMEN'S FICTION IN GRANADA PAPERBACKS

C L Skelton

Hardacre	£1.50	☐
The Maclarens	£1.25	☐
Sweethearts and Wives	£1.25	☐

Christina Savage

Love's Wildest Fires	£1.25	☐

Nicola Thorne

The Girls	85p	☐
Bridie Climbing	85p	☐
In Love	95p	☐
A Woman Like Us	95p	☐

All these books are available to your local bookshop or newsagent, or can be ordered direct from the publisher. Just tick the titles you want and fill in the form below.

Name ....

Address ....

....

Write to Granada Cash Sales, PO Box 11, Falmouth, Cornwall TR10 9EN.
Please enclose remittance to the value of the cover price plus:
UK: 40p for the first book, 18p for the second book plus 13p per copy for each additional book ordered to a maximum charge of £1.49.
BFPO and EIRE: 40p for the first book, 18p for the second book plus 13p per copy for the next 7 books, thereafter 7p per book.
OVERSEAS: 60p for the first book and 18p for each additional book.
Granada Publishing reserve the right to show new retail prices on covers, which may differ from those previously advertised in the text or elsewhere.

M5181